AN AR W9-BJZ-106

Longbow said, "The Vlagh's the mother of all the creatures, and they'll do anything she tells them to do—even if it's impossible. They only live for about six weeks or so, but the Vlagh constantly replaces them. Even if we kill a million of them, there'll be another million coming toward us in about a week or so. In most ways, the Vlagh is just another variety of insect, but she experiments, and that makes her unique—and extremely dangerous. When she sees a characteristic that might be useful, she duplicates it. That's why we keep coming up against insects that look like people—or turtles, spiders, bears, wolves . . ."

"What's making her come out of the Wasteland?" Two-hands asked. "What's she after?"

"She wants the land. All of it."

ACCLAIM FOR
THE EPIC OF THE DREAMERS

THE TREASURED ONE

"This husband-and-wife writing team once again produces a winning combination of congenial characters, beastly villains, and top-notch storytelling."
—*Library Journal*

"Filled with plenty of action . . . will excite fans of the Eddingses."
—*Baryon Magazine*

more . . .

"A zippy read."
—*Amazing Stories*

THE ELDER GODS

"Believable and engaging."
—*Library Journal*

"This sardonic series opener bodes well for its successors."
—*Booklist*

CRYSTAL GORGE

By David and Leigh Eddings

THE DREAMERS
Book One: *The Elder Gods*
Book Two: *The Treasured One*
Book Three: *Crystal Gorge*
Book Four: *The Younger Gods*

THE BELGARIAD
Book One: *Pawn of Prophecy*
Book Two: *Queen of Sorcery*
Book Three: *Magician's Gambit*
Book Four: *Castle of Wizardry*
Book Five: *Enchanters' End Game*

THE MALLOREON
Book One: *Guardian of the West*
Book Two: *King of the Murgos*
Book Three: *Demon Lord of Karanda*
Book Four: *Sorceress of Darshiva*
Book Five: *The Seeress of Kell*

BELGARATH THE SORCERER
POLGARA THE SORCERESS
THE RIVAN CODEX

THE ELENIUM
Book One: *The Diamond Throne*
Book Two: *The Ruby Knight*
Book Three: *The Sapphire Rose*

THE TAMULI
Book One: *Domes of Fire*
Book Two: *The Shining Ones*
Book Three: *The Hidden City*

THE REDEMPTION OF ALTHALUS
HIGH HUNT
THE LOSERS
REGINA'S SONG

DAVID & LEIGH
EDDINGS

CRYSTAL GORGE

BOOK THREE OF THE DREAMERS

GRAND CENTRAL
PUBLISHING

NEW YORK   BOSTON

Cover design by Don Puckey
Cover illustration by Matt Stawicki
Handlettering by Ron Zinn

Grand Central Publishing
Hachette Book Group
237 Park Avenue
New York, NY 10017
Visit our website at www.HachetteBookGroup.com

Grand Central Publishing is a division of Hachette Book Group, Inc.
The Grand Central Publishing name and logo is a trademark of Hachette Book Group, Inc.

Printed in the United States of America

Originally published in hardcover by Hachette Book Group
First International Paperback Printing: May 2006
First US Paperback Printing: August 2006

10 9 8 7 6 5 4

CRYSTAL GORGE

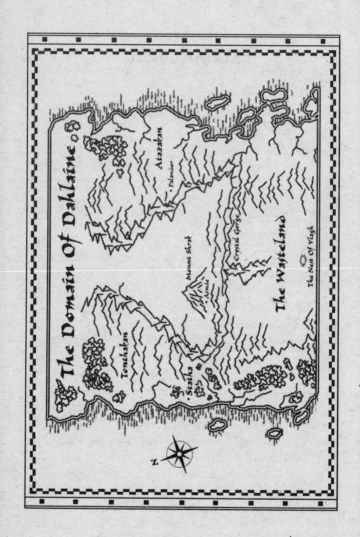

Preface

And now were we confounded, for even as had happened in the land of the sunset, our migration into the land of longer summers had met with disaster. The man-things of that region had proved to be even more cruel than those we had encountered in the land of the sunset, and our dear Vlagh shrieked in agony as we swiftly bore her away from the broad water which grew larger and larger with each passing of that which brings light to her realm.

For behold, the man-things of the land of longer summers brought forth water, even as the man-things of the land of the sunset had brought forth the hot light which had spewed up from the mountains, and the loss of the servants of our beloved Vlagh had been even greater than our loss in the land of the sunset.

And the overmind of which we are all a part shriveled because of this loss, for we were all made less.

And great was our grief by reason of this.

*　　*　　*

Now those of us which seek knowledge are much different from those whose sole task is caring for the mother which spawned us all, for we have gone forth into the lands of the man-things and have seen much that may prove useful. Those which care for mother move only by instinct, while we who seek knowledge have gone beyond instinct, and now we have reached the land of thought.

Much have we discovered in the land of thought, and we faithfully presented this to the mother which spawned us all, and the overmind shared what we told to mother.

At first the overmind which guides us all was much confused by what we had found. Horrified was the overmind to discover from what we told it that the man-things can perform tasks even when they are not under the control of any thought other than their own. More horrid still was the knowledge that those man-things which had defeated us again and again were potential breeders, rather than potential egg-layers such as *we* are. Truly, the man-things are an abomination which should no longer be permitted to exist, for, as all the world knows, breeders should have no task other than the mating with those which lay the eggs which expand the number of the servants of the she which has spawned them all.

There is yet still another peculiarity among the man-things. They make noises by which they give others of their kind information. Some of those who seek knowledge have duplicated those noises, but they soon discovered that the man-things will often make noises which are not true. And it came to us that if the man-things have no way to know which noises are true and which are not-true, we could make the not-true noises also, and thereby could we conceal truth from the man-things, and this could give us great advantage.

As we have learned, much to the sorrow of the overmind, the man-things have many sticks with teeth with which they can cause hurt—and even death—to the servants of the Vlagh, but these sticks with teeth are *not* parts of their own bodies, but are separate and may easily be carried away by those of us which serve our dear Vlagh, and the overmind in its wisdom advised us to gather up those sticks with teeth which had been carried by man-things which had died during our struggles with them.

But then it came to the overmind that we still lacked the most powerful of the things which kill us, and that is the thing which flickers and lays clouds close to the ground or far up into the sky. And as the overmind came to understand the thing which flickers and puts out light and clouds which lie near the ground or rise up into the sky, we all came to know of it as well, and we knew full well that the thing which flickers and puts out light might be the best of the things which kill, for if we could have *that* thing which kills, we could kill the man-things from far off, and thus it would be that the sticks with teeth of the man-things could not reach us.

But though we sought far and wide, we found none of that which flickers and puts out light, and so we were confounded.

But then it came to the overmind that we should search not for the flickers or the light, but rather for the clouds which lie close to the ground or rise up into the sky, for these clouds are a sure sign that the thing which flickers and puts out light must lie at the source of those clouds.

And many were the clouds we sought rising from the nesting places of the man-things, but we dared not to enter those nesting places, for the man-things which live in those nesting places have many of the sticks with teeth and should they see us near their nesting places, they will surely take up their sticks with teeth and kill us one and all.

But then it came to those of us which had sought knowledge of the man-things in the land of longer summers that the man-things had often used a certain kind of low-tree to drive us away from their things-to-eat, for the low-to-the-ground clouds which come from that particular low-tree make it hard for us to breathe, and over the passage of many periods of light and darkness, many of our kind have died when they could no longer breathe.

And so it was that many of the seekers of knowledge circled around the new body of water which had brought death to many of the servants of our Vlagh to seek out a low-tree which was still putting forth the clouds which make it difficult to breathe. And after much searching, they saw a thin, dark cloud rising from a single low-tree. Then they carefully burrowed through the ground around that low-tree to loosen the limbs it had put down into the ground to hold it in place, and when the low-tree could no longer cling to the ground, they brought it back from the land of longer summers. And now we had that which flickers and puts out light—but only one of them.

Then it came to the overmind that we should have many of the flickers which put out light. And so we closely examined that single low-tree and returned once more to the land of longer summers to gather more of those low-trees, and we carried them back to the place where our single low-tree was flickering and putting out light and a thick cloud as dark as that part of the day when the light in the sky has gone away. And then we laid many of the low-trees we had found upon the single low-tree that flickered and put out light, and behold! Where before we had had only one, we now had many.

* * *

And then there came a time of confusion for the overmind. The land of the sunset and the land of longer summers were now beyond our reach by reason of the red liquid spouting from the mountains in the land of the sunset and the water rushing down the slope in the land of longer summers. There still remained two lands where we might go — the land of the sunrise and the land of shorter summers. Now the land of the sunrise was much closer for us, but it was also closer for the man-things that had killed so many of the servants of our dear Vlagh. The land of shorter summers was far away from where we were now, but it would also be far away for the man-things.

Many of the seekers of knowledge said "sunrise!" and many others said "shorter summers!" And the overmind could not decide between them.

And then it was that the seekers of knowledge took up the sticks with teeth for the first time, and the seekers who said "sunrise" killed those who said "shorter summers" while the ones who said "shorter summers" killed those who said "sunrise." And so it was that the servants of the Vlagh grew even fewer, and our dear Vlagh cried out in agony as her children killed each other, for this had never happened before.

We will never know what it was that moved our dear Vlagh to make the decision, but she pointed in the direction of the land of shorter summers and said, "Go there!"

And then the killing stopped and we took up our cause-hurt things and we all turned and went on toward the land of shorter summers, carrying our many low-trees that flickered and put forth light, and left many dark clouds lying behind us as we went.

THE
RELUCTANT
CHIEFTAIN

1

It was summer in the lands of the west, and the young boy with red hair woke up even before the sun had risen above the mountains to the east of the village of Lattash and decided that it might be a good day to go fishing in the small river that flowed down from the mountains. There were quite a few things that he was supposed to do that day, but the river seemed to be calling him, and it wouldn't be polite at all to ignore her—particularly when the fish were jumping.

He quietly dressed himself in his soft deerskin clothes, took up his fishing-line, and went out of his parents' lodge to greet the new summer day. Summer was the finest time of the year for the boy, for there was food in plenty and no snow piled high on the lodges and no bitterly cold wind sweeping in from the bay.

He climbed up over the berm that lay between the village and the river and then went on upstream for quite a ways. The fishing was usually better above the village anyway, and he was sure that it wouldn't be a very good idea to be right out in plain sight when his father came looking for him to remind him that he was neglecting his chores.

The fish were biting enthusiastically that morning, and the boy had caught several dozen of them even before the sun rose above the mountains.

It was about midmorning when his tall uncle, the eldest son of the tribal chief, came up along the graveled riverbank. Like all the members of the tribe, his uncle wore clothes made of golden deerskin, and his soft shoes made little sound as he joined his young nephew. "Your father wants to see you, boy," he said in his quiet voice. "You *did* know that he has quite a few things he wants you to do today, didn't you?"

"I woke up sort of early this morning, uncle," the boy explained. "I didn't think it would be polite to wake anybody, so I came on up here to see if I could catch enough fish for supper this evening."

"Are the fish biting at all?"

"They seem to be very hungry today, uncle," the boy replied, pointing toward the many fish he'd laid in the grass near the riverbank.

His uncle seemed quite surprised by the boy's morning catch. "You've caught *that* many already?" he asked.

"They're biting like crazy this morning, uncle. I have to go hide behind a tree when I want to bait my bone hook to keep them from jumping up out of the water to grab the bait right out of my fingers."

"Well, now," his uncle said enthusiastically. "Why don't you keep fishing, boy? I'll go tell your father that you're too busy for chores right now. A day when the fish are biting like this only comes along once or twice a year, so I think maybe our chief might want all the men of the tribe to put everything else aside and join you here on the river-bank." He paused and squinted at his nephew. "Just exactly what was it that made you decide to come here and try fishing this morning?"

"I'm not really sure, uncle. It just sort of seemed to me that the river was calling me."

"Any time she calls you, go see what she wants, boy. I think that maybe she loves you, so don't ever disappoint her."

"I wouldn't dream of it, uncle," the boy replied, pulling in yet another fish.

And so it was that all of the men of the tribe came down to the river and joined the red-haired boy. The fishing that day was the best many of them had ever seen, and they thanked the boy again and again.

The sun was very low over the western horizon as the boy carried the many fish he'd caught that day up over the berm to the lodges of Lattash, and all of the women of the tribe came out to admire the boy's catch, and even Planter, who seldom smiled, was grinning broadly when he delivered his catch to her.

And then the boy went on down to the beach to watch the glorious sunset, and the light from the setting sun seemed almost to lay a gleaming path across the water, a path that seemed somehow to invite the boy to walk on out across the bay to the narrow channel that opened out onto the face of Mother Sea.

"Are you still sleeping, Red-Beard?" Longbow asked.

"Not anymore," Red-Beard told his friend sourly. He sat up and looked around his room in the house of Veltan. It was a nice enough room, Red-Beard conceded, but stone walls were not nearly as nice as the lodges of Lattash had been. "I was dreaming about the old days back in the village of Lattash, and I'd just caught enough fish to feed the whole tribe. Everybody seemed to be very happy about that. Then I went on down to the beach to watch the sunset, and I was about to stroll on across the bay to say hello to Mother Sea, but then you had to come along and wake me up."

"Did you want to go back to sleep?" Longbow asked him.

"I guess not," Red-Beard replied. "If I happened to doze off now, the fish would probably start biting my toes instead of the bait I'd been using. Have you ever noticed that, Longbow? If you're having a nice dream and you wake up before it's finished, your next dream will be just awful. Is there something going on that I should know about?"

"There's a little family squabble in Veltan's map-room is about all. Aracia and Dahlaine have been screaming at each other for about an hour now."

"Maybe I *will* go back to sleep, then," Red-Beard said. "You don't need to tell anybody I said this, but the older gods seem to be slipping more and more every day."

"You've noticed," Longbow said dryly.

"Do you have to do that all the time?" Red-Beard demanded, throwing off his blanket and struggling to his feet.

"Do what?"

"Try to turn everything into a joke."

"Sorry. I didn't mean to poach in your territory. Shall we go?"

"It's fairly certain that the creatures of the Wasteland will come east now, Dahlaine," Aracia was saying as Red-Beard and Longbow entered Veltan's map-room. "After Yaltar's volcano destroyed the ones in Zelana's Domain, they turned south to attack the nearest part of the Land of Dhrall, and east is closer to south than north. They'll attack *me* next. That should be obvious."

"You're overlooking something, Aracia," Dahlaine disagreed. "The servants of the Vlagh are cramming thousands—or even millions—of years of development into very short periods of time. If we assume that they're still thinking at the most primitive level, I think we'll start getting some very nasty surprises. I'm almost positive that their 'overmind' has come to realize that the attack here in the south turned into a disaster, and that would make 'closer' very unattractive. I'm quite certain that their next attack will be as far from here as possible."

"Aren't we wandering just a bit?" Zelana suggested. "We won't know which way the bugs will move until one of the Dreamèrs gives us that information. I'd say let's wait. In the light of what happened in my Domain and Veltan's, we just don't have enough information to lock *anything* in stone yet."

"Zelana's right, you know," Veltan agreed. "We can't be sure of anything until one of the children has one of 'those' dreams."

"May I make a suggestion?" the silver-haired Trogite Narasan asked.

"I'll listen to anything right now," Dahlaine replied.

"I'm unfamiliar with the lands of the north and the east, but wouldn't it make sense to alert the local population to the possibility of an incipient invasion? If the people of *both* regions know that there's a distinct possibility that the bugmen will attack, they'll be able to make some preparations."

"That makes sense, Aracia," Dahlaine conceded. "If what happened here and off to the west is any indication of what's likely to happen in your Domain or mine, the local population will probably play a large part in giving us another victory."

Aracia glared at her older brother, but she didn't respond.

Longbow tapped Red-Beard's shoulder. "Why don't we go get a breath of fresh air," he quietly suggested.

"It *is* just a bit stuffy in here," Red-Beard agreed. "Lead on, friend Longbow."

They went on out of the map-room and then some distance along the dimly lit hallway.

"Is it just my imagination or is Zelana's older sister behaving a bit childishly?" Longbow asked.

"I don't really know her all that well," Red-Beard said, "and I think I'd like to keep it that way. It seems to me that she's got an attitude problem."

"Or maybe even something worse. Remember what happened back in the ravine? Suddenly, for no reason at all, Zelana jumped up, grabbed Eleria, and flew on back to her grotto on the Isle of Thurn."

"Oh, yes," Red-Beard said. "Sorgan almost had a fit when she ran off like that without giving him all that gold she'd promised him. If I remember right, it finally took a bit of bullying by Eleria to bring her back to her senses."

"I don't know very much about Aracia," Longbow admitted, "but I'm starting to catch a strong odor of irrationality in her vicinity. Her mind doesn't seem to work anymore."

"I wouldn't be too sure about that, Longbow," Red-Beard disagreed. "It might just be working very well. From what I've heard, anybody in her Domain who doesn't want to do honest work joins the priesthood and spends all his time adoring her."

"That's what I've heard too."

"Soldiering is one kind of honest work, isn't it?"

"Not as hard as farming is, maybe, but it's still harder than adoring somebody."

"If that's the way things are in her Domain, doesn't that sort of suggest that she doesn't have anything at all like an army over there? Wouldn't that explain why she wants *all* the soldiers Zelana and Veltan hired to come on over to her territory to protect her if the bug-people decide to come her way?"

"Very good, Red-Beard," Longbow said. "Maybe she's not quite as irrational as it might seem. If her Domain is totally undefended, she'll need just about everybody with a sword or a bow to come there to protect her. It's very selfish, of course, but I don't think that would bother her. She seems to believe that she's the most important thing in the whole world, so from her way of looking at things, we're all obliged to rush to her defense."

"There's not much that we can do about it right now, friend Longbow—except possibly to suggest to Zelana that she'd better keep a close eye on her big sister."

"I'm sure that Zelana already knows about her sister's peculiarities, but we might want to caution Sorgan and Narasan about this."

"You're probably right. Should we go on back and listen to the screaming? Or would you rather go fishing?"

The squabbling of Dahlaine and Aracia continued for another half hour or so, and then Ara, Omago's beautiful wife, joined them on the balcony of the map-room. "Supper's ready," she announced.

"That's just about the best news I've heard all day," Sorgan Hook-Beak declared. "Let's go eat before everything gets cold."

They all trooped on down the hallway to Veltan's impromptu dining-room. That was one of the characteristics of the elder gods that Red-Beard had never fully understood. There was a certain practicality involved in their lack of a need for sleep, for if some kind of emergency came up, a sleeping god might not be able to deal with it. But Red-Beard couldn't for the life of him see why they didn't eat. They didn't need nourishment, of course, but there was more to eating food than just satisfying the grumbling in the belly. Dinners in particular were generally a social event that brought people closer together and smoothed over various disagreements. Red-Beard was almost positive that the elaborate dining-room in Veltan's house hadn't even been there before the outlanders had arrived, and he was fairly sure that the dining-room Veltan had added to his house had originally been Ara's idea. Omago's wife was quite probably the best cook in the entire world, but she was wise enough to know that getting people together and establishing friendships was even more important than eating. There were several peculiarities about Ara that Red-Beard didn't fully understand—yet.

He was still working on it, though.

Oddly, Veltan and Zelana were accompanying them to the dining-room. Since they didn't need—or want—food, they obviously had something else on their minds.

The conversation at the dinner table was fairly general, but after they'd all eaten—more than they really needed, of course—Zelana and Veltan took Sorgan and Commander Narasan aside and spoke with them at some length.

Red-Beard nudged his friend Longbow after supper. "I could be wrong about this, I suppose, but I think Zelana and Veltan might have come up with a way to make peace in their family, and it's probably going to involve Sorgan and Narasan."

"What a peculiar sort of idea," Longbow murmured.

"You saw it too, didn't you?"

"It *was* just a bit obvious, friend Red-Beard. I think it might disappoint Holy Aracia a little, though."

"What a shame," Red-Beard said with a broad grin.

"That's a nasty sort of thing to say."

"So beat me."

When they returned to the map-room, Sorgan Hook-Beak cleared his throat as a sort of indication that he was about to make a speech. "Narasan and I talked this over, and I think we might have come up with a way to deal with the problem that's been nagging at us here lately," he announced. "Since we can't be certain exactly where the bug-people will strike next, we'll have to cover both possibilities. Since Lord Dahlaine's territory is farther away than his sister's is, Narasan and I pretty much agreed that *I* should cover that part of the Land of Dhrall—not because my men are better warriors, but because our ships move faster than Narasan's can. Of course, that's why we built them that way. Chasing down Trogite ships and robbing them is the main business in the Land of Maag, but we can talk about that some other time. Since my people will cover the north, Narasan's will cover the east." He gestured down toward Veltan's "lumpy map." "If that map's anywhere at all close to being accurate, it'll only take Narasan's fleet a few days to reach Lady Aracia's territory, and he can protect *that* region. That means that we'll have people in place to hold the bug-people back in either the east or the north, and our employers can zip from here to there in no time at all. If the attack strikes the east, I'll sail on down around the south end and join up with Narasan in just a couple of weeks. But, if the bug-people come north, my people will be able to hold them back until Narasan arrives to help *me*. When we add the horse soldiers in the north and the women warriors in the east, we'll have enough people to bring any bug invasion to a stop. Then, when the rest of our friends arrive, we'll be able to stomp all over the invaders and win the third war here in the Land of Dhrall."

"It'll be something on the order of the way we handled things before the war in Lady Zelana's Domain," Narasan added. "There'll be enough of our people in either region to hold off the invasion until our friends can join us. Then we'll move directly on to stomp-stomp."

"What a clever way to put it, Narasan," Sorgan observed.

"I've always had this way with words," Narasan replied modestly.

"I don't want to intrude here," the scar-faced Ekial said, "but how are we going to get *my* people—and their horses—up to Lord Dahlaine's territory? Horses can run fast, but probably not quite fast enough to gallop across the top of the sea."

"I think I know how we can do that," Narasan said. "Gunda's got that little fishing yawl that *almost* knows how to fly. He can take you on down to Castano and hire ships. Then the two of you can sail on over to Malavi and pick up your men and horses. Then you'll go north to Lord Dahlaine's territory."

"I think that maybe I should go with them, Commander," Veltan added. "When you hire Trogite ships, you need gold, and I know of a few ways to keep that much gold from sinking Gunda's yawl."

"I think we've pretty much solved all the problems now,"

Narasan said, looking around at the others. "When do you think we should start?"

"Have you got anything on the fire for tomorrow?" Sorgan asked him.

"Not that I can think of," Narasan replied.

"Tomorrow it is, then," Sorgan announced.

Red-Beard had been watching Zelana's sister rather closely as Sorgan and Narasan smoothly cut the ground out from under her. It was quite clear that she wanted to protest, but the two clever outlanders hadn't left her much to complain about. She obviously still wanted *all* of the outlanders to go east to protect her Domain, but Sorgan and Narasan— at Zelana's and Veltan's suggestion, evidently—had dismissed any protest she could raise.

"I don't know if you've been watching, friend Red-Beard," Longbow said quietly, "but doesn't it seem to you that the warrior queen called Trenicia is staying very close to Commander Narasan, and she appears to be *very* impressed by him."

"Do you think it's possible that she's having *those* kind of thoughts about dear old Narasan?" Red-Beard asked.

"I couldn't say for sure," Longbow replied, "but that would be a *very* interesting sort of thing to crop up along about now, wouldn't you say?"

"Not as long as my head was on straight, I wouldn't."

2

At first light the following morning, the farmers of Veltan's Domain began carrying large amounts of food down to the beach to stock the ships of the two fleets. There was a steely quality about that early-morning light that always made Red-Beard's instincts seem more intense. "This might be a good day for hunting," he said to Longbow as they watched the farmers come down the hill.

"I don't think Veltan would like it much if you started shooting arrows at his farmers," Longbow replied.

"Funny, Longbow, very funny," Red-Beard said. "There's something about this first light before the sun comes up that always makes me feel that this might be one of those perfect days—you know, a day when nothing can go wrong."

Longbow looked up at the still colorless sky. "You might be right, friend Red-Beard," he agreed, "and if you're very lucky, things won't start to fall apart until midmorning." He looked out at the ships of the Trogites and Maags. "It's likely to take them most of the morning to load all that food on their ships," he said. "Let's go talk with Zelana and find out if there's something she wants us to do before we leave Veltan's territory."

Zelana and her two brothers were watching the farmers from a hilltop some distance back from the beach when Red-Beard and Longbow joined them.

"I'm not trying to tell you what to do, baby brother," Zelana told Veltan, "but I think you might want to consider a bit of 'tampering' to get Gunda and Ekial down to Castano as quickly as possible. We won't know for sure exactly where the creatures of the Wasteland will mount their next attack until one of the children starts dreaming. It's only a short distance from here to Aracia's Domain; so Narasan should arrive there in just a few days, and it's just a short voyage from Aracia's temple to the Isle of Akalla where Trenicia's warriors live. It's much farther from here to Dahlaine's Domain. Sorgan's ships are fast enough to reach that part of the Land of Dhrall in plenty of time, but you'll be spending quite a few days in Castano hiring Trogite ships and more days sailing on down to the land of the Malavi. Then you'll have the long voyage from there to Dahlaine's country on those wallowing Trogite ships."

"I'm very good at tampering, dear sister," Veltan told her with a faint smile. "Mother Sea is lovely at this time of the year, and I'm sure that the Malavi will enjoy their voyage enormously, but sightseeing isn't really all that important right now, so we'll hit a few high spots and hustle right along. It's going to *seem* to Ekial's Malavi that big brother's Domain isn't really all that far north when they get there, but that's not particularly important." Then he turned to look at his older brother. "Will the local people in your Domain be at all useful if the creatures of the Wasteland decide to go north?"

"The natives of the Tonthakan region are fairly good

archers," Dahlaine replied. "Their territory's very much like sister Zelana's Domain, so the Tonthakans are primarily hunters. The central region, Matakan, is open grassland and the game animals there are bison. They're quite a bit larger than the deer in the forest, and their fur's a lot thicker. Arrows wouldn't be too effective against animals like that, so the Matans use spears rather than bows and arrows."

"Wouldn't that limit the effective range?" Longbow asked.

"Bison aren't as timid as deer are," Dahlaine explained. "They don't panic the way deer do. The Matans use what they call 'spear-throwers' to increase the range."

"I don't think I've ever heard of a 'spear-thrower,'" Red-Beard admitted. "How does it work?"

"Basically, it's an extension of the hunter's arm. It's a stick with a cup on the end. The hunter sets the butt-end of the spear in that cup, and then he whips the stick forward. The added length increases the leverage, and it nearly doubles the range of the spear. The stone spear-head's quite a bit heavier than your arrowheads are, so it cuts through the fur and the thick skin of the bison. It sounds just a bit crude and primitive, but it *does* keep the Matans eating regularly. You'll probably have an opportunity to see how well it works when we get there."

"Isn't there a third region up there as well?" Veltan asked.

Dahlaine made a sour face. "I should have done something about Atazakan quite some time ago, but I've been just a bit busy here lately. The Atazaks have an elevated opinion of themselves—which probably derives from what's referred to in that region as 'the royal family.' I've never had occasion to study the notion of 'hereditary insanity,' but the term seems to fit in the case of Atazakan. The current chief, leader, king—whatever—is totally crazy. He's absolutely convinced that he's a god, and that I'm just a usurper, and that I'm trying to steal what's rightfully his."

"Oh?" Zelana said. "What *is* this precious thing you've filched, Dahlaine?"

"The world, of course—or possibly the entire universe."

"Why don't the citizens just remove him—with knife or axe?" Red-Beard asked.

"Because he has thousands of guards," Dahlaine replied. "I'd say that every third man in Palandor is a member of what Holy Emperor Azakan calls 'the Guardians of Divinity'—which gives those 'guardians' an easy life. About all they have to do is stand around scowling threateningly at sunrise and sunset."

"What's the weather like up there?" Red-Beard asked.

"Autumn isn't too bad," Dahlaine replied. "There's a warm stream of water out in Mother Sea that modifies the autumn weather, but it sort of veers off at the end of autumn, and things get very cold. Blizzards go on for weeks at a time, and the spring thaw comes much later there than in the rest of the Land of Dhrall. Summers are fairly nice, but every now and then we get spells of bad weather. Huge storms build up in the sea to the east of my Domain, and they come screaming in to hit the coast of Atazakan." He smiled faintly. "Holy—or crazy—Azakan always tries to order those storms to go away, but they never seem to listen for some reason."

"Storms don't ever seem to listen, big brother," Zelana said. "When Mother Sea gets grouchy, it's time to take cover."

"Fortunately we should be near the end of what the people of Matakan call 'the whirlwind season.'"

"My people call those storms 'cyclones,'" Veltan noted, "probably because of the way they spin around."

"We don't see those very often in my part of the Land of Dhrall," Zelana said.

"You're lucky, then," Dahlaine replied. "Those spinning windstorms tend to rip things all to pieces. They're fairly common in Matakan, because that region doesn't have very many mountainous ridges to disrupt them. The Matans usually take shelter underground."

"Caves?" Longbow asked.

"Not exactly. The Matans dig deep cellars with thick roofs, and when they see a whirlwind coming, they all go underground to sit it out."

Rabbit came up from the beach at that point. "The Cap'n told me to tell you that the *Seagull*'s ready to go whenever you say it's all right," the clever little ironsmith said.

"Tell him that we'll be along in just a few minutes," Dahlaine said. Then he looked at his brother and sister. "We could probably go on ahead," he told them, "but it might be better if we stayed with the Maags. They'll want directions, and we can give them information they'll probably need before long while we're sailing on up to my Domain. It's going to take quite a while to get there—even on those fast Maag longships—so we might as well use that time to our advantage."

"Could you have a word with Narasan?" Longbow asked Veltan as they walked on down to the beach. "I think we might want to have Keselo with us in the north country. He spent a great deal of his time studying when he was younger, and he carries a lot of information in his head that we might need in Dahlaine's Domain." Longbow smiled slightly. "Rabbit and I came to realize that if we named something, Keselo had probably studied it."

"He *is* quite learned," Veltan agreed. "I'll have a talk with Narasan before I join Gunda and Ekial in that little yawl.

I'm fairly sure that Narasan will agree. I'm sure you noticed that Narasan's going off to the east just to mollify sister Aracia's sense of having been offended because everybody didn't rush over to her Domain to defend her."

"I don't think that's entirely true, Veltan," Longbow disagreed. "Red-Beard and I were talking outside your map-room when Aracia and Dahlaine were arguing, and we sort of agreed that your older sister's problem wasn't so much offense as it was fear. If the descriptions we've heard of her part of the Land of Dhrall are anywhere close to being accurate, she doesn't have anything that even remotely resembles an army. She has farmers, merchants, and priests, but no soldiers. If the creatures of the Wasteland attack her Domain, there's nobody there to resist. *That's* why she wanted both the Maags and the Trogites to go east. She's more than a little self-centered, of course, but it was fear that was driving her."

"Now *that's* something we hadn't even considered," Veltan admitted. "It *does* sort of fit, though. We all get a bit strange and confused at the end of one of our cycles, and the rest of the family assumed that she was being driven by pride, and that being adored by all those priests had dislocated her mind. We never even considered the possibility of fear. You might want to pass this on to Dahlaine and Zelana and see what they think. It could explain Aracia's odd behavior here lately."

Things were a bit crowded on board the *Seagull* as they sailed south from the house of Veltan in the late summer. Sorgan obviously wasn't too pleased when Zelana and Dahlaine appropriated his cabin, but it *did* make sense, since they had the children—Eleria, Ashad, and Yaltar—with them. Maag sailors frequently spoke to each other in colorful terms, and it was probably best to keep the children in a place where they couldn't hear certain words.

Also, for some reason that Red-Beard couldn't really see, Dahlaine had insisted that Omago and his beautiful wife, Ara, should join their party. There was something about Ara that Red-Beard couldn't quite understand. She was beautiful, of course, but very peculiar things seemed to happen quite frequently when she was around. It could just be coincidence, of course, but Red-Beard was more than a little dubious about that.

For right now, however, Red-Beard had something a bit more serious to worry about. Once the *Seagull* and the rest of the Maag fleet were past the south coast of Veltan's Domain, they'd be sailing north along the coast of Zelana's part of the Land of Dhrall, and there was a distinct possibility that they'd pull into the bay of Lattash for any one of a dozen or so reasons.

It took him a while to work up enough nerve to speak with Zelana about the matter.

"Are you busy?" he asked her one bright, sunny morning as the *Seagull* raced down along the east coast and Zelana was standing alone near the bow.

"Are we having some sort of problem?" she asked him.

"Well, I hope not," he replied. "Do you think you could see your way clear to persuade Sorgan Hook-Beak to avoid the bay of Lattash?"

"Is there something wrong with Lattash, Red-Beard?"

"*New* Lattash," he corrected her. "Old Lattash was just fine, but it's not there anymore. It's *New* Lattash that's got me worried."

"And why's that, dear boy?"

"Boy?" Red-Beard found the term to be a bit offensive.

"It's just a relative term," she said, smiling. "What's troubling you so much, Red-Beard?"

"I'd really be much happier if word that I'm here on the *Seagull* didn't leak out anywhere in the vicinity of the new village."

"It's your home, isn't it?"

"Well, it *used* to be. After my uncle White-Braid came apart when Old Lattash was buried by that lava flow, the villagers decided that *I* should be the chief."

"It seems that I'd heard about that. Did I ever congratulate you?"

"No, and I think I'd like to keep it that way. To be honest about it, I didn't *want* to be the chief, and I still don't. If I'm lucky, these wars in the other parts of the Land of Dhrall will go on and on for years. I've never wanted to be the chief of the tribe, and I still don't."

Zelana laughed. "You and my sister make a very odd pair, Red-Beard. She *wants* all that authority and adoration, but you keep running away from it."

"How can she *stand* all that foolishness?"

"It makes her feel important, Red-Beard, and being important takes some of the sting out of the fact that our older brother outranks her in this particular cycle." She paused, looking thoughtfully at Red-Beard. "You *do* know about our cycles, don't you, Red-Beard?" she asked.

"Sort of. As I understand it, you and your family stay awake for a thousand years, and then you hand your task off to some younger relatives and take a long nap. Is that anywhere close to what happens?"

"Fairly close—except that your number isn't quite right. Our cycles are twenty-five times longer than *one* thousand."

Red-Beard blinked. "You've been awake for *that* long?" he asked her in a voice filled with wonder.

"Not quite yet, but it's getting closer to naptime. When our current cycle began, people—your species—were at a very primitive level. They hadn't even discovered fire yet, and their most sophisticated weapon was the club. In many ways, this is the most important period in the history of the world. The man-things—your species—spend most of their time changing things. That makes this particular cycle very significant—*and* very dangerous. There are some things that should *not* be changed—and that brings us to the Vlagh. Do you know anything about bees?"

Red-Beard shrugged. "They make honey, and they sting anybody who tries to steal it. Honey tastes good—but not so good that I'd want to get stung a thousand times just to gather it up."

"Wise decision, Red-Beard. Bees—and a number of other varieties of insects—have developed very complex societies that are designed to expand their territories and their food supply. That's what these wars here in the Land of Dhrall are all about. Unfortunately, the Vlagh is an imitator. When one of the creatures of the Wasteland sees a characteristic that seems useful, the Vlagh starts experimenting, and its next hatch will have a variation of that characteristic."

"So we end up with bug-men who know how to talk."

"Not exactly bug-*men*, Red-Beard. Bug-*women* would come closer to what's really happening. There aren't really very many males among the creatures of the Wasteland. They're almost all females, *but* the Vlagh herself is the only one that lays eggs—thousands and thousands of eggs at a time."

"I don't think baby bug-people would be very dangerous," Red-Beard scoffed.

"Maybe not, but they grow very fast."

"How fast?"

"They're adults within a week. Of course, they only live for about six weeks, but a new generation is already in the works. The outlanders we've hired to help us don't fully understand this, but it's not really necessary for them to understand. It's probably better that they don't. If they knew that the Vlagh can replace all the ones our friends kill in about two weeks, there isn't enough gold in the whole world to have persuaded them to come here and help us."

"Why are you telling me all this, Zelana?" Red-Beard asked her.

She shrugged. "A few people need to know what's *really* happening, Red-Beard, and you just happened to be in the right place at the right time. I'll have a word with Sorgan about your problem, and if it's really necessary for the *Seagull* to go on into the bay of Lattash, we'll find someplace to hide you so that the people of your tribe won't be able to find you."

"That definitely takes a load off my mind." Red-Beard hesitated. "You *do* understand why I don't want any part of being the chief of the tribe, don't you?" he asked her.

"It has something to do with freedom, doesn't it?"

"Exactly." He frowned slightly. "You went right straight to the point, Zelana. How did you pick it up so fast?"

"I've already been there, Red-Beard. That's why I went off to the Isle of Thurn a long time ago. If you think that being 'chief' would be unbearably tedious, take a long, hard look at being 'god.' Just like you, I didn't want any part of that, so I ran away. I spent thousands of years in my pink grotto composing music, writing poetry, and playing with my pink dolphins. Then my big brother brought Eleria to me, and my whole world changed."

"You love her, though, don't you?"

Zelana sighed. "More than anything in the whole world. That's what Dahlaine had in mind when he foisted the Dreamers on us in the first place. In a certain sense, it was very cruel, but it *was* necessary."

"Well, I'm not really all that necessary where the tribe's concerned. They can find somebody else to sit around being important." Then a thought came to Red-Beard, and he suddenly burst out laughing.

"What's so funny?"

"I know who'd make the best chief the tribe's ever had," he replied. "The tribe might not *like* it very much—at least the men wouldn't—but Planter really should be the chief."

Zelana smiled. "She already is, Red-Beard. She doesn't need the title. The tribe does what she wants done, and that's what really counts, wouldn't you say?"

"Not out loud, I wouldn't," Red-Beard replied.

The wind was coming out of the east when Sorgan Hook-Beak's fleet of longships rounded the first peninsula jutting out from the south coast of Veltan's Domain, and when that wind caught the sails, they billowed out with a booming sound. It seemed to Red-Beard that the longships almost flew toward the west. He had a few suspicions about that. Zelana and her family frequently spoke of "tampering," and a wind coming from the east was very unusual. West winds and south winds were fairly common at this time of the year, but east and north? Not too likely.

The *Seagull* rounded the third and last peninsula on the

south coast of Veltan's Domain a few days later, and then the
Maag fleet turned north. The weather seemed to have a faint
smell of early autumn now, and Red-Beard began to feel that
seasonal urge to go hunting. Autumn had always been the
time to lay in a good supply of food to get the tribe through
the coming winter.

He was standing near the slender bow of the *Seagull* with
Zelana's older brother about midmorning one day, when
Sorgan Hook-Beak came forward to join them. "I got to
thinking last night that it might be a good idea for me and
my men to know a bit about the people of your Domain,
Lord Dahlaine," he said. "My cousin Skell discovered that
it's not a good idea to turn Maags loose on the natives of this
part of the world when they haven't got the faintest idea of
what the local customs are."

"You could be right about that, Captain," Dahlaine
agreed. "I suppose a little conference in your cabin might be
in order along about now. There *are* a few peculiarities in
my Domain that you should all know about."

Sorgan's cabin at the stern of the *Seagull* wasn't really
very large, so things were just a bit crowded when they gathered there about a quarter of an hour later.

"Captain Hook-Beak spoke with me a little while ago,
and he wanted to know a few things about the people of my
Domain," Zelana's big brother told them. "It's not a bad
idea, really. I'll give you a sort of general idea about my people and the general layout of the country up there, and then
I'll answer any questions you might have."

"He sounds a lot like a chief of one of our tribes, doesn't
he, Longbow?" Red-Beard said quietly to his friend.

"Some things are always the same, friend Red-Beard,"

Longbow replied. "A chief is a chief, no matter where he lives."

"When we get to the north of sister Zelana's Domain, we'll go ashore in the Tonthakan nation," Dahlaine began.

"Nation?" Zelana asked curiously.

"It's an idea I came up with quite some time ago, dear sister," Dahlaine replied. "It was the best way I could think of to put an end to those silly wars between the various tribes. There are three significantly different cultures in my domain, so I set up three 'nations'—Tonthakan, Matakan, and Atazakan—and the various tribes in those nations settle their differences with conferences instead of wars."

"What an unnatural sort of thing," Red-Beard said in mock disapproval.

"Be nice," Zelana chided him.

"Sorry," he replied, although he didn't really mean it.

"The nation of Tonthakan lies along the western coast of my Domain," Dahlaine continued, "and it's very similar in terrain—and culture—to sister Zelana's Domain. The mountains are steep and rugged, the forests are dense and mostly evergreens, and there are several varieties of deer roaming through those forests. The Tonthakans are primarily hunters, and they're quite good with their bows. I'm sure that Longbow and Red-Beard will feel pretty much at home in that region—except that the winters are longer and colder than they are farther to the south. It won't be quite as noticeable in the autumn, but the days are longer in the summer up there and shorter in the winter." He glanced at Keselo. "I'm sure our learned young friend from the Trogite Empire can explain that for us."

"It has to do with the tilt of our world, Lord Dahlaine," Keselo replied. "Our world isn't exactly plumb and square in relation to the sun, and that's what accounts for the seasons. She spins, and that's what gives us days and nights, and she travels around the sun in what scholars call an 'orbit.' If she didn't spin, half the world would live in perpetual daylight, and the other half would live in the dark, but it's that slight lopsidedness that gives us the seasons."

"I've always known that there was something wrong with this world," Rabbit said with no hint of a smile.

"I wouldn't really call it 'wrong,' Rabbit," Keselo told him. "If it weren't for the changing of the seasons, I don't think anything alive could be here. Perpetual summer might *sound* nice, but I don't think it really *would* be."

"Pushing on, then," Dahlaine said. "The central region of my Domain is a large area of meadowland that's primarily grassland with very few trees."

"That turned out to be very useful last spring," Longbow said.

"I don't think I quite follow you there, Longbow," Dahlaine said with a slightly puzzled look.

"It has to do with certain customs in Zelana's Domain," Longbow replied. "There are certain tasks that we call 'men's work' and others called 'women's work.' Men are supposed to hunt and fight wars, and women are supposed to plant vegetables and cook supper. It might *sound* sort of fair, but it seems to give the men of any tribe a lot of spare time to sit around talking about hunting and fighting. When the fire-mountains won the first war for us, Red-Beard's village, Lattash, was buried under melted rock, so the people had to move to a place on down the bay from the old one. There was open land that should have given the women plenty of room for planting—except that it was covered with thick sod. Cutting away the sod would normally be 'women's work,' but Old-Bear, the chief of my tribe, told us that he had once visited that grassland you just described, and that while he was there, he saw the lodges made of sod rather than tree limbs. Building lodges is 'men's work,' so after Red-Beard's tribe had settled in their new village, the men built the traditional tree-limb lodges, but the wind blew quite a bit harder where the new village was located, and one night, all of the lodges were blown down."

"That must have been a very strong wind," the farmer Omago said.

"Not quite *that* strong," Longbow replied with a grin. "Red-Beard and I gave it a bit of help. Then the next morning we put on long faces and told the men of the tribe that tree-limb lodges weren't strong enough to stand up in 'windy-village,' and we suggested sod instead. The men grumbled a bit, but they went on out into the meadow and started digging up sod for all they were worth, while the women came along behind them planting beans and other things that are good to eat. Nobody was offended, and nobody will starve to death this coming winter."

"You two are a couple of very devious people," Omago's wife, Ara, observed.

"One should always do one's best when the well-being of the tribe's involved," Red-Beard replied sententiously.

The pretty lady actually laughed.

"Pushing on, then," Dahlaine continued. "There are a few herds of those various deer near the western mountains in Matakan, but the most numerous creatures in Matakan are the bison. They're quite a bit larger than deer, and they have horns instead of antlers. Since the winters are very cold in my Domain, the bison have dense fur, and their hides are quite a bit thicker. Arrows *might* penetrate that fur and hide, but spears seem to work better." Dahlaine went on to describe the Matans' "spear-thrower" again.

"Something like that would be very difficult to aim, it seems to me," Rabbit said.

"The Matans practice a lot, and they're good enough to bring home a lot of bison meat."

"That's what counts," Longbow said. "Their spearheads are stone, aren't they?"

"Of course," Dahlaine replied. "The only metal we have anything to do with here in the Land of Dhrall is gold—and I don't think gold would make very good spearheads."

"I'd say it's almost time for me to go to work again," Rabbit added with a glum sort of look.

"About all that's left now is 'crazy land,' right?" Red-Beard suggested, being careful not to smile.

"Does he always have to do that, Zelana?" Dahlaine asked his sister.

"Do what, dear brother?"

"Turn everything into a joke."

"It keeps him happy, Dahlaine, and happy people are nicer than gloomy ones. Haven't you noticed that before?"

He gave her a hard look, but she just smiled.

"All right," Dahlaine continued. "The nation on the east of my Domain is Atazakan, and as our friend who hasn't yet learned how to shave just suggested, the ruler of that region is fairly insane—which isn't really his fault, since the last five generations of his family have also been crazy. The current ruler of Atazakan has taken crazy out to the far end, though. He's absolutely convinced that he's god. He goes out to the public square in the city of Palandor every morning and gives the sun his permission to rise. Then, late in the afternoon, he goes back to the same place and permits her to set."

"She'll do it without his permission, won't she?" Rabbit asked skeptically.

"Of course she will," Dahlaine replied with a faint smile, "but that absurd business makes 'Holy Azakan' feel more goddish."

"I don't think there's such a word as 'goddish,' Dahlaine," Zelana suggested.

"You understood what I meant, didn't you, dear sister?" Dahlaine asked her.

"Well, sort of, I suppose."

"That means that it's a word, doesn't it?"

"Not one that *I'd* ever use."

"You're a poet, Zelana, so your language is nicer than mine. Anyway, crazy old Azakan desperately *wants* divinity. Whether he truly believes that he has it might be open to some question, but his subjects—or maybe worshipers—have learned to accept his announcement that he's a god, because their very lives depend upon it."

"Is there anything at all resembling an army in that part of your Domain?" Sorgan asked.

"Not really," Dahlaine replied. "Azakan has a goodly number of guards that call themselves 'the Guardians of Divinity.' Their primary duty involves intimidating the populace of Palandor so that they'll applaud and cheer each time the sun rises or sets at Azakan's command. They carry poorly made spears and clubs, but they don't really know how to use them. I'd say that their primary contribution to a war with the creatures of the Wasteland will involve staying out of the way."

3

The *Seagull* and the rest of the Maag fleet sailed on past the narrow channel that opened out into the bay of Lattash without bothering to stop, and Red-Beard heaved a vast sigh of relief—touched with just a faint hint of shame. He was fully aware of the fact that he was evading certain responsibilities, but he knew that the tribe would survive without Red-Beard of Lattash serving as chief.

As they moved on farther north it became more and more obvious that summer was coming to a close. There were aspen trees and birch scattered among the pine, fir, and spruce, and the leaves of those particular trees had begun to turn, spattering the evergreen forest with patches of red and gold. Autumn was the most beautiful season in the forest, but it also gave a warning. Winter was not far away, and only fools ignored that silent warning.

It was about three days after they'd passed the bay of Lattash when Longbow advised Sorgan Hook-Beak that he was going to paddle his canoe ashore so that he could speak with Old-Bear, the chief of his tribe. "If anything unusual is happening up in the land of the Tonthakans, Old-Bear will have heard about it."

Sorgan seemed to be just a bit surprised. "Are your people really *that* familiar with the natives of Lord Dahlaine's territory?" he asked.

"I've gone up there a few times myself," Longbow replied. "It's always a good idea to get to know the neighbors. There *are* a few restrictions, of course, but we can usually step around them. As nearly as I can determine, we won't need the archers of Zelana's Domain up in her brother's country—*unless* the creatures of the Wasteland attack in millions, but it's probably a good idea for us to stay in touch with Chief Old-Bear. If an emergency comes along, he'll be able to pass the word to the other tribes. Help will be there if we happen to need it."

"I'll lend you a skiff, if you'd like."

"Thanks all the same, Sorgan, but I'm more comfortable in my canoe."

"Could you use some company?" Red-Beard asked his friend. "Boats are nice, I suppose, but I'd like to put my feet on solid ground for a little while."

"Ships," Sorgan absently corrected.

"You missed me there, Sorgan."

"We call them 'ships,' not 'boats.'"

"Well, *excuse* me."

"I'll think about it," Sorgan replied.

Red-Beard followed his friend out onto the deck of the *Seagull*, and then the two of them carried Longbow's canoe up out of the forward hold and lowered it over the side.

It felt good to be in a canoe again, and Longbow's canoe was one of the smoothest Red-Beard had ever sat in. He rather ruefully conceded that no matter what Longbow did, he was always the best. Some people might have found that irritating, but it didn't particularly bother Red-Beard. Longbow was his friend, and he almost never tried to compete with him.

It was a balmy autumn day, the waves were gentle, and Longbow's canoe seemed almost to skim across the surface toward the pebbly beach.

Red-Beard noticed that the men of the tribe seemed to avoid Longbow, which wasn't really all that unusual. He'd noticed in the past that *most* people tried to avoid Longbow. "It's probably that grim expression of his," Red-Beard said to himself. "I'm sure he'd be more popular if he'd just learn how to smile now and then."

Chief Old-Bear's lodge stood alone on a small hillock that looked down over the beach. Red-Beard thought that was very unusual. Most tribe-chiefs set up shop right in the center of the village, but Old-Bear seemed to want to be separate—and alone.

He greeted Longbow rather formally, it seemed to Red-Beard, but different tribes have different customs.

"How did things go in the Domain of Zelana's brother, my son?" Old-Bear asked.

Longbow shrugged. "It was a bit more complicated there than it was here, My Chief," he said, "but things turned out quite well. It seems that we have a friend who can do things that Zelana's family can't, and she does them without the help of the Dreamers."

"The old myths are true, then," the chief observed.

"So it would seem, and she was using *me* as her spokesman. That got to be just a bit tiresome after a while, and it took me a while to catch up on my sleep."

Old-Bear looked a bit startled. "I must have misunderstood the myth. I'd always assumed that she'd use one of the Dreamer-children to pass her commands on to the out-landers. What did she want you to tell our friends?"

"Her speech in my dreams was just a bit formal, My Chief, but it more or less boiled down to 'get out of the way.' She knew what she was doing, and she didn't want us to interfere. We had two separate enemies, and they were very busy killing each other—right up until she destroyed them both."

"Fire or water?"

"She used water this time—a *lot* of water. The creatures of the Wasteland won't be going south anymore, because there's a large inland sea between them and Veltan's Domain."

Chief Old-Bear laughed. "I imagine that might have upset the Vlagh just a bit."

"More than a bit, My Chief," Longbow replied. "We could hear her screaming from miles away."

"Is there something happening that I should know about?" Red-Beard asked curiously.

"It's a very old story that's been handed down in our tribe for years and years," Longbow explained. "It has to do with a crisis that lies off in the future and what we'll have to do to meet that crisis. There are some references to strangers in the myth—probably Sorgan and Narasan—and to some el-emental forces—fire, water, wind—that sort of thing. The story's possibly been garbled just a bit over the years, but down at the bottom, it seems to be very close to what we've encountered so far."

"Are there any hints about what we ought to be looking for up in the north or off to the east?"

"Nothing very specific," Longbow replied. "Visions of one kind or another tend to get just a bit disrupted as time goes by."

"Do you think the outlanders will need our help if the creatures of the Wasteland attack the Domain of Zelana's older brother, my son?" Old-Bear asked.

"Probably not, My Chief," Longbow replied. "The Ton-thakans are fairly good archers, and if the Maag smiths cast bronze arrowheads for them, they should be able to do what needs to be done. If things start getting out of hand, though, I'll send word to you." He paused. "How is One-Who-Heals getting along?" he asked.

"Not too good, my son," Old-Bear replied. "It would seem that age is one of the diseases that he can't heal."

"That's too bad," Longbow said. "He is—or was—a very good teacher." Then he looked at Red-Beard. "I'll be back in just a little while and then we can paddle on back to the *Seagull* and join our friends." Then he left Chief Old-Bear's lodge.

"Where's he going?" Red-Beard asked Longbow's chief.

"To visit Misty-Water's grave, probably," Old Bear replied.

"Oh," Red-Beard said. "I don't think he's ever mentioned her to me—or anybody else—but some of the men in your tribe spoke of her on occasion. People who don't know about her don't understand Longbow, and he frightens them. Of course, sometimes he frightens even *me*."

"He was not always like he is now, Red-Beard," Old-Bear said. "The time will come, I think, when he'll draw his bow with the Vlagh for his target."

"I hope he doesn't miss when that day comes."

"I wouldn't worry, Red-Beard," Old-Bear replied. "Long-bow never misses when he draws his bow."

"I've noticed that."

"I'm sure you have. Everybody who's ever met him notices that."

CASTANO

1

The meadowlands of the clan of Ekial of Malavi lay near the north coast, and that gave the clan a certain advantage over the clans that lay farther to the south. The cattle-buyers from the Trogite Empire did business in the coastal towns, which were surrounded by extensive cattle-pens and with loading piers jutting out into the sea. This made things very convenient for the northern clans, since there were no long cattle-drives involved when the time came to sell cows.

The village of the clan was a pleasant place near the southern edge of the clan territory where a sparkling brook came tumbling down out of the hills which lay to the south. The meadows surrounding the village were lush and green, so the cattle had little reason to wander off.

The pavilions in the village were made of leather, of course, and there was a certain advantage to that. The Trogite cattle-buyers in the coastal towns lived in houses made of wood, and once those houses had been built, they stayed where they were. Leather pavilions, however, can be moved without much difficulty if necessary.

It was not uncommon among the Malavi for a proud father to announce that his son had been riding horses since before he learned how to walk. That was probably an exaggeration, but Ekial couldn't remember a day when he hadn't spent most of his time on horseback.

There were several other boys of about the same age as Ekial in the village, and, quite naturally, the boys spent much of their time racing. The horses their fathers had given them when they were still quite small had been rather old and tired, so they didn't run very fast, but the boys still enjoyed those races. Ekial had several friends among the boys of the clan, and those friends were about the same age as he was. Ariga was maybe a year younger than Ekial, and Baltha and Skarn were a bit older, but they all got along well with each other.

Ekial wasn't quite sure just why it was that the other three boys deferred to him as they played together. He wasn't the biggest, certainly, and the horse his father had given him wasn't the fastest, but for some reason, they seemed to expect him to make the important decisions—"Let's race," "Let's give the horses time to catch their breath," or, "Isn't it just about lunchtime?"

As the years moved on, the boys learned many things by listening to the conversations of their elders around the fire after the sun went down. The standard myth in the meadowland of Malavi was that in times long past, horses had been a gift from the god Mala. It was an entertaining story that was often repeated around the fire after supper, but Ekial and his friends were quite sure that there was little truth in the story. An untamed horse could hardly be called "a gift."

Ekial learned that the hard way when he was about twelve years old. Custom demanded that every man should tame his own mount before he could be recognized as a *real*

Malavi. The wild horse his father gave him on his twelfth birthday was "spirited," a common term among the Malavi that glossed over the true nature of wild horses. Ekial privately believed that "vicious," "savage," and "evil" might come closer to the truth.

Of course, the fact that his gift horse broke his right arm the first time he tried to mount the beast might have played some part in his opinion. After his arm healed, Ekial approached his "gift" with a certain caution. He had a fair amount of success with twisting the horse's ear—very hard—but then the problem of biting came up. Ekial learned never to turn his back on his horse, and he took to carrying a stout strap. After he'd slashed the horse across the nose with the strap a few times, the beast evidently decided that biting his owner wasn't a very good idea.

In time, Ekial and "Beast" grew to know each other better, and a wary sort of peace was established. Ekial still avoided turning his back on Beast, but otherwise things went rather well.

Ekial even developed a certain pride when it became increasingly obvious that Beast could outrun any other horse in the clan. Races were quite common in the meadowland, and there was usually quite a bit of betting involved. Ekial was hardly more than a boy at that time, and Beast was obviously still about half wild. The men of the clan spoke rather disparagingly of "that little boy and his barely tamed horse," and they feigned a certain reluctance to put any sizeable amount of money on them. They always insisted on what the Malavi called "odds." Two for one was fairly common in Malavi horse-races, but the men of Ekial's clan usually demanded four for one, and the men of other clans almost always agreed.

The men of Ekial's clan won a great deal of money that first summer, but the word that Ekial and Beast could probably outrun their own shadows spread rapidly, and the odds turned around significantly. The men of *some* tribes even went so far as to demand ten for one. But, since Ekial and Beast never lost, the men of the clan still won money.

By the third summer, however, nobody in any other clan would accept *any* odds at all, and Ekial and Beast retired—undefeated.

Despite the fact that the clans of the meadowland of Malavi found the racing of horses most entertaining, their primary business involved the raising and selling of cattle. It was generally known in that part of the world that the lush meadows of Malavi produced the finest beef to be found anywhere at all. There had been occasional attempts by the Trogites off to the east to incorporate Malavi into their growing empire, but that hadn't turned out at all well for the men who called themselves "civilized." Since the Trogites had no horses, they couldn't move as fast as the clansmen of Malavi could, and their occasional incursions into the meadowland had turned into unmitigated disasters.

The most recent incursion by the Trogites had occurred when Ekial and his friends were still boys, and the response of the clans had been brilliant. Rather than fight the invaders, the clans sent word to the Trogite cattle-buyers along the north coast that they would not sell so much as a single cow to *anybody* until all the soldiers had been removed from the meadowland.

Since all Trogites worshiped gold, the cattle-buyers were able to persuade the Palvanum, the ruling body of the empire, to pull their armies out of the meadowland and keep them out.

After that incident, the Malavi realized that *they* controlled the cattle-market, and that they did *not* have to accept the first price for their cows offered by the unscrupulous cattle-buyers. And so it was that the clan-chiefs of the meadowland gathered together each spring to decide what price they would demand when the Trogite cattle-buyers came to the land of the Malavi.

The complacent, superior expressions on the faces of the cattle-buyers faded to be replaced by expressions of horror when the clans all rejected the buyers' offers and came back with a much higher price. And the flat statement "That's the price, take it or leave it" cut off all the haggling.

Rumor had it that the price of beef in the empire went up significantly that year, and that there were many speeches denouncing the Malavi delivered in the hallowed halls of the Trogite Palvanum.

A few Trogite adventurers saw what they thought to be a glorious opportunity to make huge amounts of money in what had come to be called "the beef crisis." There were cows by the millions in Malavi, and it appeared that nobody was watching them. The cattle trade could be enormously profitable if they weren't required to pay for the cows they sold. There *were* a couple of problems, however. The Trogite adventurers overlooked the fact that cows have horns, and that despite what *appeared* to be the fact, the Malavi—armed with sabres and long, sharp lances—*always* kept watch over their herds. There were several unpleasant incidents, and the notion of "free cows" was quickly abandoned.

Ekial's clan elevated one bad-tempered old bull who had

gored five Trogite cattle thieves in rapid succession to the status of "defender of the herd," and they'd fed him much more than was really good for him. He died not long after his elevation—either of old age or overeating.

The clan gave him a very nice funeral, though.

Ekial and the other young men of their clan found the story of "one price" to be very amusing, but they had other, more serious things on their minds just then. The herding of cattle might *appear* to be quite simple, but the young men of the clan soon discovered that it was extremely complicated. Cows are not the world's brightest or bravest animals, and it doesn't take very much to frighten a cow. One frightened cow isn't much of a problem, but a hundred frightened cows could quickly turn into a disaster. The standard practice involved "turning the herd," and that was extremely dangerous. Ekial's boyhood friend Baltha was killed when his horse stumbled and threw him during one of those stampedes.

There were other things involved in the lives of Malavi herdsmen that had very little to do with cows. Disagreements about the ownership of streams and lakes were quite common, and there were frequent disputes about which clan owned a stray cow. Those arguments were quite often settled with sabres or lances.

As Ekial, Ariga, and Skarn matured, the older men of the clan gave them instructions in how to use the sabre. " 'Slash,' don't poke," was the cardinal rule. As one scarfaced old man put it, "If your sabre happens to get tangled up in your enemy's innards, there's a fair chance that it'll get jerked right out of your hand as your horse runs past him, and that's a very good way for you to wind up dead."

The lance, on the other hand, was made for poking. The Malavi lance was about twenty feet long, and its original purpose had been to turn a running cow. Back in those days, the Malavi lance had been blunt-ended, and it could literally push a cow in a different direction. The addition of a sharp metal point was a recent development that had appeared during the Trogite invasion, and that in turn had led to the extension of the Trogite shield. The world of weapons seemed to be changing all the time.

As the seasons passed, Ekial's reputation became based more upon his skills as a herder and warrior than upon those early years when he and Beast won every race they entered. The older men of the clan approved of his growing maturity and skills as a herder.

And then, not long before his twenty-eighth birthday, there arose a dispute with a neighboring clan about the other clan's decision to dam off a small brook. There was no question that the brook originated in the other clan's territory, but damming off streams of water that flowed into the lands of a neighboring clan had always been considered to be an act of war.

Ekial's response, however, was somewhat unusual. Instead of mounting a daylight attack on horseback, Ekial, Ariga, and Skarn waited until nightfall and then followed the now-dry streambed into the other clan's territory on foot.

"This is so *unnatural*," Ekial's friend Ariga muttered as they quietly clambered over the large dry rocks and through the dense brush.

"Quit complaining so much, Ariga," Skarn said. "One of the main rules when you go to war is 'always surprise your enemy.' The last thing those water-stealers are likely to expect is just exactly what we're doing now. We're not attacking them on horseback in broad daylight. We're attacking their dam at night on foot."

"The moon's coming up," Ekial whispered. "We'd better stick to the shadows until we get farther on up this draw. The enemy clan's probably got patrols out along the border."

The pale moon rose up over the meadowland, and it seemed to Ekial that she was leaching all color out of the surrounding countryside, and everything looked different now. The bushes along the now-dry streambed were not green as they were supposed to be, but rather were black, and almost threatening. Ekial didn't like bushes very much. They always seemed to get in the way, and they seemed to irritate horses—probably because they didn't smell like grass. In the present situation, however, the bushes were quite useful, since they filled the dry streambed with shadows, and shadows concealed him and his friends from the dam-builder clan.

The pale moon rose higher and higher in the star-studded night sky, and she was almost directly overhead when Ekial and his friends reached the enemy dam.

"Maybe we should have started just a bit earlier," Skarn whispered. "It's going to take us quite a while to tear that thing down."

Ekial studied the dam in the bright moonlight. "Not quite as long as you might think, Skarn," he disagreed. He kicked a fairly substantial boulder in the center of the structure. "*This* is the real dam. The rest of this gravel was piled up around it to keep the water from dribbling on down into the streambed." He looked at his friends. "Do either of you know how to swim?"

Ariga laughed. "Where have you been, Ekial? We ride horses, not fish."

"If we manage to pry this boulder out of place, that pond

behind the dam's going to start going downhill in a hurry," Ekial said. "I think we'd better be just a little careful here."

Ariga shrugged. "All we'll have to do is use longer poles, Ekial, and longer poles will give us more leverage." He muffled a sudden laugh.

"What's so funny?" Skarn demanded.

"The dam-builder clan's going to go wild when they see what we've done," Ariga chuckled.

"They're the ones who broke the rules," Ekial replied. "All we're doing is putting things back to the way they're supposed to be."

"You know that, and I know that, but I don't think they'll see it that way. They must have spent weeks building this thing, but it won't be here tomorrow morning."

"You *do* know that this will probably start a war, don't you, Ekial?" Skarn said.

Ekial shrugged. "We haven't had a good war for quite some time, Skarn. The horses are starting to get lazy, and a nice little war should pep them up a bit."

"That's true," Skarn agreed, "and, since we're doing this for the benefit of the horses, nobody should really object, wouldn't you say?"

"Of course," Ekial piously agreed. "Looking after the horses is one of our main obligations. Let's see if we can work that center boulder loose. I'm sure that once we roll that one out of the way the whole dam will collapse, and our little brook will come back to where she belongs."

It took them the better part of an hour to pry the center boulder loose, and then the pond behind the dam quite suddenly took over. Ekial and his friends got very wet as they scrambled on up out of the streambed, and they stood staring in awe at the huge wave that went roaring on down toward their own clan lands.

"I hope the cows aren't bedded down too close to the streambed," Ariga said.

"This *would* be a quick way to deliver a herd of cows to the Trogite cattle buyers out on the coast," Skarn noted speculatively.

"I don't think you'd get a very good price for drowned cows, Skarn," Ariga disagreed.

"I'd say that we've pretty much taken care of what we came here to do," Ekial told them. "Why don't we go on back home and get some sleep?"

"What a great idea!" Ariga said. "I think we might just want to step right along. If the dam-builder clan has patrols out, that wall of water running on down the hill will probably get their attention in a hurry. I don't want to be too obvious here, but there *are* only three of us, and we *are* on foot."

"Shall we go, then?" Ekial said.

The neighboring clan mounted their first attack about midmorning on the following day, but Ekial and his friends beat them back without much difficulty, since they'd more or less expected that response.

All in all, it turned out to be a rather nice little war. The lands of Ekial's clan lay somewhat to the north of the lands of their enemy, and they were able to block the enemy's customary route to the north coast where the Trogite cattle-buyers eagerly waited to buy cows. The enemy clan didn't make very much money that year, but from the point of view of the northern clans, that turned out to be very nice. Since there weren't as many cows for sale that summer, the price went up.

It was during a skirmish along the southern edge of the clan-lands that Ekial picked up his first sabre-scar. It was a rather nice scar on his left cheek, running from just below his ear down to the point of his chin. He was quite proud of it, and he kept one of the ears of the enemy who'd slashed him across the face as a memento.

The clan-war continued for about two more years, and then the wiser heads in the enemy clan prevailed. Their cattle-herds had continued to expand during the war, but since they no longer had access to the Trogite cattle-buyers, their meadows had been grazed almost down to the roots.

The negotiations continued for quite some time, because the elders of Ekial's clan imposed some fairly harsh conditions upon their enemy. They were required to deliver five hundred cows for every man of Ekial's clan who'd been killed during the war, and one hundred cows for every injury.

That produced a great deal of screaming, but not nearly as much as the demand that the border between the two clans should be adjusted so that the source of that brook would now and forever be in the lands of Ekial's clan. The alternative, "back to war, then," reduced the screaming to a few whimpers, and the matter was settled right then and there.

Ekial thought that all in all it had been a rather interesting war, but now it was time to move on. Wars are rather nice, but they tend to interfere with more important matters.

As the years plodded on, Beast began to slow down quite noticeably, and Ekial decided that it was probably time for him to train a new mount and put Beast out to pasture.

It took Ekial several weeks to choose his new mount, but he ultimately chose a chestnut stallion with a white patch on his forehead. The owner of the young horse called him "Bright-Star," probably because of that patch. Bright-Star was not as aggressive as Beast had been, but he ran nearly as fast, and he seemed to have a great deal of endurance. That was very important in the Land of the Malavi. It didn't take Ekial nearly as long to break Bright-Star in as it had taken him to train Beast, and the two of them got along quite well. Bright-Star was more playful than Beast had been, but he was obviously younger than Beast was when Ekial had begun *his* training.

There were several other clan-wars in the next few years, and Ekial collected more sabre-scars—and ears—as time moved on. His reputation seemed to grow with each scar— and ear—and by the time he reached his midthirties, he was generally believed to be the finest horse-warrior in the Land of the Malavi.

In all probability it had been that reputation that had persuaded a foreigner named Dahlaine to seek him out in one of the north-coast enclaves where the Trogite cattle-buyers had set up shop. Dahlaine was an older man with burly shoulders and an iron-grey beard. "I've been told that you're the finest horseman in the entire Land of Malavi," he said.

"That's probably true," Ekial replied, "but I don't get involved in horse-races anymore."

"I wasn't really talking about horse-races, Ekial. There's a war in the Land of Dhrall, and I need soldiers. Have you been involved in many wars?"

"Once in a while, yes. Not very many here lately, though. The word seems to have been spread around that it's not a good idea to get involved in a war where I'll be a member of the opposing clan."

"Are you really all that good?"

"I'm the best. Of course, my horses probably have something to do with that. Bright-Star isn't *quite* as good as Beast was, but he's still better than any other horse in the Land of Malavi."

"Isn't 'Beast' a peculiar sort of name for a pet?"

"I didn't really think of Beast as a pet. The first time I tried to ride him, he threw me off and broke my arm. It took me quite a while to persuade him to behave himself. He was the fastest horse in the Land of Malavi, though, so we won every race we ran."

"What sort of weapons do the Malavi use?"

"Sabres and lances. We slash with the sabre and stab with the lance."

"You seem to have quite a few scars on your face. That sort of suggests that you've lost a few fights, doesn't it?"

Ekial shook his head. "I came out of those fights alive; my enemies didn't. That's how we define winning and losing here in Malavi. I don't really think I'd be very interested in fighting a war in some foreign land, Dahlaine. Wars are fun, I suppose, but we make our money by selling cows to the Trogites—for gold."

"I think we'll get along just fine, Ekial," Dahlaine said with a faint smile. "You *like* gold, and I *pay* with gold." He reached under his furry tunic and pulled out a bright yellow block. "Pretty, isn't it?" he asked with a sly smile as he handed the block to Ekial.

Ekial noticed that his hand was trembling violently as he hefted the block. "Why don't we go someplace quiet and talk about this?" he suggested.

2

They went a short way out into the meadow where nobody was near and then stopped.

"I've heard some of the men of your clan referring to you as 'Prince Ekial,'" Dahlaine said. "That means that you're the ruler here, doesn't it?"

"Well, sort of, I suppose," Ekial replied. "Actually, it's a term we picked up from the Trogites a while back. It impresses the Trogite cattle-buyers, so we use it to get the price we want when we sell cows to them. When you get right down to it, the clan doesn't really have what other people call 'rulers.' We talk things over before we make any decisions. The clan-chief is older than the men and boys who do the work, and we usually follow his suggestions, but we're quite a bit more relaxed than the Trogites are. Let's talk about this war that's going on in your part of the world and how much gold you'll be willing to pay us to go there and fight your enemies."

"How many horsemen would your clan be able to send to help us?"

Ekial squinted across the open grassland. "I'd say about ten thousand—or so. We can't take *all* of the men, you understand. At least half of the men of the clan have to stay here to tend the cattle." Ekial hefted the gold block. "I'm sure that I'll be able to get the interest of other clans if I show this to them, though," he added.

"We can get into that somewhat later," Dahlaine said. "There's a war in progress in my brother's Domain right now, and I think it might not be a bad idea for me to take you there as an observer. That should give you a chance to see the enemy and come up with some tactics that might help us push them back."

"That's not a bad idea," Ekial agreed. "Now, then, how are we going to get there?"

"Leave that to me, Prince Ekial," Dahlaine replied with a faint smile.

It seemed to Ekial that he'd drifted off to sleep for some reason during his conversation with Dahlaine, and he woke up suddenly just outside a strange-looking structure that quite obviously was not anywhere in the meadowland. It was also quite obvious that it was nighttime here. "What's going on, Dahlaine?" he demanded suspiciously.

"Don't get excited, Ekial," Dahlaine replied. "We just made a little journey, that's all. We're in the southern part of the Land of Dhrall, and our enemies will begin their attack before long. That building is the house of my younger brother, Veltan, and there are people in that house that you need to know."

"Just exactly what do you mean by 'a journey,' Dahlaine? I'm not going anyplace until you tell me what just happened."

Dahlaine sighed. "We went from one place to another in a very short period of time. I just happen to have a mount that can go even faster than Beast. She's a little noisy, but she can take me to where I want to go almost instantly."

"I don't think I'd call it 'instantly,' Dahlaine," Ekial persisted. "It was morning when we were talking in the Land of Malavi, but it's nighttime here."

"That's because we traveled east. We're quite a ways to the east of your homeland."

"A couple hundred miles, maybe?"

"Quite a bit farther than that. We can talk about that later, Ekial. It's nighttime now, so you'll need a place to sleep—and probably something to eat as well. Let's go on inside and get you settled in for the night. You'll be meeting people tomorrow that you should get to know. They're on our side in this war, and that means that they'll be your friends."

Ekial shrugged. "You're the one who's paying," he said, "so we'll do things your way—for now, anyway."

They went on into the stone house and down a long, torch-lit corridor that appeared to be totally deserted.

"Just how late at night is it, Dahlaine?" Ekial asked in a quiet voice.

"About midnight, I'd say. Why do you ask?"

"We're a lot farther east of the meadowland than I thought, then."

"Don't worry about it. Let's stop by the kitchen and get you something to eat."

"I don't really need anything," Ekial replied. "I ate breakfast an hour or so ago." He shook his head. "I think it's going to take me a while to get used to this place."

Then a young fellow came along the hallway from the

other direction. He was obviously a Trogite, but the black leather clothes he wore almost exactly duplicated the standard clothing of Malavi horsemen, and that didn't sit too well with Ekial.

"How are things going, Keselo?" Dahlaine asked the young man.

"They just got a lot better, Lord Dahlaine. Commander Narasan revoked Jalkan's commission and put him in chains yesterday, and getting rid of Jalkan made the whole world seem brighter." He looked somewhat inquiringly at Ekial.

"This is Prince Ekial of Malavi, Keselo," Dahlaine said. "It's quite likely that he'll be joining us somewhat later, and I brought him here to observe the war here in my brother's Domain."

"A horse-soldier?" Keselo asked. Then he bowed. "I'm honored to meet you, Prince Ekial."

"Am I supposed to talk to this one?" Ekial asked Dahlaine.

"It wouldn't hurt, Ekial," Dahlaine replied. "I'm fairly sure you two will be working together before long."

"Not *all* Trogites are as corrupt as the cattle-buyers I'm sure you've encountered in the past, Prince Ekial," the young man said. He hesitated slightly. "Just out of curiosity, what price will the Malavi demand for a cow this season?"

"We haven't quite decided yet. I'd imagine that it'll be about the same as it was last year."

"I rather thought that might be the case. When you go home, you might want to tell your friends that you could get four or five times as much as the cattle-buyers have been paying you. The cattle-buyers have been swindling your people for generations now. When they sell one of the cows you sold them, they demand ten times as much as they paid you. I've seen the cattle-markets, Prince Ekial, so I know what I'm talking about. The cattle-buyers will scream and wave their arms about, but they *will* pay what you demand."

Ekial stared at the young Trogite, and then he suddenly laughed. "I think I just found a friend, Dahlaine," he said. Then he looked at the youthful Trogite. "We can talk about this later, Keselo. What moved you to tell me this, though? I thought that all Trogites are swindlers."

"Not quite *all* of us, Prince Ekial. You'll meet Commander Narasan before long, and he's probably the most honorable man in the world." Keselo smiled faintly. "There are bad Trogites, and then there are good ones."

"We come up against the same sort of thing in the Land of Malavi," Ekial agreed.

"That's been going around a lot lately," Keselo said with no hint of a smile.

As Ekial settled down to sleep in the room somewhere near the back of the huge stone house, he realized that he actually liked the young Trogite. Of course, the information Keselo had just given him could very well turn out to be incredibly valuable when he got back to the meadowland. Evidently, not *all* the Trogites in the whole wide world were scoundrels. That jarred Ekial's view of the world just a bit, but he was fairly sure that he could learn to live with it.

It was just after dawn the following morning when Dahlaine came into the room where Ekial had intermittently slept, and he had a very handsome young man with him. "This is my younger brother, Veltan, Prince Ekial," Dahlaine said. "This is his house—and his Domain, of course. I think it might be best if he were the one who introduced you to the outlanders."

"I'm honored to meet you, Prince Ekial," Veltan said.

"Likewise," Ekial replied shortly. He looked at Dahlaine. "Are all these formalities really necessary?" he asked.

"Well, sort of, I think," Dahlaine replied. "We've got a wide variety of people here, and formality seems to keep the fights from breaking out every time we turn around. In just a few minutes you'll be meeting Queen Trenicia of the Isle of Akalla. I'd advise you to step around her rather carefully. She's a warrior woman—which might seem a bit peculiar to you—but I wouldn't make an issue of it. She's a proud, bad-tempered woman, and she reaches for her sword any time somebody says anything she doesn't like."

Ekial smiled faintly. "A friend of mine—Ariga—rides a mare, and I'd swear that she's the worst-tempered horse in all of Malavi. Females—animals as well as people—tend to get peculiar every so often."

"I wouldn't say anything along those lines in front of our sisters, Prince Ekial," Veltan said with a grin.

"I'll try to remember that," Ekial said, rolling out of his bed. "I've given this a bit of thought, and I don't think I should say very much to the local people or the outlanders during these little get-togethers. I'm here to learn, not to teach, so I'll just watch and listen."

"That might be best, Prince Ekial."

"Do we *really* have to keep waving 'prince' around like that?" Ekial demanded.

"It's probably useful," Veltan replied. "Rank seems to be terribly important to the outlanders, so let's keep 'prince' right out where they can all see it."

The discussions in what Veltan called his "map-room" seemed just a bit silly to Ekial. The Trogites and Maags seemed to enjoy all sorts of picky little details when they were planning a war, and the term "forts" seemed to come up every time they turned around. Evidently the notion of making things up as they went along had never occurred to them. Of course, they had to walk to their wars and back again. The horses of the meadowland made things much simpler, *and*, probably even more significant, the Malavi could take advantage of the unexpected when it happened to crop up. Ekial carefully covered his mouth with his hand every time he felt a yawn coming up.

"Tedious, aren't they?" the tall native, Longbow, asked.

Ekial flashed him a quick grin. "I noticed that myself. Do they really think that they can predict every single thing that's going to happen when they encounter their enemy?"

"The Maags are a little more flexible," Longbow said. "The Trogites are very efficient, but they don't like surprises."

Ekial had been a bit curious about the clothing of the natives. Their clothes were made of leather, much like the clothes of the Malavi, but they were softer and more flexible, and they had a golden color.

"Does all this 'venom' business come anywhere at all close to the truth?" he asked the native.

"Oh, yes," Longbow replied. "Our enemy uses venom instead of swords, spears, and bows. That makes minor wounds—or even scratches—deadly."

"That might cause my people some very serious problems," Ekial said. "If this venom can kill our horses, we'll have to learn how to walk. That might take a lot of the fun out of this war."

"How long ago was it when your people started to tame horses?"

"I haven't the foggiest idea, Longbow—hundreds of

years, I'd guess. The meadowland of Malavi is the natural home of animals that eat grass. We ride horses, and we eat cows—or sell them to the Trogites." Ekial paused. "Do you happen to know that young Trogite called Keselo?"

"Quite well," Longbow replied.

"Would you say that he's honest?"

"Yes. He always tells the truth. Why do you ask?"

"I met him last night, and he told me that the Trogite cattle-buyers have been cheating my people for a long time now. Why would he betray his own people like that?"

"Honesty. Keselo doesn't like people who cheat."

Ekial grinned. "When these wars are all over, you might want to keep one of your ears pointed in the direction of the Land of Malavi. It's quite some distance away from your part of the world, but you might still be able to hear the screaming when we tell the cattle-buyers how much they're going to have to pay for the cows they want."

"Screaming *is* rather musical, I suppose," Longbow said.

"I sort of like it," Ekial agreed, "particularly when it's coming from somebody who thinks he can swindle me. How much longer do you think it's going to be until somebody here decides to go on up into the mountains to look at the *real* ground instead of that imitation Veltan laid out?"

"A few more days is about all."

"I think I'd better have a talk with Dahlaine," Ekial said. "I'd like to go along with those people. I need to see where this war will *really* take place. My people wouldn't be very comfortable in a land covered with trees."

"I'll have a talk with Veltan," Longbow said, "but if Dahlaine's description of his Domain is at all accurate, he'll want you and your friends in the central part—what his people call Matakan. It's mostly grassland there."

"*Now* this is starting to make some sense," Ekial said. "When the people here were talking about that first war, the word 'trees' kept coming up, and I was just about to tell Dahlaine that I wasn't the least bit interested. If there's open grassland in his part of the Land of Dhrall, I'll go along with him—*if* we can reach an agreement about how much he'll be willing to pay, of course."

3

Ekial felt just a bit queasy during the voyage north to the mouth of the River Vash on board Skell's ship, the *Shark*. The Maags advised him that what they called "seasickness" was not at all uncommon. Even men who'd spent most of their lives at sea had occasional bouts of the malady.

His stomach settled down when the *Shark* sailed into the River Vash, and he started to feel better as soon as the ship stopped bouncing up and down on the waves.

There were some fairly extended discussions about just how many men should form what was called "the advance party," but Ekial had already decided that he wanted no part of creeping through the trees to reach the land at the top of the narrow draw the shepherd had discovered. "I wouldn't be much good at that," he advised Longbow. "I don't like trees and bushes all that much. I start to get very jumpy when I can't see for at least five miles."

"I think I can understand that," Longbow said. "I feel much the same way when there *aren't* any trees in the immediate vicinity. I'll let you know what it's like up there after I've had a chance to look it over."

The scouting party left at first light the following morning, and Ekial drifted on over to the *Lark*, the ship of Skell's younger brother. "I wonder if you could give me any details about the war last spring," he said to Torl.

"It made me just a little nervous," Torl admitted. "I guess trees are very pretty when you look at them from some way off, but when they're gathered up all around me, it tends to tighten up my nerves."

"I know the feeling," Ekial said. "There aren't very many trees in the meadowland, and I think we'd like to keep it that way." He hesitated. "As I understand it, you Maags have been at war with the Trogites for quite a long time now."

"I wouldn't exactly call it a war, Ekial. We don't have to fight them very often. When a Trogite ship-crew sees one of us coming, they usually just jump over the side into the water. They know that all we really want to do is rob them. We'll kill them if it's necessary, but we want their gold, not their lives."

Ekial laughed. "It seems that civilization is much more confusing than I'd thought."

"The Trogs would probably be offended if you called *us* civilized," Torl said. "Do you have many wars in the Land of Malavi?" he asked.

"A few, but only occasionally—usually when somebody tries to change the shape of the land. There were some fools a while back who wanted to try farming, but that didn't turn out too well for them, since the horsemen kept burning off their crops. Then there was a clan just to the south of ours that dammed up a brook that had been our source of water for generations. I took a few friends along and we walked on up the streambed and tore their dam down. Now that I think about it, that's the longest walk I've ever taken. The war lasted for a couple of years, but, since our land lay between their territory and the coast—where all the cattle-buyers do business—they couldn't get rid of their cows. They gave up at that point."

"Did you ever have to fight the Trogites?"

Ekial shrugged. "They invaded us once, but our clan-chiefs all went off to the coast and told the cattle-buyers that we wouldn't sell them any cows until all their soldiers went home. That stopped their invasion right then and there. It would seem that the cattle-buyers pull a lot of weight in the empire, because the invading armies were ordered to go back home immediately."

"Money *is* sort of important to the Trogs, I guess," Torl agreed.

"Particularly when they can cheat people out of it," Ekial added. Then he told Sorgan's cousin about what young Ke-selo had told him about how much the Malavi *should* be demanding for their cows. "As soon as this war's over, I'm quite sure that there'll be quite a bit of weeping and wailing in the cattle-towns along the coast. When the price of a cow suddenly goes up to where it really *ought* to be, every cattle-buyer in those towns will break down and cry."

"Poor babies," Torl said with mock sympathy. Then he squinted at Ekial. "As I understand it, your horses are usually just wild animals—until you and your people tame them. Is taming a horse very hard?"

"That sort of depends on the horse," Ekial replied. He told Torl about Beast and his nasty habits. "Poor old Beast died last year, and I sort of miss having him around," he admitted.

"Nothing lasts forever, Ekial," Torl replied, "—except for the sea, of course."

The war in the basin above the Falls of Vash turned out to be much more complicated than Ekial had expected. The invasion of the bug-people was pretty much as Dahlaine had told him it would be—except that the bugs were larger but not quite so agile. Gunda's wall and Keselo's breastworks seemed to be doing what they were supposed to do, and the machines that threw fire at the enemies would have made horse-soldiers redundant.

It was the second invasion that involved Trogite soldiers which opened all sorts of possibilities. It seemed to Ekial that the second invasion almost invited the standard Malavi "slash-and-run" tactics. Foot soldiers sort of plodded along without paying too much attention to what was going on around them, and that would have made them almost perfect victims had there been any Malavi horsemen in the vicinity. Ekial frowned then and made a slight correction. *If* the red-uniformed Church soldiers had been carrying bows and quivers of arrows, a Malavi charge could have turned into an absolute disaster. A sudden storm of bronze-tipped arrows raining down on a charging body of Malavi would kill men and horses indiscriminately, and the charge would never reach its goal. He made a mental note of that. No horsemen should *ever* attempt a charge against an enemy armed with bows.

The thing that disturbed Ekial the most, however, was what Longbow called "The Sea of Gold." Even after the little smith called Rabbit had more or less proved that it *wasn't* gold, Ekial could not take his eyes off what appeared to be the greatest deposit of the precious metal in the entire world.

"Don't keep looking at it, Ekial," Keselo advised. "It might just scramble your brains if you look too long."

"But it's so pretty."

"I think that was the whole idea, but it's out there for the Church soldiers to look at—*not* you or me. *We* know that it's almost worthless, but *they* don't. I think that was the whole idea. The Church of Amar is filled to the brim with greed, and that imitation gold out there raises that greed to the boiling point. As far as we've been able to determine, the Church soldiers—and the priests—aren't even thinking coherently anymore, and that seems to have been the idea. The Church people will charge down that slope right into the hands—or whatever—of the bug-people. The men will kill the bugs, and the bugs will kill the men. When it's all over, there won't be any enemies of either kind left alive. It's nothing but an elaborate trap, and you *don't* want to be one of those caught in it."

"You speak very well, Keselo," Ekial conceded. "Maybe I *should* go look at the mountains for a change."

"*I* would, if I were you."

Ekial found the discussions of "the unknown friend" more than a little confusing. It had seemed from the very beginning of this war in the southern part of the Land of Dhrall that Dahlaine and his family had been more or less in control of things, but it appeared that someone else had stepped in without any kind of warning, and this someone else could do things that were far beyond the capability of Dahlaine and the others. Dahlaine's older sister seemed to take that as something in the nature of a personal insult, and Ekial found that to be a matter of great concern. He'd caught a few hints that Dahlaine and the others were nearing the end of what were called "cycles," and they were no longer completely aware of what was happening.

He began to have some second thoughts about having anything to do with this ongoing war in the Land of Dhrall. The pay promised to be very good, but still—

The Maags and Trogites, with the help of Longbow and the archers, seemed to have things pretty much under control. The bug-people weren't making much headway in their charges up the slope to the north of Gunda's wall, and the soldiers of the Trogite Church were rushing up from the south with their minds shut down because of that "sea of gold." The "unknown friend's" command to stand aside made good sense to Ekial, but it seemed to stir up even more bickering and wild speculation among the leaders of the Land of Dhrall.

Then when they were in the vicinity of the geyser that was the source of the Falls of Vash there came a deep rumble from far below the surface of the earth, and Dahlaine appeared out of nowhere in a blinding flash of light and told them to get clear of the area near the spouting geyser.

The earth began to shudder violently under their feet as they ran off toward the comparative safety of the east rim of the grassy basin, and that convinced Ekial that he wanted no part of these wars in the Land of Dhrall. He was more than willing to take on people in any war in any part of the world, but when the world itself began to rumble and shudder, it was time to go home.

"These geysers are not uncommon, I've been told," Keselo advised them all as they stood on top of the easternmost tower of Gunda's wall staring in awe at the thundering spout of water blasting out over the north slope. "They're the result of vast pockets of water far below the surface of the earth—water that's under extreme pressure. When there's an earthquake in the region, the solid rock that's holding all that water in place will crack, and the water will suddenly come blasting up from far down below."

"The next question is how long it's going to take for that underground pond to run dry," Sorgan Hook-Beak said.

"I wouldn't hold my breath, Captain," Keselo replied. "I've heard that there's a geyser off to the south of the empire that's been spouting up into the air for several hundred years now. There's no way that we could verify this, since those bodies of water are several miles below the surface, but *some* people who've studied them tell us that there are vast seas down there waiting for the chance to come up to the surface."

"Well, good for them," Padan said with a broad grin. "If that part of the Wasteland is lower than the rest of it, and the water's going to keep spouting out the way it's doing right now, there'll be a lake down there by the end of the week, and by this time next year, the lake will have become an inland sea."

"Well, gentlemen," Dahlaine said then, "I guess that pretty much takes care of everything up here. I suppose we might as well pack up and go on back down the hill."

There was a certain amount of celebration when they returned to the house of Veltan. They *had* won yet another war against the bug-people, but it seemed to Ekial that the celebrators all tended to gloss over the fact that "unknown friend" had stepped around them and won the war all by herself.

There were some extended discussions about which part

of the Land of Dhrall would be attacked by the bug-people next, but Ekial found the bickering between Dahlaine and his sister rather tiresome and more than a little silly—an opinion he was almost positive was shared by Zelana and Veltan.

Ekial began to avoid the map-room and frequently left Veltan's house to look over the farmland nearby. It was late summer now, and the farmers had begun to harvest their crops. The concepts of plowing and planting were alien to Ekial, but he could understand the value of having enough food to get through the coming winter. Beef was pleasant to eat, but after a few months of a steady diet of nothing but beef, even a turnip might be a welcome change.

As he wandered through the nearby farms, he began to have some second thoughts about his decision to tell Dahlaine that he wanted no part of any war here in the Land of Dhrall. The earthquakes up in the basin had occurred for a specific purpose and hadn't really threatened *him*. The gold Dahlaine had offered would greatly enrich the horsemen of the meadowland, and Ekial was fairly certain that if things began to get out of hand in the north, their "unknown friend" would almost certainly step in and straighten them out. He might not understand just how she'd accomplish this, but she'd be there if he really needed her help. That more or less convinced him that it would be foolish to throw away what promised to be an easy war for good pay.

There *was* a certain problem, though, and he went back to the house of Veltan to discuss that problem with Dahlaine. He went directly to the map-room, where Sorgan and Narasan were talking with each other.

"I don't want to intrude here," he said to them, "but how are we going to get *my* people—and their horses—up to

Lord Dahlaine's territory? Horses can run fast, but probably not quite fast enough to gallop across the top of the sea."

Narasan squinted up at the ceiling of the map-room, and told Ekial that they could hire ships from Castano to transport the men and horses to Dahlaine's Domain.

"As long as we can get there before the war breaks out, everything should be all right," Ekial replied.

Then Veltan advised Narasan that he'd go along, since it would probably take quite a bit of gold to hire that many ships.

"I take it that you've changed your mind, Ekial," Dahlaine said then. "You were looking quite doubtful when things started to get noisy up near the Falls of Vash."

"I've had time to think it over a bit," Ekial replied. "Things turned out quite well up there, and the pay you offered is very attractive. You people have already won two wars here in the Land of Dhrall, so there's no real reason to think that you'll lose the next one. Easy wars for good pay always get my attention." Then he looked at the balding Trogite Gunda. "When did you want to leave?" he asked.

"How does first thing tomorrow morning sound to you?" Gunda asked.

"About right," Ekial replied. "But let's be sort of careful. I don't really know how to swim, so I'd rather that you didn't tip your little boat over."

"I wouldn't dream of it, friend Ekial," Gunda replied with a broad grin.

4

There was a steel-grey quality about the early-morning light when Gunda led Veltan and Ekial out of Veltan's house the next day, and Ekial felt that everything was flat for some reason. Then he realized that it was the lack of shadows that flattened things. Shadows don't serve any purpose, but they *do* add a certain depth to the scenery.

When they crested the hill that stood between the house of Veltan and the beach, Ekial noticed that the sea was also grey.

"The tide's gone out," Gunda said when they reached his yawl. "We'll have to drag the *Albatross* on down to the water."

"I know that the tides rise and fall as the day goes by," Ekial said to Veltan as the three of them took hold of the slender little boat, "but I have no idea of what causes that."

"The moon," Veltan replied. "It gives her something to do when she gets bored."

"I don't exactly understand," Ekial admitted.

"It's a bit complicated," Veltan said. "Let's get the *Alba-*

tross out into deeper water first, and then I'll see if I can explain it."

It took the three of them a while to get the *Albatross* out into deeper water, and then, wet to their hips, they clambered into the narrow yawl. Gunda took his place at the oars and rowed them on out into the open sea. "That's about far enough," he muttered half to himself. Then he laid the oars aside and pulled on a long rope that raised the sail. "The wind takes it from here," he explained to Ekial. "And the nice part of that is that I don't even have to pay her."

"What if she's not blowing in the direction you want her to?" Ekial asked.

Gunda shrugged. "It's back to the oars, then. I haven't found a way to bribe the wind yet, but I'm working on it."

"You were talking about how the moon makes the sea go up and down," Ekial said to Veltan then.

"Oh, yes," Veltan said, "I was, wasn't I?" He squinted at the horizon. "I think that maybe the term 'gravity' might make it more clear." Then he went on at some length about something that didn't make much sense to Ekial.

It all became much more clear, however, when Veltan mentioned "attraction."

"Oh," Ekial said. "That makes much more sense than what you said before."

"It *does*?" Veltan seemed a bit surprised.

"Of course. It's a lot like what happens to a female cow at mating time. The sea notices that the moon's passing by, and she gets those 'urges' to—well—" he faltered. "You know what I mean." He was just a bit embarrassed by what he'd just said.

"Now *that* makes a lot more sense than all that talk about 'gravity,' I'd say," Gunda added.

"Are you saying that the sea gets mating urges twice a day?" Ekial demanded with a certain surprise.

"*I* most certainly wouldn't," Veltan replied. "I learned a long time ago that nobody in his right mind offends Mother Sea. You don't want to make her angry."

"It does make a certain amount of sense, though, Veltan," Gunda said. "I've heard that Mommy Sea is where all life comes from—people, animals, fish, and all that—so she's probably getting urges all the time, wouldn't you say?"

"Not out loud when I'm sitting in a boat a mile from shore, I wouldn't," Veltan replied.

It took them several days to reach the port city of Castano on the north coast of the empire, and Gunda led them to a place he called an "inn." "I'll spread the word along the waterfront that you're hiring and that the pay's good, Veltan," he said. "I'd make a point of letting them see those gold blocks." Then he looked at Ekial. "How many horse-soldiers are we talking about here?"

Ekial squinted at the busy street outside. "There are six clans along the north coast," he replied, "and if I understood what Dahlaine told me correctly, he might need us up in his part of the Land of Dhrall before too much longer. There *are* more clans farther south, but it might take a while to get word to them. I'm quite sure that the north clans can provide about fifty thousand men—and horses, of course. The clans have more men than that, but they won't let us have them all. Most of them will have to stay behind to tend to the cattle."

Veltan scratched his cheek. "If we can crowd five hundred men on each ship, we'll need a hundred ships."

"You're forgetting the horses, I think," Ekial said. "Horses need more room than the men do."

"That's going to be quite a large fleet, Veltan," Gunda said. "You'll need a lot of those gold blocks."

"That's not really a problem, Gunda," Veltan replied. "I can put my hands on as many as we'll need."

"How? We're here, and the gold's back in your home country."

"I'll have to cheat a little, that's all. I'm an expert when it comes to cheating."

"I should have known that something like that would crop up," Gunda said. "I'll go pass the word that you're hiring ships, and then I think I'll nose around Castano just a bit. The Amarite Church might be just a bit miffed about what happened in that basin up in your part of the Land of Dhrall, and if they're planning anything, we probably should know about it."

"Good idea," Veltan agreed, "but get the word out that I'm hiring men and ships first. My big brother might start getting grumpy if we take too long."

It didn't take long for the word to get out in Castano that Veltan was hiring ships and that he was paying more than twice as much as was usual in this part of the world. Try though he might, Ekial never actually saw Veltan pull any of the blocks of gold out of the air—or wherever it was that he had them stored—but the gold blocks were always there when he needed them.

Most of the shipowners—or captains, or whatever else it was that they called themselves—eagerly accepted Veltan's first offer. Right at first, a fair number of the Trogites seemed to want to haggle, but Veltan cut that off by abruptly dismissing the hagglers with "next, please."

At the end of the first day, Veltan turned to Ekial. "I seem to have lost count," he admitted. "How many did we pick up today?"

Ekial ran his finger down the stick he'd been notching with his dagger. "Twenty-three," he said.

"Maybe we should speed things up a bit tomorrow," Veltan mused.

"You let them talk too much," Ekial said. "They all want to tell you long stories about how nice their ships are and their skilled crews and all sort of other things that don't really matter. There are ways that you can cut that off."

"Oh?"

"We've had dealings with Trogites on the north coast of the Land of Malavi, and we've found a way to cut off all the chatter."

"I'd be happy to hear about that."

"Try 'Take it or leave it.' It gets right to the point, and it lets them know that you're not interested in any fairytales. I think you might be just a little too polite." He hesitated. "I don't want to offend you, Veltan, but is it really wise to just hand one of those blocks to anybody who comes in here claiming that he owns a ship? They could be lying, you know."

Veltan smiled. "I have a way to take care of that, Prince Ekial. Any Trogite who *doesn't* own a ship won't have the gold block I gave him when we sail away from Castano."

"It might take quite a while to track all those cheaters down, you know."

"I won't have to do that. You may have noticed that the gold blocks appear when I want them to."

"Well, as a matter of fact I have, and I can't for the life of me see how you do that."

"The gold blocks come when I call them, Prince Ekial. All I'll have to do is call the ones I gave to the cheaters, and they'll come right back to me."

"What if the cheater's got his block inside one of those iron boxes?"

"It won't really make any difference, my friend. They *will* come back when I call them."

It was two days later when Ekial's stick had seventy-eight notches cut into it. "We'll probably finish up tomorrow, Veltan," Ekial said. "You might want to let the ones you've already hired know that we'll be leaving here on the day after tomorrow." Then he remembered something. "We *will* need ships for the horses as well, you know."

"I've already come up with a way to take care of that, Prince Ekial," Veltan replied.

"Oh? How's that?"

"Have you ever heard the expression 'You don't really want to know'?"

"You're going to cheat, I take it."

"I wouldn't exactly call it 'cheating,' Prince Ekial. Let's just say 'adjusting' instead."

Just then, Gunda came into their room in the inn, and he was grinning broadly.

"You look all bright and bubbly today, Gunda," Veltan noted.

"The Amarite Church seems to be getting purified, Veltan," Gunda replied, still grinning.

"That might take quite a bit of doing, Gunda."

"It appears that the new Naos—that's the title of the head

man in the Church—has a real bad case of decency, and he's spreading it around. He's been confiscating the palaces of the assorted high-ranking Church-men and turning them into homes for the very poor, and the former owners of those palaces are now required to live in those tiny little cells in the basements of the churches where they serve."

"I'd imagine that's caused quite a bit of screaming," Veltan said.

"Not anymore," Gunda said. "The high-ranking Church-men who make *too* much noise are investigated by a new breed of 'Regulators'—if that's the right word. Anyway, there probably aren't more than three or four of those Adnaris who've been even moderately honest. Most of them are guilty of assorted high—and low—crimes, and they're dragged before a church court, with the Naos, Udar IV, passing judgment. There's no death penalty for churchies, but holy Udar has come up with something even worse."

"What can be worse than the death penalty, Gunda?" Veltan asked.

"He sells them as slaves. They probably aren't very *good* slaves, but he doesn't charge very much for them, so the slaveowner probably gets his money's worth."

Veltan stared at Gunda for a moment, and then he burst out laughing.

It was two days later, not long after dawn, when the *Albatross*, followed by a fleet of the huge, lumbering Trogite merchant ships, set sail from the port of Castano, sailing toward the west. Ekial still had a few doubts about this, but Veltan seemed to be fairly certain that everything would turn out as they'd planned.

Ekial wasn't entirely certain just how far off to the north Dahlaine's part of the Land of Dhrall lay, or how long it would take the slow-moving Trogite ships to make the journey, but Veltan kept telling him not to worry.

Ekial found that to be quite irritating, for some reason. He had every right to worry just as much as he wanted to.

The Voyage to the East

1

The faint light above the eastern horizon announced the approach of dawn in the harbor near the house of Veltan, and Sub-Commander Andar was standing near the bow of the *Victory* enjoying the silence that always seemed to settle over the sea as she awaited the arrival of a new day. Andar found an enormous beauty on the face of the sea during those silent moments. It sometimes seemed to him that the sea almost held her breath as she awaited the coming of the sun.

As he looked out across the hushed water of the harbor, he saw the pirate, Sorgan Hook-Beak, rowing a scruffy-looking little skiff toward the anchored *Victory*.

"Would you go advise Commander Narasan that there's a Maag coming to see him?" Andar quietly asked a passing sailor.

"Yes, sir!" the sailor replied, snapping to attention and saluting smartly.

"That's not really necessary, young man," Andar said quietly. "It's too early in the morning for all that formality."

"The cap'n told us all that we're supposed to act respect-ful, sir," the sailor replied apologetically. "Of course, the cap'n ain't out of bed yet, so we can do this any way you want us to."

"I appreciate that, young man," Andar replied, still looking out at the approaching pirate. There was a bulky quality about Sorgan, quite probably because, like all Maag seafarers, he'd spent much of his youth pulling on an oar when the wind wasn't feeling frisky. Just the thought of spending day after day rowing made Andar shudder. Life at sea didn't really appeal to him very much. The sea was beautiful, of course, but she extracted a great deal of hard labor from those who chose to follow her.

"*Now* what does he want?" Commander Narasan mur-mured as he joined Andar at the rail.

"He hasn't gotten around to telling me yet, sir," Andar replied. "I'm sure he'll get to it—eventually."

"Ho! Narasan!" Sorgan bellowed as his skiff neared the *Victory*.

"You're up early, Sorgan," Commander Narasan called back. "Is something wrong?"

"Not yet," Sorgan replied. "Of course, it's early. There's still plenty of time for things to get wormy. We'll be going off in different directions before long, so I thought we might want to kick a few things around before we haul out of this harbor."

"Come on board, Sorgan," Narasan said, pushing a rolled-up rope ladder over the rail.

The pirate tied the bow of his skiff to the ladder and climbed on up. Then he looked around. "Is Lady Zelana's sister anywhere nearby?" he whispered.

Narasan shook his head. "I don't *think* so," he replied. "Of course, when you're talking about *that* family, it's kind of hard to say for sure. They can be almost anyplace, and you can't always see them."

"I've noticed," Sorgan said in a sour tone of voice. "Did she pay you yet?"

"Oh, yes. Those people throw gold around like it didn't mean a thing."

"How much?" Sorgan demanded. "I'm not trying to pry something out of you that's none of my business, Narasan. I just want to make sure that Dahlaine's not trying to cheat me."

"I think our employers all got together and agreed on certain numbers, Sorgan. Aracia gave me twenty-five of those lovely gold blocks just last evening."

Sorgan nodded. "Dahlaine gave *me* twenty-five yesterday too. You've got twice as many men as I have, though. You should have held out for more, don't you think?"

"I didn't really feel like haggling with her, my friend. That shrill voice of hers sets my teeth on edge. How long do you think it's going to take your fleet to get on north to Dahlaine's part of the Land of Dhrall?"

Sorgan shrugged. "Three—maybe three and a half weeks. It sort of depends on the weather. We're getting fairly close to autumn, and the weather can turn sour without much warning. Anyway, we've both been through these wars a couple of times, so we know how to hold the bug-people back when it's necessary, and we can count on some help from our employers. Once we know for sure which part of the Land of Dhrall the bug-people will hit next, we should be able to join forces before things get out of hand."

"Probably so, yes," Commander Narasan agreed. "How's your supply of that bug-venom holding out?"

"We've got plenty, Narasan," Sorgan replied. "That poison's almost worth its weight in gold."

"I've noticed, yes."

"Did Veltan give you any kind of idea about how long it's going to take him to deliver those animal riders that he's bringing up there to help me?"

"Horses, Sorgan," Narasan said. "They call them horses."

Sorgan shrugged. "Whatever," he said. "I don't really think they'll be very useful when the bug-men attack."

"I wouldn't be too sure about that, Sorgan," Narasan disagreed. "I've heard some stories about what happened over in the Land of the Malavi. The horse-soldiers' speciality is surprise attacks. They whip in, kill about half of the foot-soldiers on the opposing side, and then they ride away—at a dead run. In many ways, they're very much like you Maags. You both specialize in speed."

"I hadn't really thought of it that way," Sorgan conceded. "I'll have to see them in action before I make any decisions. When do you think Veltan's going to be able to get them up to the north country?"

"He wasn't very specific, Sorgan." Narasan shrugged. "You know how he is sometimes. I don't think he sees time in quite the same way as we do."

"That's probably because that pet thunderbolt of his has fried his brains," Sorgan said. "Try to keep Lady Zelana's sister from flying apart, if you can. Oh, one other thing."

"Yes?"

"Would it be all right if I borrow that young officer Keselo? He and Rabbit and Longbow make a good team, so we probably shouldn't separate them."

Commander Narasan gave his friend a sly smile. "Of

course, Sorgan," he said. "We can talk about how much he's going to cost you some other time, can't we?"

"You *wouldn't*!" Sorgan exclaimed.

"Fair *is* fair, Sorgan," Commander Narasan said with mock seriousness.

Commander Narasan prudently let the Maag fleet leave the harbor first. The Maags had a longer voyage ahead of them, of course, but Andar was fairly certain that the commander's decision was based on something a bit more significant than simple courtesy. The Maags were fiercely competitive, and Andar had noticed that Sorgan's control of the other ship-captains in his fleet was marginal at best. Andar was almost positive that if Commander Narasan had ordered the Trogite fleet to set sail, some—if not all—of the Maags would have taken that to be a challenge, and a boat-race right now was the last thing they needed.

After the Maag ships had cleared the harbor, Commander Narasan ordered the Trogite fleet to set sail. The sun was well up now, and Andar was obliged to shade his eyes as the fleet came out of the harbor. That was the one thing about sailing that Andar didn't like. There wasn't any shade, and the sun always seemed to be just out in front of the ship upon which he was stationed. He turned then and walked on back to the stern of the *Victory*. The rest of the fleet was wallowing along behind, so Andar went to the main cabin to report the progress to the commander.

Veltan's older sister was in full voice as Andar entered the cabin. "Any fool can see that the creatures of the Wasteland will attack *my* Domain next," she told Commander Narasan and Queen Trenicia in a shrill voice. "My older brother is just trying to assert his authority by robbing me of half the forces I'll need before too much longer."

"Sorgan and I have been through this twice before, Lady Aracia," the commander assured her. "We have ways to delay the enemy if it's necessary. Maag ships are almost as fast as the wind. If the enemy attacks your Domain, my people will be able to hold them back until Sorgan joins us." He turned to Andar. "How's it going?" he asked.

"The last of the ships have cleared the harbor, Commander," Andar replied, "and we've got a favorable wind. I'm fairly sure that we'll make good time today."

"Could you give me an estimate of just how long it's going to take us to reach Lady Aracia's temple?"

Andar scratched his cheek. "If the wind holds, I'd say about ten or eleven days. If what we've been told about the bug-people is anywhere close to the truth, it's going to take them at least twice that long to move a significant force into Lady Aracia's Domain, and that should give us all the time we'll need to build fortifications. Then, too, once our ships have unloaded our men, they'll be free to sail on down to the Isle of Akalla and pick up Queen Trenicia's army and bring it on up here. I'd say that Lady Aracia's Domain's going to be well-protected before the bug-people show up in any significant numbers."

"There you have it, Lady Aracia," Narasan told their distraught employer. "If all goes well—and I'm sure it will—Sorgan's Maags would just be redundant. We won't really need them when we get right down to the point."

"Well—maybe," Aracia reluctantly agreed. "Let Dahlaine keep those pirates. They aren't *real* soldiers anyway, and that grubby country off to the north is all they're really fit to defend. *My* Domain is the very heart of the Land of Dhrall, so it's vital that we protect it from the incursions of the servants of the Vlagh."

"We'll have it well covered, My Lady," Andar assured her.

"You gentlemen are busy," Aracia said then. "If you encounter any problems, let me know about them. I'm sure I'll be able to deal with them for you." And then she left the cabin.

"I think I'm in your debt, Andar," Narasan said after Aracia had left. "That woman's starting to irritate me with all that screaming, and you seem to have a gift for quieting her down."

Andar shrugged. "I have an older sister who's at least as excitable as Aracia is," he explained. "I learned ways to calm her early in life. As I recall, my father was most grateful."

"You people have very complicated societies," Queen Trenicia of Akalla observed. "Things are much simpler on our island."

"Complications make life more interesting, Queen Trenicia," Commander Narasan replied with a faint smile.

"I much prefer simple, Lord Narasan," the warrior queen replied with a broad smile.

"Has Veltan's older sister always been like this, Queen Trenicia?" Narasan asked.

"I haven't known her 'always,' Lord Narasan. She came to the Isle of Akalla last spring with bars of that yellow lead she calls 'gold' that everybody seems to think is valuable. I refused, of course, but then she offered diamonds, rubies, emeralds, and sapphires. I'll work for jewels, but not for yellow lead."

"I don't want to offend you, Queen Trenicia," Narasan

said then, "but a society where women are the leaders—and the warriors—is most unusual. How did it happen to come about?"

The warrior queen shrugged. "From our way of looking at things, societies dominated by men are the unusual ones. The men of the Isle of Akalla are useless—except as breeding stock. They spend hours sitting in front of mirrors trying to make themselves look pretty by painting their faces."

"You're not serious!" Narasan exclaimed.

"Oh, yes," Trenicia replied. "In a certain way, looking pretty is their only way to stay alive. Ugly men don't live very long on the Isle of Akalla." Then she laughed. "I had a predecessor who ruled the isle several years ago who didn't really care much for men. She mated with quite a few of them, but when she grew tired of one of them, she'd cut off his nose and push him out of her house. She had quite a collection of noses by the time she was killed in a war with the women from another part of the Isle."

Commander Narasan looked at her in horror.

"Don't worry, Narasan," she said with a wicked little smile. "Your nose looks fine right where it is."

Andar swallowed hard. This was a very, very strange woman, and she seemed to spend a lot of her time looking at Commander Narasan. "Better him than me, I guess," he muttered to himself.

2

As the *Victory* sailed along the east coast of the Land of
Dhrall, Andar spent more and more of his time looking at
the trees.

"Are you having some thoughts about going into the lum-
ber business, Andar?" his lean, dark-haired friend, Brigadier
Danal, asked on their fourth day out from the harbor near
Veltan's house.

"Not really," Andar replied in his deep, rumbling voice.
"What I'm really looking for is color. Autumn isn't too far off,
and the leaves of certain trees change color when autumn rolls
around. Red leaves mean winter uniforms, wouldn't you say?"

"I *hate* those winter uniforms," Danal replied. "That wool
makes me itch all over."

"Itching's better than freezing, isn't it?"

The boundary between Veltan's Domain and Aracia's
wasn't really clear, but after three or four days at sea, Andar
was fairly certain that they were now in Aracia's part of the
Land of Dhrall.

Aracia and her little girl, Lillabeth, came out on deck a

few times, but they spent most of their time in the cabin near the bow of the *Victory*. Andar didn't really miss Veltan's older sister that much. Her superior attitude and shrill voice didn't sit very well with him, so he tried to avoid her as much as possible.

As the *Victory* and the rest of the fleet continued sailing in a generally northeasterly direction, Andar saw several farming villages and even a few small cities along the coast. The cities seemed sort of unfinished to Andar, largely because they didn't have walls like cities should. Of course, the Land of Dhrall was generally peaceful, so walls weren't really necessary, but still, that unfinished look made them appear incomplete, for some reason.

The wheat fields appeared to have no boundaries, and that was something else that seemed most unusual. Property owners back in the Trogite Empire always marked the edges of their land with fences, but so far as Andar was able to determine, "mine" and "yours" didn't really mean all that much to the people here. It seemed most unnatural to Andar, but it might just be that "ours" was the guiding principle here.

It was approaching autumn now, and the endless wheat fields lay golden under the late-summer sun. The soil here must be quite a bit richer than the soil back in the empire, Andar concluded, since the wheat stalks stood almost twice as high as was normal back home. "It looks to me like they won't run out of food around here," he murmured.

"That's ridiculous, Narasan," Padan protested when they were all gathered in Narasan's cabin for their daily meeting a few days later. "The city *has* to have a name."

"I don't think she sees it as a city, Padan," Narasan disagreed. "She refers to it as 'the temple.' There *are* some shops there, I understand, but we're still talking about a land without money, so what *we* might call a 'business' wouldn't be exactly the same here. Anyway, Aracia's temple is the only significant part of the town as far as she's concerned. Maybe a few of you should nose around in the city outside the temple walls a bit after we get there. The word 'temple' suggests a priesthood, and sometimes priests haven't got a very firm grip on reality. Let's find out what the *real* people think. We'll *also* need to know if there's anything at all resembling an army in this part of the Land of Dhrall. Omago built a fair military in Veltan's Domain, and Longbow's archers did their share of the work in Zelana's. There *might* just be some sort of defensive force here, but I don't think Aracia would even be aware of it. She's too busy being important to pay very much attention to what's going on around her."

Andar was fairly sure that Narasan had been glossing over a goodly number of Aracia's faults. Of course, *if* what they'd heard about the Elder Gods was anywhere close to being accurate, they were nearing the end of their cycle, and there was a distinct possibility that some ugly terms like "dotage," "senility," and "foolish" might apply, despite the fact that, with the exception of Dahlaine's grey hair and beard, they showed none of the usual signs of extreme age—on the outside, at least.

It was about midafternoon on the following day when the *Victory* led the fleet into what civilized people would call the "harbor" of Aracia's temple-town. There were a couple of crudely constructed docks jutting out from the beach, but nothing at all resembling the piers of Castano. There were several small buildings above the tide-line, but the major structure in the town—if anyone could call it a town—was quite obviously the temple.

"I don't think letting the men go ashore here would be a very good idea," Narasan told them as they gathered again in the large cabin near the stern of the *Victory*. "We know very little about the people of this part of the Land of Dhrall, so let's not take any chances. Let's keep things sort of formal until we get to know the people here a little better."

"Should we leave our swords behind, Commander?" Brigadier Danal asked a bit dubiously.

"I don't think so, no," Narasan replied. "We *are* soldiers, after all, and we *have* been hired to fight a war. Just the presence of our swords should let everybody in the temple know why we're here and what we're capable of doing. No jokes or laughing, Padan. I'm sure it'll hurt your face just a bit, but force yourself to look grim and bleak. We want the high-ranking people—priests, most likely—to know just exactly what we are and why we're here." He looked around at them. "Any questions?" he asked with one raised eyebrow.

Nobody answered.

"All right, then. Andar, would you be so good as to go advise 'holy' Aracia that we've arrived and that we're ready to go ashore whenever she wants us to?"

"I'll see to it, Commander," Andar replied a bit reluctantly. Then he went out onto the deck of the anchored *Victory*.

He tapped on the door of Aracia's cabin. "We've arrived at your temple-town, ma'am," he called out. "Commander Narasan wants to know if you'd like us to escort you to your temple."

"I don't think that would be a good idea," she replied through the door. "I'd better go on ahead and prepare my people to meet you. They aren't used to seeing soldiers, so let's not frighten them."

"Whatever you think best, Lady Aracia," Andar said in a neutral tone. Then he went back to Narasan's cabin. "She's not ready for us to go ashore yet," he reported. "She wants to prepare her people before we make our appearance."

"Or maybe clean house," Padan suggested. "You know— mop the floors, dust the furniture, wash the windows, order the servants to put on clean clothes—all those important things a lady absolutely *must* do to impress the visitors."

"That's absurd, Padan," Danal scoffed.

"I know," Padan conceded, "but unfortunately, it might just come very close to being the truth."

It was almost noon on the following day when a rather awkward canoe approached the *Victory*. Unlike the canoes of Lady Zelana's Domain, this one appeared to be a hollowed-out log with a dozen or so paddlers on each side. A grossly fat man wearing a black linen robe and an ornate miter was standing at the front—which didn't seem to be a very good idea to Andar. Standing up in a canoe could be a very good way to get wet in a hurry.

"Holy Aracia invites you to her temple, mighty warriors," the man announced in an almost oratorical manner. "Welcome are you in her Domain in this time of crisis, forasmuch as we, her servants, are ill-prepared to meet the unholy invaders which most certainly even now are preparing to assault this precious land with evil intent, and though we would all joyfully die in her defense, beloved Aracia has most wisely chosen a different course, and you, O mighty warriors, have generously agreed to stand in our stead and to wreak destruction unimaginable upon our foes. Welcome, then, one and all, to the holy Domain of Divine Aracia, and at her command I have come here to advise you that she eagerly awaits your coming that you may speak with her of diverse crucial matters in preparation for the coming conflict."

Padan turned rather abruptly and hurried over to the other side of the *Victory*, and Andar heard his muffled laughter.

"You may advise Holy Aracia that we shall come forthwith, revered sir," Narasan said, accepting the invitation with no hint of a smile.

"Most kind are you, mighty warrior," the fat native replied, "and I shall most quickly return to Holy Aracia's temple to advise her of your coming." He signaled the men holding paddles, and the hollowed-out log boat turned awkwardly around and went back toward the beach.

"Not a sound!" Commander Narasan hissed sharply. "I don't want to hear so much as a giggle—at least not until that pompous fool gets out of earshot."

"Is it my imagination, or does it look to you like this town was built on some sort of mound?" Brigadier Danal asked Andar as they started up from the beach.

"It *does* seem to be a bit higher than the rest of this coast," Andar agreed. "It's probably just a hill of some kind."

"You don't see too many hills this close to a beach in flat country," Danal reminded his friend. "I hate to say this, but isn't it possible that it's man-made?"

Andar looked around, and his mind shuddered back from an ugly possibility. "Something like that would have taken *centuries*, Danal, and what purpose would it have served?"

"A temple built on high ground *would* be a bit more impressive than one on flat, coastal ground, and impressing people is very important to Veltan's older sister, I've noticed."

"I think you gentlemen may be overlooking something," Padan said then. "If Lady Aracia wants something to happen, it probably *will* happen. All she'd have had to do was to say, 'Rise up,' and the ground would have been tickled to death to obey her."

"Maybe," Danal said a bit dubiously, "but if some of the things I've heard came even close to being the truth, fully half of the people in this part of the Land of Dhrall are priests, and taking on a project like building a mound that's several miles across would have given them something to do in their spare time."

"Close up, gentlemen," Commander Narasan told them. "Let's at least *try* to look military."

So far as Andar could tell, the town that appeared to have grown up around Aracia's temple was the closest thing to a city in the entire Land of Dhrall. The buildings had white-plastered walls and red tile roofs, and the streets were paved.

The temple rose up from the top of the mound, of course, and there were tall spires—probably decorative—reaching high up into the air. It seemed grossly overdone to Andar, but he realized that Aracia *needed* something like this. There had been more than a few hints during the campaign in Veltan's Domain that Aracia deeply resented her older brother's status as the highest-ranking god in the Land of Dhrall, and her ostentatious temple here was little more than a form of self-aggrandizement. It was rather sad, but not really all that uncommon.

The steps leading up to the temple were wide, and the massive doors were sheathed with what appeared to be gold. That took ostentation out to the far end, Andar concluded.

The stout orator who'd spoken to them in the harbor was waiting at the door, and he unleashed his vocabulary again as he greeted them.

Andar chose not to listen.

It took them quite some time to reach the central room of the temple, which did not even remotely resemble a Trogite convenium, since the central feature was a throne rather than an altar. That was one advantage the Dhralls had that the Trogites did not. They knew what their gods looked like, since they were usually present in the immediate vicinity.

Andar was fairly sure that neither Zelana nor Veltan would have enjoyed all the adoration Aracia's priesthood kept shoveling all over their goddess, but Aracia seemed to revel in the long, tiresome speeches.

Commander Narasan nudged Andar, and the two of them drifted on to the back of the ornate throne-room. "I'd say that they're just getting warmed up," Narasan said quietly, "so this will probably take most of the day. Why don't you and Danal go drift around this town and take a look at things? What we really need to know is whether this place is at all defensible. I'm having some serious doubts about that. Why would anybody in his—or her—right mind build a city and then neglect to build a wall?"

"I wouldn't say that 'right mind' is an applicable term, Commander," Andar replied. "It looks to me like our esteemed employer doesn't have a very firm grip on reality. I'll have a look around, but I wouldn't get my hopes up too high, Commander. These people probably don't even know what the word 'war' means."

"You could be right, Andar," Narasan conceded, "but go have a look, and talk with the locals. We need to know if the people of Aracia's Domain have anything at all resembling an army. If the bug-people *do* decide to come this way, we're going to have to hold them off—at least until Sorgan can get here, and that might take a while."

"I'll see what I can find out, Commander, but I'm not very optimistic."

3

Andar and Brigadier Danal quietly left Aracia's throne-
room and went on out of the temple. "That fat one who
makes long, windy speeches is called the 'Takal of Aracia,'"
Danal advised his friend.

"How did you find that out?"

Danal shrugged. "I asked a young fellow who was off to
one side," he replied. "He told me that he only recently
joined the priesthood, and he was trying his best to impress
me. You know how novices are. They'll talk forever if you
give them half a chance. Anyway, if I understood him correctly, 'Takal' is something on the order of what the Trogite
Church calls 'the Naos'—except that he has four wives, and
that would send the Amarite priesthood right up the walls."

"It *would* disturb them a bit, I'd imagine," Andar agreed.
"Did the young fellow give you that high priest's name?"

"Bersla, I think was the name he mentioned. The young fellow was talking so fast that I had a little trouble keeping up
with him. He told me that the fat one was rich, but I'm not sure

just how a man can be 'rich' in a land without money. For all I know, it could be a reference to the size of his belly."

They split up after they'd left the temple grounds, and Andar went on out to the western edge of the city. His uniform drew many puzzled looks, and the natives tried to avoid him for some reason. He *did* manage to get a few answers from a couple of them, though, but the answers weren't very clear. When he said "wall," the local people seemed to think he meant the side of a house. It was quite obvious that the concept of a protective wall surrounding the city was completely alien to them, and most of them, it appeared, had never heard the word "war" before.

He methodically went on around the outskirts of the town, asking each native willing to speak with him the same questions. When he reached the beach again, Danal was waiting for him. "There's not one tavern in the entire town," Danal complained. "When I asked them where I should go if I wanted something to drink, they kept pointing at the wells. Evidently, water's the only thing they drink."

"Their religion might have something to do with that," Andar suggested. "Their god *is* a woman, and women have strange ideas sometimes. Were you able to find out anything about this 'barter economy' business?"

"Not much that made any sense. I wouldn't swear to it, but I *think* they use fruit or grain when they want to buy something—so many apples for a yard of wool and that sort of thing. There's quite a bit of haggling going on in those shops. Did you happen to come across anybody who understood what you meant when you asked them about a wall?"

"They all seemed to think I was talking about house walls," Andar replied. "The notion of a stand-alone wall doesn't seem to have occurred to any of them. Let's face it,

Danal, these are very primitive people. The only metal most of them have encountered is gold, and they use gold for ornaments, not for money."

"Pitiful," Danal said. "Have we seen enough yet?"

"I think we've covered just about everything the commander wants to know about."

"Let's go on back to the temple, then."

"Must we?" Danal replied plaintively.

Bersla, the fat high priest of the temple, was orating again, and Lady Aracia had a dreamy sort of look on her face as she sat on her throne.

Andar and Danal joined Commander Narasan and the warrior queen.

"Any luck?" Narasan asked them quietly.

"I wouldn't really get my hopes up, sir," Danal replied. He glanced around at the nearby priests. "Do you think Aracia would be offended if we went outside for a breath of fresh air—or something? There are some things you should know, and I don't think the priesthood there would be very happy if any of them overheard our reports."

"I don't imagine she'll even notice if we leave," Narasan replied. He snapped his fingers, and Padan, who was standing nearby, looked over at them. Narasan gestured toward the door at the far side of Aracia's throne-room, and Padan joined them as they moved toward the main door of the temple. "What's afoot?" he asked quietly.

"Let's hold off until we get outside," Narasan replied. "I don't think we want the natives to hear us."

They moved rather casually through the crowd of overdressed priests and then went on outside, with the warrior queen Trenicia close behind.

"What did you find out, Andar?" Narasan asked when they went out through the golden doors.

"There's nothing at all even remotely resembling any kind of defenses, sir," Andar replied, "and the local citizens don't seem to understand the meaning of the word 'wall.' If we want a wall, we'll have to build it ourselves. The wall around the temple itself is no more than a decoration. The way things stand right now, I'd say that 'Holy City' is completely indefensible."

"Why bother?" Padan asked. "I'd say that 'Holy City' isn't really worth the trouble. What we *really* need right now is another one of those 'lumpy maps.' If we can pinpoint the most probable route the bug-people will take when they invade, we should be able to stop them before they reach open country. Once they spread out on the farmland, we'll have lost the war."

"That *does* make sense, Commander," Andar agreed. "If we can find a good place to build a fort that the bug-people can't get past, we'll win this war."

"I know," Narasan replied glumly, "but 'Holy Aracia' wants us to concentrate on defending 'Holy Temple.' It's the only thing that's the least bit important to her, and she wants to have multitudes of soldiers right here where she can see them. Did either of you come across anything at all like a local army—something on the order of those farmers in Veltan's Domain?"

"They don't even have police here, Commander," Danal said, "and as close as I was able to determine, the word 'weapon' is beyond their understanding."

"I'm not sure if this would work, Commander," Andar said, "but as soon as we can determine the most probable route for the bug-people invasion, maybe we should start waving the term 'protective wall' around. Then we tell 'Holy Aracia' and 'Fat High Priest' that bricks made of clay and straw wouldn't do the job. We'll need rocks, and from what I've seen, rocks are very rare in this coastal region. If we put a couple thousand men to work carrying rocks here from the mountains off to the west, it *might* persuade the lady who hired us that we're making preparations to build a protective wall around her temple. That might keep her happy, and then she'll be able to concentrate on being adored while *we* concentrate on building a *real* wall where we're going to need one."

"This one is very clever, Narasan," Trenicia observed. "The one who concentrates on listening to speeches isn't going to pay *too* much attention to the details, and as long as the pile of rocks near her temple keeps growing, she'll relax and listen to more speeches while you and your men do what really needs to be done."

"The first thing we need, though, is a map," Padan insisted, "and I'm not sure if our employer has ever taken the trouble to even *look* at the rest of her Domain. Being adored is evidently a full-time job."

They had to wait until suppertime before they could speak with Lady Aracia, of course. Takal Bersla filled the entire afternoon with adoration, but eating was probably even more important for him.

Aracia, of course, remained on her throne, most probably impatient for the adoration to resume.

"We need to talk, Lady Aracia," Commander Narasan said as soon as Bersla had left.

"Is it important?" Aracia demanded.

"Extremely important, My Lady," Narasan replied. "If

I'm going to defend your part of the Land of Dhrall, I'll need a map. I must know what the ground looks like before I can make any decisions."

"It's fairly flat near the coast," she replied almost indifferently. "Then the foothills begin to emerge off to the west. Then the mountains rise up even higher to separate my Domain from the Wasteland. That's about it, Commander."

"Details, Lady Aracia," Narasan insisted. "I can't make any plans without details. I'm quite sure that we're going to need one of those 'lumpy maps' that have been so useful in the past two wars."

"We'll talk about this some other time, Commander," she replied. "My Takal will be coming back soon, and I'm sure he has more to say to me."

"He can wait," Narasan said bluntly. "I can't. Let me put it to you in simpler terms, Lady Aracia. If I don't have a map of your Domain by tomorrow morning, I'll give all those pretty gold blocks back to you and take my army back home."

"You wouldn't!" she exclaimed, the imperious expression sliding off her face.

"Try me," Narasan said bluntly.

Takal Bersla appeared to be seriously discontented the following morning, quite probably because his after-dinner oration had been canceled somewhat abruptly by divine Aracia. It was very likely that his discontent had been elevated by his discovery that his luxurious "contemplation chamber" had been usurped, and that it now had a lumpy floor.

"Our defenders required a map of my Domain, my devoted Takal," Aracia explained. "The map, of necessity, is quite large, so we needed a sizeable room."

"What is a 'map,' most holy?" Bersla demanded.

"A picture of the ground," Aracia explained. "Our friends wanted to study the shape of my Domain so that they will be able to defend it when the creatures of the Wasteland attack us."

"It is the temple that must be defended, holy Aracia. The empty ground outside the temple is not significant."

Andar was startled by Bersla's lack of understanding, but he approached the fat man rather carefully. "I'm just guessing here," he said, "but I gather that your family has served holy Aracia for many generations."

"We have served in her temple for centuries," Bersla declared with some pride.

"Ah," Andar said. "That might explain why you've overlooked something rather important."

"I overlook very little, outlander."

"Good. Now tell me which part of the temple you'll eat when the supply of food runs out."

"There's always food here. It's the primary obligation of the commoners to provide food for the priesthood."

"But if they don't have any food to give you, there won't be anything here for you to eat, will there? If you think about that just a bit, I'm sure you'll realize that the farmland out there is much more important than this temple."

"How *dare* you?" Bersla flared.

"Truth sometimes has a very bad taste," Andar said. "How many times a day do you eat?"

"Thrice, of course. All people eat three times a day."

"And where does the food you eat come from?"

"Well, the farms, I suppose, but there are many farms in holy Aracia's Domain. We'll *always* have food."

"Not if we don't stop the invasion of the bug-people, you

won't. The bug-people eat *everything*—vegetables, fruit, meat-animals, trees, and the farmers themselves. Once the bug-people start eating, it won't be long before everything out there will be gone. That's when you and the other priests here in this holy temple will begin to starve to death. I've been told by people who know about such things as the process of starvation that it would probably take a man of your girth about three months to die, and it's likely to be the worst three months of your entire life. You'll have to be very watchful after the supply of food runs out, because your fellow priests are very likely to decide that a plump fellow like you might taste very good after they've gone without food for a few weeks."

"That's monstrous!" Bersla exclaimed.

"I know, but it *does* happen in these situations. Now, then, if your fellow priests *don't* kill you and eat you, your body will begin to absorb your flesh. In a certain sense, you'll be eating yourself, and your skin will start to sag like a wet blanket. I wouldn't worry *too* much, though, because after the bug-people have eaten everything out in the farmland, they'll come here, and then *they'll* eat you. You should probably keep a nice sharp knife handy so that you can kill yourself *before* the bugs arrive. Bugs don't seem to think it's necessary to kill something before they eat it, and being eaten alive would probably be even worse than dying of starvation. If you'd like, I'll show you exactly where to drive in your knife to kill yourself quickly with the least amount of pain. Or maybe you could hide yourself long enough to finish starving to death before the bugs find you. But make no mistake, great priest, when the food runs out, you *will* die— one way or another."

Bersla was staring at Andar with a look of sheer horror,

and Aracia's expression was much the same. "He's just making this up, isn't he, Narasan?" she demanded.

"Actually, I think he put it rather mildly, Lady Aracia," Narasan replied. "When famine strikes, horrors beyond imagination begin to crop up. Starvation is even worse than a war, and when a really severe famine breaks out, *everybody* dies—eventually—and the longer people live, the more they suffer. Now that you understand what's likely to happen here, maybe we should talk about how we're going to prevent it. I'd say that we should concentrate on keeping the bug-people out of your Domain. Once they come down out of the mountains and spread out, we'll have lost this war, and all of your people will become nothing more than something the bugs will have for lunch."

THE
NORTH
COUNTRY

1

At first light Captain Hook-Beak rowed a skiff across the harbor near Veltan's house to speak with Narasan. Rabbit was standing near the bow of the *Seagull* when his young Trogite friend Keselo came out on deck. "Where's your captain going?" he asked.

"He wants to get a few things straightened out with your commander before we split up and sail off in different directions," Rabbit replied. "We're likely to be separated for a month or two, so the cap'n wants to be sure that we'll all be ready if trouble breaks out, I guess." He looked at Keselo. "Do you know very much about these horse-soldiers that everybody seems to be so excited about?" he asked.

"I've never been in that part of the world," Keselo replied, "but I've heard a few stories, and if those stories come anywhere close to being accurate, I definitely wouldn't want to face them in a war."

"Just exactly what is a horse?" Rabbit asked curiously.

"It's one of the animals that eats grass," Keselo replied. "It's not very much like a sheep or a cow or a deer, though.

It's quite a bit larger, and it can run faster. The Malavi have somehow managed to tame them, and they sit on the backs of horses when they're moving their cattle-herds from one place to another. Horses can run faster than cows—even when they've got a Malavi sitting on them. Over the years, the horses have turned out to be very useful, and the Malavi cow-herds have proved to be extremely valuable."

"Do the horse people have any unusual weapons?" Rabbit asked.

"Their swords and spears are a bit different from ours. They call their swords 'sabres,' and they slash with them rather than stab. Their spears are called 'lances,' and they're quite a bit longer than ours. I think they might have some problems if they encounter the bug-people, though. Venom would kill a horse just as fast as it kills people, I think, and a Malavi without his horse wouldn't be very effective."

"Do they wear armor of any kind?"

Keselo shook his head. "It would probably just get in their way, and the extra weight would slow their horses down. Speed is very important in Malavi war tactics. In many ways they're very much like your people, Rabbit. They rely on speed." Keselo smiled briefly. "Now that I think about it, the Malavi are almost a land version of the Maags, and the horse is very much like the *Seagull* here."

"I think we'll get along with them fairly well, then," Rabbit said. Then he sighed. "I guess I'd better fire up my forge. Longbow told me that the archers up north will probably want bronze arrowheads as soon as they see the ones he has."

"Wouldn't iron be even better?"

"Maybe, but not all that much. Bronze is *almost* as good as iron when you're talking about arrowheads, and it's a lot easier to work with. The fire in my forge doesn't have to be as hot to melt down bronze. I can turn out ten times as many bronze arrowheads in the same amount of time as it'd take me to make a few out of iron."

"Do you have that much bronze here on the *Seagull*?" Keselo asked, sounding a bit surprised.

Rabbit grinned at his friend. "There's quite a bit down in the hold," he said. "Trogite ships usually carry spare anchors just in case they happen to break the rope on the main one, but those spare anchors have been disappearing here lately for some reason. Isn't that odd?"

Keselo laughed. "You're a pirate, Rabbit," he declared.

"Of course I am. I'm a Maag, after all, and piracy's what we're all about. Everybody knows that."

It seemed to Rabbit that there was a kind of dusty quality about the air as the Maag fleet sailed along the southern coast of Veltan's Domain. He'd noticed that on several occasions in the past. Autumn was often pretty when the leaves were turning gold or red along the coast, but there was a kind of sadness about the season that followed summer.

"You're looking sort of gloomy today, Bunny," Eleria said as she joined him near the bow of the *Seagull*.

"Winter's coming," Rabbit said. "That's the gloomy time of the year."

"We could ask the Beloved to make winter go away, if you'd like," she said with one of those sly little smiles.

"I don't know if that would be a very good idea, baby sister," Rabbit replied. "If she starts playing with the seasons, Mother Sea might send her off to the moon like she did to Veltan that time."

"Mother Sea wouldn't do that to the Beloved," Eleria

replied. She held out her arms. "I need a hug, Bunny. Everybody's so busy talking in that hut where we're staying that they don't have time for me."

"It's called a 'cabin,' baby sister, not a 'hut.' "

"What's the difference?"

"I'm not really sure," Rabbit admitted, "but I think 'hut' would upset the cap'n almost as much as when somebody calls his ship a 'boat.' That sends him right straight up the wall."

"You're not hugging, Bunny," she scolded.

"Sorry, baby sister. I'll get right on it." He picked her up and wrapped his arms about her.

"That's *so* much nicer," she said, kissing his cheek.

Later that day, Longbow came out on deck and joined Rabbit at the bow of the *Seagull.* "It's good to be moving again," he said quietly. "I was starting to get a little tired of all that bickering."

"What was that all about, anyway? I never *did* get the straight of it."

Longbow shrugged. "Zelana's older sister wanted *all* of the outlanders to defend *her* Domain, but her big brother wouldn't hold still for it. He feels that his Domain is just as important as hers—if not more. Zelana and Veltan thought that they were both being a little silly. We sometimes forget that the Elder Gods are nearing the end of their cycle, and they're starting to get just a little strange."

"More than a 'little,' sometimes," Rabbit said. "Eleria's going to take over for Zelana before long, isn't she?"

"I believe so, but the gods might have a different definition of 'before long' than we do. I'd imagine that the younger gods will have to grow up before their elders can hand things off to them."

2

I see that you're working again, Rabbit," the farmer Omago said when he came forward later that day.

"Just trying to stay a little bit ahead of Longbow," Rabbit said. "He thinks that the Tonthakans will want bronze arrowheads when we reach Lord Dahlaine's part of the Land of Dhrall. I'm not really doing anything very important now anyway, and if I'm banging on my anvil, Ox and Ham-Hand won't be sitting around trying to come up with things for me to do." He laid his hammer down on the anvil. "What's Ara been doing here lately?" he asked. "We haven't seen very much of her."

"She's in the kitchen, of course," Omago said with a faint smile. "She's been giving that one called 'the Fat Man' some cooking lessons."

Rabbit laughed. "I should have known she'd do something like that," he said. "The Fat Man's not really one of the world's greatest cooks, that's for sure. He usually gets grouchy when somebody goes into his galley, though."

"Nobody stays grouchy very long when Ara stops by,"

Omago said. "After she'd tasted a couple of the meals he'd served up, she decided to educate him. I'm almost positive that he'll be a much better cook by the time we reach Dahlaine's part of the world."

"That won't hurt my feelings very much," Rabbit said. "I'm not sure how much she'll be able to teach him during this trip, though. There isn't much stored down there in the galley except beans, and there's only so much you can do with beans."

"I think you're in for a pleasant surprise, Rabbit," Omago said. "Ara *is* the finest cook in the world, after all, so I'm sure she'll find *some* way to make beans taste better."

The fleet rounded the last peninsula on the south coast a few days later and turned north. There was a good following wind, and the longships seemed almost to fly. Rabbit found that to be quite exhilarating. This was what sailing was all about. He spent most of his daylight hours out on the deck near the *Seagull*'s bow heating bronze in his forge.

"Breezy, isn't it?" Longbow said as he joined him at the rail.

"It's a fair wind," Rabbit agreed as he tested the iron pot filled with pieces of bronze on his forge. "If it keeps this up, we'll make better time than the cap'n thought we would. Have we reached Zelana's territory yet?"

Longbow squinted at the coast. "Not quite, I think. Give it another day or so." He glanced at Rabbit's forge. "Your bronze is starting to melt."

"I know," Rabbit said. "I want it to get a little soupier before I pour it into the molds, though. If I pour too soon, there'll be lumps sticking out of the arrowheads. How far would you say it is to the bay of Lattash?"

"About two days, I think."

Then the bull-shouldered first mate Ox came forward to join them. "Lady Zelana's brother's going to tell us some things about his part of this country," he said, "and the cap'n wants you two to sit in. I guess things on up north are just a little different from the places we've seen so far."

"It wouldn't be much fun if it was all the same, would it?" Rabbit said.

"We're here for gold, Rabbit," Ox said sourly, "not for fun."

"Gold and fun don't always go in different directions, Ox," Rabbit said with a grin.

"Just go on back to the cap'n's cabin, Rabbit," Ox said a bit wearily. "If you want to have fun, do it on your own time."

The cabin at the stern of the *Seagull* was a bit crowded, but they all managed to squeeze themselves in.

Zelana's grey-bearded big brother looked around. "I guess that's everybody," he said. "Captain Hook-Beak wants to know a few things about the people of my Domain, and I thought that maybe it'd save time in the long run if you were all here. I'll give you a sort of general idea about my people and the layout of the country up there, and then I'll answer any questions you might have." He paused, looking around at them. "When we get to the north of Zelana's Domain, we'll go ashore in the Tonthakan Nation. There are three significantly different cultures in my Domain—the Tonthakans, who are very much like the people of sister Zelana's Domain, the Matans, who dwell on the grassy plain in the center, and the Atazakans. The Tonthakans are primarily hunters, the northern Matans have vast grain fields, and the Atazakans are totally worthless."

"Are we likely to hit bad weather?" Sorgan asked.

"Not immediately," Dahlaine replied. "There's a warm current that comes up the west coast in the autumn that sort of holds winter back. When winter finally *does* arrive, it's fairly brutal. We get snowstorms that last for weeks. Fortunately, the whirlwind season is almost over for this year."

"We come across those out at sea sometimes," Torl said. "We call them 'water-spouts.' We use some other terms as well, but I don't think we should repeat those words in the presence of Lady Zelana."

"I appreciate that, Torl," Zelana said.

"Are there mountains of any kind standing between your part of the Land of Dhrall and the Wasteland?" Sorgan asked.

Dahlaine nodded. "If the creatures of the Wasteland come north, I don't think they'll enjoy it very much. The mountains of Zelana's Domain and Veltan's are gently rolling hills by comparison, and with winter coming, things are likely to get very unpleasant in those mountains without much in the way of a warning of any kind."

The wind held steady for the next several days, and Sorgan's fleet moved briskly on up the west coast of the Land of Dhrall. It was about midmorning of an autumn day while Rabbit was busy forging more bronze arrowheads for the natives of the Tonthakan region of Dahlaine's territory when Longbow joined him. "How's your supply of bronze holding out?" he asked.

"I've still got enough to keep me going for another week or so," Rabbit replied. "The smiths on board the other ships are *supposed* to be working, too, but I couldn't swear to it that they are."

"There's something I've been meaning to ask you," Longbow said. "I've heard about what you did to that Regulator called Konag. When did you decide to take up archery? I thought your job was to *make* arrows, not to shoot them."

"It just sort of popped into my head one day," Rabbit replied. "I'd been spending days and weeks *making* arrows, and then one day I realized that I'd never pulled a bow even once in my whole life. The more I thought about it, the more I wanted to give it a try."

"I was busy someplace else when you killed Regulator Konag, but from what I've heard, you did a very good job."

"All I really did was follow your instructions, Longbow. It seemed like every time I turned around, you were talking about 'unification.' After I'd trimmed and shaped my bow and got the bowstring in place, I took a few arrows and went out into the woods to make sure that my bow—or the bowstring—wouldn't break the first time I tried to shoot an arrow. There was a patch of moss on a tree a ways away from where I was standing, and I looked at it for a while, and then I shot an arrow at it. Somehow I *knew* that the arrow would go exactly where I wanted it to go. I stuck quite a few arrows into that moss-patch, and they all went exactly where I wanted them to go. That's when I decided that Konag would look much prettier with an arrow sticking out of his forehead, and, as it turned out, he did." Rabbit frowned. "When you get right down to it, though, I wasn't really thinking about shooting him until I actually saw him. As soon as I saw him, I suddenly just *had* to kill him."

"I'm starting to catch a faint smell of dear old 'unknown friend' again," Longbow said with a thoughtful expression on his face. "Konag was causing some problems, and she wanted him dead. You and your bow were right there, so she borrowed you."

"Borrowed?"

"She was doing the same thing to me for several weeks. I wasn't in the immediate vicinity when Konag started to get in her way, so she just reached out and grabbed you."

"Can she really *do* that? I mean, I don't think that even Zelana could have done *some* of the things your friend was doing up in that basin above the Falls of Vash."

"I'm getting a strong feeling that our unknown friend can do things that make Zelana and her family look like children by comparison. She grabbed that geyser and moved it several miles off to the north of the place where it had been happily bubbling up out of the ground for thousands of years, and then she unleashed it to drown thousands of bug-people and church-people all at the same time. Even Dahlaine couldn't have done that."

"I'm glad she's on our side, then," Rabbit said. "We wouldn't really want to have her as our enemy, would we?"

"Not even a little bit, friend Rabbit," Longbow agreed.

"Do you suppose we could talk about something else?" Rabbit said. "Just the thought of that kind of power makes me go cold all over." He frowned. "Did I hear it right? As I understand it, you've actually visited the part of Dahlaine's territory he calls Tonthakan."

"I've gone up there a few times, yes," Longbow replied. "I'd pretty well thinned out the bug-people in our territory, and I was sort of wondering if I'd frightened them so much that they'd started to sneak around off to the north."

"Dahlaine says that they're archers—just like you and Red-Beard. Are they any good at shooting arrows?"

"They're not bad," Longbow replied. "They're good enough to keep eating regularly, at any rate. There's a man up there—Athlan, his name is—who's quite skilled. He's a funny sort of fellow, and I like him. I'm sure he'll be delighted with these bronze arrowheads you're forging for him."

"A man should always help his friends, Longbow," Rabbit said. "We're getting a start on this, but as soon as we go ashore in that place called Tonthakan, we'll set up an arrow factory like we did at Lattash, and then we'll be able to turn out bronze arrowheads by the thousands. I don't think the bug-people will like that very much, but we can't please everybody, I guess."

Since the Maag fleet was sailing north along the coast at a good rate of speed, it seemed to Rabbit that autumn was coming on much faster than it should. There were birch trees and oak scattered among the pines and firs of Zelana's Domain, and their leaves were changing color now at what appeared to be an unnatural speed as he worked at his anvil.

"Would it be all right if I stayed out here with you for a while, Bunny?" Eleria asked after she'd come out of Sorgan's cabin about noon one day. "I'm getting very tired of all the talking that's going on in Sorgan's cabin. All they want to do is talk-talk-talk."

"They're making plans, baby sister," Rabbit told her.

"No, they're just wasting time. We won't know what's *really* going to happen until one of the Dreams comes along."

"Are *you* going to do the dreaming again this time, baby sister?" Rabbit asked her.

"I don't really think so, Bunny," she replied. "It's possible, I suppose, but I think it's just about time for Lillabeth to do her share of the work. Yaltar, Ashad, and I've been doing all the dreaming so far, so I think it's Lillabeth's turn."

"Won't that be just a little inconvenient? I mean, if she's way off to the east and we're on up north, it's going to be a long way from where we are."

"Distance doesn't really mean anything, Bunny," Eleria replied. "You should know that by now."

"Well—maybe—but I think we'd all be a lot happier if you or one of the boy-dreamers were telling us what was going to happen. Zelana's sister won't be very happy if *her* Dreamer is the one who tells us that we'll be fighting the next war up north instead of off to the east. You don't need to tell Zelana I said this, but I don't really like her sister very much."

"You don't *have* to like her, Bunny. The only one you're supposed to like is the Beloved. She *is* the one who's paying Hook-Big, after all."

"Are we still playing that tired old 'Hook-Big' game, baby sister?" Rabbit asked with a faint smile.

"The old ones are the best, Bunny," Eleria replied with a toss of her head. "Do you think you might be able to spare me a kiss-kiss along about now?" she asked then.

"Oh, I think so," Rabbit replied. "I've got quite a few of them stored up in the little room where I keep my hugs and kisses locked away so that nobody can steal them."

"Oh, goodie!" Eleria said, clapping her little hands together.

And then they both laughed, and Rabbit picked her up and kissed her soundly several times.

3

W hat's afoot?" Rabbit asked Kryda Ham-Hand, the second mate of the *Seagull*, a couple of days later when they veered off from the main fleet and anchored just off the beach of a small village about three days to the north of the bay of Lattash.

Ham-Hand shrugged. "Longbow wants to go ashore and have a few words with his chief. He's fairly sure that Chief Old-Bear will know if anything's happening on up to the north of here. As I understand it, the natives of the coastal region of Lord Dahlaine's country stay in touch with Old-Bear's tribe, so if anything's happening up there, Longbow's chief will know about it. The cap'n thinks it might not be a bad idea to find out if the bug-people have started to move yet. Red-Beard's just going along for the ride. It shouldn't take them very long, and the information could be very useful."

"It makes sense, I guess," Rabbit agreed. "Good information can sometimes be worth more than gold when you're fighting one of these land wars with the bug-people."

"Bite your tongue, Rabbit," Ham-Hand said. "*Nothing's* worth more than gold."

"Could you accept '*almost* worth more than gold'?" Rabbit asked.

"I'd have to think about that for a while," Ham-Hand said. "I'll get back to you about it—one of these days."

Longbow and Red-Beard paddled back on out to the *Seagull* after about an hour or so, and they went directly to Captain Hook-Beak's cabin to report. Longbow's face seemed to be just a bit bleak, but there was nothing particularly unusual about that.

After a while, though, Red-Beard came out of the cabin alone and joined Rabbit near the anvil.

"Are the bugs moving yet?" Rabbit asked him.

"Not so far as Chief Old-Bear knows," Red-Beard replied. "A few things cropped up, though, that you should probably know about."

"Oh?"

"It seems that there's been an old story floating around up here in this region that has to do with Longbow's 'unknown friend.' Chief Old-Bear was just a little surprised when Longbow mentioned her. If the myth—or story—or whatever you want to call it—comes anywhere close to being truth, Longbow's 'unknown friend' can do things—or arrange to have them done—that Zelana's family couldn't even come close to doing. It was Dahlaine who came up with the idea of the Dreamers, I guess, but 'unknown friend' tells the children what they're going to dream about. Zelana's family has some fairly rigid limitations, but she— whoever she is—doesn't. The story mentions 'strangers'— you, Sorgan, Narasan, and all the others—who'll come here to help, but I guess there'll be times when she'll deal with the bugs all by herself. That's why she kept telling Longbow to get out of the way. When you get right down to it, all we were doing was cluttering things up. Back in the first war, she gave Eleria the flood dream and Yaltar the fire-mountain dream, but during the war in the basin above the Falls of Vash, she didn't even bother with the Dreamers. She made that 'sea of gold' to drive the church armies crazy, and then when the church-soldiers started to run all over the bug-people, she told that river to turn around and go the other way—and it did exactly what she told it to do. She killed all of our enemies and created an ocean with little more than a snap of her fingers."

"I'd say that if she can do things like that, Zelana and her family don't really *need* all the armies they've been hiring," Rabbit mused.

"It might just be that you outlanders are important for something else," Red-Beard said with a slight frown. "Maybe she wants a lot of outlanders here just to watch while she's turning the world inside out. Then, when they go back home, they'll be able to tell all their friends that trying to come here to the Land of Dhrall could be the worst thing they could ever do, because if they try, they won't live long enough to spend any of the gold they steal."

"I think she's already convinced me," Rabbit declared with a shudder. "It might take her a little longer to get through to the cap'n and some of the others, but I think they'll get her point—eventually."

"The only trouble there is that time might run out for them before 'eventually' gets here."

          *   *   *

The Maag fleet continued to sail north along the coast for the next several days, and at some indeterminate point they left Zelana's territory and moved on up into the Domain of her older brother. Rabbit had noticed that the borders here in the Land of Dhrall were seldom marked by rivers or any other significant—or even noticeable—landmarks. It seemed that boundaries in this part of the world existed in the minds of the people rather than on the ground itself. The natives didn't seem to have any problems with that informality, but it appeared to bother Sorgan Hook-Beak quite a bit, and he came out on deck quite often to ask Longbow or Red-Beard if they'd moved out of Zelana's territory yet.

Then about midmorning on a hazy autumn day the *Seagull* rounded a jutting point of land, and there was what appeared to be a fishing village just ahead. Dahlaine came out of the cabin near the stern and joined Sorgan up near the bow. "We'll stop here, Captain Hook-Beak," he said. "Now we get to start walking."

Sorgan looked at the village. "That's not much of a town, Lord Dahlaine," he said.

"I wouldn't even call it a town, Captain," Dahlaine replied with a faint smile. "We have to go inland several miles before we'll reach the home of the local tribe. The fishermen here usually pack up and go on back home when winter arrives. Winters aren't very pleasant out here."

"That makes sense, I suppose," Sorgan agreed.

Rabbit noticed that the somewhat scruffy-looking huts of the village were almost identical to those in Lattash and the village of Chief Old-Bear, and the natives standing on the beach were dressed in leather clothes much like those of Longbow and Red-Beard. They might live in a different Domain, but their cultures appeared to be nearly identical.

Then a tall, lean native with dark hair pushed a canoe down the sandy beach to the water, nimbly stepped into it, and paddled on out toward the *Seagull*. As he drew closer, he slowed. "Ho, Longbow!" he called out, "what are you doing in that floating house?"

"Resting my feet, Athlan," Longbow called back. "Walking isn't all that much fun anymore."

"You know him, I take it?" Rabbit said quietly.

"I've known him for a long time, Rabbit," Longbow replied. "His name's Athlan, and he's a good hunter. I'm just guessing, but I'm fairly sure that he was sent here to guide us inland to the main tribal village."

"What's afoot, Longbow?" the native in the canoe called.

"War lately. The creatures of the Wasteland are starting to get restless."

"I thought you'd have killed them all by now."

"I left a few of them alive to give you something to shoot arrows at. Dahlaine's here, and he wants to talk to you."

"I'm not the chief of the tribe, Longbow," Athlan protested, pulling his canoe in beside the *Seagull*.

"I know that, but Dahlaine wants you to see enough of our outlander friends so that you can tell the members of your tribe why they've come here and what they can do to help them. Is your old chief still alive?"

"Just barely. His son, Kathlak, is sort of filling in for him. He goes into the chief's lodge and when he comes out, he tells us that the chief wants us to do this, that, or something else. We all know that the chief probably isn't even awake, and that the orders are coming from Kathlak himself, but we don't make an issue of it."

Longbow dropped a rolled-up rope ladder down to his

friend, and Athlan climbed on up. "Where did this thing come from?" he asked, looking around at the *Seagull*.

"There's a land off to the west of here, and Zelana went on over there to hire outlanders to help defend her Domain. I'm sure that the man in charge of those outlanders will want to talk with you, but this little fellow here is much more important."

"He's not very big, is he?"

"He doesn't have to be big, Athlan. He makes arrowheads that are probably the best in all the world."

"Is he really strong enough to split rocks?" Athlan asked a bit dubiously.

"He doesn't split rocks or chip points and edges. He makes arrowheads out of something else." Longbow handed his friend one of the bronze arrowheads Rabbit had forged.

Athlan carefully ran his thumb over the arrowhead. "What is this," he asked Rabbit, "and where can I find some?"

"You won't need to find any of it," Rabbit told him. "I've got several hundred of them already, and there's more on the way. It's a metal called bronze, and I heat it in my forge until it melts down into a liquid. Then I pour it into a baked clay mold. After it cools off, it stops being liquid and goes back to being solid, but it's in the shape that you've got right there in your hand."

"Where does this 'bronze' come from originally?"

"I haven't got the faintest idea," Rabbit admitted. "When I need some of it, I buy it—or steal it, if nobody's watching. People have told me that bronze is a mixture of two different metals that aren't very good by themselves, but once they're mixed together, they're much better. There's another metal called iron that we use for knives and axes, but it takes a much hotter fire to melt iron."

"There aren't any of these peculiar things here in the Land of Dhrall, are there?"

"I'm sure that there are. I've even seen red-colored rocks that are almost certainly iron ore. I can heat iron in my forge to make it soft enough to work with, but my forge doesn't get hot enough to melt it."

"What would you want me to give you for a dozen or so of these?" Athlan asked, holding up the bronze arrowhead.

Rabbit shrugged. "Nothing. I've come here to help you fight the bug-people, so the arrowheads are a gift." Rabbit shuddered. "I can't believe I just said that," he told Longbow.

"It sounded all right to me," Longbow replied.

"I'm not the only one in the tribe who'll need these new arrowheads," Athlan said. "It's likely to take you a long time to make enough of them for us, don't you think?"

"I won't be working alone," Rabbit said. "There's a smith on every ship in the fleet. Back in the war last spring we set up what we called the 'arrow factory' while we were waiting for the snow to melt off. We made enough arrowheads there to give every archer in Zelana's Domain all that he needed."

"I think this one just got a lot taller, Longbow," Athlan said. "I might have to twist a few arms to persuade the other men in the tribe that these new arrowheads are better than stone, but I'm sure they'll get my point."

"Let's go talk with Dahlaine, Athlan," Longbow said. "There are a few things you need to know so that you can pass them on to Kathlak."

"Lead the way, friend Longbow," Athlan replied.

*   *   *

"All creatures change with the passage of time, Athlan," Dahlaine told Longbow's friend. "The changes usually take so long that the creatures aren't even aware of them. The Vlagh has been tampering with the natural order of things here lately, though. When one of the creatures who serve the Vlagh sees a characteristic that might be useful, that characteristic will probably appear in the next hatch. During the war in the south, the Vlagh added turtle shells to a new hatch to protect them from the arrows my sister's archers had been using to kill them. Back before these wars, the servants of the Vlagh were all very much the same, but now we're facing six or eight varieties of enemies—that we know about. For all we know, there could be several new varieties when we encounter them here."

"Are you certain that they'll attack our part of Dhrall next?" Athlan asked.

Dahlaine shook his head. "They could come north," he said, "but they might go east instead. We don't know for sure yet, so we're covering both areas."

"That makes sense," Athlan agreed. "I think that maybe we should go on up to Statha now. It might be best if Kathlak hears about this as soon as possible, and we've had another problem that you should know about. The Reindeer Hunter Tribes started breaking the rules while you were off to the south. We drove them off, so they've more or less started to behave themselves. They might just be waiting until we go to war with the creatures of the Wasteland so that they can attack us when we're not looking."

Dahlaine's face blanched, and he stood up. "Let's go to Statha," he said. "I need to get to the bottom of this."

4

The region to the east of the fishing village was marshy, with thick grass at the water's edge, and dead trees sticking up out of shallow, brown water. Rabbit was more than a little startled when he saw that the swamp seemed to be on fire. It wasn't an ordinary fire, though. Most of the fires Rabbit had seen were orange or red, but this one was blue.

"Don't be concerned, friends," Athlan told them. "That's just swamp-fire. It shows up in these marshy areas all the time."

"How do you go about setting a swamp on fire?" Ox asked. "Swamps *are* mostly water, aren't they? And I don't think I've ever come across a patch of water that burns."

"It's not the water that's on fire," Keselo explained. "I've heard about this, but this is the first time I've ever seen it. Our instructors told us that there's a gas called 'methane' that rises up out of stagnant water. I guess it also shows up in coal mines. Swamp-fires aren't really very dangerous, but a fire in a coal mine can turn into a disaster."

"I don't think I've ever seen blue fire before," Ox said.

"It *is* sort of pretty, though," Rabbit observed.

"I'll stick to red fire," Ox said. "Blue fire looks kind of spooky to me."

"It *does* frighten the native population in some parts of the world," Keselo told him. "They believe that blue flame is a sign that there are ghosts in the vicinity, and they won't go near a burning marsh."

"Why would *anybody* want to wander around in a swamp?" Sorgan demanded.

"It might be a good place to hide, Cap'n," Rabbit said. "If somebody happens to be chasing you, and he believes that blue fire means that the swamp's haunted, he won't go near it."

"I think I'll stick to open water," Sorgan said.

"I burn coal in my forge," Rabbit told Keselo, "but I don't think I've ever seen it burn blue."

"It probably wouldn't," Keselo said. "The methane sort of grows out of the coal when there isn't very much fresh air around. The people who dig coal up out of the ground are really afraid of it. I've heard that there's one coal mine in the southern part of the empire that's been burning for about seventy years now. The owners of the mine have tried everything they can think of to put the fire out, but it's still burning all their coal, and that turns their profit into smoke."

The village of Statha was almost as big as the original village of Lattash had been, but unlike Lattash, it stood in a deep forest of huge trees. Rabbit saw a certain practicality there. The trees protected the lodges from the wind and weather to some degree, but the mud-and-wattle structures were widely scattered, since nobody in his right mind would try to chop down a tree with a stone axe when the tree was thirty feet thick at the butt. There was a rambling sort of quality about the village that made it almost impossible to determine just exactly where it started or where the end might be.

"Interesting idea," Keselo murmured as they followed Longbow's friend toward the center of Statha. "If this region's periodically struck by cyclones, those huge trees would offer a great deal of protection, and the people who live here were clever enough to lash their lodges to the trees with strong ropes. They might lose a roof once in a while, but it looks to me like the walls will stay intact."

Rabbit shrugged. "I prefer living on board a ship," he said. "A steady drizzle of pine needles might be sort of irritating after a while."

"They *would* keep the streets—if you could call them streets—from turning into mud when the rainy season rolls in," Keselo pointed out.

The center of the village had several structures that were quite a bit larger than Rabbit had seen to the south in Zelana's Domain. "Are they trying to build palaces?" he asked Longbow.

"Not really," his friend replied. "Those are what the Tonthakans call 'Nation Lodges.' It's part of what emerged when Dahlaine established what he calls 'the Nations' as a way to put an end to the tribal wars. The Tonthakans are supposed to talk rather than fight. There are three groups of tribes here, and they have general meetings every five years. There are 'Nation Lodges' here, others in a village to the north, and more in a village in the mountains. Any time a disagreement occurs, they gather in those 'Nation Lodges' and talk at each other until they reach some sort of agreement. Athlan told me about a meeting that lasted for three years on one occasion."

"Three *years*?" Rabbit exclaimed.

"I think they forgot what they were arguing about after about six months, but they kept on talking anyway. They finally agreed that they'd think about it and then get together again. From what Athlan told me, I guess the subject never came up again."

"That's ridiculous, Longbow."

"Maybe so, but nobody was killed. I think that was what Dahlaine had in mind in the first place. As long as people are talking instead of fighting, nobody loses very much blood—unless he happens to bite his tongue."

They entered one of the large structures, and there was a tall, grim-faced native of middle years with silver-touched hair waiting there.

"What's going on off to the north, Kathlak?" Dahlaine asked.

"We don't really know for sure, Dahlaine," the native replied. "The northern tribes keep shouting about 'insults' and 'violations,' but they refuse to be specific. They seem to think that somebody from one of the southern tribes did something that's forbidden, but they won't tell us who it was or what he did. Of course, it's a little hard to hear what they're saying, because they won't come within bow range of any of our people, and they start howling threats if we try to get anywhere near them."

"I seem to be catching a faint smell of tampering here, big brother," Zelana said. "Somebody appears to be just a little bit unhappy with your 'nation' concept." She frowned. "I'd almost suggest that it *might* be one of the servants of the Vlagh, but wouldn't that be just a little complicated for them?"

"I wouldn't swear to that, sister. They're developing much faster than any of us thought was possible. If they can somehow manage to stir up some intertribal wars, they might be able to use that to their advantage. I'm not going to discard any possibilities at this point."

"I think maybe I'll drift on up to that part of your Domain, brother mine, and see what I can pick up."

"That's *my* responsibility, Zelana," Dahlaine objected.

"It's mine as well, Dahlaine," she said, "and I can move around more quietly than you can. I'm sure that your pet thunderbolt is very nice and terribly impressive, but she's noisy. I'll ride the wind, and none of the people up there will even know that I'm around."

"You're going to insist, I take it."

"How terribly perceptive of you, dear brother," she said, fondly patting his cheek.

And then she was gone.

"It's something Rabbit came up with during the war in Zelana's Domain last spring," Longbow explained to Athlan and Kathlak. "Sorgan Hook-Beak called it 'a lumpy map,' and it turned out to be very useful. Red-Beard had been hunting in that ravine for years, and he knew exactly where every streambed and outcropping of rock was located. It saved a lot of lives."

"Where did you come up with that idea, Rabbit?" Athlan asked curiously.

"I'd been making molds for arrowheads out of clay," Rabbit explained, "and when Red-Beard told the cap'n and Commander Narasan that a flat map didn't have enough details, I suggested that he could add the details he thought we'd need if he carved the map out of clay instead of drawing it with a pen. That's when Red-Beard started building a little duplicate of the ravine. It showed us exactly where everything was up there—how steep the slopes were, how wide the river was, and all sorts of other things. We all studied it, so we knew *almost* as much as Red-Beard did about that ravine. Things went pretty well—right up to the time when we found out that the bug-people had been burrowing tunnels in that area for centuries. That *really* worried us, but it turned out to be *their* mistake instead of ours. The fire-mountains filled those tunnels with boiling rock, and that cooked thousands of our enemies."

"I've heard about 'fire-mountains' a few times," Kathlak said. "Do they *really* spout liquid rock hundreds of feet up into the air like some people told me?"

"I'd say that 'hundreds of feet' doesn't even come close," Longbow said with a slight smile. "Five miles would be more accurate."

"I've never seen one of them," Kathlak admitted.

"You've been lucky, then," Rabbit told him. "It's one of those things that you *don't* want to see—particularly when it's uphill from the place where you're standing."

"Did fire help you win the second war as well?" Athlan asked curiously.

"Not all that much," Longbow said. "Water was more important in *that* war. The first war was fairly simple. The second one was very complicated."

"You won, though, didn't you?"

"I'm not really sure," Longbow replied. "Our main job *that* time involved getting out of the way. It seems that we have a friend who can make very peculiar things happen."

"What's your friend's name, Longbow?" Kathlak asked.

"I really don't know, but when she says 'get out of the way,' you'd better start running."

"It's a *woman*?" Kathlak sounded startled. "Can a woman actually *do* things like that?"

"You might have to change your way of looking at the world, my friend," Longbow told him. "Zelana is a woman, and she can do things that you wouldn't believe. Then, too, our enemies are *also* females. There aren't really very many males in the world of bugs."

"But women are weak!"

"Not in the world of bugs, they aren't. A female bug can pick up something that weighs ten times more than she does, and then she can carry it all day without even working up a sweat. You're going to have to change the way you look at the world, Kathlak, and your life could very well depend on how fast you can make that change."

Zelana returned to the village of Statha the following morning. "This is very nice country you have up here, Dahlaine," she said to her brother. "I passed over a birch forest that was absolutely glorious."

"Did you find out just *why* the northern tribes are behaving so peculiarly, Zelana?"

"No, actually, I didn't. Of course, *they* don't know, either. They *think* that the southern tribes insulted them in some way, but they can't quite remember just exactly what the insult was all about—but they're positive that it was just awful. I'd say that we've encountered 'tampering' again. It's not *quite* as extreme as 'the sea of gold' or the 'Kajak affair,' but it comes close. I browsed around just a bit, and the men of the northern tribes are outraged by the insult, but they have no memory of it."

"It's nothing but a hoax, then?" Dahlaine asked.

"I thought I just said that. I'd say that the servants of the Vlagh have come up with a way to set off certain emotions in your people without providing them with details. The emotions are very primitive, and they're without any justification, but they *have* set off this war. If it continues the way it's going right now, you won't have any Tonthakan warriors available when the creatures of the Wasteland attack. I'd say that right now you'd better concentrate on exposing these hoaxers before this war goes much further. You're going to need these bowmen, and right now I don't think you can count on having them when the time comes."

"You're all sweetness and light, baby sister," Dahlaine growled at her sourly.

"Just trying to brighten up your day, big brother," she said with a sly little smirk.

TONTHAKAN

1

Athlan of Tonthakan was born in the village of Statha near the southern edge of the Tonthakan Nation, and he was a member of one of the eight "Deer Hunter Tribes." The seven "Reindeer Hunter Tribes" lived farther to the north, and the five reckless "Bear Hunter Tribes" lived in the mountains to the east which formed the natural boundary between the Tonthakan and Matakan nations.

Athlan's father, Athaban, was a highly skilled archer, and he began his son's training quite early. It soon became evident that Athlan would probably grow up to be one of the finest archers in all of the Statha tribe, a prediction that was verified when the boy took his first deer when he was only seven years old with a running shot at a hundred paces.

"This boy will go far," Dalthak, the tribal chieftain, predicted when the hunters who had witnessed Athlan's phenomenal accuracy described the near-impossible shot.

The other boys of Athlan's age viewed him as something

in the nature of a hero, but the older boys of the tribe sneered and tried to shrug the shot off as "pure luck."

Athlan took that to be something in the nature of a challenge, so he took three more deer in rapid succession and threw "pure luck" right back in the teeth of the older boys.

The sneers began to wither just a bit after that.

As Athlan grew older, he began to pick up some hints of discontent among the tribal elders about Dahlaine's decision to unify the twenty tribes of Tonthakan into what he chose to call a "Nation." It seemed that the elders felt that the unification was unnatural, and even offensive. The Deer Hunter Tribes had always viewed the Reindeer Hunters and Bear Hunters as their natural enemies, and they devoutly wished that Dahlaine would discard the "Nation" absurdity and let them go back to "the good old days," when arrows were made for killing enemies as well as deer.

As Athlan grew older, he noticed that others were also aging, but it appeared that age fell much more heavily on those who were already carrying a heavy burden of years. Chief Dalthak's hair moved from grey to white, and his once-powerful voice turned squeaky. The members of the tribe of Statha began to refer to their chief as "Ancient Dalthak," a term which was supposedly one of profound respect. Athlan, however, was quite sure that he wouldn't like "Ancient" attached to *his* name. It seemed to him that "Ancient" carried strong overtones of crumbling, decaying, and wasting away, but the elders seemed to think that it was just splendid. Of course, Chief Dalthak wasn't too spry, and he tended to fall asleep in the middle of a speech—even when *he* was the one who was talking. By the time that Athlan had reached his tenth year, old Chief Dalthak's son Kathlak had more or less assumed his father's duties. To maintain appearances, Kathlak would go into his father's lodge "to consult with our chief." And when he emerged, he'd announce that "our chief says this," and that technically justified any orders he might give to the members of the tribe. It was fairly obvious to Athlan that Kathlak himself was issuing all the commands, but his little game maintained his father's dignity, and his own reputation quieted any objections.

When Dahlaine had decided to unify the tribes of Tonthakan into one Nation, the Deer Hunter Tribes had chosen to designate the village of Statha as the site for the Nation Lodges of the southern tribes. Many men in the tribe viewed that as a great honor, but Athlan caught a few hints that the more sensible tribe members saw it as a great inconvenience. The tribe had been obliged to build the oversized lodges and to maintain them, and, of course, they had to provide food and shelter for the visitors during those meetings. There were annual meetings of the Deer Hunter Tribes, and they were always rather informal, but when Athlan reached his twelfth year, the "Nation Meeting" took place in Statha, and it seemed to Athlan that it positively drooled formality. Kathlak gathered the boys of the tribe some days before the event, and he sternly laid down some arbitrary rules—"No laughing, no smiling, and no talking during the meetings. The various chieftains of the twenty tribes will make speeches—long speeches. Do *not* go to sleep during those speeches. Pretend to be interested. Sit up straight and nod your heads once in a while. The meeting will last for three days, and then everybody will go back home."

"Does this happen every five years?" Athlan asked.

"Yes," Kathlak replied, "but the next meeting will take

place in Bear Hunter territory, and the one after that will be in Reindeer Hunter land."

"Is anything important likely to happen?"

"No, not really."

"Why bother with it, then?"

"It keeps Dahlaine happy."

"Oh. I guess that sort of makes it all right."

"I'll let him know that you approve, Athlan," Kathlak said with no hint of a smile.

"Ah—I don't know if you need to bother him with that, Kathlak," Athlan said a bit anxiously. "He's probably busy right now with other things. Why don't we all just forget that I said anything at all about this?"

"I suppose that if you really want us to do that, we'll just let it lie, Athlan, but if you think that your opinion is really important, I'll bring it to his attention the next time I see him."

Athlan was squirming by then, but he *had* learned a few things that were quite important during their little exchange. First of all, it might not be a bad idea to think things through *before* he started making suggestions, but even more important, he'd learned never to cross Chief Dalthak's grim son Kathlak if he could possibly avoid it.

By the time Athlan reached his fourteenth year, his growing reputation began to attract the attention of the fathers of young, eligible girls in the tribe, and those fathers spoke frequently with Athlan's father, Athaban, about certain "interesting possibilities."

Athlan took to the woods at that point. His mother had died when he'd been very young, and he'd become quite comfortable living with only his father. Someday, perhaps, mating might be appropriate, but for right now he chose freedom instead. He roamed out in the forest alone with only trees and animals for company, and that suited him right down to the ground. His skills as a hunter increased tremendously during those years, and he found that if he moved slowly and quietly through the forest, the animals didn't even notice him.

It was about midmorning on a glorious summer day when Athlan was moving through the forest near the coast when he saw a stranger smoothly paddling a canoe northward some distance out from the beach. The stranger was quite obviously not a member of one of the Deer Hunter Tribes. There was no fringe on the sleeves of his buckskin shirt, and no beads sewn to its front. Athlan was quite certain that he was out of sight, but the stranger laid his paddle down and held up his hands to show Athlan that he was not holding his bow.

Athlan was curious enough not to just fade back into the forest. He slung his bow over his shoulder and held out his hands to show the stranger that he wasn't feeling hostile, and walked on down to the edge of the water. "I am Athlan of the tribe of Dalthak," he called to introduce himself as the stranger paddled in closer.

"And I am Longbow of the tribe of Old-Bear," the stranger replied in a quiet voice. "I come here in peace, and I have no hostile intent."

"Welcome, then, to the Domain of Dahlaine of the North," Athlan greeted the quiet stranger.

"I am from the Domain of Zelana of the West, and I thank you, Athlan of the North."

"Do you think we've managed to pile up enough formality yet?" Athlan asked.

"I think we've covered the requirements of stuffy," Longbow agreed with a faint smile.

"Come ashore, then, and we can talk about the weather or something."

Longbow smoothly drove his canoe up onto the sandy beach and stepped out.

"Are you just exploring, or did you want to have words with one of the local chieftains?" Athlan asked.

"I think *you* might be the one I came up here to see. You're a hunter, aren't you?"

Athlan shrugged. "It gives me something to do when I'm not busy sleeping or eating. Was there something you wanted to know about?"

"Have the creatures of the Wasteland been nosing around in your territory at all?"

"I've heard about them occasionally, but I've never actually seen one," Athlan replied. "Let's get your canoe out of sight and then go back into the forest a ways. Standing right out in the open like this makes me just a bit fidgety."

"Oh? Is there somebody you don't want to encounter?"

"I'm not in trouble or anything like that. It's just that I'm not ready to settle down just yet. I'm a fairly good hunter, and there are some older men in the tribe who think I'd be suitable to mate with their daughters so that I could provide food for their families while they just relax and let me do all the work."

"That *does* seem to crop up now and then," Longbow agreed with a wry smile as he took hold of the front of his canoe.

They pulled the canoe into a patch of bushes and then went on back under the trees. "Now, then," Athlan said, "what is it about the creatures of the Wasteland that concerns you? From what I've heard, they're nothing but midgets that go sneaking around in the woods—probably looking for things to steal."

"It goes just a bit further, Athlan. What they're *really* looking for is information, and they don't want us to know that they're intruding into our territory. They may *look* like nothing but people, but they're *not* people at all. Actually, they're servants of the Vlagh."

"I've heard about that one, but I thought that it was just a story that somebody made up to frighten children."

"It's not a story, Athlan. There really *is* a thing called the Vlagh, and it wants to rule the world. That's why it's sending the little ones into *our* lands to find out if we have any way to resist when it sends its warriors here to conquer us."

"How did you happen to find out about all this?" Athlan asked a bit skeptically.

"They killed she who was to be my mate, so now I kill them every time I encounter them. If you ever happen to come across one of them, be very careful. If you let them get too close to you, they'll bite you, and you'll die. They have venomous fangs, and their venom is deadly—even if they happen to bite one of their own friends. The shaman of our tribe has studied them for quite a while and he showed me how to take the venom from dead ones and anoint my arrowheads with it. The tiniest scratch from one of my arrows kills them instantly."

"Would it kill a deer in the same way?" Athlan asked.

"I'm sure it would."

But then Athlan realized that his clever idea might *not* be quite as clever as he'd thought at first. "It could be a very easy way to hunt deer," he said a bit ruefully, "but there might just be a bit of a problem there. The poison would kill the deer immediately, but it might just make the deer meat poisonous as well. What do you think, Longbow?"

"I'm not really sure," Longbow admitted. "Cooking the meat *might* neutralize the poison, but I wouldn't want to bet my life on 'might,' would you?"

"We could always feed some of the meat to a dog, I suppose," Athlan mused. "If the dog's still alive the next day, that would mean that the meat's safe to eat."

"Does your tribe have many dogs?"

"Lots of them. When we're snowbound in the dead of winter, the dogs give us something to eat. Dog meat doesn't taste very good, but it's better than tree meat." Then Athlan looked off toward the west where a rosy sunset was lying low over the face of the sea. "I'd say that it's just about time to set up a camp for the night, and then maybe tomorrow we can go hunting—deer, not the creatures of the Wasteland." Then he hesitated. "You *do* have some arrows that haven't been dipped in poison, don't you?"

"A few," Longbow replied.

"Are you sure you can tell the difference between a poisoned arrow and a clean one?"

Longbow nodded. "The clean ones have white feathers. The dirty ones are red." Then he frowned slightly. "Or is it the other way around?" he added without the slightest hint of a smile.

It was still dark in the forest when Athlan woke up the following morning, roused by the sound of Longbow stirring up the fire. "Isn't it just a bit early?" he asked.

"Probably not," Longbow replied quietly. "I'm not at all familiar with the deer up here in the north, but the ones on down the coast feed at night and return to their bedding places at first light. If we happen to be in the right place at the right time, we'll have fresh meat before the sun rises.

Smoke-cured meat is all right, I suppose, but I'm starting to get hungry for real meat."

"I shall be guided by you in this," Athlan vowed quite formally.

"I think you might have been spending too much time with the elders of your tribe, Athlan."

"We're supposed to honor them, aren't we? That doesn't mean that we have to pay any attention to them, of course, but we *should* respect them."

"I suppose so. Are all the deer up here of the same kind? We have two fairly different kinds of deer in the western forest. The timid ones aren't quite as large as the stupid ones, and their antlers are more evenly matched. They also run smoothly. The larger, silly ones bounce when they run."

"I don't think I've ever encountered a silly deer."

"They always run uphill, and after they're fifty or so paces above you, they stop and look back to see what you're doing."

"That *would* be sort of silly, I suppose."

"They also have much bigger ears. In some ways they almost look like a rabbit with horns."

"We don't have any deer up here that look like that," Athlan said. "I'd say that *our* deer are the timid ones. The reindeer off to the north gather up in very large herds, so if you see one of them, there are probably several hundred in the same region. The meat doesn't taste as good as the meat of our deer, so I wouldn't waste any arrows on them."

"If you're ready, we might as well go to the hunt."

"Aren't you going to eat breakfast first?"

Longbow shook his head. "I always hunt better when I'm just a bit hungry, don't you?"

"Well—maybe, but I start to get just a bit shaky if I go *too* long without eating."

There was a faint band of light along the eastern horizon as the two of them moved quietly out into the forest of enormous trees.

"Maybe we should stop for a while and give our eyes a chance to adjust to the dark before we go much farther," Longbow suggested in a soft voice. "Fire's nice, I suppose, but it does peculiar things to a hunter's eyes, or had you noticed that?"

"Oh, yes," Athlan agreed. "Any time I walk away from a campfire after dark, I have to hold my hands out in front of me to keep from bumping into trees. Trees absolutely *hate* it when you bump into them in the dark."

They moved quietly through the forest as the dim light of dawn gradually increased among the huge trees.

"Not very many bushes," Longbow observed, looking around.

"The needles from these trees have been piling up for a long time," Athlan explained. "That pretty much chokes out any late-coming plants. Their seeds won't sprout if they don't reach dirt, and I'd say that the layer of needles we're walking on right now is at least three feet thick. Are there many bushes down in your part of the Land of Dhrall?"

"The brush cover's fairly dense along the coast," Longbow replied. He shrugged. "It gives the deer and other animals plenty of food to eat, so I guess it's all right."

"The deer around here have to do their grazing in the meadows. There's a fairly large meadow just on ahead of us. I thought we might want to have a look at that one first. There are several other meadows nearby, but the one just ahead is closer to our camp, so if we take a few deer there, we won't have to drag them so far. I always do my best to make life easier."

"I don't see anything wrong with that," Longbow replied.

They stepped across a narrow brook that wandered through the deep forest, and Athlan saw the edge of the meadow about a hundred paces ahead. "We're coming up on that meadow I was telling you about," he whispered.

"I sort of thought we might be," Longbow replied softly. "I've been catching a faint smell of deer for a little while."

Athlan sniffed at the air. "I think you might be right," he agreed. "Your nose must be almost as sharp as your eyes, Longbow."

They crouched down at the edge of the forest and looked out at the meadow.

"It's still just a little too dark," Athlan whispered. "I'd say that we're about a quarter of an hour early."

"Better early than late," Longbow replied.

"What a clever thing to say," Athlan declared sardonically. "That's almost as good as 'the early bird gets the worm.' Of course, I don't eat worms very often, so it doesn't hurt my feelings too much if I happen to miss them."

The darkness gradually faded as the light along the eastern horizon grew almost imperceptibly brighter.

"They're out there, all right," Athlan said. "I can make out four or five deer already."

"Fairly small, though," Longbow replied, "probably just fawns. The bigger ones are most likely farther out in the meadow."

"I'm starting to get hungry, Longbow," Athlan complained.

"Breakfast's only about a hundred paces away, Athlan," Longbow assured him.

Athlan could see farther out into the meadow now, and he

was a bit surprised by how many deer were grazing out there, and it seemed that every time he blinked, there were still more.

"That one," Longbow declared. "It's just on the other side of that tree snag."

Athlan peered out into the meadow and finally located the large, massively antlered deer Longbow had chosen. "He's a big one, all right," he whispered, "but he's a long way out there, don't you think?"

"I can reach him," Longbow said confidently.

"Now *this* I want to see," Athlan said. "I wouldn't waste an arrow trying to hit a deer who's *that* far away."

"You should learn to trust your bow, Athlan," Longbow said, slowly rising to his feet and peering on out across the still dimly lighted meadow. Then he nocked an arrow and smoothly drew his bow. Then he released it, and his arrow arced out over the meadow in the faint predawn light and struck the large deer he had chosen. The deer dropped as if the ground had suddenly been cut out from under him.

"Amazing!" Athlan exclaimed. "I've never *seen* a shot like that before! That deer had to be at *least* two hundred paces away."

"Closer to two hundred and fifty," Longbow replied. "Of course, there's no wind blowing, and that made it easier. Did you want to take one as well, Athlan? There are still plenty of deer out there."

"The one you just took should be enough, Longbow. It's a fair distance back to our camp, and your deer's probably heavy enough to wear us both out by the time we drag him there. Of course, I suppose we could just camp where he's lying and eat on him for the next week or so."

Longbow shook his head. "Let's get him back in the

shade," he said. "If we leave him out in the sun, he'll start to rot before too long."

It took the two of them until almost noon to drag the heavy deer back to their camp, and then they went through the tedious process of skinning the large buck-deer.

"How in the world did you ever learn to shoot arrows that accurately, Longbow?" Athlan asked. "Was it maybe Dahlaine's sister who gave you instructions?"

"I've never met Zelana," Longbow replied. "She doesn't really like people, so she went off to the Isle of Thurn a long time ago."

"Now *that's* very unusual," Athlan said. "Dahlaine—her older brother—wanders around up here in the north country all the time. He comes up with a lot of silly ideas, and we're supposed to obey his orders. You don't need to tell anybody that I said this, but the gods are very foolish sometimes."

"As far as I'm concerned, they can be just as foolish as they want to be," Longbow replied. "I *know* what *I'm* supposed to be doing. I kill the creatures of the Wasteland, and I'll keep on killing them until I'm old and grey. It's the only reason that I'm alive, and if I stay at it long enough, I *might* be able to kill them all." There was a kind of intensity in Longbow's voice and a bleak look on his face that sort of filled Athlan with awe.

They remained in their forest camp for the next several days, and then Longbow decided that it was time for him to take his canoe and go on back home.

Athlan stood on the sandy beach watching as his strange new friend paddled his canoe on out into deeper water and turned south. For some reason, Athlan was almost positive that they'd meet again. "And maybe next time, *I'll* be the one who takes the deer," he muttered to himself.

2

Early in the autumn of that year Athlan discovered a small cave in the south side of a wooded hillock a mile or so to the south of Statha. After some thought, he decided to abandon his lodge out in the forest and move into the cave. Lodges were traditional in Tonthakan, of course, but Athlan was positive that a cave could not fall down no matter how strongly the wind blew.

Winter held off for some reason that year, and the hunting was very good in the vicinity of Athlan's new home. He was quite certain that his new residence was the finest place for him to dwell in all the world.

It was just after the first significant snow in that year when a young hunter named Zathal came through the forest to advise Athlan that his father had recently died. "It didn't seem to anybody that he was sick or anything like that, Athlan," Zathal said. "He was busy chipping out some new arrowheads, and he suddenly grabbed his chest and then fell over dead. Chief Kathlak sent me out here to find you and to tell you that we'll go through the burial ceremony tomorrow, if that's all right with you."

"Tell Kathlak that I'll be there," Athlan replied shortly.

The ceremony took most of the day, naturally. Athlan's father had been a mighty hunter, and the men of the tribe made many speeches praising him. The sun was nearing the western horizon when the ceremony concluded, and Chief Kathlak joined Athlan at the side of the grave. "Will you be returning to Statha now?" he asked.

"I don't believe so, My Chief," Athlan replied.

"The fathers of the young women of the tribe won't pester you now, Athlan. Your time of grief will last for as long as you want it to. You can keep them away from you, if that's what's bothering you."

"That's not why I won't be coming back, My Chief. I've found a quiet place to live, and the hunting's very good there. In a peculiar sort of way, I'm almost grateful that those fathers drove me away from Statha. I'm a hunter now, and I don't need—or want—company. If a war comes along, I'll be here to help as best I can. Otherwise, I'd prefer to be left alone."

"What do you want us to do with your father's lodge?"

Athlan shrugged. "Give it to somebody who needs it—or tear it down. It doesn't matter to me. Be well, My Chief."

And then he turned and went back into the forest.

Early the next spring, Longbow returned to the land of the Tonthakans, and he found Athlan's cave without much difficulty. "Have you decided to become a bear, Athlan?" he asked. "Taking a long nap might be nice, I suppose, but I'm fairly sure that your stomach will start to growl at you after a few weeks."

"It gets windy around here, Longbow," Athlan explained, "but almost never windy enough to blow a cave down."

"I see your point," Longbow replied. "Is the hunting good around here?"

"Very good. We're far enough away from any village that the deer don't even realize that we want to eat them. When they're hungry enough, they'll even graze in the meadows in broad daylight. That means that I don't have to get up in the middle of the night anymore."

"You're lazy, Athlan."

"I need my sleep, Longbow. I *am* just a growing boy, you know."

"The trouble there is that you've stopped growing *up*. Now you're starting to grow *out*. Give it a couple more years, and you won't be able to squeeze through your cave mouth anymore."

"Did you want to go hunting," Athlan asked, "or would you rather stand around making funny remarks?"

"Lead the way, friend Athlan," Longbow replied.

It was several years later when Dahlaine came to the Tonthakan Nation to advise the archers that the Domain of his younger sister Zelana had been invaded by the creatures of the Wasteland. Athlan was fairly sure that Longbow was having a wonderful time by now, but he had other things on his mind just then. Dahlaine's "Nation" idea was beginning to fall apart. Old Chief Dalthak was pretty much over the hill now, and Kathlak had discarded his previous practice of pretending to discuss matters with his father and had begun to issue commands without "consultation," and right now the Deer Hunter Tribes needed a leader who knew what he was doing. There had recently been a number of incursions into

Deer Hunter territory by the Reindeer Hunters, and they refused to explain why.

In keeping with Dahlaine's "Rules," Kathlak issued a call for an "Emergency Meeting" to track down and correct any problems. The Bear Hunter Tribes came to the village of Statha to attend the meeting, but the Reindeer Hunter Tribes didn't bother. The raucous chieftains of the mountain-dwelling Bear Hunter Tribes suggested what seemed to Athlan to be the best response. A few punitive incursions into Reindeer Land would quite probably get Dahlaine's immediate attention, and then *he* could deal with the matter. From Athlan's point of view, that was one of the obligations of the gods.

Kathlak didn't see it that way, unfortunately. It appeared that he was willing to go along with Dahlaine's absurd "Nation" idea. Peace was nice enough, Athlan conceded, but every now and then, peace didn't work, and it seemed to Athlan that the Reindeer Hunters had decided to fall back on the good old idea of war.

The "Emergency Meeting" didn't accomplish much, and the Reindeer Hunters continued their raids down into Deer country, burning villages, killing men, and abducting women. Athlan and his friends began to make preparations for an extended war to teach the Reindeer Hunter Tribes a few lessons about good manners.

The incursions of the Reindeer Tribes into Deer Hunter territory continued throughout the rest of the spring and well into the summer, while sketchy, and probably exaggerated, reports of the wars in the West and South arrived from time to time.

It was quite obvious to Athlan that Kathlak was keeping a tight lid on his anger about the incursions of the Reindeer Tribes into Deer Tribe territory. Dahlaine's establishment of the "Nations" had been intended to bring peace, and Kathlak was doing his best to keep that peace intact. To Athlan's way of looking at things, however, Kathlak's refusal to retaliate just encouraged the Reindeer Tribes.

It was about midsummer when Athlan came up with a way to avoid direct retaliation while still letting the Reindeer Tribes know that their incursions were a very bad idea.

"All right, then," he told a goodly number of his friends one hot summer day when they'd gathered in the forest to discuss the matter, "Chief Kathlak has ordered us not to retaliate, but he didn't say a word about 'defend,' did he?"

"Not that I remember," the young archer named Zathal said. "What did you have in mind, Athlan?"

"There are only four or five trails leading down from Reindeer Land into Deer Land," Athlan explained, "and not really all that many villages up there. If we had a good number of archers hidden in the woods near those trails and villages, a very large number of those intruders from Reindeer Land could suddenly turn up dead, wouldn't you say? We don't really *have* to go up into Reindeer Land to find targets, since the Reindeer Hunters are coming on down *here*. All *we'd* have to do is wait for them and then kill them before they can even set fire to the villages. We know that country up there much better than they do, so we'll have all the advantage. I don't think we should waste time shouting war cries or any of the other things people do when they're fighting with each other. Just drive arrows into them and then disappear back into the forest. We won't violate the border of Reindeer Land, but we *will* stop them dead in their tracks when they come across *our* border. There might be a hundred or so of them that'll come across that border, but I'd say that they'll be very lucky if two or three manage to get home again. The Reindeer Tribes aren't really all that bright, but I think they'll get the point—eventually."

"Would it offend you if I made a suggestion, Athlan?" young Zathal asked.

"Probably not. What did you have in mind, Zathal?"

"Dead things start to rot after a while, and they don't smell very nice. After we've killed those Reindeer Hunters, we could drag them all on up to the border and just leave them there. The wind *usually* comes up from the south at this time of the year, so after a little while, that border area's going to stink pretty bad, don't you think? That stink might persuade the Reindeer Hunters to go play somewhere else, wouldn't you say?"

"It *would* make it easy to find the border, Athlan," another young archer said, "even in the dark."

"I *like* it!" Athlan said. "Let's do it that way."

The incursions of the Reindeer Tribes into the northern part of Deer Hunter country continued for the next few weeks, but Athlan's "silent ambushes" and Zathal's "stinking bodies" notion seemed to disturb the invaders more and more as time went by, and as autumn approached, the intrusions became fewer and fewer.

Then, on a cloudy morning, Kathlak came up from the village of Statha to speak with Athlan. "What are you doing, Athlan?" he demanded.

"Hunting, of course," Athlan replied with feigned innocence. "Isn't that what I'm supposed to do?"

"I just received a complaint from the chief of one of the Reindeer Tribes about a foul smell coming up from our territory. He says that it's making the people of his southern villages sick."

"That was sort of what we had in mind, Kathlak," Athlan replied. "The Reindeer Tribes have been attacking villages on our side of the border, so we came up with a way to make them stop."

"Oh?" Kathlak said. "What's that?"

Athlan shrugged. "We kill them and then drag the carcasses back up to the border and leave them there. If Dahlaine doesn't like what I'm doing, tell him to order the Reindeer Hunters to stay on their own side of the line."

Kathlak glanced around to make sure that they were alone. "Don't change a thing, Athlan," he said very quietly. "All I'm doing here is following Dahlaine's orders. I'm supposed to reprimand you, so consider yourself reprimanded."

"Did you want me to weep and wail and bang my head against a tree, or something?"

"I don't think you need to go quite *that* far," Kathlak replied. "Keep me advised about how things are going up here. If the Reindeer Tribes learn to stay where they belong, you probably won't have to go any further, but if they keep on coming down here, we might have to take some more drastic steps."

"I'll let you know, My Chief," Athlan promised.

The incursions of the Reindeer Tribes into Deer Hunter territory had more or less come to a halt by the end of the following week, so Athlan went on back to Statha to advise Kathlak that things were quiet again. "It took them a while to get the point, My Chief," Athlan concluded as they spoke together in Kathlak's lodge, "but when they realized that we'd kill every one of them who came across the line, and we wouldn't make any noise, they decided to go find something else to do."

"You're very good at this sort of thing, Athlan," Kathlak observed.

Athlan shrugged. "I'm a hunter, My Chief, and a good hunter's quiet. You won't take very many deer if you yell at them before you shoot your arrows."

There was a sudden shattering crash just outside Chief Kathlak's lodge.

"I *wish* he wouldn't do that!" Kathlak growled.

"Who is it?" Athlan demanded, his ears still ringing.

"Dahlaine, of course. He roams around in the world on a thunderbolt. He says it's fast, but the noise it makes irritates me for some reason. Let's go see what he has to say."

"Has he managed to get over his grouchies about what my people were doing to the Reindeer Hunters?" Athlan asked a bit apprehensively.

"We can ask him, if you'd like. Come along, Athlan."

They went on out of Kathlak's lodge, and Dahlaine was waiting nearby.

"How are things going in your brother's Domain?" Kathlak asked.

"Even better than we'd hoped, Kathlak," Dahlaine replied. "The war's over down there, and the Vlagh doesn't have nearly as many servants as she had when it started. There was another enemy involved as well, and now *they're* gone, too."

"Fire again?" Kathlak asked.

"No. This time it was water." Dahlaine grinned broadly. "Things don't seem to be going too well for the Vlagh this year, for some reason."

"Which way do you think the Vlagh will strike next?" Kathlak asked.

"We don't know for sure," Dahlaine replied. "We've

managed to block off the West and the South, so that leaves only two regions of the Land of Dhrall still open. My older sister's positive that the Vlagh will attack *her* Domain next, but I think she might be wrong. We've all been hiring outlanders to help fight the Vlagh, though, so we can cover Aracia's Domain and mine as well. There's a sizeable fleet of Maag ships on the way up here, and they should arrive before very long. Have there been any sightings of the creatures of the Wasteland up here lately?"

"What are *they*?" Kathlak asked.

"That's what the servants of the Vlagh are called, My Chief," Athlan explained. "They're very small, and they sneak around, watching what we do. Longbow told me that they've got poisonous fangs—sort of like some snakes, so you don't want to get too close to them."

"You know Longbow?" Dahlaine asked with some surprise.

"We met a few years ago," Athlan replied. "He came up here to find out if the creatures of the Wasteland were snooping around up here like they were down in Zelana country. He comes by every so often, and we usually go hunting. He's awfully good with his bow, isn't he?"

"He's the best," Dahlaine said. "He's coming up here with the Maags, so you'll be able to renew your acquaintance." Then Dahlaine squinted at Athlan. "You're the one who's been murdering the members of the Reindeer Tribes, aren't you?" he asked.

"I wouldn't exactly call it 'murder,' Dahlaine," Kathlak stepped in. "The Reindeer Hunters are coming down here into *our* country to rob and kill members of *my* tribe. Athlan gathered up some archers to hold them off—and he did a very good job. I approve of almost everything he did. Piling dead Reindeer Hunters on the border and leaving them to rot *might* have been a little extreme, but it got the point across. The Reindeer Hunters stopped attacking our people at that point, and that was the whole idea. If you want to scold somebody, you can scold me."

Dahlaine frowned. "I wasn't aware of what was happening up here," he admitted. "I think I'll have a word or two with that Reindeer chief. He didn't tell me what was *really* going on up here. All he said was that those rotting bodies were making life unpleasant for his people."

"That was sort of what we had in mind," Athlan said. "How long would you say it's going to take Longbow and his friends to get here?"

"No more than a week," Dahlaine replied. "There'll be some others coming as well, but it might take them quite a while to get here. I'm sure they'll surprise everybody in this part of the world. They've managed to tame an animal called 'the horse,' and they sit on his back when they want to go somewhere."

"You mean that they're too lazy to walk?" Kathlak asked.

"Not really. It's just that horses run very fast, so those people can go from here to there much, much faster than just about anybody else. They're very good warriors, so I'm sure that they'll be useful when our enemies invade our part of the Land of Dhrall."

3

Athlan went on down to the temporary village the fish hunters of the tribe set up on the coast every summer. Fish meat didn't taste as good as deer meat, but once it had been dried, it didn't rot, and it kept the tribe eating regularly during the winter.

The outlander boats came up the coast a few days later and Athlan was surprised by the size of them, *and* by the fact that the outlanders didn't use paddles to move their boats. They'd come up with a way to put the wind to work, and their boats moved very fast.

The boats came closer to the fish hunter village, and Athlan saw his friend standing at the front of the leading boat. He pushed his canoe off the bank and paddled on out to greet his old friend. When he climbed up the rope ladder, Longbow introduced him to a small man who appeared to be playing with a fire for some reason that Athlan couldn't understand. Then Longbow and his little friend showed Athlan something so remarkable that the world seemed almost to turn itself upside down. It was an arrowhead unlike any other one he'd ever seen, and he saw its value almost immediately. Then the man called Rabbit advised him that there would soon be more of those arrowheads available than he could even count—*and* that they'd be a gift.

Then Longbow advised him that Dahlaine wanted to speak with him.

After Athlan told Dahlaine that the Reindeer Hunters Tribe would probably continue their attacks, Dahlaine decided that it was time to get to the bottom of that.

The strangers seemed to be quite surprised by the swamp-fires dancing over one of the marshes, but the young soldier called Keselo explained it, using some terms Athlan had never heard before.

When they reached Statha, Kathlak was waiting for them in one of the Nation Lodges, and he and Dahlaine spoke at some length about the attacks of the Reindeer Hunters Tribe to the north, and then Dahlaine's sister told them that she'd drift on up to that part of the Tonthakan Nation to find out just why the Reindeer Hunters had suddenly decided to go to war.

"I don't really think that's a very good idea, Longbow," Athlan said to his friend, "particularly not if she's going up there alone. It could be dangerous for her up there, you know."

"I wouldn't be too concerned, Athlan," Longbow replied. "Our Zelana can listen without being seen. She'll be able to find out what's really going on up there, and the Reindeer Hunters won't even know that she's been there."

"I take it that she doesn't ride a thunderbolt like Dahlaine does," Athlan said.

"She rides the wind instead," Longbow replied. "It's not as fast as a thunderbolt, but it's a lot quieter."

"Just exactly when was it that she decided to leave that island where she was hiding?"

"Last winter. She and her little girl chased me down and persuaded me to help when she went on over to the Land of the Maags to hire an army to fight the creatures of the Wasteland."

"I've heard a few things about that war, but it seemed to me that there might have been a lot of exaggeration in those stories."

"They probably were *under*statements, Athlan," Longbow said. "There *was* a fire-mountain that cooked thousands of the creatures of the Wasteland, and later there was a flood that drowned even more of them."

"Did Zelana do that?"

"No, actually, Eleria and Yaltar did it. Have you heard the old story about 'the Dreamers'?"

"When I was younger, yes." Athlan blinked. "Are you trying to tell me that the story was really *true*?"

"It came very close, my friend. So far, we've won *two* wars that we couldn't possibly have won if it hadn't been for the Dreamers—*and* with the help of somebody we didn't even know about. That's *another* old story that you probably heard when you were a child." He smiled. "As they always say, 'the old ones are the best.' That should brighten up your whole day, Athlan. We're getting so much help that we can't possibly lose."

Dahlaine's sister returned to Statha the following morning with a slightly puzzled look on her beautiful face.

"Well?" Dahlaine asked her.

"Somebody's tampering, big brother," she replied. "The Reindeer Tribes are all convinced that the southern tribes insulted them dreadfully, but they can't quite remember just exactly what the insult was. I browsed around a bit, and they're all certain that the insult was dreadful, but they can't remember a word of it. I'm fairly sure that the servants of the Vlagh have come up with a way to instill a sense of outrage in the Reindeer Tribes with no real basis in fact. If this continues the way it's going right now, you won't have any Tonthakan archers to help you when the creatures of the Wasteland attack."

Then the farmer from Veltan's Domain came forward. "Excuse me," he said, "but I just remembered something that might be useful here. It seems that there are certain sounds that the bug-people can't pronounce. The shepherd Nanton told me that they lisp, and they can't correctly pronounce the sound at the beginning of the words 'cat,' or 'cow,' or 'kill.' It comes out as a peculiar sort of 'click' that sounds very much like a hiccup."

"Now *that* might be the answer to our problem right there," Longbow said. "If there just happen to be several people with hiccups standing around any of the chieftains up in Reindeer country, it might just explain what's happening. The bug-people have been able to manipulate quite a few ordinary people in the past."

"Like Kajak, you mean?" Rabbit suggested.

"He was *one* of them, that's for certain."

"How?" Athlan demanded. "How in the world could a bug-man convince a chief that he'd been insulted when it really didn't happen?"

"Let's not throw the idea away," Dahlaine said, frowning slightly. "Sometimes the bug-people use certain scents to set off reactions that aren't really appropriate. It's entirely possible that some scent made a chief of that Reindeer Hunter Tribe believe that something happened when it really hadn't."

"I'd say that it might be time for some of us to go up into Reindeer Land and listen for clicks and sniff the air," Longbow suggested. "If there's somebody smelly who clicks when he says 'Tonthakan,' it might just explain what's going on up there."

With Dahlaine in the lead, Athlan and Longbow, along with several outlanders, went north from Statha toward the border between Deer Hunter Land and the home of the Reindeer Tribes. It was a cloudy day, and for some reason that made Athlan just a bit edgy.

There weren't any archers of the Reindeer Tribe guarding the border, and that was unusual. Since the path they were following went directly up from Statha, the border here was usually well guarded by both tribes.

"Peculiar," Longbow observed. "If the Reindeer Tribe's feeling belligerent, they should be watching this border very carefully."

"Maybe they've come up with a plan of some kind," the bulky sea-warrior Ox suggested. "They could have pulled back like this to lure Athlan and his bowmen into a trap. That would be very much like what Athlan here's been doing to *them* lately, wouldn't it?"

"It is possible, Lord Dahlaine," the young Trogite Keselo agreed.

Dahlaine frowned. "There aren't any of them in the immediate vicinity," he said. "If they're trying to lure us deeper into their territory, it would make sense to leave the border unprotected. The one we're looking for is Chief Kadlar. He's the one who was complaining about the stench coming from his dead archers a while back. He's the one we want to track down, because he's almost certainly the one who started all this. Let's keep moving, gentlemen. I'll be able to sense them if they're hiding in the forest, and that's probably all the warning we'll need."

They pushed on through the alien-looking forest. Athlan noticed that there were many more hemlock trees here than there were in the forests of Deer Hunter Land. He didn't really care much for hemlock trees, since they gave off an unpleasant odor.

The small, wiry Rabbit moved on ahead of them, and after a while, he came scampering back out of the hemlock forest. "They're just ahead of us," he reported quietly to Dahlaine. "They're gathering in a large meadow about a half mile to the north."

"Archers?" Dahlaine asked.

"They all have bows," Rabbit replied. "That says 'archer' to me. I didn't count them, but I'd say there are a thousand or so."

"Is there any open ground between us and that meadow?" Dahlaine asked. "I want them to see me coming so that they don't start showering us with arrows. Kadlar may not *like* me all that much, but he *does* know that I'm the one who's giving the orders around here."

"There's a dry creekbed that leads down into that meadow," Rabbit replied. "It's a little brushy, but I'm sure they'll be able to see us if we stand up and walk instead of creeping through the brush."

"Lead the way, Rabbit," Dahlaine said. "When we get close to the normal range of a well-shot arrow, I'll unlimber my pet thunderbolt to let Kadlar's people know that it's me.

She's terribly noisy, but she lets people know that I'm really who I say that I am."

They veered off through the hemlock woods and then followed the dry streambed on down to the meadow.

"Kadlar!" Dahlaine roared in a voice people probably heard ten miles away, "I want to talk with you—*now*! Come here!"

The chief of the Reindeer Tribe was a large man of middle years who was fairly paunchy, and he appeared to be more than a little reluctant to obey Dahlaine. He approached warily, followed by several of his tribesmen.

"Why are you doing this, Kadlar?" Dahlaine demanded.

"The Deer Hunter Tribes insulted us, My Lord," the paunchy chief replied. "We won't tolerate that."

Athlan noticed that most of Kadlar's men were grouped up around him with their bows ready. There *were* two men, however, who seemed to be backing slowly away, and they were holding their bows rather awkwardly. "I think those two don't really want to get too close to us, Longbow," Athlan told his friend in a very quiet voice.

"You could be right," Longbow agreed, his eyes going narrow. "Ox, why don't you see if you can persuade those two who seem to want to leave to join us."

Ox hefted his heavy iron axe a couple of times. "Do you think this might get their attention?" he asked.

"I'm sure it will," Longbow said.

"Just exactly what was it that the Deer Hunter Tribe said that you found so offensive, Kadlar?" Dahlaine demanded.

"I won't repeat it, Dahlaine. It was absolutely foul and uncalled for."

"And who was it who used that language? Was it Chief Kathlak himself?"

Chief Kadlar frowned. "No, it wasn't Kathlak," he said.

"It was somebody who was standing very close to him, though."

"Give me a name, Kadlar," Dahlaine insisted. "I can't punish him if I don't know his name."

Kadlar looked a bit puzzled. "The name's right on the tip of my tongue, but I can't seem to remember it."

Ox was herding the two reluctant natives back to the little group surrounding Chief Kadlar. "Here are those two bashful ones, Longbow," he said with an evil grin.

"Good," Longbow said. "Why don't you have a word with them, Rabbit?" he added.

"My pleasure, Longbow," the little fellow said. Then he walked over to the two that Ox was holding. "I seem to be all mixed up, friends," he said with feigned confusion. "Could you tell me just exactly what part of Lord Dahlaine's country this is?"

"I don't understand," one of them said.

"I'm sure that it has a name, friend," Rabbit said. "I'm sure that I've heard it but I just can't seem to remember what it is."

"I don't know either," the captive replied sullenly.

"You know perfectly well that this is the Tonthakan Nation," Chief Kadlar declared.

"Oh, that's right," the captive replied. "It must have just slipped my mind."

"Why don't you say it a few times, friend?" Rabbit suggested. "That might help you to remember."

"I don't take orders from strangers," the fellow said.

Ox raised his broad-bladed axe. "This tells you that Rabbit's *not* a stranger," he growled. "It says that you're going to do exactly what he tells you to if you want to keep your health. Now say 'Tonthakan,' or you'll make my axe very grouchy."

The fellow glowered at Ox and mumbled something.

"I can't *hear* you!" Ox said.

"Tonthakan!" The fellow sort of spit it out, and Athlan definitely heard the click-sound Keselo had described, and he caught a peculiar sort of odor that somehow removed what they were supposed to be listening for from his memory.

"Very nice," Ox said, patting the fellow's shoulder with his free hand. Then he turned to the second man. "Now it's your turn," he said.

"Tonthakan," the second one said, sounding a bit relieved.

"I didn't hear anything all *that* peculiar, did you, Longbow," Athlan said.

Then, without any warning whatsoever, Ox brained the two with his axe, splashing blood all over everybody standing nearby.

The strange odor was suddenly gone, and Athlan vividly remembered the loud click he'd heard when the two had said the word "Tonthakan."

"What's going on here?" Chief Kadlar demanded. He looked down at the two bleeding bodies. "I thought that I knew these two, but I've never even seen them before."

"These two are—were—servants of the Vlagh, Kadlar," Dahlaine told him, "and they tricked you into believing them."

"How?"

"They were emitting a peculiar smell that convinced you that they were telling you the truth. The smell *also* persuaded you you'd been insulted, when nothing had been done—or said—by any member of the Deer Hunter Tribes. There's a war coming this way, and these two are—were—

enemies. They were trying their best to trick you into going to war with the Deer Hunter Tribes so that there wouldn't be any archers to hold off their friends when they invaded." Dahlaine frowned and looked at Ox. "How did you manage to avoid being tricked by that odor they were putting out?"

"I didn't smell a thing, Lord Dahlaine," Ox replied. "I never do when I'm ashore at this time of the year. I sneeze a lot, and my eyes start running, and I can't smell anything at all. When I'm out at sea, I don't have any problems, but just the sight of land at this time of the year makes me start sneezing."

Dahlaine suddenly laughed. "I think we owe you for every sneeze, Ox," he said with a broad grin.

"I'll start keeping count, then," Ox said with a chuckle.

"I *must* go down to Statha and apologize to Chief Kath-lak," Kadlar declared. "I just hope that he'll forgive me."

"You can do that later, Kadlar," Dahlaine said. "What you really need to do now is to go tell all the other chiefs of Reindeer Land that we've got an enemy that's trying to trick them into going to war with the Deer Hunter Tribes." He reached inside his furry jacket and took out a white object that looked very much like a piece of rock-salt. "Wave this under their noses. It'll erase that scent the servants of the Vlagh use to deceive your people. Tell them to kill the smelly ones and then gather up all their warriors and archers and go on down to the village of Statha. We're just about to go to war with the creatures of the Wasteland, and we want to be ready when they attack."

"I shall do as you have commanded, Lord Dahlaine," Kadlar promised.

"Good boy," Dahlaine replied.

4

They returned to Statha the following morning, and the people of the tribe all seemed to view the seasonal malady which had made it impossible for Ox to catch even a hint of the strange scent the creatures of the Wasteland had used as a gift from Dahlaine.

"Actually, I didn't have a thing to do with that," Dahlaine confessed to his sister. "Ox told us that he sneezes and coughs every autumn if he happens to be on dry land. Once he's out at sea, it goes away. It was definitely useful up in Reindeer country, though. It turned out to be almost as valuable as gold."

"I don't think I've ever heard of golden sneezes before, dear brother," Zelana replied, smiling.

"Now that we've broken the grip the servants of the Vlagh had on the Reindeer Tribes I think we'd better advise all the tribes that it's time to prepare for war. Just the fact that there were servants of the Vlagh tampering with the Reindeer Tribes is a fairly strong indication that the Vlagh will come north before long."

"You could be right, Dahlaine," Zelana agreed.

"I'd say that it's just about time for you to set up your arrow factory again, Rabbit," Red-Beard suggested. "Would you rather set it up on the beach or here in Statha?"

"All of our equipment is on the ships," Rabbit replied. "I think it'd be better to do it there—unless it starts to rain."

"How long is it likely to take?" Dahlaine asked.

Rabbit squinted at the roof of the lodge. "The casting won't take all that long," he said. "I've got all those baked clay molds we used back in Lattash stored in the hold of the *Seagull,* so all we'll have to do is melt the bronze we brought up here and pour it into the molds. I'd say that we'll have barrels full of arrowheads in about a week or so. Then Longbow and Red-Beard can show Athlan and his friends how to replace their stone arrowheads with the bronze ones and we'll be ready to fight another war."

"I'll send runners to all the tribes in Tonthakan," Kathlak said. "We should let them know that we're just about to go to war *and* let them see these new arrowheads. This might take a while, but I'm sure that we'll have about fifty thousand archers available when the invasion begins."

"How long would you say it's likely to take before you're ready?" Dahlaine asked.

Kathlak scratched his cheek, squinting at the floor. "If the weather holds, it'll probably take a month or so. I'm sure that a lot of them are out in the forest hunting winter meat, and hunters are sometimes hard to find when they're busy."

Dahlaine considered it. "I think we should all home in on Mount Shrak," he decided. "It's centrally located, so we can go from there to any likely invasion route. I'll get word to the Matans, and they'll be there in a week or so."

"What about the Atazakans?" Kathlak asked.

"I don't think they'd be very useful. Gather as many archers as you can chase out of the forest and then come to Mount Shrak." Then Dahlaine smoothed his beard. "I think we'd better leave somebody who's familiar with Gunda and Veltan here to guide the Malavi horsemen when they arrive up here," he said.

"I can take care of that," Red-Beard said, "but I'll need somebody to show *me* the way to Mount Shrak."

"I know the way," Athlan volunteered.

Kathlak shook his head. "I want you and Longbow to come with us. He's familiar with the outlanders, and he can advise you when I make any mistakes, and then you can warn me."

"Zathal knows the way to Mount Shrak, My Chief," Athlan suggested. "He can show Red-Beard and the horse-soldiers how to get there."

Kathlak nodded. "I think that just about covers everything, Dahlaine," he said.

"Let's get started, then," Dahlaine said.

They went off toward the southeast through the deep forest Athlan had hunted since he'd been very young. He knew all of the trees, of course, and he knew the shortest route they should take. There was a slight breeze blowing in from the west, and, as always, the breeze set the eternally green trees to sighing almost as if the approach of winter made them sad and regretful.

"Mournful, aren't they?" Longbow said quietly.

"Probably not," Athlan replied. "It's just the wind. Now the *wind* might be feeling sort of down, but I wouldn't make any wagers on that. Weather goes through here all the time, and the trees sing to it as it goes by. For all I know, they're trying to sing it to sleep."

"If you happen to come across a song that puts the weather to sleep, you might want to remember how it goes. That could be very useful." Longbow paused. "Deer," he said quietly, pointing ahead of them with his chin.

"Not too big," Athlan noted. "I don't think I'd take that one. Let him grow up a bit."

"Good idea," Longbow agreed as the deer flicked his ears and ran off into the forest.

The burly outlander called "Sorgan" or sometimes "Captain" joined them. "I thought the trees down in Lady Zelana's country were about as big as a tree could get," he said, "but the ones around here are so tall that they probably tickle the moon's tummy when she goes by."

"Now *that's* something I'd like to see," Longbow said. "Do you think she might giggle if a tree happened to tickle her tummy?"

"I wouldn't want to put any bets on it, Longbow," Sorgan replied. "Around here, almost anything can happen—and sooner or later, it probably does." He turned to Athlan. "Just how far would you say it is from here to Lord Dahlaine's mountain?" he asked.

"Six days," Athlan replied. "Maybe a week. It sort of depends on how steep the mountains between here and Matakan are. I've never been up in those mountains, so I'm not familiar with them."

"Haven't you ever hunted up there?"

Athlan shook his head. "The mountains are the country of the Bear Hunter Tribes. It wouldn't be proper for me to go roaming around up there."

"I don't think I've ever seen a bear," the farmer Omago said.

"You've been lucky, then, Omago," Athlan said. "Bears aren't the nicest animals in the world. They've got big, sharp teeth, and their claws are longer than a man's fingers. The mountains between here and Matakan are safe in the wintertime, because the bears aren't awake then. Come spring, though, things start getting dangerous in bear country. When a bear wakes up from his winter nap, he'll eat anything that moves—or so I've been told."

"How big would you say that they are?" Omago asked.

"I saw a bearskin that was twelve feet long once," Athlan replied. "The bear was probably about that tall."

"Twelve *feet*?" Omago exclaimed.

"About that, yes. A full-grown bear isn't the sort of animal that anybody with good sense wants to play with."

"I can see why," Omago said in an awed tone of voice. "Do those mountain tribes actually hunt monsters like that?"

"I'm told that they hunt in groups," Athlan said. "If there are eight or ten men shooting arrows at a bear, they'll probably be able to take him down. I wouldn't really want to try it with only three or four, though."

They came to another marshy area the following day, and this one was also on fire with flickering blue swamp-fire dancing across the stagnant water.

"Are all of these swamps on fire like this?" Sorgan asked.

"Most of them I've seen, yes," Athlan replied.

"What sets them off?"

Athlan shrugged. "A spark of some kind, I'd guess. We get thunderstorms fairly often around here, and Dahlaine rides that pet thunderbolt of his when he's in a hurry. Then, too, when the forest gets dry, it catches fire fairly often." He looked around to get some idea of their exact location, then he smiled wryly. "Actually, though, this particular one was *my* fault. I was just a little too close to the marsh when I was setting up my camp one evening a few years ago, and when

I tried to start my campfire, I suddenly had a lot more fire than I really wanted. I left in a hurry about then."

"I wonder why," Sorgan said.

They skirted around the north side of the marsh and crossed the indeterminate border into the rugged Bear Hunter territory late that afternoon.

They'd gone about a mile or so up a steep slope when they saw a burly fellow wearing a shaggy fur cloak sitting beside a small campfire. He stood up when Dahlaine approached him. "What took you so long?" he asked.

"There was some trouble along the border between Deer Hunter territory and Reindeer Land, Agath," Dahlaine replied. "It took a while to get it straightened out. Is there a problem of some kind?"

"Not that I know about. There's a young Matan over on the other side of our mountains who wants to talk with you, but he's afraid of bears, so he won't come into the mountains."

"Are the Matans having problems of some sort?"

"I think maybe they are. The young one said a few *very* ugly things about the Atazaks. Of course *everybody* dislikes the Atazaks, so there wasn't anything in what he said that I haven't heard before."

The young Matan was named Tlingar, and it was fairly obvious that Dahlaine's young Dreamer, Ashad, knew him very well. They spoke with each other at some length, but Athlan wasn't really listening. He looked rather closely at the young Matan's "spear-thrower" instead. So far as he could tell, it was just a long stick with a slightly hollowed-out cup at one end. He couldn't exactly see how it worked. He'd frequently heard about the Matan spear-throwers, but this was the first time he'd ever seen one.

"Tlantar thought that you should know that the Atazaks have been raiding across our border, Dahlaine," Tlingar reported. "They haven't caused us too much trouble yet, but Tlantar says that they've got a *huge* army, and if they really wanted to, they could send more men than we could handle. What's the matter with their chief, anyway?"

"He's crazy, Tlingar," Dahlaine replied bluntly. "He thinks that he's a god. He goes out of his palace every morning and orders the sun to rise. Then, when evening comes along, he goes out again and tells her that it's all right for her to set."

"That *does* sound sort of crazy, all right," Tlingar said. Then he grinned. "You *could* turn your thunderbolt loose on him, couldn't you?"

"I'm not allowed to kill people—or things—Tlingar," Dahlaine replied. "You know that."

"You wouldn't really have to *kill* him, Dahlaine. If your tame thunderbolt started to bounce around on the ground near his feet when he was commanding the sun to rise, he'd probably give up the idea that he's a god, don't you think?"

Dahlaine's answering grin covered the front of his face.

"I think you might get in trouble if you tried that, big brother," Zelana said.

"I wouldn't *hurt* him, little sister. It *would* frighten him, though, don't you think?"

"Probably, yes, but if your thunderbolt happened to miss even just a little bit, she'd burn him down to ashes right there on the spot." She frowned. "I think I'm catching a faint smell of more tampering, aren't you? First we have bug-people telling Kadlar of the Reindeer Tribe that he's been insulted, and now we've got somebody who should know better thinking that he's a god. A little squabble between two tribes in the

Tonthakan Nation is one thing, but a religious war between the Atazak Nation and the Matans could be disastrous."

Dahlaine frowned. "I think we'd better move right along, Zelana," he said. "Let's get our friends settled down at Mount Shrak. Then I'll go out and see if I can find out what's going on around here."

Athlan was more than a little awed by the sheer size of Mount Shrak. Of course the fact that Dahlaine's mountain rose up alone out of the plains of Matakan made it appear even larger. He was fairly certain that there were mountains almost as tall in the coastal range of Tonthakan, but the surrounding peaks sort of concealed their size.

"Impressive," Longbow said, "but it looks just a little bare to me. Not very many trees on its sides. I don't think the hunting would be very good, do you, Athlan?"

"As I understand it, the Matans don't hunt deer the way we do. They hunt bison instead. I've heard that bison meat tastes very good, and an animal that large would feed a lot of people." He turned to speak with the young Matan, Tlingar. "I've heard tell that the bison here in Matan are herd animals," he said. "How many of them would you say would it take to make up a herd?"

Tlingar shrugged. "It sort of depends on what part of Matan you're talking about. The herds around Mount Shrak aren't usually very large—four, maybe five hundred. Chief Tlantar told me that he saw a herd up in central Matan once that took three days to run past the hill where he'd set up his camp. I can't come up with a word for that many bison. A thousand is about as far as I can count, and the herd Chief Tlantar saw that time went quite a bit past a thousand, I'd imagine."

"That would be a *lot* of meat," Athlan said.

"They aren't meat until after you kill them, Athlan, and it usually takes three or four spears to kill one bison. It's worth the trouble, though. The meat tastes very good, and we make our winter robes out of their hides. A good bison robe will keep a man warm no matter how cold the winter is."

"We might want to look into that, Athlan," Longbow said. "There aren't any trees here to hold back the cold, and we might be here for quite a while."

Dahlaine led them around the base of Mount Shrak, and they reached the mouth of his cave in the late afternoon of a chilly day.

"I'd say that Dahlaine's cave's quite a bit larger than your cave back in the forest, Athlan," Longbow observed.

"Do you actually live in a cave, Athlan?" Zelana asked.

"It holds off the weather much better than a lodge does," Athlan replied.

They followed Dahlaine into the large cave, and Athlan saw that the cave was even larger than he'd thought at first. "What are those things hanging down from the ceiling?" he asked Zelana.

"It's a form of rock," she explained. "Water seeps down through the mountain, and it picks up small amounts of certain minerals along the way. When it reaches the cave the minerals sort of stick together."

"Judging from the size of those things, I'd say that *small* amounts of minerals wouldn't come very close to what's getting washed on down here."

"It's not the sort of thing that happens overnight, Athlan," Zelana replied. "It *might* take as long as a thousand years for just a foot of one of those to develop."

Athlan swallowed very hard.

"I wouldn't pursue that much further, Athlan," Longbow advised. "Zelana has a habit of answering questions, and if you ask her the wrong ones, you might have a lot of trouble with the answers."

Athlan glanced up at the small light that seemed to be floating in the air above them.

"That would *definitely* be one of the things you don't want to ask any questions about, my friend," Longbow said. "Dahlaine has quite a few pets here in his cave. Let's just call that light a 'pet' and let it go at that, shall we?"

"Right!" Athlan agreed fervently.

They reached what appeared to be living quarters of some kind about a quarter of an hour later.

"I'm awfully tired, Beloved," the little girl Eleria said to Zelana when they reached that part of the cave. "If I don't get some sleep fairly soon, I think I'll start to fall apart."

"Is there some side chamber nearby, Dahlaine?" Zelana asked. "The children need some sleep. We've been pushing them for the past few days, you know."

"What about my playroom, uncle?" Ashad suggested. "It's warm there and I've got several bison robes we could use to sleep on."

"Good idea," Dahlaine agreed. "Why don't you show Yaltar and Eleria where it is? I think the other grown-ups and I'll be talking for quite some time about things that don't really concern you children."

"We'll see you in the morning then, uncle," Ashad said, and the three children went off into a side tunnel in the cave.

"All right, then," Dahlaine said, "if Zelana's right—and she usually is—the creatures of the Wasteland are stirring up trouble just as hard as they can up here." He smiled faintly. "I'll borrow a term from our Maag friends here. I'd say that we've 'whomped' them hard twice so far, and now they're trying to stir up trouble here in my Domain to distract us enough that we'll be too busy to 'whomp' them again."

"It sounds about right to me," Sorgan Hook-Beak agreed. "Every time the bug-people or the snake-men tried to whomp us, we turned things around and whomped *them* instead. I don't care how fast the Vlagh thing can lay eggs, we've still come out ahead, and even the stupidest thing in the whole wide world could see that if we go into a regular war, we'll win and they'll lose. Just about the only way they can avoid another 'whomp' will be to distract us from what we're supposed to be doing. Right now I'd say that they're doing everything they possibly can to stir up the natives of this part of Dhrall to make them fight each other instead of the servants of the Vlagh." He looked directly at Dahlaine. "Have you got any strong feelings about that fellow off to the east who thinks that he's god?"

"*Very* strong feelings, Captain Hook-Beak," Dahlaine replied. "If you'd like, I can give you a few hints about how you'd go about reaching down his throat and tearing out his heart. Then if you want, I wouldn't be at all disturbed if you cooked it and had it for supper."

"I'll save you a couple of bites, Lord Dahlaine," Hook-Beak promised with an evil grin.

Athlan was roused from his sleep early the next morning by the smell of cooking meat. "What is that?" he asked Longbow. "It doesn't smell at all like deer meat."

"It wouldn't," Longbow replied. "Bison aren't related to deer. There's a Matan village near Dahlaine's mountain, and the villagers brought food here earlier this morning."

"If bison meat tastes as good as it smells, I can see why the Matans spend their time hunting those animals. If they're going to provide the food while we're here, this might just turn out to be a pleasant war."

The little girl Eleria came out of the side tunnel into the large chamber. "I need a kiss-kiss, Longbow," she said.

"You're up early, Eleria," Longbow said, lifting her and holding her in his arms.

"I need to talk with the Beloved. Where is she?"

"Outside with her brother. The sun's coming up, so Zelana and Dahlaine are having breakfast. Did you sleep well?"

"Not really. Something happened in the middle of the night that sort of upset Ashad and Yaltar and me."

"Oh? What was it?"

"I'm not sure if I should tell you about it, Longbow," she said. "It's one of those family things. Of course, you *are* part of the family, aren't you?"

"Not quite, little one," Longbow replied with a faint smile.

"Here she comes now," Eleria said, pointing toward the chamber entrance.

"You're up early, Eleria," Zelana said. "Breakfast should be ready in just a little while."

"We can worry about breakfast later, Beloved. Lillabeth had one of 'those' dreams last night, and I think it might cause some problems."

Zelana looked a bit startled. "How do *you* know about Lillabeth's dream?"

"We *always* know, Beloved. I thought you knew that we share our Dreams with each other. Anyway, Lillabeth is very upset because when she told your sister that the creatures of the Wasteland were moving toward the land of the north, your sister Aracia decided not to let anybody know about the dream."

"She did *what*?" Dahlaine exclaimed.

"Lillabeth told us that your sister's afraid that if you find out that the bug-people will be coming *here* instead of into *her* country, you'll pull Narasan and his army out of her part of this land, and there won't be anybody there to protect her. Lillabeth isn't very happy about that. We're supposed to warn people when we have those Dreams, but your sister won't let Lillabeth do what she's supposed to do."

Dahlaine's eyes suddenly bulged and his face turned pale.

"*I'll* take care of this, big brother," Zelana told him quite firmly. "You've got to make preparations for a war, so you'll be very busy. I'm going on down to Aracia's silly temple and straighten her out—once and for all. We don't *do* things like this, and Aracia's going to answer to me for this idiocy! Then I'll find out about the Dream from Lillabeth herself and come right back here to tell you."

A
FAMILY
AFFAIR

1

Zelana followed Eleria back to the children's sleeping chamber off to the side of Dahlaine's central cave. Eleria's announcement had startled her more than a little, and she thought it might be best to speak with Ashad and Yaltar to get a few more details before she went on down to confront her sister.

"We thought you all knew that we shared our Dreams with each other," Yaltar said. "We weren't trying to keep it a secret or anything. It all started when Eleria had that first Dream about the time when the world was just a baby. That was an awfully noisy time, wasn't it?"

"Very noisy, yes. Are you saying that all four of you had exactly the same Dream at the same time?" Zelana asked, feeling more than a little startled.

"Not really, was it, Ashad?" Yaltar asked his brother.

"No, Eleria was doing the dreaming," Ashad replied. "We could *see* it, of course, but everything was coming from her. I think that Eleria's pink pearl might have had something to do with that. Her jewel was the very first one any of us found, so she had the first Dream. We were all just sort of tagging along behind her, watching what was happening. Later on, Yaltar found his opal, and then *he* had *his* first Dream, and we all watched that one—in the same way that we'd watched Eleria's. Then I found my agate, and I had *my* Dream. Now *Lillabeth's* doing the dreaming, and the rest of us are watching. We all sort of know that it's going to happen, though. The pretty lady wants it that way, I think."

"Pretty lady?" Zelana asked, somewhat baffled.

"We aren't supposed to talk about her, Beloved," Eleria said. "She loves you and your sister and brothers, but she doesn't want us to upset you right now because you're very busy. Anyway, your sister's trying to keep Lillabeth's Dream a secret, because she's afraid that if you and your brothers know about it, you'll take all those soldiers away from her and bring them on up here to help your big brother. Your sister's terribly afraid right now, and she wants lots and lots of soldiers in her country to protect her from the bugs. I think she was hoping that the next Dream would tell everybody that the bugs would attack *her* part of the world next and that everybody would run on over into her country to fight them off. Lillabeth's Dream didn't say that, though, so now your sister's trying to hide it from everybody else."

"I think she might be worried about how many soldiers the bug-people will kill when they come north," Ashad said. "If all those soldiers get killed up here, there won't be any left to protect her. That's kind of silly, isn't it? The soldiers haven't lost any of these wars yet, so there'll still be plenty of them left after they win the war up here. I don't want to make you mad at me, Zelana, but your sister's kind of silly, isn't she?"

"I think it's just about time for me to go on down there and slap the silly out of her," Zelana said.

"Can we come along and watch?" Yaltar asked eagerly.

"I don't think that would be a very good idea," Zelana said grimly. "I'll need Eleria, probably, but I think you boys should stay here. We never know when one of these Dreams are going to come along, and if one of you boys starts dreaming, Dahlaine will need to know about it immediately. Come along, Eleria. Let's go on down and teach Aracia a few things." She reached out and picked Eleria up and went on out of Dahlaine's cave.

"Are you going to hit your sister, Beloved?" Eleria asked eagerly.

"Behave yourself, Eleria," Zelana scolded the little girl as she walked up the steep side of Mount Shrak toward the peak. "You know that we never hit each other."

"You could spank her, though, couldn't you? Spanking and hitting aren't exactly the same thing, are they?"

Zelana laughed almost in spite of herself. "We'll see, child," she said. "If nothing else works, maybe I *will* have to spank my sister." She reached out with her mind in search of a good strong wind that was going in the right direction. "Now, I want you to just relax and stay calm, Eleria. We'll be a long way up in the sky, and we'll be moving very fast. I'll hold you tight, so you won't be in any danger at all. It might be best if you don't look down—at least not right at first. After a while, it won't bother you anymore."

"I trust you completely, Beloved," Eleria replied, "and I think that flying might be fun after I get used to it."

"I've always enjoyed it. In a certain sense, flying's a lot like swimming—except that you don't get wet." Then Zelana briefly touched a strong wind blowing down out of the northwest. "*That* one, I think," she said, taking Eleria in her arms. Then she reached up to grasp the wind, and she and

Eleria rose smoothly up into the sky, frightening a flock of geese as they went.

"Are those birds anything at all like Meeleamee and the other pink dolphins, Beloved?" Eleria asked.

"Not really, dear. Birds aren't very clever at all."

"Oh, my," Eleria said, looking down at the forest far below.

"What is it, dear one?"

"Those trees are all red and gold, Beloved. They're beautiful, aren't they?"

"Indeed they are, Eleria," Zelana said. "It's autumn now, and sometimes autumn is the most beautiful time of the year."

"Why do some trees stay green while others change their color?"

"Certain trees need to show off, dear. I'm sure that my big brother could explain why it happens. Dahlaine *loves* to explain things, and he can be very tedious about it. I prefer simpler answers. The trees are sad because summer's almost over."

"It *will* come back, though, Beloved. The trees know that, don't they?"

"I'm sure they do. Some trees stay green all year because they stay awake. The trees that change color sleep through the winter."

"Then those bright colors are just their way of saying 'good-night' to each other, isn't it?"

Zelana laughed and pulled Eleria even closer. "I *love* you, child," she said.

"And I love you, Beloved. How much farther is it to your sister's country?"

"Not too far. We were lucky enough to find a wind that knows where it's going. Every so often I encounter a wind that wanders off in all directions when I'm in a hurry."

"Spank it, Beloved. That would make it do what it's supposed to do, wouldn't it?"

"I'm not sure that I'd know how to spank a wind," Zelana said, laughing. "We should reach Aracia's temple in just a little while. We'll drift on in quietly, and I'll drop you off in Lillabeth's room before I confront Aracia. I don't want you to be alarmed. I'm going to shout at my sister and call her nasty names. I want her to get excited enough to start saying ridiculous things right in front of Narasan and Trenicia. I'm fairly sure that she'll deny everything that I say. You'll have had time enough by then to explain things to Lillabeth, and when Aracia starts screaming, you two can come into the throne-room and cut the ground right out from under my silly sister. I want Narasan and Trenicia to realize that they shouldn't believe anything Aracia tells them."

"I think Lillabeth's even unhappier with your sister than you are, Beloved," Eleria replied. "We're *supposed* to tell people about our Dreams. That's why we have them, isn't it?"

"Indeed it is, child," Zelana agreed. "I think it's just about time for me to show my sister that telling lies will get her into trouble."

"You don't like her very much, do you, Beloved?"

"Not when she's lying, I don't."

"Then we'll have to teach her not to lie."

They reached Aracia's marble temple just as the sun was sinking down over the western horizon, and Zelana carried Eleria to Lillabeth's room first. Then she rose up into the air again and listened carefully to her sister's conversation with the Trogite called Narasan and the warrior queen Trenicia. The outlanders seemed to be having some trouble explaining things to Aracia and the fat man who spent all of his time making speeches.

Zelana drifted down through the polished marble dome of Aracia's temple and then quite suddenly appeared as if out of nowhere in front of her sister's throne.

Aracia flinched back and half rose from her throne.

"Don't even think about it, Aracia," Zelana said. "We're going to settle this once and for all right here and now."

"What are you talking about?" Aracia demanded.

"You're lying, and you know it. What on earth possessed you to try to conceal Lillabeth's Dream? Didn't you know that the other Dreamers knew all about it?"

"That's not possible!"

"Then how do you explain why I'm here and how I know that Lillabeth's Dream told us that the creatures of the Wasteland were going to attack Dahlaine's Domain next? I think you've been awake too long, Aracia. You're starting to slide over the line into senility."

"What's this all about, Zelana?" Aracia demanded.

"Betrayal, Aracia. This idiocy of yours has put the entire Land of Dhrall in terrible danger. What were you thinking? You *do* know that if the servants of the Vlagh overrun Dahlaine's Domain, the entire Land of Dhrall will fall into their hands, don't you? In spite of that, you tried to keep Lillabeth's Dream a secret."

"I most certainly did *not*!"

"More lies, Aracia? Are you insane?"

"What's this all about?" the warrior queen Trenicia demanded.

"You *do* know that the Dreamers are here to warn us when the creatures of the Wasteland are about to attack, don't you?" Zelana replied. "Or did my idiot sister try to hide that from you? I wouldn't be surprised if she had. Sister Aracia seems to be making a career out of lying and hiding the truth."

Trenicia's eyes narrowed, and she glared at Aracia. "What do you have to say about this?" she said.

Aracia had gone pale. "My sister's just making this up to discredit me! She hates me! She's always hated me!"

"That's not true and you know it," Zelana said in a voice filled with contempt.

"How dare you?" the fat priest standing to one side of Aracia's throne exclaimed. "Holy Aracia *never* lies."

Just then Eleria and Lillabeth, walking hand in hand, came into Aracia's ornate throne-room. "I have dreamed," Lillabeth announced, "and in my Dream, the creatures of the Wasteland moved up through a deep valley lined with crystal toward the lands of the far North."

"Stop!" Aracia shouted. "I forbid you to say any more!"

"Greatly troubled were the people of the North," Eleria picked up where Lillabeth had stopped, "for there were many signs that *some* of their friends were no longer loyal to the Elder God who holds dominion in the North."

"Stop! Stop! Stop!" Aracia shrieked.

Eleria, however, continued, and Lillabeth joined her voice with Eleria's, and they spoke as one. "And there was a plague that was *not* a plague, and many, many in the North died. And for the first time the servants of the Vlagh bore with them weapons which were *not* parts of their bodies. But in time, the creatures of the Wasteland that serve the Vlagh were consumed by a fire unlike any fire we have ever seen, and thus was the Dream ended, for victory was once more ours."

"It's a lie!" Aracia howled. "A lie! A lie! A lie!"

"No, Aracia," Zelana said sadly, "you're the one who's

been lying. We all know that now." Then she looked at Commander Narasan. "I think you just got your marching orders, Commander. I'm sure that Sorgan will be happy to see you."

"You can't leave, Narasan!" Aracia screamed. "I forbid it."

"Forbid all you want, sister mine," Zelana said, "but Narasan goes north—now."

Then the warrior queen Trenicia glared at Aracia. "I see that you're not to be trusted," she said. "You lied to me, and I won't have anything more to do with you. I'm going north with my dear friend, Narasan."

"You can't do that! You're leaving me alone and unprotected! I *paid* you!"

Trenicia began to rip various jewels off her clothes and to throw them on the floor at Aracia's feet. "Take back what you paid me, Aracia," she said in a voice filled with loathing.

"It didn't work, did it, Aracia?" Zelana said then. "Your lies and foolish attempts at deception just fell apart, and now you're all alone. Our brothers and I *will* come here to protect your Domain when the servants of the Vlagh attack, but we won't do it because we love you. When you get right down to it, *nobody* really loves you. Your fat, lazy priests *pretend* that they love you, but they really don't. All they want is a life of luxury, and they'd sooner die than work for it. You're pathetic, Aracia—stupid, arrogant, and pathetic. I think it's time for you to grow up and look at the *real* world, but that's up to you. I don't really ever want to see you again."

Aracia stared at her in horror, and then she wailed and fled, weeping uncontrollably.

"Just a bit extreme there," Narasan suggested with a faint note of disapproval.

"She'll get over it," Zelana replied. "I know my sister very well. She'll twist it around for a while, and then—in her own mind at least—she'll come to see this as a victory. It's much too late for Aracia to look reality right in the face." Then she turned and looked at Eleria. "How did you manage to pick up Lillabeth's Dream that way?" she asked. "I knew that you had a general idea of her Dream, but I didn't know that you could recite it word for word like that."

"When I told you that we could share our Dreams, I meant *share,* Beloved. I knew exactly everything that was happening, and I also knew the words Lillabeth would use to describe her Dream. That's been going on since my very first Dream. If you want, we can go back to Dahlaine's cave, and you'll find out that Ashad and Yaltar can tell you exactly the same story, and they'll use the same words that Lillabeth and I used. It's not really something that we're doing our-selves, Beloved. Our jewels take care of that part. Didn't you know that?"

"No," Zelana replied, "actually, I didn't. I think you might have forgotten to tell me about it."

"Oh, maybe I did at that." Then Eleria smiled. "Every-thing's all right now, though. You might want to tell your brothers about it as well. It's not nice to keep secrets from your family, you know. Your sister just tried to do that, and look how angry that made you."

THE
MALAVI

1

It was early autumn in the Land of Malavi, and the little clumps of birch trees had turned golden, while the tall grass was now a pale yellow, sure signs that winter was not far away. Since Ekial had run off to some place to the east of Malavi, Ariga was obliged to take over his friend's duties, and he wasn't the least bit happy about that. The annual cattle-drive was no particular problem. Ariga had been involved in those drives for years now, so he knew what had to be done. It was the prospect of being obliged to deal with the Trogite cattle-buyers in the coastal village that irritated him. Always before, he'd gone off with his friends to celebrate at the end of the drive, but *this* time he wouldn't be able to do that.

That just didn't seem fair to Ariga.

The village on the coast was a shabby sort of place with rickety buildings where assorted Trogites desperately tried to swindle the Malavi herdsmen with watered-down beer and scruffy-looking prostitutes. There were piers jutting out into the harbor and each pier had a little shack on its shoreward side where the cattle-buyer waited, obviously hoping that he could cheat the Malavi herdsmen out of a few pennies.

Ariga swung down from his horse to one side of the pier where Ekial usually did business and went on up to the canvas door of the Trogite shack.

"Is anybody in there?" he called.

"Come in, come in," somebody inside called eagerly.

Ariga braced himself and went on in.

The Trogite was a scrawny-looking man with one eye that seemed to be looking off to one side while the other one appeared to be looking at the ceiling. He was dressed in fancy clothes that weren't very clean, and he didn't smell too good. "Welcome! Welcome!" he greeted Ariga. Then he squinted slightly. "I don't believe we've ever met before," he said.

"My name is Ariga, and I am of the Clan of Prince Ekial."

"Is the prince ill?"

"He's busy right now," Ariga replied curtly. "I drove our herd here this time. Let's get down to business, shall we? I've got five thousand prime cows. I'm sure that you know what price the elders have set for this year, so we won't have to argue about that."

"I think maybe we should get to know each other a little better," the Trogite said, his off-center eyes narrowing slightly.

"Why? I'm selling, and you're buying. That's the only thing that matters."

"I have a cask of very fine ale, Ariga. Why don't we have a few tankards before we get down to business?"

Ariga was tempted, but this was the one thing Ekial had warned all his friends about. "Don't *ever* accept a drink of anything—even water—from a Trogite cattle-buyer," was the first rule. "I'm not really all that thirsty," Ariga said.

"Let's get this over with, shall we? I have other things to take care of today."

"Well—" the wall-eyed Trogite said, "I think maybe the Malavi elders overlooked a few things when they set the price for this year. We've already bought more cows than we'll probably be able to sell when we sail on back to the empire, so I won't be able to pay you the full price your elders demanded this year. The market goes up, and it goes down. You know how that is."

"It's been nice talking with you," Ariga said, turning abruptly and starting toward the door.

"Where are you going?" the Trogite almost screamed.

"Anyplace but here. I don't think we'll be able to do business this year, and I don't really have time to dicker with you—particularly since my price just went up."

"You can't *do* that!" the Trogite protested.

"I just did. And I'll keep on doing it every time you try to play these silly games. Have a nice day." Ariga pushed the canvas flap aside and went on back outside.

"Come back!" the Trogite screamed from his doorway.

"No. I'm not going to waste any more time with you. Maybe next year—or possibly the year after that."

"But I've hired all these ships to carry your cows back to the empire!"

"That's *your* problem, not mine." Ariga went back to where his horse was waiting, mounted, and rode on down to the next pier and a different Trogite cattle-buyer. He was fairly sure that word of what he'd just done would get around among the Trogites rather quickly, so the next time he and his friends drove a herd of cows down to the coast, the cattle-buyers would know enough not to try to play games with him.

He was a bit surprised to find that he'd actually enjoyed himself when he'd jerked the wall-eyed Trogite up short. This was turning out very well.

Ekial returned to the lands of the clan a few weeks after Ariga had trounced the wall-eyed Trogite, and Ariga was very happy to see his friend again. "What took you so long?" he asked.

"I had to watch a war," Ekial replied. "Then some friends and I had to go to a place called Castano to hire enough ships to carry our men and their horses on up to the north end of a place called 'The Land of Dhrall.' From what I saw during that war I mentioned, we shouldn't have too many problems, and the pay's very good. How did the cattle-drive go this year?"

"No problems," Ariga replied. "I had to jerk that wall-eyed Trogite cattle-buyer up short, though." With a chuckle he described the encounter to Ekial.

"He thinks he's the cleverest man in the whole wide world, and he always tries to cheat—particularly when he has dealings with somebody for the first time. Did you find a dealer willing to pay the right price?"

"I had to go through a couple more cheaters before I found an honest buyer, but I'm fairly sure that the word's been passed around, so nobody's going to try to cheat me again. I got the full price for our herd, and then we all came back here. What's this business about a war off in some other part of the world?"

"*This* is what it's all about, Ariga," Ekial said, pulling a yellow block out from under his tunic and handing it to his friend.

The block was very heavy, and Ariga almost dropped it. "Is this what I think it is?" he demanded in a trembling voice.

"It *is* gold, yes."

Ariga hefted the block. "This weighs almost fifty pounds, Ekial," he exclaimed.

"That's fairly close, yes, and I've got several more. You and I and our friends are going to have to visit several other clans. The fellow who's hiring armies right now wants about fifty thousand men—and horses—to help his people fight off an enemy who's trying to take over his part of the Land of Dhrall. They're just a bit unusual, but they're foot-soldiers, so we shouldn't have any trouble dealing with them. Have you had anybody ride Bright Star lately? If he's feeling frisky, I might have to wear him down just a bit. Then you and I should ride on back to the coast and talk with a Trogite named Gunda and our employer's younger brother, Veltan. He's the one who hands out the gold."

"How many guards has he got with him? A man with several of these gold blocks needs *lots* of protection."

"He keeps it very well hidden, Ariga," Ekial said with a faint smile. "It doesn't show up until he needs it."

"How does he manage that?"

"I haven't got the foggiest idea. Get word to the other clans here in the north. We'll need about fifty thousand men—and their horses, of course—and we're just a bit pressed for time. Dahlaine's not sure just exactly when his enemies will attack, so he wants us up there in his territory as soon as possible."

"I'll pass the word, Ekial," Ariga said. Then he patted the heavy block of gold. "I'm fairly sure that this pretty little thing will get *everybody's* immediate attention."

*　　*　　*

"I'm not really sure *who* it was that came up with the idea, Gunda," Ariga told Ekial's bald Trogite friend a few days later when the two of them were sitting in one of the shabby taverns, in the coastal village where the cattle-buyers did business. The crews of the huge Trogite ships were busy building raftlike floating piers so that they could load men and horses, so Ariga and Gunda had stopped by the tavern to pass some time away.

"I'm sure that it was a long time ago, though," Ariga continued. "As far as I've heard, we've been riding horses for hundreds of years now."

"I'm sure that it's easier than doing your own walking," Gunda said.

"And faster, too," Ariga said. "I don't want to offend you, Gunda, but you don't act at all like the Trogites we come across here on the north coast. The only thing *they* seem to be interested in is finding new ways to cheat us."

"They refer to themselves as 'businessmen,' Ariga," Gunda said. "It's a nicer word than 'thieves,' I guess, but it means the same thing when you get right down to the bottom of it. I grew up in an army compound, and we were taught not to lie, cheat, or steal. We're so honorable that we make other Trogites sick to their stomachs."

"I can imagine," Ariga said. "Just exactly who *is* this fellow who took Ekial off to the west after he decided to hire us to fight his war for him?"

"That would be Dahlaine," Gunda said. "That one scares me just a little bit. Veltan is pleasant, and Zelana is beautiful—even if she is a little silly sometimes—but Dahlaine's as bleak as a mountain, and Aracia's crazy."

Ariga swallowed hard. "Why are we working for them, then?" he demanded.

"For the gold they pay us, Ariga. I thought you knew about that. I'll work for anybody—well, *almost* anybody—if the pay's good."

"Just exactly who—or what—are we going to be fighting, Gunda?" Ariga asked. "Ekial wasn't too clear when he was describing the enemy in that last war."

"That's probably because we were fighting two separate and different enemies in Veltan's Domain. The ones we came up against in the first war—the one in Lady Zelana's part of the Land of Dhrall—were what Sorgan Hook-Beak called 'snake-men.' "

"No arms or legs? They wouldn't be much of a problem."

"Oh, they had arms and legs, Ariga," Gunda said. "Sorgan was talking about their fangs and the venom that came out of those fangs. Are there any poisonous snakes here in Malavi?"

"I've heard about them," Ariga said, "but there aren't any around here—at least I *hope* not. Who—or what—was your second enemy?"

"The Trogite Church," Gunda replied, "—which isn't really around anymore. If you think *we're* interested in gold, we don't even come close to the Trogite Church. They *invented* greed—and that's what finally killed them—well, most of them, anyway. When the Church found out that the Land of Dhrall had mountains of gold just lying around for anybody who wanted it to just bend over and pick it up, they went completely insane. When you get right down to it, the Church fought that second war for us. All *we* really had to do was get out of the way." Gunda laughed then. "There's *somebody* in the Land of Dhrall who can do things that you wouldn't *believe,* Ariga. We *think* that she's a woman, but as far as I know, nobody's actually seen her. The Wasteland in the center of the Land of Dhrall is a desert—all sand and rocks—and this mysterious lady somehow made the whole thing look exactly like gold. The snake-men were charging *up* a slope that led into Veltan's territory, and the Church-men were charging down. They were busy killing each other, but then a solid wall of water came out of the ground, and drowned every single enemy on that slope."

"Where did the water come from?"

"The way I understand it, there's an underground sea five or six miles down below that part of the Land of Dhrall, and it broke loose just exactly when we needed it. I guess there was a bit of what the Dhralls call 'tampering' involved. Dahlaine's family tampers with things all the time, but even *they* seemed to be more than a little startled by that vast amount of water that suddenly came blasting up out of the ground to wash away all of our enemies."

"How long did that water keep on running down that slope?" Ariga asked.

"If I understood it correctly, it'll keep on running like that for several hundred years at least. The last time I looked, there was a huge lake at the bottom of the slope, but that lake's still growing. Give it a few more years, and it'll be an ocean. The bug-people won't be able to attack the southern part of Dhrall again."

"I think you just lost me, Gunda," Ariga said. "First you called our enemies 'snake-men,' but just now you called them 'bug-people.' Just exactly what are we going to have to deal with when we reach the Land of Dhrall? Are they bugs, or are they snakes? Or are they some odd mix of both breeds?"

"They're all kinds of things, Ariga. We even came up against a variety of them that appeared to be bats—and you don't *ever* want to encounter a venomous bat that does its hunting in the dark." Gunda laughed suddenly. "There's a clever little fellow called Rabbit on one of those Maag ships, and he came up with the idea of holding the bat-things back with fish-nets. I've heard that the nets snared thousands of the bug-bats, and they didn't come around after that." Gunda frowned slightly. "I'm a soldier, Ariga. I can follow orders, and I know how to use my weapons, but there are a lot of things going on in the Land of Dhrall that I don't understand. I've heard that 'the Vlagh' is the leader—or maybe the mother—of the snake-bug-bat things that live out in the Wasteland. It lays eggs—like a chicken—but when the eggs hatch, the new little chicks aren't anything at all like their older brothers and sisters. I guess that this Vlagh thing tampers even more than Dhalaine or his brother and sisters do. We kept coming up against things that seemed to be impossible—but we keep on winning, and I can't for the life of me understand how we did that. If the dice suddenly go sour on us, though, I think we'll be in a whole lot of trouble."

"You're just full of good news, aren't you, Gunda?" Ariga said just a bit sourly.

Ariga found it to be very crowded on the big Trogite ships that had been hired to take them to the Land of Dhrall. He'd had to help Ekial lead the newly hired horsemen from several other clans down to the coast, so he was among the last of the Malavi to go onto one of the ships. When Ekial's other friend—the one with all the pretty gold blocks—told them that he was going to put fifty thousand horses on a single one of those ships, Ariga laughed right in his face. "That's ridiculous, Veltan," he said. "You'll need twice as many ships to carry the horses as it took to load up the men."

"That might be true, Ariga," Veltan replied, "*if* the horses stayed as big as they are now. Are you at all familiar with the word 'tampering'?"

"Gunda mentioned it to me. He said that you and your family can play games with reality, and he referred to that as 'tampering,' and he said you do it all the time."

"Interesting definition, there," Veltan said. "Anyway, I'll tamper with *size* this time. Your horses will be quite large *before* they go onto that Trogite ship, but as soon as they go on inside, they'll be a lot smaller, and they won't need nearly as much food."

"How *much* smaller?" Ariga demanded.

Veltan squinted at the huge Trogite ship. "Oh," he said then, "probably about the same size as mice are. There's more than enough room on that big ship for fifty thousand mice, wouldn't you say? And there'll also be plenty of room for their feed as well."

"Why did you hire so many ships, then?"

"To carry fifty thousand men, of course."

"If you can shrink horses, can't you shrink people as well?"

Veltan blinked and then he suddenly flushed with embarrassment. "I never even *thought* of that," he admitted. "Now that you mention it, though, I probably could." He put one hand on Ariga's shoulder. "I'd take it as a kindness if you didn't tell this to any of your friends, Ariga. For some reason, my mind seems to have blanked out. It's probably one of the signs of old age."

"You aren't really all *that* old, are you?"

"I'm quite a bit older than I look, Ariga. I think it's just about time for me to take a long nap—a very, very long nap. It appears that my mind's already gone to sleep."

2

They sailed from the north coast of Malavi at first light the next morning, and the blond-haired Veltan had suggested that Ariga might as well join them on Gunda's fishing-yawl, which he referred to as the *Albatross*. Ariga had a few suspicions about that. Veltan had been quite embarrassed by Ariga's suggestion that he could have saved time and money if he'd gone ahead and shrunk down the Malavi in the same way that he'd shrunk their horses. Evidently, Veltan didn't really want Ariga telling stories to the other Malavi.

The weather was nice that day, so they'd covered a fair distance by the time evening was approaching. "Those big tubs you hired back in Castano don't really move very fast, do they, Veltan?" Ekial said when the herd of Trogite ships lowered their sails and dropped the heavy bronze weights they called "anchors" into the water.

"I wouldn't blink if I were you, Ekial," bald Gunda suggested. "Our friend Veltan here is a master of cheating, so we're probably a lot farther north than it might seem."

"'Cheating' is such an ugly word, Gunda," Veltan said

rather plaintively. "We much prefer 'tampering.' I'm not *really* cheating anybody. All that I'm really doing is modifying time just a little bit—and distance as well, of course. The coast of sister Zelana's Domain is pretty enough, I suppose, but we're not really here to look at the scenery. My big brother needs us on up to the north, and I think we'd better do our best to make him happy. He tends to get grouchy when things don't go the way he wants them to."

"Did he ever manage to get his older sister calmed down?" Ekial asked.

"We hope so. Aracia's having some problems, and Dahlaine sent Commander Narasan on over to her Domain to make her feel just a bit more secure. We don't know for sure just where the creatures of the Wasteland will strike next, so we more or less have to cover the East and the North at the same time. Narasan will have the help of the warrior women from the Isle of Akalla, and we're going north to help Sorgan Hook-Beak."

"Now *that's* a very peculiar name," Ariga said. "Do all of those Maags have those odd names?"

"It's a cultural peculiarity," Veltan explained. "Most Maags have names that sort of describe them. The one called Ox is a huge man with big shoulders and a thick neck."

"He doesn't have horns, though, does he?" Ariga asked.

"Not yet, I think," Gunda said with a faint smile. "I haven't checked his head lately, though."

"Ox is a good sailor," Veltan said, "and the crew on Sorgan's ship, the *Seagull*, usually do what he tells them to do. He's the second in command on the *Seagull*, and Sorgan depends on him to get things done."

"That little one they call Rabbit is very clever, I noticed," Ekial said, "and he seems to get along with the archer called

Longbow. Now *there's* a man that you don't want to irritate, Ariga. I'd say that he's probably the finest archer in the whole world—probably because he doesn't know how to miss when he shoots an arrow. If Dahlaine had ten men like Longbow, he wouldn't need anybody else."

"Longbow has a very personal reason to hate the creatures of the Wasteland," Veltan said. "He's turned killing them into his life's work." Then he looked off toward the western horizon. "The sun's going down, gentlemen. Why don't you have some supper and then get some sleep? We've got a full day ahead of us tomorrow."

"Would beans be all right for supper?" Gunda asked Ekial and Ariga. "I hope so, because that's just about the only thing I know how to cook."

"What would *you* prefer, Veltan?" Ariga asked.

"Veltan doesn't really matter, Ariga," Gunda said. "He doesn't even know how to eat—or to sleep either."

Veltan shrugged. "Family peculiarity," he said without bothering to explain. "Eat and get to bed, my friends. Tomorrow promises to be a very long day."

"You're going to cheat some more, I take it," Gunda said with a broad grin. "Didn't that get you into a lot of trouble once? I've heard that once you spent quite a few years camped out on the moon."

"It was just a misunderstanding," Veltan replied. "I got everything straightened out last spring. Mother wasn't really that angry with me, but the moon lied through her teeth to keep me there because she was lonesome." He looked at Gunda with one raised eyebrow. "Did you want any more details, Gunda?" he asked. "I'd be more than happy to fill you in if you're really curious."

"Ah—no, Veltan," Gunda replied. "I think I know just

about as much as I really want to know. Why don't I go get started on supper?"

"Excellent idea, Gunda," Veltan replied without changing his expression.

It was a couple of days later and the good weather showed no signs of changing. The wind continued to come up from the south, and Gunda's sleek little fishing yawl seemed almost to fly along the west coast of an island Veltan called Thurn. "My sister Zelana lived here for many years," he told them. "That was before our brother drifted around with the 'gifts' that changed our lives."

"What would people who own tons of gold need with gifts?" Ekial asked curiously.

"They were children, Prince Ekial," Veltan replied, "and they were the most precious things in our lives. I'm sure that you encountered sister Zelana's little girl Eleria a few times when we were in that basin above the Falls of Vash."

"Oh, yes," Ekial replied with a sudden grin. "She's the one who goes around kissing people into submission, isn't she?"

"That's Eleria, all right," Veltan agreed. "She started that kiss-kiss game when she was just a baby. My sister had some very close friends who were dolphins, and she persuaded them to feed Eleria. After Eleria started thanking the dolphins with kisses, they'd argue with each other for hours about whose turn it was to nurse the child. She's even managed to soften Longbow, and he's the hardest man in the whole world. Eleria didn't learn how to talk the language of people until just a couple of years ago. She spoke dolphin instead."

"It seems that I heard something about that during the

war in your Domain," Ekial said. "I was fairly sure it wasn't really the truth, though."

"Oh?"

"The fellow who told me about it said that the dolphins were pink. There's no such thing as a pink dolphin, is there?"

"There's one hopping around just ahead of us, Ekial," Veltan replied, pointing toward the bow of Gunda's yawl. "It looks to be pink to me."

Ekial turned quickly, and Ariga leaned out over the rail just to one side of his friend. "It looks pink to me, Ekial," Ariga said. "Just because you've never seen one before doesn't mean that they don't exist. If you really like that color, I'll see if I can find you a pink horse when we go on home after this war's over—or maybe you'd prefer a blue one. A blue horse would really make you stand out in a crowd, wouldn't you say?"

Ekial glared at his friend, but he didn't say anything.

"This one's almost as bad as Red-Beard, isn't he, Veltan?" Gunda said with a broad grin. "I think he and I are going to get along just fine."

The fleet of Trogite ships continued north for the next several days, and Ariga was a bit startled by the size of the trees in that region. They were immense and they seemed to rise up almost like columns. "How long would you say it takes a tree to grow that big?" he asked Veltan.

"Several thousand years at least," Veltan replied. "Until recently, the people of sister Zelana's Domain made their tools out of stone, and an axe with a stone blade wouldn't work very well if you decided to cut down a tree of that size. That means that the trees just keep growing and getting bigger every year."

"They're pretty enough, I suppose," Ariga said, "but I don't think I'd want to live in a place like this."

"Oh?"

"I don't see any grass growing in those woods, and that means that there wouldn't be anything for our cows to eat. Cows are what the Malavi are all about. What do the people around there eat?"

"Wild animals, for the most part. Zelana's people are primarily hunters. The people of my Domain are farmers." Veltan peered on ahead. "Well, finally," he said. "I'd say that we've reached the place that we've been looking for."

"How can you tell? The forest here looks about the same as it was farther south."

"Pretty much, yes, but there's a man in a canoe just ahead of us, and I think it's Red-Beard. My older brother told me that Red-Beard would guide us to Mount Shrak—Dahlaine's home."

"You're not going to have any trouble unshrinking our horses, are you?"

"Not really." Veltan straightened. "Ho, Red-Beard!" he called. "I'm over here."

"What took you so long, Veltan?" the man in the canoe called back, digging his paddle into the water.

"Have you encountered any of the creatures of the Wasteland yet?"

The native pulled his canoe in beside the front end of the *Albatross*. "We came across a few of them," he answered. "We didn't know what they were right at first, but once we recognized them, we did what needed to be done. They were trying to stir up trouble between the tribes around here, but now that they're all dead, things are going more smoothly." He looked out at the fleet of Trogite ships following the *Al-*

batross. "It's going to take a while to get your people out on dry land, I'd say. There's a little fishing village just on ahead. I'll lead you there, and then I'll tell you the wonderful story about how we got rid of those nasty bug-people."

"I can hardly wait," Veltan replied.

"That one exaggerates things a bit, doesn't he?" Ariga observed.

"He's a funny sort of fellow," Veltan replied, "but we all like him. He's Longbow's closest friend, and that makes him quite important."

"Ekial mentioned Longbow," Ariga said. "It'll be good to get my feet back on dry land again. Boats are all right when you have to cross water, I guess, but I still prefer dry land. There's something you should probably know, Veltan," he said then. "It's going to take us a little while to get our horses settled down after we unload them. Horses start to get a little belligerent if they haven't been ridden for a few days."

"I thought that they'd all been tamed."

"Well, *sort* of tamed. If a horse is really any good, though, he's quite spirited, and it takes a little while to remind him that *we're* the ones who make the decisions. He'll get the point—eventually—but it *does* take some time."

Ekial's face had a slightly awed expression as what appeared to be an endless string of horses came down the wide ramp from the Trogite ship. "How did Veltan *do* that?" he asked Ariga.

"He didn't go into too many details, Ekial," Ariga replied. "He just said that he reduced the size of the horses when they went from the pier into that ship."

"Reduced?"

"He shrank them down until they were about the size of mice—or so he told me. I'd say that he's *un*shrinking them now. It's going to take a while to get that many horses off of one lone ship, I'd say."

Ekial shuddered. "That's making my hair stand straight up," he said. "Let's go talk with Red-Beard. Veltan told me that they had some problems when they first came here. If we can persuade him to stop joking around, we might be able to get a few details about what happened."

The two of them went a ways on down the beach to the shady grove where the native called Red-Beard was talking with Veltan, telling him about how the bug-people had deceived the Tonthakans and how their "clicking" that the farmer Omago had described gave them away. "I'm not sure just exactly how the 'clickers' persuaded that Tonthakan chief that he'd been terribly insulted, but, evidently, he believed them, even though they never told him just exactly what that insult had been all about. His mind cleared up immediately after Ox brained those 'clickers' with his axe."

Veltan winced. "Wasn't that just a little extreme?" he asked.

Red-Beard shrugged. "You know how Ox is. He doesn't waste any time when he encounters an enemy. With Ox, it's bash first and *then* talk. The chief who'd been causing all of the trouble apologized all over the place, and everything went back to normal again. I'm not trying to frighten you or anything, Veltan, but it looks to me like the bug-people are getting a lot smarter than they were in those earlier wars. We might want to start being a little more careful this time. A clever enemy is a dangerous enemy, so I don't think we'll want to rush into anything."

"You *had* to go and say that, didn't you, Red-Beard," Veltan reproached his friend.

"I just thought you ought to know, Veltan," Red-Beard replied. "Aside from this 'Nation' foolishness your big brother devised, the people here in Tonthakan are pretty much the same kind of people that those of us who live farther south are. They use bows and arrows and they spend a lot of their time hunting. Longbow has a new friend now. His name's Athlan, and he's a fair hunter. He's not as good as Longbow, of course, but who is?"

3

He's a pretty tired old horse, Red-Beard," Ariga told the native from Zelana's part of the Land of Dhrall. "He just sort of plods along, but he *will* get you to where we're going. If Veltan was right about how far it is to this mountain, you probably won't want to walk."

"I *do* know how to walk, Ariga. I can cover a lot of ground when it's necessary. What happened to the fellow who owns this tired old beast?"

Ariga shrugged. "He and some other men were playing dice on one of those Trogite ships, and they were using *his* dice. Things were going very well for him until one of the other players checked the dice rather carefully and found out that they'd been weighted on one side. If a man knew how to roll them just right, he could make any number he wanted come up every time."

"Isn't that cheating?"

"Indeed it is, my friend," Ariga replied. "The other players weren't very happy, so they threw him into the water behind the ship. I guess he'd never learned how to swim, so he sank like a rock. Now we've got a horse that doesn't have anybody to ride him."

"Oh, the poor thing," Red-Beard said in mock sorrow.

"We wouldn't want that horse to feel neglected, now would we?" Ariga said, grinning.

"I'll sacrifice myself to make him feel happy, then," Red-Beard said. "Sometimes I'm so noble that I just can't stand myself."

"I've noticed that. Now, you want to be certain that your foot's firmly in place in the stirrup *before* you mount. If that foot slips out, you'll wind up face-down on the ground, and the horse will run off and leave you behind."

"Let's try it and see what happens," Red-Beard said. He took hold of the saddle, jammed his foot into the stirrup, and hauled himself up onto the horse's back. "It's sort of awkward, isn't it?" he said.

"You'll get smoother with practice."

"How do I persuade him to start walking?"

"Nudge his sides with your heels—gently right at first. You want him to walk. If you thump his sides *too* hard, he'll run."

"How do I tell him that I want him to stop?"

"Pull back on the reins. He knows what that means."

"All right. Let's give it a try and see what happens."

Red-Beard fell off the horse a few times, but by the end of the day he'd grown more proficient, and if the horse wasn't running *too* fast, he managed to stay in the saddle.

"It's going to take a few more days to get all of the men off those ships," Ariga told Red-Beard, "so you'll have time to practice and grow more proficient."

"Does this horse have a name?"

"I think he's called 'Seven,' " Ariga replied. "His original owner was *very* interested in dice games, and seven's very important when you're playing dice."

"I wouldn't know about that, but I'll take your word for it," Red-Beard said. He patted his horse on the neck. "You're a good boy, Seven," he said. "Why don't you go rest your feet for a while, and I'll go rest my bottom." He looked at Ariga. "Does it get any easier on your backside as time goes by?"

"There are some ways you'll develop in time to keep from bouncing up and down so much. Right at first, though, you'll probably eat most of your meals standing up. Seven will get you to where you want to go quite a bit faster than your feet will, and your feet won't hurt at the end of the day."

"But my bottom will, I take it."

Ariga shrugged. "Nothing comes free, Red-Beard."

The deep forest on the Tonthakan side of the mountain range bothered all of the Malavi quite a bit. "We aren't used to see-ing trees that big, Red-Beard," Ariga said. "The trees down in our part of the world aren't nearly so tall, and they have leaves that fall off when winter arrives."

"The trees up here in Dahlaine's territory are probably the biggest ones in the whole world," Red-Beard agreed, nudging Seven along with his heels. "I always thought that the trees in Zelana's Domain were the biggest, but they don't even come close to *these* monsters. A tree that's three hundred feet tall gives a man something to think about, doesn't it? Can you imagine how *old* those things are?"

"They seem to be aging quite well, though," Ariga added. "Their limbs aren't turning grey, and they don't seem to need canes to keep them standing upright."

"I don't think trees *get* old, Ariga," Red-Beard said. "If

nothing goes wrong—a forest fire or a windstorm—they'll just stand there forever. If we looked around, we could *probably* find a tree up here that's a million years old—give or take a month or two."

"Very funny, Red-Beard."

"I'm glad you liked it," Red-Beard said. "Wait!" he hissed.

"What?"

"Deer on up ahead. Let's find out if I can shoot arrows when I'm sitting on old Seven here." He carefully took up his bow and pulled an arrow out of his quiver. "Stay right here," he whispered. "I don't think this will take too long." He lightly nudged Seven with his heels and the weary old horse plodded forward toward the deer that was feeding on a low bush.

The deer raised his head, his ears flickering a bit. Then he went back to eating.

Red-Beard took aim and loosed his arrow.

The arrow took the deer high in his neck, and the deer staggered off a few yards and then collapsed.

"Meat in the pot!" Red-Beard shouted triumphantly.

Ariga rode forward. "You're very good with your bow, Red-Beard," he said.

"Lots of practice, my friend," Red-Beard said. "Now you'll be able to taste *real* meat. Venison's richer than beef, and a meal of deer meat will keep you going. I don't want to offend you, Ariga, but beef *is* a little bland, you know."

"It's never bothered *me* all that much," Ariga said, "and the Trogites pay good money for cow meat."

"Trogites will eat almost anything," Red-Beard said, sliding out of his saddle with a knife in his hand. "I'll dress this one out and then sort of snoop around and see if I can find any others nearby. We're coming up on feeding-time here in the woods."

"You don't have to tell Red-Beard that I said this," Ariga told his friend Ekial, "but that deer meat didn't set too well with me."

"It *was* just a bit gamey, wasn't it?" Ekial agreed. "I definitely prefer beef, but let's not make an issue of it. We don't want to offend Red-Beard if we can avoid it."

They rode on up into the mountains that stood to the east of the Tonthakan country, and Ariga was somewhat awed by these rugged peaks. This wouldn't be a good place to fight a war on horseback.

When they reached the summit, however, Ariga and the other Malavi stared off to the east at what was probably the most beautiful meadowland any of them had ever seen. It stretched unbroken from the east side of the mountains to the far horizon, almost like a golden sea. "Now *that* is our kind of country, isn't it, Ekial?" Ariga said to his friend.

"Truly," Ekial agreed in an awed voice. "We could raise cows by the millions out there."

They rode on down the east slope of the mountains, and there was a native of the region waiting for them in the shade of a small grove of trees.

"Which one of you is Veltan?" the solid-looking native asked when they approached him.

"That's me," Dahlaine's brother said, nudging his horse closer.

"Your big brother wanted me to tell you a few things," the native said. "My name is Tlatan, and I am of the tribe of Tlantar. I'm supposed to warn you and your people that there's a pestilence roaming around killing people off to the north and that the Atazakans have invaded the lands of the Matans."

"You said *what*?" Veltan exclaimed.

"We've got a pestilence and an invasion," Tlatan replied. "You really should learn to listen more carefully."

"Let's set the pestilence aside for now and concentrate on the invasion. Why are the Atazakans invading?"

"Probably because their high chief is crazy," Tlatan said with a shrug. "I thought everybody knew that Azakan is crazy."

"When did this invasion start?"

"Sometime last week, I think. We haven't received too many details yet. Your big brother's quite concerned about it. You might want to hurry on down to Mount Shrak and talk with Dahlaine. He can probably give you more in the way of details."

"I want to thank you, Tlatan," Veltan said.

The native shrugged. "I'm just doing what I was told to do." He looked around at the mounted Malavi. "Do these people always sit on the animals they're going to eat for supper?" he asked, curious.

"They're called bison, Ariga," Veltan said. "The Matans hunt them—for food, primarily, but I understand that their hides are also useful."

"They're quite a bit bigger than cows," Ariga observed, "and I don't think I've ever seen an animal with horns that are all one solid piece like that."

"Dahlaine says that the bulls are quite aggressive. They don't just run away when something—or someone—attacks the herd. The bulls fight back, and they're very bad-tempered."

"That might take a lot of the fun out of hunting them. They look very shaggy, don't they?"

"That's why the Matans value their hides so much. It gets very cold up here in the winter, and shaggy garments keep the Matans warm and dry when winter arrives."

"If it wasn't for that cold weather, this would be a great place to raise cows," Ariga suggested.

"Not really, Ariga. There are wolves up here in Dahlaine's country, and I'm fairly sure that the wolves would eat all your profit."

"I've heard about wolves, but I don't think I've ever seen one."

"If you're lucky, you never will. They're very clever animals, and they hunt in packs. If a dozen or so wolves decide that you might taste good, they'll probably have you for supper."

"They'd have to catch me first, and I'm fairly sure that my horse could outrun them without too much trouble."

"Possibly so, Ariga, but how long can your horse run?"

"All day, if it's necessary."

"That wouldn't be quite long enough, I'm afraid. A pack of wolves could make your horse run as fast as he possibly could for two or three days—and nights. Sooner or later, your horse would collapse, and then the wolves would eat him, and have *you* for dessert."

Ariga shuddered. "Do you suppose we could talk about something else, Veltan?" he asked.

"Of course, Ariga. The weather maybe?"

Mount Shrak was one of those solitary peaks, much like some of those in the southern reaches of the Land of the Malavi. Most mountains had family members clustered around them, but every now and then, a lone peak would stand off all by itself—possibly because it didn't get along with its brothers and sisters. Ariga found the notion of a grumpy mountain stalking away from its family in a huff rather amusing.

Veltan spoke briefly with Ekial and then went to a large cave-mouth in the side of the lonely peak to talk with Dahlaine and with the most beautiful woman Ariga had ever seen.

"She did *what*?" Veltan exclaimed in an astonished tone of voice.

"She was trying her very best to hide Lillabeth's Dream from the rest of us, baby brother," the beautiful woman said. "She wanted everybody in the world to run on down to her Domain to protect her 'Holy Temple,' but I jerked the rug out from under her. Now she's all alone down there with no-body to protect her except for several thousand fat, lazy priests who couldn't tell one end of a knife from the other. I think we'll let her sweat for a while before we send her any help. It might be good for her."

Than a large man with a broken nose came out of the cave with a bleak-faced native beside him. "Did I hear you right, Lady Zelana?" the bulky man asked. "Is Narasan on his way up here?"

"He and his men were boarding their ships when I left, Sorgan," the lady replied. "It's going to take them a while to sail up the east coast, and then they'll have to march the rest of the way here from the beach."

"I really need him *here*, Lady Zelana," Sorgan declared. "I went down and had a look at the canyon called 'Crystal Gorge,' and we'll need a good strong fort to hold back the bug-men when they begin their attack, and Narasan's men make better forts than my men can."

"I think you might just be overlooking something, Captain Hook-Beak," Veltan said with a faint smile. "I just happen to have Sub-Commander Gunda in my party, and Gunda's the best fort-builder in the entire Trogite Empire. That wall he built down in my Domain will probably still be there a thousand years from now. If your men can follow his instructions, the creatures of the Wasteland will *never* get out of Crystal Gorge."

"Unless they decide to take up flying again," the bleak-faced native added.

"Why do you always have to do that, Longbow?" the one called Sorgan demanded.

"It keeps you on your toes, Sorgan. Always expect the worst. If it doesn't come along, it'll brighten your whole day."

"I don't think you'll be involved in the building of the fort, Captain Hook-Beak," Dahlaine said. "I think it might be a good idea for you and Prince Ekial to get to know each other. I have a sneaking suspicion that Ekial's horse-soldiers will radically change the way we'll be fighting wars from here on, and the servants of the Vlagh are going to be getting some very nasty surprises before we finish up this time."

THE
WAR
CHAMBER

1

There was an alien quality about the Domain of Veltan's older brother that Omago found to be just a bit disturbing. The huge evergreen trees in the Tonthakan region filled Omago with awe, and that might have had something to do with his problem, but the more he thought about it, the more convinced he became that it was people rather than the trees or mountains that concerned him so much. It seemed to Omago that they didn't behave the way that people were supposed to. He knew that Longbow and Red-Beard were hunters rather than farmers, but after a while he'd grown accustomed to their peculiarities, and they'd actually become fairly close friends. The outlanders were *very* different, but that was to be expected. They came from different parts of the world, after all. Even so, Omago found that there were several of the Trogites and Maags that he thought of as friends.

The natives of the Domain of Veltan's older brother, however, baffled Omago. There was a belligerence about them that seemed most unnatural, and it appeared that the slightest disagreement could start a war up here.

As it turned out, however, that belligerence had been the

result of what Veltan had always referred to as "tampering." Veltan himself was a master tamperer. He altered many things, usually to make the lives of the people of his Domain more pleasant. The tampering up in that part of Dahlaine's Domain called Tonthakan, however, had evidently been the work of their enemies, and it had obviously been designed to stir up conflict between the various tribes, and thereby to reduce the size of the force that would be needed to hold back the invasion of the creatures of the Wasteland.

All had turned out very well in Tonthakan, but it appeared that their enemies were far more clever than they'd been in the earlier wars in the Domains of Veltan and his sister Zelana. Omago remembered something that Veltan had told him when he'd been just a boy. *Most* creatures, Veltan had said, developed very slowly, and a minor change could take thousands of years to become common in all members of that species. The creatures of the Wasteland, however, could change significantly almost overnight. It was *that* peculiarity which made the servants of the Vlagh so dangerous.

After Sorgan's friend Ox had eliminated the two creatures who'd been causing the dissension in Tonthakan, things went much more smoothly, and Veltan's older brother decided that they should all go on down to his home in a place called "Mount Shrak." They left the village of Statha and crossed the mountains that the árcher Athlan called "Bear Hunter Territory" and came to the lands of Matakan.

The vast prairie-land of Matakan filled Omago with awe. The tall yellow grass strongly suggested that the soil was very fertile, and Dahlaine told them that the grain-fields to the north were extensive. The Matans of this southern region, however, concentrated on hunting the huge bison that grazed here and were the primary meat source in the lands of the Matans.

Omago had a bit of trouble with that idea, of course. There had always been a certain amount of trouble in the Domain of Veltan because of the grazing habits of sheep. A herd of hungry sheep could devour vast stretches of wheat and other crops in the space of just a few days, and Omago was quite sure that a herd of bison, an animal that appeared to be ten times larger than a sheep, could strip away an entire season's worth of hard work almost overnight. That probably caused a lot of problems.

It took them a couple more days to reach Dahlaine's home under the towering Mount Shrak. The notion of sleeping in a hole in the ground disturbed Omago more than a little. Hadn't Dahlaine ever seen a house?

As usual, however, Ara took everything in stride—right up until they reached Dahlaine's main underground chamber and she saw Dahlaine's rudimentary kitchen. She spoke with Veltan's older brother at some length about stoves and ovens, pots, pans, plates, cups, spoons, and other utensils.

Omago had to cover his mouth with one hand to keep Dahlaine from seeing his broad grin as Ara continued to scold him.

It was early on the following morning when Zelana's little girl Eleria came out into the main chamber of Dahlaine's cave looking for her "Beloved." Omago saw a certain charm in the child's use of that term, but he'd had just a bit of trouble with Zelana's explanation that the word had been derived from the term used by her pet pink dolphins. The concept of talking animals disturbed Omago more than just a little. If dolphins could talk, that probably meant that they could also think. And if they could think——? Omago shuddered back from that possibility.

Both Zelana and Dahlaine seemed to be quite troubled when Eleria advised them that the children "shared" their Dreams with each other. The notion that the children were able to step over vast distances with their minds didn't really seem all that remarkable to Omago. They *were* brothers and sisters, after all, and, given their importance in the current situation here in the Land of Dhrall, communication between them could very well be absolutely essential. Yaltar had never quite come right out and told Omago and Ara that he'd known exactly what his sister Eleria had seen in one of "those" Dreams, but he'd quite obviously been aware of the more significant details.

It was the decision of their sister Aracia to conceal Lillabeth's Dream from the other members of her family that outraged Dahlaine and Zelana the most, however. In their eyes this was an out-and-out betrayal. Omago wasn't really all that surprised, however; Aracia's arrogant, self-centered behavior during the war in Veltan's Domain quite strongly suggested that she devoutly believed that she was by far the most important creature in the entire world, and that her brothers and sister were not really all that significant.

Omago found that to be moderately offensive.

Zelana's immediate reaction was anything but moderate, however; Omago was quite certain that "divine" Aracia was likely to have a very bad day when Zelana confronted her.

"Don't concern yourself, dear heart," Ara said with a faint smile. "I'm quite sure that Zelana's just about to go turn her sister's world upside down, and then everything should be all right again."

"If you say so, dear," Omago said, but he *did* have a few doubts.

2

I'm not too sure that the idiocy down there was entirely Aracia's fault, Dahlaine," Zelana told her brother after she and Eleria had returned to the cavern later that day. "There's a priest down there who's *almost* as fat—and dishonest—as Adnari Estarg of the Trogite Church was, and he has our sister neatly wrapped around his finger. His main goal in life is to make sure that he's protected from honest work—and living in luxury, of course. Once he starts talking, Aracia's mind goes to sleep. She adores being adored, and Takal Bersla piles adoration on her for all he's worth for hours and hours every day. I wouldn't be at all surprised to find out that our dear sister 'just happened' to tell him about Aracia's Dream, and then *he* could very well have been the one who persuaded her to try to hide it from the rest of us." Then she laughed. "Do you happen to remember that fellow in Narasan's army who goes by the name of Andar? The one with the deep voice?"

"I think so, yes," Dahlaine replied.

"After Narasan and his army reached Aracia's temple

down there and discovered that 'Temple City' was completely indefensible, they tried to persuade our sister that they should determine the invasion route the bug-people would most likely follow and then block it off with their standard fortifications. Holy Bersla violently objected and announced that the *temple* was the only place in our sister's Domain that needed protection. As far as he was concerned, the rest of Aracia's Domain wasn't at all significant."

"Is he really *that* stupid?" Dahlaine asked with a certain astonishment.

"Not anymore, he isn't," Zelana replied with a broad grin. "Andar gave him a rather extended lecture on the process of starving to death after Bersla said that he'd *always* have plenty to eat. He pointed out the fact that if the creatures of the Wasteland managed to occupy the farmland in Aracia's Domain, they'd eat *everything* and leave nothing at all for Aracia's priests. He even managed to raise the possibility of cannibalism. By the time he was done, 'Holy Bersla' was in a state of near-panic. Aracia was still 'forbidding' Lillabeth to tell us about her Dream, though, but Eleria jerked the ground out from under her."

"Could you give us the gist of Lillabeth's Dream?" Dahlaine asked.

"I can do better than that, big brother," Zelana said with a broad smile. Then she looked at the children who'd been standing nearby. "Why don't you tell him Lillabeth's Dream?" she suggested to them.

"I have dreamed," the children recited, speaking in unison, "and in my Dream the creatures of the Wasteland moved up through a deep valley lined with crystal toward the lands of the far North. Greatly troubled were the people of the North, for there were many signs that *some* of their friends were no longer loyal to the Elder God who holds dominion in the North. And there was a plague that was *not* a plague, and many, many in the North died. And for the first time, the servants of the Vlagh bore with them weapons which were *not* parts of their bodies. But in time, the creatures of the Wasteland that serve the Vlagh were consumed by a fire unlike any fire we have ever seen, and thus was the Dream ended, for victory was once more ours."

"Any questions, big brother?" Zelana asked with a sly little smile, "or would you prefer to go into an extended oration about assorted impossibilities? What it all boils down to, Dahlaine, is the fact that the Dreamers will do *exactly* what they're supposed to do, regardless of how hard any one of us—or all of us put together—might try to stop them." Then she gave him a broad smile. "Isn't that neat?" she said with almost childish enthusiasm.

They gathered in the central chamber of Dahlaine's cave to consider Lillabeth's Dream. Now that all doubts had been pushed aside, Omago was certain that they'd be able to find solutions, even as they had during the war near the Falls of Vash.

"I *was* fairly sure that Crystal Gorge would be the route the creatures of the Wasteland would follow when they decided to pay me a call," Dahlaine said. "There *are* a few other passes that come up here from the Wasteland, but they're crooked, and narrow, and very steep. Crystal Gorge isn't really very wide, but it's wider than any of the others. If the servants of the Vlagh decide to follow their usual practice of charging in masses, they'll almost have to come up here through that gorge. I think that one of Narasan's forts might be the best solution to the problem. We have archers and spearmen who'll be able to defend that fort, and we'll have the Malavi horsemen who'll be able to deal with any invaders who try to sneak around behind us."

"I think we might just be coming up on 'lumpy map' time," Longbow suggested. "*You* know exactly what the ground looks like, Dahlaine, so maybe you should share it with the rest of us."

"Does he *always* do that, Zelana?" Dahlaine asked his sister in a grouchy tone of voice.

"*Almost* always, yes. Longbow's an extremely practical man, and he won't put up with *im*practicality. Keep the peace in the family, big brother. Make a lumpy map. Then we'll all be able to look at it and point out all the mistakes you've made."

"Somehow I *knew* you'd say something like that, Zelana," Dahlaine replied sourly.

"Then I haven't disappointed you, have I? Make a map, Dahlaine. Show us how beautiful your land is, and then we'll tell you what's wrong with it."

"Don't let all those clever remarks disturb you, Dear Heart," Ara said quietly to Omago. "In a peculiar sort of way this is how they express their love for each other. It's a game they've been playing for a long, long time. They *might* grow up someday, but I wouldn't count on it, if I were you."

Dahlaine conjured up his "lumpy map" in a large chamber some distance away from the one where he and Ashad spent most of their time, and he borrowed Veltan's idea and put a balcony around the chamber wall to give the people who were there to help defend his Domain a clearer view of the map. The map was much larger than the one in Veltan's house, and right at first Omago thought that Veltan's older brother might have been exaggerating just a bit in the somewhat childish hope that "bigger" might seem more impressive. The more Omago looked at the map, however, the more certain he became that it was fairly close to being an exact representation of Dahlaine's part of the Land of Dhrall.

"That's Crystal Gorge right there," Dahlaine told them, pointing at the representation of the place that had been very significant in Lillabeth's Dream.

"It looks to me like that might be a good place for one of Narasan's forts," Sorgan Hook-Beak suggested. "The one called Gunda is the expert on forts," he added. "As soon as he gets here with Veltan and the horse-people, we'll let *him* decide where we should build it, and then I'll take my men down there, and we'll construct a base so that when Narasan arrives, he'll be able to put his men to work on the fort itself." Then he looked at Dahlaine. "Can you give us any kind of guess about when the snake-men are likely to show up in that gorge?"

"I *think* we'll have enough time, Sorgan," Dahlaine replied. "It's a goodly distance from Veltan's Domain up here to mine, and the Vlagh's going to have to replace all the servants that were drowned when that river changed direction."

"Do the Matans hunt anywhere near that gorge?" Longbow asked. "I'm not trying to offend you, Dahlaine, but hunters pay very close attention to the terrain of the place where they hunt."

Dahlaine shook his head. "The Matans wouldn't hunt down there in those mountains," he said. "They hunt bison, not deer, and the bison prefer open grassland."

"I think I might know someone who could help us, uncle," the little boy Ashad said. "Long-Claw spends a lot of time down there when the fish are running."

"Who's Long-Claw?" Eleria asked.

"He's my brother," Ashad replied.

"I don't think I'll be able to help you, Ashad," Yaltar said a bit dubiously.

"I was talking about my *other* brother," Ashad said. "He and I sort of grew up in Mama Broken-Tooth's cave."

"Who's Mama Broken-Tooth?" Rabbit asked curiously.

"She's the one who fed me when I was a baby."

"One of the women from the local village, then?"

Ashad laughed. "I wouldn't exactly call her a woman, Rabbit," he said. "That might offend her, and you don't really want to do that. She gets very bad-tempered sometimes, but that's only natural, I suppose. Grouch is part of her nature."

"Just exactly what *is* she?" Rabbit asked.

"A bear, of course," Ashad said. "Bears are just about the best mothers in the whole world."

"Were you crazy, Lord Dahlaine," Sorgan Hook-Beak demanded in a shrill voice. "You actually handed a new-born infant off to a bear? You're lucky she didn't have him for breakfast."

"Quite the contrary, Captain Hook-Beak," Dahlaine said. "Ashad was right. Bears *are* very close to the best mothers in the world. Their milk is very rich, and they teach their cubs—or children—how to find berries to eat, and how to swat fish out of mountain streams, *and,* when the cubs misbehave, the mama bear spanks them to make them mind their manners. A mother bear will also tear anybody—or anything—apart if it tries to hurt her cubs. They're extremely protective."

"But Ashad wasn't *really* her cub," Sorgan protested.

"She *thought* he was, and that's all that mattered to her.

Look at it this way, Captain. If a human child has a mother who stands ten feet tall, weighs close to a thousand pounds, has claws that are long and sharp, and teeth that are even longer and sharper, that child doesn't have a thing in the world to worry about, wouldn't you say?"

"It just seems so *unnatural*," Sorgan protested.

"Don't think about it, then."

"I'll go see if I can find Long-Claw, uncle," Ashad said. "I'm sure he'll be able to tell us all kinds of things about that Crystal Gorge place." Then the boy turned and left the map-chamber.

"This 'plague that's not really a plague' concerns me, my brother," Zelana said after Dahlaine's Dreamer had left. "That sort of suggests a poison of some kind, wouldn't you say?"

"It's possible, I suppose," Dahlaine conceded, "but wouldn't that be just a bit sophisticated for the creatures of the Wasteland?"

"Using weapons that aren't a part of their own bodies *is* sophisticated, Dahlaine," Zelana reminded him. "The servants of the Vlagh are moving much faster than we'd expected, so we'd better start thinking fast, or they'll outrun us. I'm also starting to catch a strong odor of 'tampering' again. If I understood what you told us earlier, the crazy man in Atazakan has started to do things that an ordinary crazy wouldn't do. Ordinary crazies develop a certain routine, and it never changes. Going outside every morning and afternoon to give the sun her marching orders *should* fill his whole day, but quite suddenly he's decided to invade his neighbors, and that doesn't fit at all. Somebody—or something—is changing his obsession, wouldn't you say?"

"Why don't I have Ox sharpen his axe?" Sorgan suggested. "It sort of sounds to me like maybe it's 'whomp' time again."

"It probably *would* solve some problems, Dahlaine," Zelana agreed, "and Ox is probably one of the best whompers available to us."

"I think another problem just came through the door," Sorgan's cousin Torl said in an alarmed tone of voice.

Omago turned quickly and stared at the hairy animal that was shambling along beside Dahlaine's Dreamer.

"This is my brother, Long-Claw," Ashad announced. "He's agreed to tell us everything he knows about that gully down in the mountains, and he won't eat anybody here, so you don't have to worry very much."

The huge bear stood up on his hind feet, and Omago was stunned by the enormous size of the creature.

Ara, however, didn't seem to be the least bit afraid of the monster. She strolled around the balcony and held out her hands to the shaggy animal.

Long-Claw sniffed at her hands, and then she rather fondly scratched the huge bear's ears and petted him. He nuzzled at her in response. They *seemed* to be getting along quite well, but Omago *wished* that Ara wouldn't stand quite so close to the huge beast.

Ashad began to make growling sounds, and the bear squinted down over the balcony railing at Dahlaine's map. Then he shook his head and rumbled something to the little boy.

"He can't see it well enough," Ashad said. "His eyes aren't very good, so I'll have to take him on down there so that he can see it better."

"We'll watch from up here, Ashad," Dahlaine said.

"It might be better that way, uncle. Long-Claw's not

really very comfortable around people." He led his shaggy brother on out into the hall-like tunnel beyond the balcony, and in a few moments, the two of them came out onto the lumpy map below. They went on down to the part of the imitation where the mountains were and growled and rumbled at each other for quite some time.

"Uncle," Ashad called, "Long-Claw tells me that this upper part of the streambed is sort of crumbly. I don't think you'd want to build this fort-thing there."

"Go on down a ways, Ashad," Dahlaine called. "We'll need solid ground if we're going to build a fort."

"Right," Ashad agreed. Then he growled at his bear, and they went a ways farther on down the imitation valley. Then they stopped and growled at each other for a while.

"He says that this is just about the best place, uncle," Ashad called. "This is his favorite place when he's looking for fish to eat."

"Mark it, Ashad," Dahlaine called.

"Right," Ashad agreed, pulling a clump of fur off the sleeve of his tunic and poking it into a narrow crack in one of the crystal rocks.

"Thank him for us, Ashad," Zelana called, "and then tell him to go back to Mama's cave."

"I'll do that, Auntie," Ashad replied.

"Auntie?" Zelana asked her older brother.

"It's one of those 'in the family' things, Zelana," Dahlaine explained. "It's sort of like Eleria's 'Beloved.' Not quite as pretty, of course, but then what is?"

3

It was several days later when Veltan, Red-Beard, Gunda, and the horse-soldier Ekial arrived at Mount Shrak with a large number of mounted Malavi behind them. Everybody in Dahlaine's cave went outside to look at the horse-creatures, and, naturally, the Malavi began to show off. Omago had never really understood just why warrior people always seemed to want to do that.

Their friend Red-Beard was *also* riding a horse that he called "Seven," for some reason. Red-Beard was obviously not as skilled at horse-riding as the Malavi were, but he didn't fall off his horse as it trotted along with the other horses, so it appeared that horses weren't totally wild.

That raised a very interesting possibility for Omago. It seemed to him that with a bit of proper training, a horse—or several horses harnessed together—might be extremely useful. He decided that he might want to talk with Rabbit the smith about that. If Rabbit could devise the right tool, it might just make the shovel obsolete when the time came to prepare the ground for planting.

The Malavi set up a kind of camp near the foot of Mount Shrak. It was fairly obvious that camping inside Dahlaine's cave wouldn't have suited them at all. Omago was becoming a *bit* more accustomed to living inside Dahlaine's hole-in-the-ground residence, but he was never really comfortable with the idea, so he understood the reluctance of the Malavi to even go inside Dahlaine's cave-house.

Omago and the others had seen a few of the local people before the arrival of the Malavi, but now that Dahlaine's hired warriors were here, Veltan's older brother decided that it might be a good time to bring the local Matans into his cave so that the Matans, the Tonthakans, and the Malavi could become acquainted with each other.

And so it was that Dahlaine's little boy Ashad went on down to a nearby village called Asmie, and he soon came back with a young villager called Tlingar, who was about the same age as Ashad, and was obviously Ashad's close friend. There was another native with the two boys who was an older man with greying hair and was called Tlantar Two-Hands the Chief. Omago couldn't quite understand why his people had added "Two-Hands" to their chief's name.

"It's because he doesn't favor one hand over the other, Dear Heart," Ara quietly advised her mate. "The members of his tribe started to call him 'Two-Hands' when he was just a boy. He can throw his spear with either hand, and he almost always makes his spear go exactly where he wants it to go. The members of his tribe are terribly proud of that, so they've added 'Two-Hands' to his name to impress other tribes."

"How did *you* manage to pick that up, Ara?"

"I just happened to overhear one of the members of his

tribe boasting about that when he was talking with some-body who belonged to a different tribe. It's not very com-mon, but it *does* show up every so often."

Then there was a general sort of get-together in Dahlaine's war-chamber where the various warrior people examined Dahlaine's replica of Crystal Gorge, and discussed a number of possible ways to hold back the invasion of the creatures of the Wasteland.

Gunda, the Trogite fort-builder, picked a slightly differ-ent location for the fort that would be their main line of de-fense, and he patiently explained that higher ground would give them a certain advantage.

Then Ekial and Ariga pointed out several places that would be ideal for their standard "hit-and-run" tactics. It seemed to Omago that much of what they were saying to each other was fairly obvious, and it *also* seemed that they were all being excessively polite.

"It's called 'getting to know you,' Dear Heart," Ara told him. "They discuss very obvious things while they're be-coming better acquainted with the nature of the people who'll be their allies in the coming war. It's not all that un-common, and if it makes them more comfortable with each other, it's not really a total waste of time."

"If I remember correctly, there was quite a bit of that going on in Veltan's map-room back home before the out-landers went on up into the mountains."

"We're bringing a wide range of warrior people together in the same place, Omago," Ara explained. "They don't know each other very well at all, so everybody is stepping very carefully until they become more familiar."

"There *is* something that's likely to happen when we en-counter these bug-people—or whatever they're called," the horse-soldier Ariga declared. "If these enemy creatures really *do* have snake-fangs like you've all mentioned, won't they be able to kill our horses with just one little nip? We could *all* wind up walking before the first day of the war is over."

"I think there might be a way to solve that problem," Tlantar, the chief of the local tribe, said. "We hunt bison for the meat, of course, but we also make use of their hides. A robe made of bison hide is very thick, and the fur is dense enough to keep us warm through the coldest winters. If those robes can hold off the weather, isn't it possible that they'd be thick enough to keep the snake-fangs from getting in deep enough to wound your horses?"

"It might take our horses a while to get used to wearing clothes," Ekial said, "but if those animal skins will protect them, it might just solve the problem. The horses might not *like* wearing robes very much, but they don't really have to like it, I guess. They'll just have to *do* it."

"Are plagues really all that common in this part of the world?" the young Trogite Keselo asked. "The Dream mentioned a 'plague that was not a plague,' and that has me a bit confused."

"I've heard a few accounts about this new disease," Chief Tlantar told him. "Certain diseases aren't all that uncommon here in Matakan, but this new one seems to be much more deadly than the ones that make people cough or cover their bodies with little pink splotches. The people of the northern tribes have told us that anybody who catches this new disease almost always dies in about a half a day."

"That *can't* be true," Keselo objected. "No disease is *that* fast."

"You could go on up north and tell the dead that they

aren't really dead," Tlantar Two-Hands said with a shrug. "I don't think they'll listen to you, though. A man who's busy being dead doesn't usually have time to listen."

"Since the little girl's Dream mentioned this disease, wouldn't that sort of suggest that the bug-people are behind it?" Rabbit said. "If one of the Dreamers warns us about something, it usually has something to do with a scheme of the bug-people—or a warning about some kind of bad weather."

"That might be worth some examination," Keselo agreed.

"Is this invasion—or incursion—into Matakan by the Atazaks likely to cause any serious problems, Dahlaine?" Veltan asked.

Dahlaine laughed. "Not for *our* people, it won't," he replied. "The 'army' of Atazakan is composed of 'the Guardians of Divinity,' the bodyguards of crazy Azakan. They're the ones who threaten the ordinary people if they don't cheer loud enough when the madman tells the sun to set. I'd say that *most* of them aren't very sure which end of a spear is which. The Matans will probably obliterate them in about half a day. If this incursion is another halfwit scheme by the creatures of the Wasteland to divert our forces in the same way the 'clickers' tried to stir up trouble in Tonthakan, it won't work in Matan either."

"Maybe that army of incompetents isn't *intended* to cause any real trouble, Dahlaine," Veltan suggested. "Isn't it possible that their only purpose is to pull a part of our defensive force off to the north, so that they'll be exposed to this 'plague'? I'm leaning in the direction of a poison, myself. There are all sorts of plants—and mushrooms as well—out there in the Wasteland, you know. If the servants of the Vlagh have been slipping into the camps of the Matans at night, isn't it possible that they've been mixing poisons of one kind or another into the food the Matans will be eating for breakfast? They probably wouldn't have enough time to poison *all* of the food, but they could poison enough to make the Dreamers pass along this warning, wouldn't you say?"

"You *could* be right, Veltan," Dahlaine conceded. "And the poison from plants isn't *nearly* as deadly as the spores from certain mushrooms. If the wind's coming from the right direction, they could throw clouds of those spores up into the air and everybody who's downwind would breathe in enough of those spores to kill them—eventually. Breathing in mushroom spores wouldn't be *quite* as deadly as eating them would be, and it'd probably take a man about a half a day to get sick enough to die."

"If they *are* using mushroom spores to cause this pestilence, they wouldn't even *have* to sneak around at night poisoning the food, would they?" Veltan suggested. "People absolutely *must* breathe, and as long as the wind's blowing in the right direction, the bug-people should be able to foist this 'pestilence' off on the Matans, and we'd probably have to divert a sizeable portion of our armies up there to ward off the crazy man's invasion."

"Excuse me," Omago said, "but I *think* I know of a way to deal with that. Down in our part of the Land of Dhrall, we use smoke to drive ordinary bugs away from our fields. There's a greasy little tree that puts out a heavy cloud of smoke when we set fire to it, and the bugs can't stand that smoke; the only problem is that *we* choke on that smoke as well. We've found that tying a thick wet cloth over our faces gives us a certain amount of protection—particularly if we stay upwind from the burning tree."

Veltan's eyes brightened. "I think that 'upwind' might be our answer, Dahlaine. We *can* control the wind to some degree if we need to. A nice friendly little wind would blow those mushroom spores right back into the faces of those bug-people *and* into the teeth of those 'Guardians of Divinity.' I'd say that the crazy man's invasion will fall apart right there, and the bug-people will provide the weapon that we'll need."

Omago was standing on the balcony of Dahlaine's "war-chamber" carefully memorizing the details of the mountainous terrain at the mouth of Crystal Gorge.

Dahlaine was talking with Sorgan Hook-Beak not far away. "These local problems shouldn't interfere with *your* activities, Captain," he said. "I'm quite sure that the local people will be able to eliminate the crazy man's army and the bug-people who tricked him. *Your* job will be to lay that base for Narasan's fort so that it'll be ready when his people get here."

Sorgan nodded. "We know what needs to be done, Lord Dahlaine. Can you give me any kind of a guess about how long it's likely to take Narasan to get here?"

Dahlaine scratched his cheek. "I'd say that it'll probably take about seven days for his fleet to sail up the east coast to the southern part of my Domain. It's a fair distance from that coast to Mount Shrak here, so it's probably going to take eighteen or twenty days. That comes out to be about four weeks altogether."

"That's a bit longer than I'd hoped," Sorgan said. "Once we've got the base for his fort completed, I think we should put up some temporary defenses—logs and other things.

We've got plenty of archers to help us hold back the snake-men, and the horse-soldiers should be able to clear away any sneakers who try to slip around us. I'd say that we'll be able to hold the enemy off until Narasan and his men get here."

Dahlaine nodded. "We'll see," he said.

THE
TEMPLE

1

Behold! I am Divine Azakan, and I dwell now and forever in Holy Palandor, the most glorious city in all the world. Much have I heard in myth and legend of "The Dreamers," which will one day rule all the world, but I tell ye, one and all, that *I* am the *only* Dreamer, for it hath come to me in a Dream that I am not *only* the emperor of Holy Atazakan, but I am *also* god of all the Land of Dhrall, as was foretold in ages past.

And know full well, all ye who would bow down before me, that I will reward they who worship me, but great will be my punishment for those who do not.

And I have gathered about me many who will guard and protect me, and *they* will be the ones who will carry out my will, for weary am I in that my responsibilities do weigh upon me most heavily in that only *I* can command the sun and the moon and the stars to march across my heavens as they must, for in the day that I fail to perform my most burdensome task shall chaos conquer all, and my glorious universe shall be no more.

Look upon my magnificent temple, and my glorious universe, crude and rustic Dahlaine of the North, and cringe before me, for I am the *true* god of what thou hast attempted to wrench from my grasp. Flee now from me, for soon I will send forth descendants by the millions to drive thee from *my* Domain, for I have fair wives by the hundreds who joyfully present me with child-gods beyond counting to carry out my will.

Flee now, barbaric Dahlaine, for surely art thou doomed.

And Behold, it came to pass on an autumn day that there came one who was not of our kind to Holy Palandor, and, as all creatures should, he knelt before me in my holy temple and besought me to listen unto him, and, because I am most kindly and gentle, as it befits a god such as me to be, I granted his wish, and he spake unto me, saying this: "We have heard of thee in our distant home at the center of the Land of Dhrall, Holy Azakan," spake he, and a peculiar glottal sound came from his mouth as he said my name, but, gentle and kindly that I am, I did not chastise him for his error.

"We have indeed heard of thee," continued this alien creature, "for truly, thy fame doth reach out far beyond this region which Dahlaine of the North hath usurped from thee, O Divine One."

And much pleased was I that my fame had reached out even to they that were not of human kind. "Say on, devout one," I said unto him.

"I have sought thee out, Most Holy," he continued, "for it is vital to us that we know the designs of the foul usurper who says to one and all that he alone is divine in this part of the Land of Dhrall."

"He is not *my* god, gentle creature," I said unto my small

visitor, "and I know nothing of his designs, for I have no part of them."

"I do perceive that our purposes may well be much the same, Divinity, for we—even as thou—would thwart the unholy desires of he who falsely doth pretend to be divine."

"I would hear more of what thou wouldst say unto me, friendly stranger," I said unto him.

"It hath come to us that the usurper hath brought unto the Holy Land of Dhrall multitudes of heathen outlanders to do hurt to *our* people—as well as thine, Divinity. Might it not be wise of us to divide the heathens that we might more easily defeat them?"

And the words of my gentle visitor did trouble me much. "Gladly would my people come to thine aid, gentle stranger," I said unto him, "for my people are most devout, but I do fear me that they are unskilled in the arts of war."

"It hath been my purpose in coming here, Divine One, to offer unto thee a weapon which none living are able to meet."

"And, pray tell me, what *is* this mighty weapon?"

"As thou hast surely seen, Divinity," spake he, "we are not of thy species. Small are we, and we have not the strength to overwhelm the huge outlanders brought here to Holy Dhrall by the family of Dahlaine the usurper, *but*, to defend our species from these who come against us, we have within our bodies a weapon which no outlander is able to withstand. There are several ways by which we have been able to bring our weapon to bear upon our enemies, but we have most recently found a means which shows much promise. By reason of our peculiarities, we can send forth this weapon in the form of a mist, and should man or beast breathe in that mist, he will surely die. Yea, truly, should even Dahlaine the usurper himself breathe in our mist, he will *surely* die."

And I answered my small friend, saying, "It is most appropriate that he should, my dearest friend, for the air which he doth breathe in is *my* creation, and it is not proper that he should steal it. Let him then die from thy mist, and all that serve him die as well."

"Then must we lure him and his heathen supporters to the border of thine empire that we may more easily destroy him." Then paused my new, dear friend. "It seemeth me," spake he, "that they who serve thee and worship thee might well bring this to pass by going from here into the lands of the Matans, Dahlaine's most slavish adherents, and when the Matans and the outlanders rush to repel your worshipers, will I and my brethren send forth our mist, and all that march against thee and thine will most surely die."

And then was my heart filled with joy. "And thus, my dear, dear friend, shall die usurper Dahlaine, and, as it should, all of the Land of Dhrall shall surely and forever be mine!"

Great was my disappointment when they who guard my Divinity and require all who come before me to properly show their love and respect for me failed to perceive the brilliance of the plan of my new and beloved friend. And it came to me with sorrowful certainty that they who called themselves my "Guardians" were far more concerned with their own comfort and safety than they were with carrying out my commandments, and I hovered on the brink of destroying them one and all.

But then my most trusted servant, Lazakan, came for-

ward to implore me to permit him to speak with his way-
ward friends.

"Much is my disappointment in thee, one and all, my
timid companions," spake Lazakan in sorrowful voice.
"Know ye not that Divine Azakan can protect us with his
might? I must tell ye now that our new friend and I did speak
with each other at some length, and it was *I* who did advise
him that Holy Azakan might look kindly upon this proposal
whereby we might once and forever depose usurper
Dahlaine with this alliance. I urge thee, one and all, to hear
the words of our new and unexpected friend." And then did
clever Lazakan gesture to our new friend that he might explain how it might be that victory would most certainly be
ours.

And as our dear new friend came forth to speak with the
timid, I did catch a faint hint of a peculiar odor emanating from
his body, and that odor did somehow make more intense my
certainty that we would most surely emerge victorious from
this war.

More peculiar still, I did observe that my timid "Guardians"
grew less and less timid as our alien friend explained how the
deadly mist would bring us victory unimaginable.

And it came to me unbidden that the odor which had so
heightened *my* certainty was also heightening the certainty
of my timid servants. And I considered a very interesting
possibility. If I could but find the source of this odd fragrance within the body of our peculiar friend and extract it
from him, all who came within my presence would—will
he, nil he—accept me as the one and only true god in all the
world. It saddened me to some degree that my extraction of
this peculiarity from the body of my dear, dear friend might
very well kill him, but *my* needs, of course, were much more

important to the world than was his life. But, since I am brave beyond the understanding of all others, I was most certain that my grief would not be unbearable.

As the enthusiasm of they who guard me intensified, I selected brave Lazakan to lead the army of the "Guardians of Divinity" against our foes.

But then, most certainly at a suggestion from me—which I have for some reason forgotten—brave Lazakan did send the Guardians forth to gather up *all* the people of Holy Palandor to join us in our holy campaign against Dahlaine the usurper and his heathen allies.

And so it was that victory was within our grasp as we left Holy Palandor and marched to the border which most temporarily stood between my people and the Matans.

And victory was now most certainly within my grasp, and soon would I be King and God of all the Land of Dhrall, and in good time of all the rest of the world as well—as had most certainly been the intent of the world and the heavens since before the beginning of time.

THE
WARRIOR
QUEEN

1

Queen Trenicia of the Isle of Akalla no longer felt any obligation to remain here in the Land of Dhrall. Her sometime employer had turned out to be a person without the slightest hint of integrity, and Trenicia had revoked their contract by contemptuously throwing all the jewels that Aracia had given to her at her former employer's feet. Given Aracia's dishonest nature, Trenicia was fairly sure now that the jewels were little more than cheap imitations of genuine gems. In the light of that, Trenicia realized that she *should* be looking for a way to return to the Isle of Akalla, but for some reason she found that she was most reluctant to do so.

When she got right down to it, though, she was fully aware of the reason for that reluctance. In all her life on the Isle of Akalla, she had never once seen a man who was anything but a tame house-pet. The notion of a man who commanded an army struck her as most unusual, but there he stood, not ten paces away. His name was Narasan, and when he told his men to do something, they immediately obeyed him, and that would have been unheard of on the Isle of Akalla.

Moreover, Narasan had exquisite manners, and the touch of silver in his hair made him look most distinguished. It was his tight-fitting uniform that revealed a well-muscled body, however, that quite noticeably raised Trenicia's interest in this peculiar man.

There was nothing particularly pressing taking place on the Isle of Akalla right now, so Trenicia saw no real need to rush back home, and there were quite a few much more interesting things happening here in the Land of Dhrall.

"The wars on the Isle of Akalla aren't nearly as complicated as your wars are, Narasan," Trenicia said. "Of course, we don't have armies as large as yours, and we really don't have to go so far to reach enemy territory."

"What would you say would be the size of the standard army on Akalla, Your Majesty?" Andar rumbled in his deep voice.

"Probably no more than fifty warrior-women," Trenicia replied, "and it's usually only about twenty miles to the enemy's part of the isle."

"That has a familiar sort of ring to it, wouldn't you say?" Brigadier Danal suggested to the others. "It sounds quite a bit like the squabbles between those assorted barons and dukes that we used to go fight for them."

"Except that *we* were paid to do the fighting," Padan added. "It sounds to me like the women-warriors on Akalla fight their *own* wars."

"Isn't that just a little bit illegal?" Danal asked with a faint smile.

"You'll have to excuse my friends, Trenicia," Narasan said. "They all seem to think they're hilariously funny."

"Do you see me laughing?" Trenicia asked Danal quite firmly.

"Ah—no, ma'am," he replied. "There *is* one thing that's got me just a bit puzzled, though. The people here in the Land of Dhrall all seem to have weapons made of stone, but that sword of yours is made of steel. How did you come by it?"

Trenicia shrugged. "Every now and then a boat that came from some other place washes up on one of the beaches on our island, and there are all kinds of things on those boats that are made of metal. We've learned how to heat it so that we can pound it into the shape we want."

"What are all those wars on your island about?" the deep-voiced Andar asked.

"Pride," Trenicia said with a blunt honesty. "We all feel that anything we see is ours. Since I'm the proudest woman in all of Akalla, the island is *mine.* I had to kill quite a few people to persuade the others that I really *am* the queen, but now that they understand, things are much more peaceful than they used to be. Peace is nice, I suppose, but it *does* get sort of boring after a while. That's one of the reasons that I accepted Aracia's offer. I thought that if I could find a war of some kind in some other part of the world, I could keep all the other proud women busy enough that they'd stop trying to sneak up on me and kill me, and not being killed *is* fairly important, wouldn't you say?"

Several days later at about noon, the somewhat boisterous Padan came into the cabin at the stern. "I think we might have reached the place where we're supposed to go ashore," he announced. "There's a good-sized bonfire on the beach, and if I'm not mistaken, the man standing by that fire is Longbow's old friend, Red-Beard. I'm just guessing here, but I *think* that maybe Veltan's big brother sent him here to guide us to the place where Dahlaine wants us to go."

"Good," Narasan said. "Let's go talk with him. He'll probably be able to tell us how things are coming along."

They all went out onto the deck of the *Victory*, and Trenicia immediately saw the large fire on the beach.

The sandy beach was snowy white and the woods to the west of the beach were glorious in shades of red and gold. There appeared to be a mountain range beyond that wooded region, and the mountains were rounded and gentle, and much more pleasant than the rugged range in Veltan's Domain far to the south.

"Would you like to come along with us, Trenicia?" Narasan asked politely.

"Of course," she replied with a smile. "I'm just as curious as you are, Narasan."

The sailors on board the *Victory* lowered several of the small skiffs down into the water of the bay and then rowed Narasan and his friends ashore.

The native on the beach *was*, in fact, Longbow's friend Red-Beard. "What kept you?" he asked them with a faint smile.

"We stopped every so often to find out if the fish were biting," Padan replied with a perfectly straight face. "Unfortunately, they didn't seem to be hungry."

"What a shame," Red-Beard said in mock sympathy.

"If you two have finished, do you suppose we could get down to business here?" Narasan suggested firmly. "How do things stand right now, Red-Beard?"

"We had a little trouble over in Tonthakan," Red-Beard

replied. "The bug-people were trying to start a war between some of the tribes over there, but Sorgan's friend, Ox, bashed the troublemakers in the head with his axe, and a real bad case of peace broke out. We discovered that the bug-men have started to use fragrance to win people over to their side."

"Fragrance?" Narasan asked.

Red-Beard shrugged. "It's a nicer word than 'stink,' wouldn't you say? Anyway, this peculiar smell made people—the real ones—believe anything the bug-people told them. The 'grand plan' the bug-people had come up with had a small hole in it, though, and the hole's name was Ox. It seems that poor old Ox is one of those unfortunate people who start sneezing every time they see a flower, and during the sneezing season, Ox can't smell *anything*—flowers, dead bodies, or anything else—because his nose is so stopped up that he has to breathe through his mouth. The two bug-people who were trying their best to make everybody believe them were spewing out that smell of theirs for all they were worth, but their 'fragrance' didn't have any effect on Ox, because his nose doesn't work the way it's supposed to. That's when he solved the problem for us—with his axe. After he'd brained the two bug-people, everybody seemed to wake up, and that ended *that* particular problem right there on the spot."

"They've never done *that* before," Narasan observed. "It seems like every time we turn around, they've come up with something new—and even more dangerous."

"Red-Beard," Padan said curiously, "what sort of an animal is the one you've got tied to a tree on the upper side of the beach?"

"That's one of the creatures that gave the 'horse-people'

their name," Red-Beard replied with a smile. "That one's called 'Seven,' and he's mine."

"The horse-people don't even give their pets names?" Padan asked. "Do they just give them numbers instead?"

Red-Beard shook his head, and then he told Padan the story of Seven's previous owner, the gambler who cheated. "After that, poor old Seven didn't have an owner anymore, so Ekial and Ariga gave him to me."

"What's it like—riding a horse, I mean?" Andar asked.

"A lot easier than doing your own walking. Seven and I don't cover as much ground as a Malavi on horseback can in one day, but we can still cover about three times as much as I could on foot."

"What kind of terrain are we going to encounter on the way to Mount Shrak?" Narasan asked.

"There's a mountain range off to the west," Red-Beard said. "I don't know if I'd call those hills 'mountains,' though. The slopes are fairly gentle, and I didn't come up against anything that I'd call rugged. The passes we'll follow are wide enough to give your army plenty of room to march through. Then we'll go on down to the grassland of the Matakan Nation. It's pretty much like one vast meadowland with almost no trees. We *might* encounter a herd of bison out there, and that could delay us just a bit. The herds here to the south aren't as big as the ones off to the north are, though, so we won't have to set up camp and wait for three or four days the way we might have to farther north. Tlantar Two-Hands told me that he had to sit on a hilltop for a week once when a bison herd up there had him blocked off."

"Who's Tlantar Two-Hands," Padan asked, "and how did he come up with a name like that?"

"He's the chief—or headman—of a village called Asmie

in the vicinity of Mount Shrak, and I guess the people of Asmie call him 'Two-Hands' because he doesn't know one hand from the other."

"We can discuss this as we go along," Narasan said. "For right now, let's get our men ashore and prepare to march. We've got about twenty days of hiking ahead of us, so we'd better get started."

There were quite a few strange things about this part of the Land of Dhrall that troubled Trenicia a bit, but she was sure that she'd be able to adjust to them. Her main purpose right now was to more firmly establish her relationship with Narasan, and that seemed to be coming along very well.

2

It took the better part of two days for Narasan's army to come ashore and make the necessary preparations for the march to Mount Shrak. There were so many details! Sometimes Trenicia almost wanted to scream. Why didn't they just get *on* with it?

"Does he *really* have to go through all of this again and again and again?" she asked Padan, about midday on their second day on the beach.

Padan shrugged. "He made a few serious mistakes once during a war in the southern part of the empire, Your Majesty, and he learned quite a few things the hard way."

"Oh?" Trenicia was quite interested in such things. "What happened?"

Padan sighed. "After his father was killed in a senseless little war, Narasan's mother went all to pieces with her grief, and Narasan decided that he should never marry."

That got Trenicia's immediate attention.

"Anyway," Padan continued, "after he became the commander of our army, Narasan grew very attached to his nephew, Astal—a young man with an enormous potential. In many ways, Astal was the equivalent of the son Narasan would never have. Then a duke named Bergalta hired us to fight a small, meaningless war with one of his neighbors. The money was good, and it appeared that this would be one of those easy wars. As it turned out, though, it *wasn't* the least *bit* easy. Our army's the best in the entire empire, and we've made a lot of enemies over the years. Evidently, a number of those enemies got together and came up with a fairly elaborate scheme, probably in the hope of killing us down to the last man."

"You Trogites have a very complicated sort of society, don't you?"

Padan grinned at her. "Money seems to do that, Your Majesty. Rich people make enemies, and sooner or later they feel that they need an army—and they pay very well. Anyway, we marched south, and Narasan decided that his nephew should lead several cohorts in our advance force—ostensibly to give Astal a bit of experience, but actually to boost Narasan's pride. There was an ambush, and Astal and twelve cohorts were killed."

"What's a cohort?"

"A thousand men, Your Majesty. Narasan went all to pieces after that happened—even after Gunda and I hired several assassins and had every single one of the plotters killed. Revenge was sort of appropriate in that situation, but Narasan was still overcome with his grief and his guilt, so he broke his sword over his knee and set up shop as a beggar in one of the seamier parts of Kaldacin. Then Veltan came along, and somehow he persuaded Narasan to put his grief aside and go back to work." Padan sighed. "Narasan's grief is still there, though, and that's why he spends so much time going over and over all the picky little details. He most definitely doesn't want to make those same mistakes ever again."

Trenicia's eyes filled with tears. "That's the saddest story I've ever heard," she declared.

"I can tell you some even sadder ones, Your Majesty," Padan said. "If a good cry will make you feel better, I can fill your eyes with buckets full of tears any time you want."

"You're outrageous, Padan," Trenicia said, laughing in spite of herself.

"I know," Padan replied in mock modesty. "I think outrageousness is a gift from some god or other. One of these days maybe I'll look him up and thank him."

They started out early the next morning, and it seemed to Trenicia that if Narasan's army moved as rapidly as they were marching now, they'd be able to cover much more than just ten miles. After about an hour, though, things began to slow down quite noticeably. The problem Narasan had referred to as "bunching up" began to appear very frequently, and the pace slowed to a crawl.

Trenicia was not emotionally suited for plodding, so she began to range out farther and farther in front of Narasan's army. The forest to the west of the beach where they'd come ashore was quite extensive, and, since it was autumn now, the leaves of those trees were red and gold rather than the bright green of summer. She encountered several deer in that forest, and, more to entertain herself than out of any real interest, she began to move very quietly to see just how close to one of those animals she could get before the creature caught her scent or saw her move. Her experiences on the Isle of Akalla had given her a lot of opportunities to practice sneaking, so she was frequently able to get close enough to one of the grazing deer to be almost within touching distance. She found the panicky reaction of a deer when she said "Hello, Sweetie" to be quite amusing. She soon realized that a startled deer could jump much higher and farther than she'd have thought possible.

There were quite a few other animals in the forest as well. There were many hares and foxes as well as flocks of partridges scurrying through patches of bushes. Once, she even encountered a huge grazing animal that she assumed was one of the bison Red-Beard had mentioned. She was more than a little startled by the size of that creature. It was truly massive, with a shaggy coat and huge horns flaring out from the front of its head. Trenicia prudently backed away from *that* particular animal.

As evening settled down over the forest late each afternoon, Trenicia went back to rejoin the plodding Trogites who were following Red-Beard and Seven.

"Did you happen to encounter any people out there?" Narasan asked her on the third day of their march.

"Quite a few deer, and many, many hares," she replied, "and I *think* I saw a fox, but no people."

"Any more bison?" Padan asked.

"Not today, no," she replied.

"Are we getting anywhere at all close to the western edge of this forest?" Andar asked her then.

"I don't really think so, Andar," she replied doubtfully. "I climbed up a fairly tall tree, and as nearly as I could determine, we've still got four or five days of woods in front of us."

"She makes a pretty good scout, Commander," Brigadier Danal said. "She knows how to move quietly, and she sees just about everything we need to know about."

"You could get your name in a lot of history books, Narasan," Padan said then, "and you'd probably send the Church of Amar up in flames if it became known that you'd enlisted a woman to serve in your army."

"That would depend on how much Narasan would be willing to pay me, Padan," Trenicia said slyly. "I'm sure you remember that I *don't* work for gold." Then she looked at Narasan. "How are you fixed for diamonds right now, old friend?" she asked.

"I haven't checked lately," Narasan replied blandly. "There *might* be a few diamonds and pearls bouncing around in the treasury, but I couldn't say for sure."

"There goes your chance at fame, Dear Heart," Trenicia said in mock sorrow.

"Ah, well," Narasan replied with a feigned sigh of regret.

The forest began to thin out a day or so later, and Red-Beard and his horse, Seven, led Narasan's army up through a wide pass that led on into the gently rolling mountains quite some distance to the west of the seacoast. Trenicia found the area rather pleasant, but so far as she was able to determine, there were no people living in the region. Trenicia found that more than a little strange. The Isle of Akalla wasn't *densely* populated, by any stretch of the imagination, but there *were* people living all over the isle. A completely uninhabited region seemed *most* peculiar.

"Is there some reason that nobody lives here?" she asked Red-Beard late in the afternoon of their first day up in the mountains.

Red-Beard shrugged. "There *might* be, I suppose," he replied, "but there's nobody here to explain it to us. The hunting might not be very good, or the ground might not be fertile enough to grow good crops, or maybe the word's been going around that this part of the Land of Dhrall is haunted by ghosts or something. Then, too, it might just be that nobody's ever gotten around to settling here. There are vast regions in Zelana's Domain that don't have any people. I've always sort of liked open country without people cluttering it up. People can be awfully messy sometimes. Does empty country bother you, Trenicia?"

"Not all that much," she replied. "I was just a little curious, that's all. How long would you say it's likely to take us to get through these mountains?"

"A couple more days is about all. There's nothing in the way, and the peaks—if you want to call them that—aren't really very steep. If you think *this* country's empty, wait until we go on down into Matakan. There's almost nothing there but miles and miles of miles and miles, waist deep in grass and neck deep in bison. When Seven and I were crossing the meadowland while we were leading the Malavi to Mount Shrak, I saw herds of bison that were spread out almost to the horizon. I wouldn't mind hunting bison—except that my arrows would probably just bounce off them."

"Why do you always have to make a joke out of everything you say, Red-Beard?"

"Laughter's good for people, Trenicia," Red-Beard said with a grin, "but I wasn't really making a joke when I said that arrows wouldn't be very useful if I decided to hunt bison. The Matans use spears instead of arrows, because an arrow won't go deep enough into a bison to kill him—unless you happen to get very lucky. Matan spear-points are much bigger—and heavier—than my arrowheads are, so they go in deeper and leave much bigger wounds. My arrows will kill deer—or people—well enough, but they wouldn't do the job on bison."

Late the following day Trenicia was ranging out ahead of Narasan's plodding army and she reached the top of the pass they'd been following. Then she immediately saw what Red-Beard had described as "miles and miles of nothing but miles and miles." She'd never in her life seen any country so totally empty. The meadowland to the west was almost like an ocean of grass pushed into waves by a continual wind coming in from the west. In her entire life, Trenicia had never seen so much emptiness, and she stood there for a long time gazing out across that enormous vacancy.

Narasan joined her there after a while, and he also seemed almost stunned by that vast emptiness. "It might take a while to get used to that," he murmured.

"Six or eight years, at least," Trenicia agreed. "That's a lot of empty out there. Just looking at it makes me feel terribly lonely."

"I'll hold your hand, if you'd like," Narasan offered.

"We might want to talk about that," Trenicia agreed with a fond smile. Oddly enough, the uncluttered meadow lying off to the west no longer disturbed her. Things suddenly seemed to be going along very well.

Late the following day Narasan's army marched down out of the mountain range and moved on into the meadow.

"I think I'm going to need three or four cohorts, Narasan," Padan said as the army continued its westward march.

"Were you planning to declare war on the grass?" Narasan asked his friend.

"Not really, O Mighty Commander," Padan replied. "But unless you'd like to live on a steady diet of cold, uncooked beans for the next week or so, *somebody's* going to have to gather up some firewood before we get *too* far away from these mountains, wouldn't you say?"

"Good thinking there, Padan," Narasan replied. "I must have had my mind on something else." He glanced briefly at Trenicia, and then looked quickly away.

That definitely brightened Trenicia's whole day.

It somehow seemed to Trenicia that they weren't even moving as they pushed on out across the endless meadow for the next week or more, but then Red-Beard turned and galloped Seven back to join Narasan and the others. "If you look carefully off to the west, you'll be able to see Mount Shrak sticking up out of the grass," he told them. "We've still got quite a way to go, but at least we can see our destination now."

Trenicia shaded her eyes with her hand and peered off to the west at what appeared to be a small, steep clump of rocks out near the western horizon.

"Well, finally," Narasan said. "There for a while, I thought we might have to walk until the middle of winter. How far off would you say that mountain is, Red-Beard?"

"Three or four days, anyway. We still have a long way to go, I'm afraid. Dahlaine's almost positive that his pet mountain's the highest peak in the world, and for all I know, he could just be right. Don't take off your boots yet, Narasan. We've still got a lot of miles spread out there in front of us."

3

The lack of obstructions in the meadowland of the Matakan Nation had given Narasan the opportunity to spread his army out, and they were now covering much more ground each day than they had in rougher country, so it was only about two and a half days later when they reached Dahlaine's mountain.

As Red-Beard had suggested, the fact that Mount Shrak was an isolated peak rising up out of the surrounding plain made it appear to be even higher, but it was the herd of Malavi horses grazing in the vicinity of the solitary mountain that got Trenicia's immediate attention. Ekial, the head man of the Malavi, had told them that he would be able to field fifty thousand men, but fifty thousand horses covered much more land than their owners ever could. It seemed to Trenicia that the horse herd stretched almost from horizon to horizon.

Then Dahlaine, followed by Sorgan and Ekial, came out of a large hole in the side of Mount Shrak. Trenicia had heard about "caves" before, but this was the first time she'd ever seen one. For all she knew, however, Mount Shrak *might* just be an illusion that Dahlaine had conjured up to conceal a palace. Sorgan went directly to Narasan and the two of them clasped hands in that gesture of friendship that men seemed to find quite necessary.

The Malavi chieftain Ekial, however, came over to Trenicia. "Zelana told us that her sister was trying to deceive everybody and conceal her little girl's Dream. If I understood what Zelana told us correctly, you threw all those precious jewels right back in her face and told her that you weren't going to help her anymore."

Trenicia smiled. "That might have been an even better way to show her that she and I were through, but it didn't occur to me. I was just a bit angry at the time, so I wasn't thinking too clearly. I threw them at her feet instead of right in her face."

"You didn't really have to just throw them away like that, Trenicia," Ekial said with a concerned expression. "Her deception was a violation of your agreement. You *could* have kept the jewels and just walked away, you know. Once she'd put them in your hands, they were *yours*."

"As dishonest as Aracia is, I wasn't at all certain that what she'd given me were *really* all that valuable, Ekial, and I wasn't about to start decorating myself with cheap trinkets. That's why I threw them down on the floor and walked away."

"I hate to see a friend get cheated the way you were, Queen Trenicia," Ekial stubbornly declared.

"You and I are friends now, Ekial?" Trenicia asked in mock surprise.

"Of course we are," he replied. "We're fighting on the

same side in this war, and that automatically makes us friends, doesn't it?"

"You *could* be right, Ekial," Trenicia conceded. "Let's say that we *are* friends—up until we wind up on opposite sides in some war on down the line."

"You seem to have changed a bit since we left Veltan's part of the Land of Dhrall," Ekial noted. "We've been talking here for ten minutes, and you haven't once reached for your sword."

"I've got other things on my mind now, Ekial," she said. "How well did you get to know the Trogite Narasan during that war down in Veltan's Domain?"

Ekial shrugged. "We talked to each other a few times, but we got a bit better acquainted in Veltan's house before Narasan and his men—and you, of course—sailed off to the east. Judging from what I saw during that war above the waterfall, Narasan's extremely good—for a foot-soldier, anyway. He knows *exactly* what has to be done, and he does it quite efficiently."

"I got pretty much the same impression," Trenicia agreed.

Ekial gave her a lightly puzzled look. "Was there some reason why you didn't just turn around and go back home when you quit working for Zelana's sister?"

"Curiosity, Ekial," Trenicia replied. "These people don't fight wars the way we do on the Isle of Akalla. I learned a great deal during the war in Veltan's land, and I thought I might learn more during *this* war. The more we learn, the better we become. I *might* even decide to learn how to ride a horse—if you'll agree to give me lessons."

"We might want to talk about that someday," Ekial replied with a faint smile.

*   *   *

Trenicia felt a certain apprehension as they followed Dahlaine on into his cave under the towering Mount Shrak. The notion of spending days and days in a hole in the ground disturbed her more than a little.

The passageways—or perhaps tunnels—that led back into the mountain were decorated, if that was the right term, with what appeared to be icicles made of solid stone, and Trenicia shuddered at the thought of something so unnatural.

The passageway they followed finally opened out into a much larger chamber, and that relieved Trenicia quite a bit.

"We'll come back here in a while," Dahlaine told them, "but for right now, we should probably go take a look at my map. It's fairly accurate, and I think we should all examine it rather closely. If Lillabeth's Dream was correct—and I'm sure that it was—we should all look at Crystal Gorge very closely." He looked at Narasan. "Since your man Gunda is the expert on fortifications, I've got him down there working with Captain Sorgan's cousin Skell putting up a solid base for the wall your men will need to hold back the creatures of the Wasteland."

"Those two work together fairly well," Narasan agreed, "so I'm sure they'll have a solid foundation in place by the time my men get there. Let's go have a look at your map, Lord Dahlaine. I think much more clearly when I've got a map in front of me."

They trooped on back along another tunnel and entered a very large chamber with a balcony that went around the outer edge and closely resembled the balcony in Veltan's house far off to the south. Trenicia and the others were able to look down at the presentation of the mountains to the south almost as if they were standing on a cloud about a mile above the most probable battleground.

Narasan smiled faintly. "Our maps seem to be getting better and better," he said. "As I recall, my friend Hook-Beak here was terribly upset back in Lattash when he found out that Red-Beard was using gold blocks as a base for *his* map."

Dahlaine shrugged. "The more our people practice, the better they get. There's *one* feature that might start some arguments, though. It's a notion that your man Keselo came up with. There'll be Malavi horsemen stationed in your fort, and we were all beating our heads on the wall trying to come up with some sort of gate that we could open and close very fast. We wanted the Malavi to be able to ride out of the fort, of course, but we wanted a gate that we could slam shut as soon as the Malavi were clear. Keselo came up with the notion of a gate that slides up and down rather than swinging out and then back in. Keselo's positive that his new kind of gate can open or close almost instantly."

"That's our Keselo for you," Padan said with a grin. "It sounds like he's just invented a magic gate."

"Only if you want to accuse *me* of using magic," the little smith called Rabbit said, "since *I'm* the one who made the silly thing. When we put it in place after your men build the fort, there'll be a rail on each side of the break in the wall. The gate's made of iron bars, and there are two wheels on each side of it. Those wheels are supposed to ride up and down those rails. Your people will raise the gate by pulling on ropes that'll run up through pulleys on top of the wall on either side. When we want to close the gate again, we just tell your people to let go of the ropes. The gate will drop back so fast that *nobody* will be able to get through."

"Brilliant!" Narasan exclaimed.

"Keselo and I sort of liked it," Rabbit said modestly. "I

think we'll need quite a bit of grease, though. We *don't* want that gate to get stuck when it's only half-closed."

"How far apart will the bars on your up-and-down gate be, Rabbit?"

"Not far enough apart to let any snake-men wriggle through," Rabbit replied. "The gate's going to be very heavy, so the pulley crews need to be about as strong as bulls. If it won't break any rules, I'd suggest that Maags might work out better than Trogites, but that's between you and Cap'n Hook-Beak, Commander Narasan. Keselo and I *build* things. You and the cap'n decide who's going to use them."

Trenicia was leaning over the balcony railing peering down at Dahlaine's replica of Crystal Gorge. "Could you brighten the light just a bit?" she asked Dahlaine. "It's a little shadowy down there."

"Of course, Your Majesty," Dahlaine replied. He made a slight gesture in the direction of the light hanging in the air over the map, and the light grew brighter and brighter. "How's that?" he asked.

"Much better." Then Trenicia looked a bit more closely at the light, and her eyes went very wide.

"She's a pet," Dahlaine explained with a slight smile. "When Ashad was just a baby, she used to hover over him all the time, and I was never able to persuade her that he didn't feed on light the way my brother and sisters and I do. We can talk about that some other time, though. Do you see anything about Crystal Gorge that the rest of us might have missed?"

"Probably not," Trenicia confessed. "I was just wondering what all that gleaming rock is. When I first looked at it, I thought it *might* be huge deposits of diamonds."

Dahlaine shook his head. "It's quartz, Your Majesty," he

said. "You might say that it's the diamond's third cousin, but it's not as hard—nor as rare."

"It's still very pretty, though. I was just wondering if it would shatter if Narasan's people used those catapult things to throw large rocks at it and break it to pieces. A downpour of sharp fragments would make things very unpleasant for enemies who were trying to attack, wouldn't you say?"

Dahlaine frowned slightly. "It *would*, wouldn't it?" he agreed. "We could eliminate enemies by the thousands without putting any of our people in danger. I think you've just earned your pay for this day, Queen Trenicia."

"That's something we might want to discuss one of these days, Lord Dahlaine," Trenicia replied. "The way things stand right now, I'm not being paid anything at all. We really should do something about that, wouldn't you say?"

"The one thing about Lillabeth's Dream that has me completely baffled is 'the plague that is *not* a plague,' big brother," Zelana said after they'd returned to Dahlaine's main chamber. "A disease that's not really a disease is sort of a contradiction, wouldn't you say?"

"It doesn't make much sense to me," Dahlaine agreed. He looked at the native Tlantar. "Have you heard anything at all about the outbreak of some new disease anywhere here in Matakan, Chief Two-Hands?"

"Nothing particularly specific, Dahlaine," the tall chief of Asmie replied. "There've been a few rumors about an outbreak of some kind of disease that nobody can recognize on up to the north. The Atazaks have been probing down into the lands of the northern tribes. They don't really pose much of a threat, so nobody up there takes those intrusions very seriously. They set up ambushes and shower the intruders with spears, and then the Atazaks turn around and run. They aren't the bravest people in the world, after all."

"Have the people of Atazakan ever intruded into the land of the Matans before, Chief Tlantar?" Longbow asked.

"Not that I've ever heard about. The Atazaks aren't exactly what you'd call warriors, Longbow. I'd say that an ordinary Atazak couldn't tell one end of a spear from the other even if his life depended on it."

"But now they've suddenly turned aggressive?"

"I don't think I'd go *quite* so far as to describe them as 'aggressive.' They try to sneak down into Matakan for some reason, but as soon as somebody sees them, they turn around and run back across the border."

"Do you think it might be another one of those diversions, Longbow?" Keselo asked his friend. "It sounds just a bit like that tribal war the creatures of the Wasteland were trying to stir up back in Tonthakan. If they can somehow prod the Atazakans into invading Matakan, it's going to pull a lot of people out of the war down in Crystal Gorge, wouldn't you say?"

"It *is* possible, I suppose," Longbow agreed, "but I can't quite see how a disease of any kind fits into that plan."

"What we need now, then, are some more descriptions of this disease that isn't really a disease," Keselo suggested.

"I'll send more men on up there to ask questions," Chief Tlantar said. "The rumors that have been drifting down here have been sort of vague."

"That's probably about the best we'll be able to do for right now," Longbow agreed. "We'll need more information before we'll be able to start looking for a solution."

4

Trenicia *assumed* that it was late afternoon several days later when one of Tlantar's men came into Dahlaine's central chamber to speak with his chief. Of course, Trenicia hadn't seen the sky for several days now, so she really had no idea at all whether it was night or day outside. *That* was the thing about caves that bothered Trenicia the most. Day or night didn't matter at all when she was in a cave.

"A messenger just came down here from on up to the north," Tlantar told the rest of them, "and he's given us more details about this new disease that's been worrying us lately. If his numbers are at all accurate, the disease has killed several hundred of the northern Matans already. When somebody catches this disease, it seems that he has a great deal of trouble breathing, and then he starts raving almost as if he just went crazy. The messenger told my people that when somebody catches this disease, he's usually dead within a few hours."

"That's hardly possible, Chief Tlantar," the young Trogite named Keselo objected. "A disease almost always takes several days to run its course. If the northern Matans sicken and die *that* fast, it has to be something else that's killing them."

"Poison, maybe?" Sorgan Hook-Beak suggested, "or maybe even some of that snake-venom that's caused us so much trouble before?"

Keselo scratched his cheek and then shook his head. "I think we can rule out venom, Captain," he replied. "The venom we've encountered before kills people almost instantly. Various poisons take a bit longer."

"Wouldn't that suggest that somebody's been slipping into the camp of the northern Matans and sprinkling poison on their food?" Padan asked.

"I'd say that poisoning the water supply would be more likely," the little Maag called Rabbit said. "It'd be a lot easier—and safer—to pour poison into a spring or a well than it would be to slink around at night poisoning the food. Most people guard their food, since they usually have to pay for it. Water's free, though, so people take it wherever they find it."

"Isn't something like that just a bit complicated for a creature that's at least part bug?" Narasan suggested.

"I don't know that I'd lock 'stupid' in stone, Narasan," Red-Beard cautioned. "It seems to me that every time we turn around, the bug-people—or whatever they are—have been doing their best to outsmart us. Their 'fragrance game' back in Tonthakan came very close to starting a war between the Deer Tribe and the Reindeer Tribe."

"All we're doing here is guessing," the deep-voiced Andar rumbled at them. "We don't have enough information yet about what's *really* killing all those northern Matans, and I can't think of anybody who'd be able to clear it up for us."

"I wish that One-Who-Heals was here," Longbow said.

"*He* could find out just exactly what was killing those people in just a day or so."

"I could go on back to the village of your tribe and bring him on up here," Veltan said. "I'd have him here in less than an hour."

Longbow shook his head. "The trip would kill him," he said. "One-Who-Heals is very old, and he's not well. I don't think he'd survive if you carried him up here on your tame thunderbolt, Veltan."

"I'd say that we've definitely got a problem here, Narasan," Sorgan Hook-Beak said.

"Don't rush me, Sorgan," Narasan said with a troubled frown. "I'm working on it."

"I don't really have the chemicals I'd need to test the water—or food—for any of the known poisons," Keselo admitted after Padan had suggested that the young officer was the best qualified to identify the poison that was killing the northern Matans. "And then, too, if it happens to be a new poison, the chemicals that would identify one of the older ones might not work on this new one."

The pretty lady who was the mate of the farmer named Omago sighed, rolling her eyes upward. "Would it hurt your feelings if I happened to suggest a simpler solution, gentlemen?" she asked. "I'd sooner die than make you all feel very foolish, but we *do* need an answer, wouldn't you say?"

"Do you *have* to do that all the time, Ara?" Veltan complained.

She gave him a sly little smile. "Probably not, dear Veltan," she admitted, "but it's a lot of fun sometimes. Now then, we have an expert called One-Who-Heals who could probably identify this poison in about a minute and a half, right?"

"Maybe just a *bit* longer," Longbow said mildly.

Ara let that pass. "Our problem, though, is that our expert is old and sick, and he'd probably die before we could bring him up here to examine the Matans that fell over dead. Am I going too fast for anybody yet?" She looked around. "Good. Since we can't bring our expert up here, why not take a dead Matan on down to Longbow's home village and let One-Who-Heals examine him down *there*?"

"Now, why didn't *I* think of that?" Dahlaine said, looking just a bit ashamed of himself.

"You don't *really* want me to tell you, do you, Dahlaine?" Ara replied with a naughty little smirk.

It was almost certainly well past midnight when Zelania, Veltan, and Longbow returned from a journey that Trenicia was positive would have taken *her* several months at least.

"As it turns out, big brother, the Matan *was* killed with venom rather than some ordinary poison," Zelana reported to Dahlaine.

"That's not—" Dahlaine began to protest.

"Hear me out, Dahlaine," Zelana scolded him. "It appears that the creatures of the Wasteland have come up with a way to spray their venom up into the air instead of leaking it out through their fangs."

"In a sort of mist, you mean?" Dahlaine suggested.

"Exactly. The venom is still deadly, but it doesn't kill people quite as fast as the usual dose of it would if it were injected into the victim's veins. The victim breathes the mist in, and it takes a while for it to get into his blood. The old— but still very skilled—shaman of Longbow's tribe found traces of the venom in the dead Matan's nose, and that fine mist didn't kill him instantly as it would have had it gone straight into his blood. If the servants of the Vlagh can make that mist fine enough, it could probably kill several dozen Matans with the same amount of venom as it could deliver with one bite to kill just one man."

"That's terrible!" Dahlaine gasped.

"Moderately terrible, yes," Veltan agreed. "The next question that sort of leaps to mind is, what are we going to do about it?"

Were these gods children? Trenicia had almost instantly come up with a solution. Why couldn't *they* see it? "Correct me if I'm wrong here, but can't you and the other members of your family control the wind?"

"Well, up to a point, I suppose," Dahlaine conceded, "but—" He abruptly stopped. "How in the world did you come up with *that*, Queen Trenicia?"

"On occasion in the past I've used smoke to drive an enemy away," she replied. "A little bit of smoke doesn't bother people very much, but a *lot* of smoke makes it almost impossible for them to breathe. At that point, they have to run away—or stay and die."

"Omago came up with something very much like that a little while back, Queen Trenicia," Veltan said. "There's a peculiar sort of tree down in my Domain that the farmers call 'greasewood.' When they're having trouble with insects, the farmers make a large pile of those trees and then set fire to them. The bugs can't stand that smoke, so it drives them away before they can eat all the food the farmers are growing. The smoke bothers the farmers almost as much as it bothers the bugs, though, so the farmers cover their lower faces with wet cloth. If Dahlaine's Matans covered their lower faces with wet cloth, it might protect them—particularly if the wind suddenly changes direction. *Our* people would be fairly safe, but the wind would blow that mist right back into the faces of the creatures of the Wasteland *and* those Atazakans who've joined forces with them. When Omago suggested this, we thought that our enemies from the Wasteland were using mushroom spores to poison the Matans with this imitation disease, but a sudden change in the direction of the wind would blow this misty venom back into the faces of our enemies just as fast as it'd blow mushroom spores, wouldn't it?"

Sorgan the pirate chortled. "I love it when an enemy provides just exactly what we need to kill him," he said.

"It's not a bad idea," Dahlaine said, "but I think it might just break one of the rules. Mother Sea won't let us kill anybody—or anything—and changing the direction of the wind in this situation would be almost as bad as throwing thunderbolts at our enemies."

"I don't think I'd worry very much, Dahlaine," Longbow suggested. "We have this 'unknown friend,' remember? The wind will go where she *wants* it to go. If she could change the direction of a waterfall, changing the course of a breeze wouldn't give her many problems."

"But how are we going to get word to her?" Veltan protested.

Longbow shrugged. "I'm fairly sure that she knows already, Veltan," he said. "I don't think that there's very much of *anything* that she doesn't know about, when you get right down to it."

Then several things that had taken place near the Falls of Vash suddenly all fit together for Trenicia, and she stared at the wife of the stodgy farmer Omago in open astonishment.

"That was quick," Ara's voice came soundlessly to the warrior queen. "You're more clever than you appear to be,

Queen Trenicia. Some of the others have caught a few hints, but they haven't *quite* put them together yet."

Trenicia tried to speak, but her tongue seemed to have gone to sleep.

"Not out loud, dear," Ara's voice scolded. "Don't upset the children just yet."

"*Which* children?" Trenicia silently demanded.

"They're *all* children, dear. Didn't you know that? They call it 'war,' but it's really just a game. Let them play, dear. It keeps them busy and out from underfoot. You and I can talk about this some other time, Trenicia. I'm going to be occupied for a while, so this can wait."

Trenicia began to shiver and she stared at the pretty lady in astonishment.

"Don't let your mouth gape open like that, Trenicia," Ara's voice chided. "It's not very becoming."

THE
PESTILENCE

1

Tlantar was born in the village of Asmie, which was snuggled up against the south side of Mount Shrak, the home of Dahlaine of the North, the eldest of the gods of the Land of Dhrall.

Tlantar's father, Tladan, was the chief of Asmie, and Dahlaine frequently came by Tladan's lodge when he wanted to send word to other Matan villages, so Tlantar was perhaps much more familiar with him than were the children of the other villagers in Asmie.

The close proximity of the village to the towering Mount Shrak didn't seem to make much sense in the summertime, but when winter came roaring in, Mount Shrak was Asmie's dearest friend, sheltering her from howling gales and blizzards that went on for weeks at a time. The lodges of the tribe were solidly built of sod blocks and thatched roofs held in place with heavy rocks, and they were clustered tightly together with overlapping roofs. Tlantar was quite sure that winter found that to be very offensive, since there was no way she'd be able to pile her pet snowflakes in the narrow passages between the lodges. All in all, the villagers were quite smug about winter's discontent.

There was a nice little brook that giggled down through Asmie, generously giving the tribe all the water they needed, and the endless meadow to the south of the village provided fuel for the cooking fires—*if* the members of the tribe had gathered up enough of the plentiful bison droppings to get them through the following winter.

Tlantar's early childhood was a time of impatience for him. The men of Asmie spent most of their time in the hunt. There was an almost ritual quality about the hunting of the bison of Matan. They were very large animals, shaggy, humpbacked, and not really very bright. Their horns were massive, and they were joined together at the base in the center of the animal's forehead. Many of the younger men of Asmie seemed to think that the bison was a stupid and timid animal, but Tlantar had some serious doubts about that. It seemed to him that the reaction of the bison to anything that happened in their immediate vicinity was most effective. One frightened and fleeing animal posed no threat to anyone who happened to be nearby, but the bison of Matakan were herd animals, so they ran away in groups, and Tlantar was quite certain that the flight of the bison wasn't really a response to panic, but was a clever way to deal with anything that threatened the herd. The stampede of a herd of bison could kill almost anything—or anyone—who posed a threat. Any man with even a hint of intelligence knew that standing in the path of a thousand fleeing animals, each of which was at least ten times as heavy as a full-grown man, was an act of pure stupidity. The horns of the bison of Matakan were most impressive, but the older men of the tribe warned the boys that it was the *hooves* of the bison that were *really* deadly. The experienced hunters all seemed to have a habit of repeating the same warning to the novices. "Don't *ever* stand in front of them if they start to run."

It was when Tlantar was about ten years old that his father and several of the other experienced hunters returned to the village from the hunt and told the boys of Asmie that there was something not far away that they should see. They led the boys out across the grassland to a spot a mile or so to the west of Asmie and then pointed at a place where the grass seemed to be all mashed flat. "Go look," Tlantar's father commanded the boys.

When the boys reached the area of mashed-down grass, several of them began to vomit. Tlantar clenched his teeth to keep his breakfast where it was supposed to be as he stared in horror at the remains of what had probably been a hunter who hadn't been clever enough—or agile enough—to get out from in front of a stampeding herd of bison.

The splintered pieces of a Matan spear-thrower and the scraps of what had probably been the hunter's shirt confirmed the fact that what was scattered about in the mashed-down grass had been a man not too long ago, but what was left of him was not recognizable.

"All right, boys," Chief Tladan called, "that's enough. Come away from there. Now you know what's likely to happen to you if you make a mistake when you're hunting bison. It's not very pretty, but it was important for you to see it."

"Who was he, Chief Tladan?" one of the boys asked when they rejoined the older men of the tribe.

Tlantar's father shrugged. "We can't really be sure yet. When everybody comes home later, we'll count noses. *One* of the men of the tribe won't be among us, and that should let us know just who it is that's scattered around out there. We're lucky that there's only *one* dead man involved. When there are four or five, it's very difficult to keep the bits and pieces separate when you bury them, and every man should have his own grave, wouldn't you say?"

It was about a year later when Tlantar began his training with the clever device the Matans all referred to as "the spear-thrower." The experienced hunters told the boys that a man who knew what he was doing could cast a spear twice as far with his spear-thrower as he could if he just picked up his spear and threw it with his hand. As one wry old hunter told them, "Those extra yards can be very important. They give you just a bit more time to run away if you happen to miss on your first cast. Bison always seem to get sort of grouchy when people start throwing spears at them, and you *don't* want to be too close when they come running in your direction."

Tlantar began to practice with one of his father's worn-down spear-throwers, casting spear after spear at an old, worn-out bison-hide blanket stuffed full of straw. What he was doing seemed to bother the old hunter who was giving the boys instructions. "*Will* you make up your mind, Tlantar?" he demanded. "Are you right-handed or left-handed?"

"Both, I think," Tlantar replied. "Whichever hand I pick something up with seems to work just as well as the other one does. I've always sort of wondered why everybody else in the tribe only uses one hand."

"Let's find out which of your hands works best right now. One of them *has* to be better than the other."

It took Tlantar the better part of a week to convince the

old hunter that there was no significant difference between what he could do with either hand, and his teacher began to refer to him as "Two-Hands." Chief Tladan seemed to be a bit puzzled by that. "Everybody has two hands," he objected.

"Maybe so," the old man replied, "but they don't—or probably *can't*—use them the way your boy does."

Tlantar felt that they were all getting excited about something that didn't really mean very much, but if they wanted to make a big thing out of it, that was up to them.

After the boys of the tribe of Asmie had grown more proficient, the men of the tribe took them out into the grassland to give them a chance to hurl spears at live bison instead of stationary targets, and even Tlantar was a bit surprised when he felled a full-grown bison with his very first cast.

"Which hand did you use?" his old teacher asked.

"I'm not too sure," Tlantar admitted. "I was just a little bit excited, so I can't really remember."

His teacher walked away, shaking his head and muttering to himself.

There was a fair amount of discussion among the men of the tribe that evening. Tlantar was still just a growing boy, but it had long been a custom in the tribe to elevate a young man to the status of adulthood when he made his first kill. Ultimately, "first kill" won out over "just a boy," and "Tlantar Two-Hands" was now a grown-up, probably the youngest grown-up in the history of the tribe. Chief Tladan was so proud of his son that the other men of the tribe began to avoid him, since his boasting was getting to be just a bit tiresome.

Tlantar spent the next several weeks scraping and curing the shaggy hide of his first kill in keeping with yet another tired old custom. He was required to make new clothes for himself from that hide. The older men of the tribe could give him advice, of course, but the scraping, curing, and sewing were *his* responsibility. He made several mistakes, naturally, but he was able to conceal them fairly well, and he was quite proud of the winter cloak he'd put together.

Unfortunately, however, he outgrew his new winter cloak in about a year and a half, so he had to make himself a new one before his fourteenth birthday—and yet another one when he was sixteen.

He began to have a recurrent nightmare about then—a horrible dream in which he was about forty feet tall and had to make yet another winter cloak out of the hides of a dozen or so bison.

Winters were most unpleasant in the Domain of Dahlaine of the North. It turned bitterly cold, and howling blizzards swept in to bury everything in deep snowdrifts. The winter of Tlantar's seventeenth year was particularly savage. The previous summer had been a good hunting season, so there were ample supplies of smoked bison meat in Asmie, and the stores of beans had been building up for years now. The members of the Asmie tribe were quite smug about that. If winter wanted to howl and scream all around them, let her. They had food in plenty, fuel for their fires, and the thick sod walls of their lodges held the screaming winter at bay.

But there was nothing to *do*. Tlantar was a very active young man, and just sitting by the fire in his father's lodge day after day after day was almost more than he could bear.

And then there came a day when the wind seemed to have died and the bitter chill softened, and the sun even came out low over the southern horizon. The sky overhead was blue, and except for a patch of dark clouds off to the west, things seemed almost springlike.

"I need to stretch my legs, father," Tlantar said along about noon. "If I sit here for much longer, I'll probably forget how to walk."

"Just be careful, Tlantar," his father cautioned. "Don't go out into the open too far. Winter's still lurking out there, and she could come crashing back without much warning if she decides to have you for lunch."

"I won't be too long, father," Tlantar promised. "I just want to stretch the kinks out of my legs."

His father smiled faintly. "When you get a bit older, your legs won't kink up quite so bad."

"That's then, father," Tlantar replied. "This is now, and now's been piling kinks all over me since last fall." Tlantar gathered his heavy winter cloak around him and went on out into the open.

There was still a definite chill in the air, he noticed, and the sunlight gleaming from the vast sea of snow was almost blindingly bright. Tlantar squinted and tried to shade his eyes with his hand.

The howling blizzard that had savaged the village of Asmie for the past several weeks had come up out of the southwest rather than the usual northwest, and the unobstructed wind had swept most of the snow away from the village. Tlantar thought that might be a good sign. Mount Shrak normally sheltered Asmie from the wind, and snow seemed to be very fond of shelter. It hadn't been at all uncommon for the snowdrifts in Asmie to be twelve feet deep, and in shaded spots, they'd still been there in midsummer. So far *this* year, however, there wasn't more than a few inches of snow lying on the village. That promised to make life much more pleasant in early summer.

Tlantar strode away from the village, squinting out over the gleaming snow. He was just a bit surprised when he saw a herd of bison raking their hooves across the snow to uncover the grass. If the weather held steady, there *might* even be an opportunity to take fresh meat. It was something to think about, that was certain. Tlantar began to move carefully at that point. He didn't want to frighten the grazing bison, and he wished that he'd remembered to bring his spear and spear-thrower with him.

He moved cautiously, of course. He wanted to see just how close he'd be able to come to the herd of bison, but he most definitely didn't want to startle them. Startled bison usually ran, and about half the time they ran right over the top of whatever—or whoever—had surprised them.

He crouched low and moved very slowly, keeping his eyes fixed on the grazing bison, and *that* quite nearly cost him his life.

A sudden blast of cold wind struck his back and a blinding swirl of dense snow came rolling down the side of Mount Shrak to engulf him.

He prudently suppressed his sudden panic. His heavy winter cloak gave him *some* protection, but that might start to fade if the wind grew colder. What he needed right now was shelter of some kind, but there *wasn't* anything nearby that would shelter him. All that there was in his vicinity was snow. "It's the *wind* that's trying to turn me into ice," he muttered. "I've *got* to get in out of the wind."

Then "snow" and "shelter" suddenly came together. Snow wasn't *warm,* exactly, but it wasn't nearly as cold as that cursed wind. If he could somehow burrow down into a patch of deep snow, it *would* get him in out of the wind, and right now that would probably give him his best chance of surviving.

He dropped to his knees and began probing at the snow beneath him. "Not deep enough," he muttered and crawled on several yards farther, but the snow was still too shallow.

Then he came to a hilltop that the howling wind had swept clear of snow. If the snow had piled up *behind* that hill, there'd almost certainly be deep snow beyond that bare hilltop. He quickly scurried on across that grassy knob and immediately sank down to his hips in soft snow. "Now we're getting someplace," he muttered. He kicked at the snow around his feet and knees until he'd managed to open a fairly sizeable pit. Then he dropped to his knees and began to scoop out loose snow. As he went deeper, he found that tramping the snow with his leather-clad feet packed it, and packed snow didn't take up as much room as loose snow did.

He stopped to catch his breath and to think his way through what he was doing. He needed shelter from the wind, and "shelter" meant something very much like one of the lodges of Asmie—except that shelter could be made out of blocks of snow rather than sod. He was going to have to tunnel down a ways and then open up something like a chamber. Then he'd need to block off his tunnel to keep out the bitterly cold air that was driving the snow down the side of Mount Shrak. "I'll have air to breathe—if I don't stay there too long, and I can eat snow if I get thirsty." He was sure that it was going to be a bit dangerous, but the cold was much, much more dangerous.

He burrowed on down until he came to grass and then he followed the grassy slope down a bit farther, packing the snow of his makeshift tunnel with his shoulders and elbows.

It wasn't nearly as cold down here as it had been up on the surface, and he could breathe. "That's all that matters right now, I think," he said, and went back to work.

He ended up with a small, dome-shaped chamber with a partially blocked-off tunnel. It was dark and chilly, but he *was* getting fresh air to breathe, and, though it wasn't exactly warm there, it wasn't *nearly* as cold as it'd been outside in the screaming wind.

Then he remembered something and almost laughed. He untied the leather pouch hanging from his belt and found several thin slabs of smoked bison meat in the pouch. "Food, water, and a sort of warm place to sleep. It doesn't get much better than that," he said out loud.

He periodically went up through his tunnel to push away the snow that had accumulated in his tunnel-mouth *and* to find out if it was still snowing out there.

After about four days, the cold wind apparently decided that Tlantar wasn't really worth all the time she'd been spending trying to freeze him into a block of solid ice, so she moved on. Tlantar waited for a while, just to be on the safe side, and then he tied his furry winter cloak shut, crawled on out through his tunnel, and waded through the new snow back to Asmie.

When he arrived back home, he was more than a little surprised to find his friends holding a "farewell ceremony for my dear son Tlantar." It took him a while to convince his father and friends that he was *not* a ghost coming back to haunt dear old Asmie. He explained several times how he'd managed to survive, and then Dahlaine insisted that he take all the men of Asmie to his hidden hole in the snow and show them exactly how to make one of their own should it ever become necessary. "We lose hundreds of men in Matakan every winter to those deadly blizzards, Tlantar," Dahlaine said. "You've managed to come up with a way to survive. I want you to show every man in Asmie how to do it. Then we'll bring in men from other tribes, and you'll teach *them* as well. I think you've stumbled across something that'll save thousands of lives, Tlantar Two-Hands, and Matans will remember you long after you've gone to your grave."

Tlantar thought that being famous might be sort of nice, but he didn't care much for the word "grave" that Dahlaine had just dropped on him.

2

When Tlantar was about twenty, his father, Chief Tladan, was killed in a stampede of frightened bison. "He shouldn't have been out there with us, Tlantar," a hunter named Tlodal, who'd been a member of the hunting party, asserted. "He's been slowing down for the past few years—probably because his back was bothering him quite a bit. You might not have noticed it, but it was all he could do to walk when he first got up in the morning. We tried our best to persuade him to stay home, but he wouldn't hear of it. He loved the hunt, and I guess he thought that his back and legs could get him through one more season."

Tlantar sighed. "He was always like that," he said. "He was probably the most stubborn man in all of Matakan."

"I'm sure that was what made him such a good chief," Tlodal said, "but it seems to have caught up with him finally. Maybe we should make it a rule that nobody over thirty can go to the hunt."

"That might get both of us in a lot of trouble, Tlodal," Tlantar told his friend.

Chieftainship in the tribes of Matakan was usually hereditary, but the men of the tribes always had the final say when the previous chief died, and "Tlantar is too young" began to crop up fairly often after Chief Tladan's death. There seemed to be a strong odor of ambition floating around in the village of Asmie.

"We've talked it over, Tlantar," Tlerik, one of the elders of the tribe, told him, "and we pretty much agree that things will go more smoothly for you if you have a mate. The men who don't approve of you keep pointing out the fact that you aren't mated. You'll look more stable if you have a mate. A few children would probably help even more, but that usually takes a while."

"I've noticed that, yes," Tlantar agreed without even a hint of a smile.

"We strongly suggest that you should be mated, Tlantar," old Tlerik said firmly. "It doesn't have to involve any towering love or any of that other juvenile foolishness. All you really need is a mate you can get along with fairly well. You'll be offering her a significant elevation in rank, so I'm sure that many of the women in Asmie would be more than happy to join with you."

"You're starting to make it sound like some sort of business arrangement, Tlerik," Tlantar protested.

Tlerik scratched at his cheek and looked thoughtfully out at the waving grass. "That pretty much describes it, yes. You need to have a mate, and you're offering a higher rank in payment. Grand passion—or whatever else you might want to call it—really doesn't play any part in this. A lot of matings start out this way, but after a while, the man and the woman discover that they're really rather fond of each other. The nice thing about that sort of arrangement is that it's a lot quieter than the other kind of matings. Passion can be dramatic, but it's terribly noisy sometimes."

Tlantar was not particularly pleased by Tlerik the elder's suggestion. Even as a boy, all of Tlantar's attention had been focused on the hunt. Other young men of the tribe were greatly interested in unmated young women, but Tlantar had never really had time to even think about such things. Then, too, he'd noticed that mated men were more or less obliged to go home every evening—even when the hunting was very good. As things now stood, Tlantar was free to come home or stay away, and there was nobody in the tribe who might protest.

Then the thought of those of the tribe who objected to his chieftainship came to him unbidden. For the most part, the objectors were not really very good hunters, largely because they were too indolent to spend the necessary time practicing with their spear-throwers. The more he considered his detractors, the more he became convinced that their objections grew out of their hope that *they* might be chosen by the men of the tribe to occupy the station of chief so they might live a life of ease and comfort that would require no effort and even less thought.

Should it happen that one of those incompetents were to become the chieftain of the tribe, it could very well be a total disaster, and Chief Tladan had spent hours beating his son over the head with "responsibility."

Tlantar sighed and then drifted around the village of Asmie looking at the young, unmated women. It soon became quite obvious to him that old man Tlerik had forgotten how to keep his mouth shut, because it seemed that every time Tlantar turned around, there was another grossly overdressed young woman standing there fluttering her eye-lashes at him.

Though he probably never would have used that exact word, Tlantar turned and fled. He'd spent much of his life hunting, but *being* hunted made him go cold all over.

He was several miles off to the west of Asmie when he stopped to catch his breath.

"You idiot!" a shrill voice came from the grass not ten yards away. "I've been tracking that hare all morning, and you just frightened him so much that he'll probably still be running next week."

"I'm sorry," Tlantar apologized. "Something just happened in Asmie that upset me quite a bit. I'll help you chase down that hare, if you'd like."

"Forget it," the voice came crisply out of the tall grass. "He's at least a mile away by now." The speaker stood up, and Tlantar immediately realized that the person who'd just scolded him was *not* some half-grown boy. It was a young woman instead, but she wasn't wearing a dress. Her clothes were made of leather, and they fit her tightly enough to re-veal certain attributes that definitely identified her as female. She wasn't very tall, and her braided hair was pale blond.

"Are you from Asmie?" Tlantar asked her. "I've lived there all my life, and I don't think I've ever seen you there."

"I don't go into town very often," the young woman replied. "There's nothing there that interests me."

"Are you saying that you live alone out here in the meadowland?"

"I didn't say that at all. Where I live is none of your con-cern."

"I wasn't trying to pry or anything," Tlantar apologized,

"but I don't think I've ever encountered a Matan woman who lives alone and spends her time hunting before."

"There aren't too many of us," she admitted, coiling up what appeared to be a sling and tucking it under her belt. "It might seem a bit strange to you, but women *do* know how to hunt—and to fish as well. Someday, I might even make myself a spear and have a try at a bison."

"I wouldn't recommend it," Tlantar told her. "Bison can be very dangerous if you rub them the wrong way."

"I didn't intend to rub them. I'm going to kill them."

"You might want to think about that just a bit," Tlantar advised. "I lost my father in a bison stampede a month or so ago. He was getting old, so he couldn't run very fast anymore."

"I'm very sorry," she said. "I lost *my* father in the same way when I was about eight years old."

"Are you saying that you've lived alone out here since you were only eight?"

"I didn't come right out and *say* it," she replied tartly, "but that's pretty much the way my life's been. I can take these meadow hares with my sling and I've got a nice sharp fish-spear, so I usually have plenty to eat. Why were you running just now? Is there somebody after you?"

Tlantar made a wry face. "More than *one* somebody," he replied. "The tribal elders told me that I should be mated, and somehow word of that leaked out. Now every unmated young lady in Asmie has her eyes on me."

"You've already found the answer to that. Just run away, and stay out in the meadow until the young ladies find somebody else to chase."

"I wish I could do that," Tlantar replied, "but I have certain responsibilities in Asmie. There are several lazy incompetents there who'd *really* like to be the chief. If one of *them* gets the job, the village won't even *be* there after a few years."

"This is all very interesting," the young woman said, "but I need something for supper, and you just frightened off my hare, so it's time for me to go hunting again."

"What's your name?" Tlantar asked her.

"Tleri," she replied.

"I'm called Tlantar Two-Hands."

"That's a peculiar sort of name."

"It wasn't my idea."

"That happens quite often, I've heard. Parents seem to come up with peculiar names sometimes." She took her sling out from under her belt. "Maybe we'll meet again sometime," she said, and then she abruptly turned and ran on out across the grassland.

For some reason, Tlantar couldn't seem to get the young huntress Tleri out of his mind. There had been a certain directness about her that was very much unlike the women who lived in Asmie. It had always seemed to Tlantar that the women of Asmie went out of their way to be complex and never once to say anything that got right to the point. Of course, the village women weren't hunters, and Tleri was. That was also most unusual. The women of Asmie grew beans, and once planting was finished, they didn't have much to do until harvest time. They talked all the time, but it didn't seem to Tlantar that they ever said anything that got right to the point. Tleri, on the other hand, hadn't said anything during their brief encounter that *wasn't* right to the point.

The young women of Asmie continued to flutter their eyelashes at Tlantar, and to carefully arrange their schedules so that they could encounter him three or four times a day, but Tlantar generally ignored them. He had other things on his mind now.

Then, a few days later, he came out of his lodge and saw Tleri, still garbed in leather, walking along the narrow path at the center of the village.

"I see that you've decided to pay us a visit," he said with a broad smile.

"Us?" she asked.

"The village is what I meant."

"No. I just came by to see how my aunt was doing. She wasn't feeling too well the last time I was here."

"Aunt?"

"My father's sister. You probably know her. She's called Tlara."

"Oh, yes," Tlantar said. "I've known her since I was just a boy. I hadn't heard that she's been sick."

"It's a woman's ailment. We don't usually talk about those when there are men anywhere in the vicinity. Did you want any details?"

"Ah—no, Tleri, I don't really think so," Tlantar replied, feeling more than a little embarrassed.

"Are you blushing, Tlantar?" she asked with a kind of wide-eyed innocence.

Tlantar felt his face flame even brighter.

Tleri laughed with glee. "Did you want to play some more, mighty leader?" she asked.

"I don't think so," Tlantar replied. "I know when I've been beaten."

"Aren't you the darling boy?" she said, patting his cheek with one small hand.

*   *   *

Tlantar and Tleri went through the mating ceremony two weeks later, and the entire tribe turned out to watch as Dahlaine joined the pair.

In general, the tribe of Asmie was quite pleased about the joining of Tlantar and Tleri, but Tlantar noticed that several young women and a couple of slightly older men seemed just a bit resentful as the ceremony concluded..

It took the newly joined pair a while to become adjusted to each other. Tlantar had never paid too much attention to the time of day. When the sun was up, it was daytime. When it went down, it was nighttime. Tleri, however, was a bit more precise. She'd taken over the kitchen in Tlantar's lodge, and she wanted him to be *there* when the meals were ready, and she didn't make her discontent a secret.

It wasn't long after their joining when Tleri conceded that she hadn't been *quite* as indifferent as she might have appeared to be during their first few meetings. She'd known *exactly* who Tlantar was, and their first encounter had been well-planned in advance. "There wasn't *really* a hare scampering around out there in the deep grass, Tlantar. I made him up as an excuse for our little talk that day."

"I'm shocked!" Tlantar lied. "How could you have *done* such a thing?"

She gave him a sudden, stricken look and saw his broad grin. "You knew that already, didn't you?" she flared.

"Can you ever forgive me?" he said, trying to conceal his knowing smirk.

"I'll get you for this, Tlantar."

"We might want to talk about that a little later," he said rather blandly.

*　　*　　*

It was late in the following summer when Tleri began to put on quite a bit of weight, and she advised Tlantar that it had nothing to do with how much she'd been eating lately. All in all they were both very pleased that they'd soon become parents.

Strange things began to happen that autumn that Tlantar didn't fully understand. It seemed that every time the sun came up, Tleri started to vomit. She refused to talk about it, and Tlantar became more and more concerned about his mate's illness, and he told the elder Tlerik about it.

"It's nothing to worry about, Chief Tlantar," Tlerik replied. "*All* women go through this when they are with child. It's very common."

"What causes it?"

"I have no idea, Chief Two-Hands. It's one of those things that women refuse to talk about."

"Some kind of secret, you mean?"

"I don't think I'd call it a secret, My Chief," Tlerik said with a faint smile. "Women aren't put together the way we are. Many things happen to them that never happen to us, but I'd say that's all right. Life wouldn't be at all pleasant without women, wouldn't you say?"

Tlantar continued to worry about Tleri's peculiar illness, but after a while it went away, and things were all right again—except that she now wore a dress instead of her customary leather clothing. Her belly grew larger and larger, and that seemed to embarrass her, for some reason.

By early spring, Tleri's belly had grown so large that it seemed to Tlantar that it might be easier to jump over her than to walk around her.

Then there came the night when she started screaming, and it wasn't long after the screaming began that several of the women of the tribe entered Chief Tlantar's lodge and quite firmly told him to go away.

"But—" he began to object.

"Out!" a stout woman of middle years told him. "Now!" she added, pointing at the entryway of Tlantar's lodge.

Tlantar didn't know very much about the process of giving birth, but it seemed to him that Tleri was taking much longer than the other women of the tribe had when *they'd* produced children. After two days of listening to her screams, Tlantar was beside himself.

Then her screams began to subside, and Tlantar was sure that the worst was almost over.

After the women of the tribe had summarily turned him out of his lodge, he stayed in the lodge of the elder Tlerik, who spent most of the next two days talking about Dahlaine's "Nation" concept. "It *does* make good sense, My Chief," he said. "All this bickering and wars between the tribes don't make much sense when we're right on the verge of being invaded by the creatures of the Wasteland. We need to set our differences aside and start preparing for a *real* war."

"Do you suppose we could talk about this some other time, Tlerik?" Tlantar said. "I've got something else to worry about right now."

"I was trying to take your mind off that, Two-Hands," Tlerik replied. "Quite often, childbirth is harder on the men than it is on the women. Don't worry so much, Tlantar, Tleri is young and strong. She'll come through this just fine."

Tlantar awoke with a start. It had seemed to him that going to sleep while Tleri was in such pain would have been an act of profound disrespect, but all those sleepless hours had finally overwhelmed him. He had no idea of how long he had slept, but peculiarly, it had been silence that had aroused him. There were no screams now, and Tlantar heaved a vast sigh of relief. Tleri's suffering was over, and he was now a father. "Why didn't you wake me up?" he asked the elder Tlerik.

"You needed some sleep, My Chief," the old man replied.

"Is the child a boy or a girl?"

"Well, it was a boy, My Chief," Tlerik replied rather somberly.

"*Was?* What are you talking about, Tlerik?"

"Things didn't turn out well, My Chief. The birthing took too long, and Tleri was too weak to complete it. I'm sorry, My Chief, but your son was born dead."

Tlantar felt a sudden wrench in his heart. "Was there no way he could have been revived?" he asked in a choked voice.

"None, My Chief. As nearly as the women who were helping Tleri could determine, the child died before he left Tleri's womb." There was a somewhat evasive quality in Tlerik's voice.

"There's something you're not telling me, old man," Tlantar accused.

Tlerik sighed. "Your son will not go alone into his grave, Two-Hands," he said very quietly.

Tlantar stared at the old man in horror as the full meaning of what he'd just heard came crashing in on him. Then he threw back his head and howled in his grief.

3

Your mate's hips were too small," the stout woman who had tried to help Tleri said a few weeks later when Tlantar had partially regained his senses and questioned her about his mate's death. "They were so small that the baby, who was quite large, couldn't come out. Tleri tried very hard to force him out, but then she started to bleed, and much more blood came out than is usual. There was nothing we could do to stop the bleeding, so we couldn't save her. I'm very sorry, Chief Tlantar, but these things happen all the time. More women die in childbirth than most people realize."

"I'd heard that it happens now and then," Tlantar conceded.

"'Now and then' isn't too accurate, My Chief," she said in a grim voice. "I'd say that almost half of the women with child die during the delivery."

"Half?" Tlantar exclaimed.

"She's right, My Chief," Tlerik agreed.

"That doesn't happen that often with animals, does it?" Tlantar demanded.

"No," the stout woman said. "I asked Dahlaine about that once, and he told me that it happens to people more often than it does to animals because we walk on our hind legs instead of all four. Our hands are more useful than paws or hooves, but our bodies aren't as strong as they should be, since the muscles in our lower bellies haven't switched over from four legs to two yet. He told me that it might take several thousand years for our belly-muscles to change over and do things right."

"Couldn't Dahlaine just—" Tlantar left it hanging.

The stout woman shook her head. "I asked him about that myself, but he told me that he wasn't supposed to tamper with us that way."

"You might want to consider something before too much longer, Chief Two-Hands," Tlerik said, pursing his lips. "Not right at once, of course, but after your grief has subsided, you should probably consider finding another mate."

Tlantar shook his head. "No. Tleri was my mate, and in my heart she always will be."

"I just wanted to raise the issue, My Chief. You absolutely *must* have a son who'll become Asmie's chief after you pass on. If you don't have a descendant, arguments about who'll be our next chief will break out before your body even turns cold, and *those* particular arguments are the ones that usually lead to bloodshed. There have been many tribes in the past that aren't around anymore for exactly that reason."

Tlantar firmly shook his head. "I won't betray my Tleri for all this political nonsense, Tlerik. You should know me well enough by now to realize that."

"You *could* just choose somebody else's child," the stout woman suggested. "That might even be a better way to do this than hanging the title on a son who might not be bright enough to tell his right hand from his left." She hesitated. "No offense intended there, Chief Two-Hands—but just because *you're* intelligent, it doesn't really follow that your son will be as well. If everything I've heard about Atazakan is true, that's the perfect example of what happens when leadership is handed off to a long succession of descendants that are increasingly incompetent—or insane."

"She has a point there, My Chief," Tlerik said, frowning slightly. "Sometimes bloodlines grow weaker and weaker with each passing generation, and what began as genius slides down toward idiocy eventually." Then he looked appraisingly at the woman. "You seem to have an unusually firm grasp upon a fair number of unpleasant realities, good lady," he observed.

"How nice of you to say so, honored elder," she replied with a little curtsy.

"For some reason, I can't remember ever having seen you before here in Asmie," Tlerik said with a slight frown.

"That's probably because you weren't looking, old man," she replied. "If that's everything we have on the fire for right now, I have some other things that need my attention." And then she turned and left Tlerik's lodge.

One of the things Tlantar's father had told him many times was that he should always be familiar and friendly with the other men of the tribe. "A chief can't have too many friends."

Given the circumstances of Chief Tladan's death, however, Tlantar had some serious doubts about the wisdom of his father's suggestion. Chief Tladan had been aware of the fact that his back and legs were not as strong as they'd been when he was younger, and even though he'd tried very hard to keep the other men of the tribe from realizing that his legs ached almost all the time, his limping had been very obvious when he'd been alone with his son. Given his condition, he should never have agreed to go to the hunt with his friends, but once someone had suggested it, he'd felt obliged to join in. Casual friendship might be nice, Tlantar admitted to himself, but it definitely wasn't nice enough to die for.

Tlantar's recent bereavement gave him a sound reason to distance himself from the other men of the tribe, so he made a point of maintaining a somber expression when he was in the presence of others and going straight to the point in his discussions with the men of the tribe. Even the more boisterous tribe members took him seriously. It seemed to Tlantar that even now Tleri was helping him.

Despite Dahlaine's concept of "The Matakan Nation," there were still periodic outbreaks of tribal war, and the usual reason for these outbreaks of violence had to do with what the Matans referred to as "poaching." Tribes were supposed to do their hunting within the bounds of their *own* territory, but the bison were not even aware of boundaries, and once they'd been frightened, they would run, and the hunters who'd frightened them would run after them.

That started many arguments and quite a few wars. Tlantar took a rather stiff-necked approach in these situations, pushing aside the "hot pursuit" justification many nearby tribes tried to assert, and firmly announcing, "When you reach our boundary, you stop. If you don't, we'll fight you."

It took several rather bloody demonstrations to convince the neighboring tribes that Chief Tlantar Two-Hands meant exactly what he said.

As time went on, Dahlaine continued to push the south-

ern tribes toward what he called "Nationhood." Tlantar, despite some serious reservations, met with the chieftains of
several nearby tribes to examine the possibility, and his
growing reputation helped to persuade them that Dahlaine's
peculiar notion *might* have a certain value. "If Dahlaine's
right—and he usually is—we have a much more dangerous
enemy out there in the Wasteland," Tlantar advised his fellow chieftains. "In the not too distant future, it's very likely
that hordes of creatures that aren't anything at all like us will
come up into our part of the world with the intent of killing
us all. If the tribes remain separate and hostile to each other,
our alien enemies will be able to take us one tribe at a time,
and we'll all be gone in a very short period of time. At that
point, our little squabbles about who owns that particular
herd of bison won't mean much anymore. We must learn to
live together, or we'll die alone."

It was not long after Tlantar had turned thirty-four when
Dahlaine came into possession of an infant child he called
Ashad. Tlantar had not the faintest idea of where the child
had come from, and he was very disturbed when the local
god advised him that he'd placed the child in the care of a
she-bear called "Broken-Tooth."

"As soon as she wakes up, she'll eat your little boy,"
Chief Two-Hands told his friend.

Dahlaine shook his head. "Oh, no, Tlantar," he disagreed.
"Mama Broken-Tooth will believe that Ashad is her cub, and
she'll destroy any creature that tries to hurt him. You don't *ever*
want to get between a she-bear and her cub. Ashad will be fed
and protected by the most savage creature in the vicinity."

"Well, maybe," Tlantar said dubiously. "Have you been

picking up any hints about when the creatures of the Wasteland are likely to attack us?"

Dahlaine shook his head. "Noting that's very specific, Chief Tlantar," he replied. "I'm getting a strong feeling that their attack is still several years away, though. They don't really know very much about us, but they've been sneaking around in the forests of my sister's Domain trying to find out as much as they can about her people. I'm fairly sure that they'll attack Zelana first."

"Will her people be able to drive them off?"

"We're working on that. Keep talking with the other tribes, Tlantar. The time's not too far off when they *must* be unified into a single Nation."

"They're starting to come around, Dahlaine," Tlantar assured his friend. "I've been waving a few horror stories in their faces, and joining up with other tribes doesn't seem quite as unnatural as it did before. When I start talking about thousands and thousands of enemies charging up out of the Wasteland, friendship between the tribes starts to look very nice."

"It might look even nicer if you were to say 'million' instead of 'thousand,' Tlantar."

"I don't think I've ever heard that word before. How many *is* a million?"

"A thousand thousands, Tlantar," Dahlaine replied.

"There aren't that many of *anything*, Dahlaine!" Tlantar exclaimed.

"You're wrong, I'm afraid. There probably isn't a word that even *begins* to describe how many of those creatures are *really* out there in the Wasteland. Keep working on the other tribes, Chief Two-Hands. The time isn't too far off when we'll need all the help we can get."

*   *   *

Tlantar realized that the more tribes he had loosely joined together in his rudimentary "Nation," the more anxious the still-independent tribes would become. In theory, at least, Tlantar could bring several thousand warriors to any battle that might arise. Tlantar didn't make a big issue of that, but he was certain that the other tribal chieftains could count almost as well as he could.

Dahlaine's little boy had grown teeth, so he no longer lived on a steady diet of bear's milk. He still spent much of his time playing with the bear-cub he called Long-Claw, but after a couple of years he found a new friend in the village of Asmie. His *human* friend was a boy called Tlingar, and the two of them seemed to get along fairly well.

It was when Ashad was five or six years old that Dahlaine came by in the early spring to advise Tlantar and the other tribal chieftains that the creatures of the Wasteland had invaded his sister Zelana's Domain. Dahlaine was a bit vague about the outlander armies that had come to Zelana's Domain to help with the fighting, and he also glossed over a couple of natural disasters that had proved to be quite helpful. "I think you'd better order your assorted soldiers to practice with their spear-throwers, Tlantar. They work very well, but our people will be much safer if they can throw their spears farther."

"I'm not sure that ordering them to practice with their spear-throwers will accomplish very much, Dahlaine. They may all *say* they've been hard at it for hours and hours every day, but if I'm not right there watching them, they'll probably exaggerate the amount of time they *really* spent practicing." He gave it some thought. "Maybe a contest of some kind would encourage them to do what we want them to do. There are twenty tribes in this general vicinity, and they've been more or less at war with each other for as long as I can remember. If I suggested competition—which tribe can throw their spears farther and more accurately or something like that—it *might* just be seen by those tribes as a substitute for war, except that nobody gets killed. If I were to tell them that you want to find out who's the finest spearman in all of Matakan, they'll start practicing day and night. Eventually, I suppose, somebody *will* turn out to be the best, but by the time we find out just who he is, they'll *all* be better than they are right now."

"That's *brilliant*, Tlantar!" Dahlaine exclaimed. "Animosity suddenly turns into friendly competition, and we get what we want without shedding any blood."

"None of *ours* anyway," Tlantar added.

"I almost never ask Dahlaine *why* he wants something, Chief Tlartal," Tlantar told the chief of one of the western tribes. "When he wants something, I just do what I can to make sure that he gets it. Right now, he seems to have a burning desire to find out just who the best spearman in Matakan is. That's why I came up with this 'contest' idea. I don't know if it really *means* very much, but if it makes Dahlaine happy, we should go ahead with it, wouldn't you say?"

"I don't suppose you could just 'accidentally' forget that *my* tribe's part of your 'Nation,' could you, Two-Hands?"

"I'm afraid not, Tlartal. Besides, it just wouldn't be the same without you. Tell your men to start practicing. It's early spring now, and Dahlaine would like to find out just *who* the best spearman in Matakan is sometime in the autumn, so your men have all summer to practice. You might want to make an issue of 'the best in all Matakan.' If your men start yearning to be famous, they'll probably practice even harder."

"We'll see, Tlantar," Tlartal replied without much enthusiasm.

As Tlantar Two-Hands had been quite certain would be the case, the younger Matans enthusiastically accepted the challenge he'd placed before them, despite the nearly unanimous skepticism of the tribal chieftains. Being "the best" can be tremendously important to men who had only recently left their childhood behind them, while the notion that some gangly juvenile was far more likely to reach that goal than a middle-aged, flabby chief probably gnawed at the innards of almost every chief in all of south Matakan.

As Dahlaine had suggested, Tlantar laid a great emphasis on "greater accuracy" and "farther away." As he'd been sure would be the case, the taller young men of almost every tribe outperformed their shorter friends. Longer arms made longer casts in most cases. The shorter men concentrated on accuracy, and even though they couldn't cast a spear as far as their taller companions could, they almost universally drove their spears into the exact center of their targets. Longer range and greater accuracy almost never came out of the same hand.

Tlantar had some other things that he needed to consider. People who hunt with spears almost never carry more than one spear, but he quickly realized that there were many differences between the hunt and a war.

It was later that spring when Dahlaine briefly returned to North Dhrall to advise Tlantar Two-Hands and other leaders of his Domain that the war in his sister's Domain was going quite well—largely because of the presence of the outlanders.

"Just exactly how are those outlanders and your sister's warriors dealing with the invaders?" Tlantar asked.

"They're building things called 'forts' for the most part," Dahlaine replied.

"What exactly *is* a fort?"

"Basically, it's a wall that's made out of rocks—a fairly high wall, actually."

"And is it likely that they'll do things the same way when they come here?"

"I'm sure they will. Why do you ask, Tlantar?"

"It came to me several weeks ago that Matan hunters usually carry only one spear, and once they throw it, they're out of business. That had me more than a little worried, but these fort things the outlanders build might solve that problem. If our people make lots and lots of spears, they can carry bundles of them to the fort, and the creatures of the Wasteland will run out of people before we run out of spears."

"That's not a bad idea, Tlantar," Dahlaine said approvingly. "Oh, there's one other thing you should know about. The outlanders make their weapons out of metal, not stone, and they'll be bringing a *lot* of that metal with them when they come here. It may not be as pretty as stone, but there's a little fellow called Rabbit who can turn arrowheads out by the hundreds in a single day. Spearheads are larger and heavier than arrowheads, but I don't think that will mean anything to Rabbit and the other metalworkers. All that you and your men will have to provide will be the shafts, and then Rabbit and his friends will set up a 'spear factory' right there in the fort. I'd say that they'll probably be able to make them faster than your men will be able to throw them." He hesitated slightly. "Tell me, Tlantar, what's your opinion of the archers of the Tonthakan Nation?"

Tlantar shrugged. "Their arrows are probably good

enough to kill deer, but I don't think they'd work very well on bison."

"I don't think that's going to be much of a problem, Tlantar," Dahlaine said. "The bug-people we've seen in the ravine above Lattash are all smaller than a deer that's only half grown, so Rabbit's arrows in the hands of the Tonthakans will almost certainly kill most of our enemies. I'm almost positive that there are much larger bug-people, though, and that's when your men—and their spears—will come in. Don't waste your spears on the little ones. Save them for the big ones."

"As you desire, Dahlaine," Tlantar replied without a smile.

"You should try to get over that, Tlantar," Dahlaine said sourly.

"And maybe *you* should try it as well. You irritate people when you say obvious things to them. You *did* know that, didn't you? I'll send the southern tribes down into the woods that lie along your southern border to gather up spear-shafts so that we'll be ready when the one called Rabbit arrives."

"There's one other thing you should know about, Tlantar. The creatures of the Wasteland are venomous—much like certain snakes are. We don't *have* venomous snakes this far to the north, so you might not quite realize just how deadly that venom can be. There's an archer called Longbow down in my sister's Domain who pokes his arrow points into the venom sacs of the dead enemies, and that makes his arrow points as deadly as the snake-fangs are. Over the years, he's killed thousands and thousands of the bug-people by using their own venom."

"Now *that's* the man I want to meet," Tlantar declared.

"You will, Tlantar," Dahlaine replied. "He'll be coming up here as well. He's not doing it out of any affection for *us*, though. He'll be coming here to kill more of the bug-people. He wants to kill them *all*. I'm not sure exactly *why*, but his hatred for the bug-people goes far beyond anything I've ever encountered before."

"Will he be coming north before much longer?" Tlantar asked.

Dahlaine spread out his hands almost helplessly. "I have no way of knowing, Chief Two-Hands," he replied. "Things are looking very positive in Zelana's Domain—so far, at least—but we can't even guess which direction the bug-people will decide to attack next. They could come *this* way, or go south, or maybe even east. We'll have to wait until the Dreamers tell us where before we can make any decisions."

Dahlaine periodically returned to Mount Shrak and Asmie to keep Tlantar and the other Matan chieftains advised of the progress in his sister's Domain. Tlantar *liked* Dahlaine, of course, since they'd been friends since Tlantar's boyhood. Tlantar chose not to make an issue of it, but he definitely wished that Dahlaine would find a quieter way to travel.

It was almost summer when Dahlaine briefly stopped by to advise Tlantar that the war in his sister's Domain had come to a rather abrupt conclusion. "I think I might have underestimated the capabilities of the Dreamers, Tlantar," he said in a troubled tone of voice.

"Oh? What happened down there?"

"The creatures of the Wasteland turned out to be burrowers, and they had tunnels running below the ground all over that ravine where the fighting was going on. Then, without any warning at all, my brother's little boy blew the tops off of a couple of dormant volcanos at the head of the ravine, and a wave of molten rock came pouring down the ravine—

and through all the burrows where the bug-people were hiding. I don't think we'd have won that war without that Dream, but I go cold all over just thinking about it."

"How hot a fire does it take to melt rock?"

"Probably about a thousand times hotter than any fire *you've* ever seen, Tlantar. The bug-people hiding in those burrows turned into puffs of smoke when the molten rock went boiling on down the ravine, and the little river that followed that ravine turned into steam, and it's not there anymore. Has Ashad told you about *his* Dream?"

"He's been pretty much staying in your cave, Dahlaine. We don't bother him when he's in there—except to make sure that he's got enough food."

"I appreciate that, Tlantar. Sometimes I forget that he has to eat real food. Anyway, the last time I came home, he told me that he'd been dreaming about my brother Veltan's Domain, and it's beginning to look like things are getting a bit more complicated. Ashad's Dream strongly suggests that there'll be *two* invasions of the South instead of just the one we met in Zelana's Domain."

"Two different kinds of bugs, you mean?"

Dahlaine shook his head. "The way Ashad described it, the second invasion involved people rather than bugs, and they came here to the Land of Dhrall in boats from somewhere off to the south of Veltan's Domain. Anyway, Zelana offered more gold to the Maags if they'd sail on down to help the Trogites Veltan had hired to fight off the creatures of the Wasteland, and then she sent many of her own people on down there to help as well."

"Then it's not very likely that *we'll* be invaded before autumn, is it?" Tlantar asked. "That might work better for us here in the North. I've had the men of the various tribes practicing with their spear-throwers, but most of them can't get the distance we'll probably need. They'll get better, I'm sure, but it's going to take them a while. If we're lucky, the war in the South will last longer than the other one did. I don't think *anything* will move once the snow starts."

"We'll see, Tlantar, but keep your men practicing—even after the snow flies. The better they get with their spear-throwers, the more chance we'll all have of living long enough to see next summer."

Dahlaine seldom returned to his Domain during the war in his brother's part of the Land of Dhrall, and Tlantar had a distinct feeling that things were not going as well as Dahlaine had hoped they would, but along toward the end of summer Dahlaine came crashing home on his pet thunderbolt, and he seemed to be greatly relieved—but deeply puzzled at the same time. "We won the war in the South, Tlantar," he said, "but I haven't the faintest idea of how. Somebody—or, for all I know, some thing—stepped in when everything was starting to fall apart on us, and that whatever or whoever it was started to do things that I didn't even understand. As Ashad's dream had told us, there *were* two invasions, but what Longbow called 'our unknown friend' instructed us to just step aside. Then she—we're all positive that 'unknown friend' is a woman—started to do some unbelievable things that pitted our two enemies against each other in what *I'd* call a war of mutual extinction. Then, just when things were starting to get interesting, she moved a geyser that'd been spouting from the same place for almost twenty-five thousand years about five miles to the north of its original home and swept away *both* of our enemies at the same time. Her geyser produced a lake that's getting bigger every day and will permanently block off any possible new incursions into Veltan's Domain by the creatures of the Wasteland. The way things stand right now, we've won two wars—or had them won for us—and we have no idea of which way the creatures of the Wasteland will come next. All we know for sure is that fire and water have blocked off the West and the South. We haven't a clue about where the creatures of the Wasteland will come next or what we'll use to stop them."

"Probably earth and air, Dahlaine," Tlantar suggested. "There *are* only four elements, and we've got two that haven't been used yet."

"Interesting notion," Dahlaine said. "Anyway, we've split up the armies Zelana and Veltan hired. The Maags are coming here, and the Trogites are going east to protect sister Aracia's Domain."

"Why not the other way around?" Tlantar asked curiously.

"Maag ships move much faster than the Trogite ships can move, and this part of the Land of Dhrall is much farther away from Veltan's Domain than Aracia's is. There'll be another fleet coming here a bit later, and that's the one that's going to bring the soldiers that *I* hired up here. I think just about everybody here—the Tonthakans, the Atazakans, and you Matans—are going to be very surprised when the Malavi get here. They have animals called horses that carry them to wherever they want to go, and the Malavi ride those animals into wars as well. Horses can run about four times faster than men can, so the Malavi strike fast and then fall back. Then they strike again. They cut their enemies all to pieces, and their enemies can't even protect themselves, because the Malavi move so fast."

"I'm glad they'll be on our side whenever the war comes here, Dahlaine," Tlantar said fervently. "There's one thing I've been meaning to ask you, though. How did you and your brother and sisters persuade these outlanders to come here and fight our wars for us?"

Dahlaine shrugged. "We offered them gold, Tlantar, and the outlanders will do *anything* for gold."

"I've seen it a few times," Tlantar said. "Isn't it awfully soft to make tools from?"

"The outlanders call it money, Tlantar, and they'll do *anything* if you offer them enough of it."

"These outlanders are very strange, aren't they?"

"Indeed they are, Tlantar. They think that *we're* the strange ones, though."

Autumn came just a bit later than was usual that year, and Tlantar ordered the tribes to the south of Asmie to continue practicing with their spear-throwers.

Dahlaine had sent word that the outlanders known as the Maags had reached the Tonthakan Nation and that they'd soon be coming overland to Mount Shrak, and Tlantar's curiosity about these strangers grew with every passing day.

It was on a cloudy day in early autumn that a messenger from one of the northern Matan tribes came down to Mount Shrak, and he seemed to desperately want to speak with Dahlaine.

"He's over in the Tonthakan Nation right now," Tlantar told the messenger. "I *might* be able to get word to him, but he can be just a little hard to find sometimes. What seems to be the problem?"

"It goes quite a ways past 'seems,' Chief Two-Hands," the messenger replied. "There's been an outbreak of some kind of new disease up north, and it's like no other disease we've ever seen. Our healers are baffled. I think that what bothers them the most is the speed of this particular ailment. A man can be perfectly healthy at breakfast, but he's dead before lunchtime. Just about everybody up north is afraid to go near anybody else. They've started to go on out into the meadows and set up individual camps, and they threaten anybody who comes near their camp. The tribes are coming apart because nobody wants to have anything to do with anybody else."

"I'll do what I can to get word of this to Dahlaine," Tlantar said. Then he squinted at the messenger. "Have *you* been anywhere near any of the sick people?" he asked.

The messenger shuddered. "I've got much better sense than that, Chief Two-Hands," he said. "Up north, we don't even talk to each other anymore. We yell instead, because nobody wants to get anywhere closer to anybody else than about a hundred paces. The only *good* thing about this particular ailment is that anybody who comes down with it doesn't live long enough to pass it on to others. A solitary life makes a man sort of lonely, but lonely's better than dead, wouldn't you say?"

The outlanders and what appeared to be most of the Tonthakan Nation arrived at Mount Shrak a couple days later, and Dahlaine came down to Asmie to speak with Tlantar. "The Maags and Tonthakans are getting along together fairly well," he said. "I think we should let them get settled in before *too* many members of your tribe come up to the cave. Sometimes people who don't know each other don't get along too well right at first. I'll need *you* there, of course, but let's ease the others of your tribe into contact with the outlanders and Tonthakans rather slowly. Oh, there's something else, too. Tell your womenfolk to avoid any contact with the Maags. The presence of women seems to bring out the worst in the Maags for some reason."

"That tends to crop up every so often, Dahlaine," Tlantar said with a faint smile, taking up his spear and spear-thrower.

"I think *you* should come back with me to my cave, though. There are several people I want you to meet, and you'll need to explain the spear-thrower to them. They understand bows quite well, but most of them have never seen a bison up close, so I'm quite sure they won't understand just exactly why you need such a heavy spear-point when you go to the hunt."

"I think my cloak might show them why," Tlantar replied. "When they see how thick and shaggy bison hide is, they'll probably understand why arrows are too light."

"Good point, Chief Two-Hands," Dahlaine agreed. "Shall we go?"

They went around the rocky base of Mount Shrak, and Tlantar was startled by how many outlanders and Tonthakan deer hunters were encamped on the broad plain stretching out from the foot of Dahlaine's home. The camp seemed to go out for miles.

There were several strangers gathered around the mouth of Dahlaine's cave. Tlantar recognized the Tonthakans, of course, since they were all wearing their traditional deerskin shirts, but there were several others as well, and their clothes seemed more than a little peculiar. Tlantar was much more impressed by their size, however. These outlanders appeared to Tlantar to be perhaps the biggest people in the world.

"This is Chief Tlantar of the Matakan Nation," Dahlaine told the strangers. "Some of you may find his weapon of choice just a bit peculiar, but it was designed to kill a very large animal with thick skin and dense fur. When the creatures of the Wasteland attack us, *some* of them might have very thick skin—or even those protective shells that caused so much trouble down in Veltan's Domain. I'm quite sure that the Matan spear will solve that problem—particularly if Captain Hook-Beak's clever smith can make metal spearheads for the Matans."

Then Dahlaine introduced Tlantar to his beautiful sister Zelana and his youthful-looking brother Veltan.

Then a burly outlander with a broken nose came up to Tlantar. "Have the bug-people been snooping around up here yet?" he asked.

"Bug-people?" Tlantar asked.

"Captain Hook-Beak has some very colorful names for the creatures of the Wasteland, Tlantar," Dahlaine explained. "*Some* of them are so colorful that he doesn't use them in the presence of my sister. The creatures of the Wasteland are descendants of a peculiar kind of insect, but the Vlagh has been modifying them to the point that they're not really insects anymore."

"Ah," Tlantar said. "If that's what's been happening, 'bug-people' sort of fits, I suppose." He turned to the big-shouldered outlander. "We haven't seen anything unusual down in the mountains, Captain Hook-Beak," he said. "We don't go down there very often, though. We hunt bison when we want meat, and the bison don't go down there. They eat grass, and there isn't very much grass in the mountains. I've asked the southern tribes to keep an eye on Crystal Gorge, but they tell me that they haven't seen anything unusual down there so far."

"It's probably too early, big brother," Zelana said. "It's a long, long way from Veltan's Domain up here to yours, and the Vlagh probably had to wait for her most recent hatch to mature before they could start."

"We know that there *have* been a few of the servants of the Vlagh roaming around up here," Dahlaine said. "There were at least two of them tampering with the Reindeer Tribes over in Tonthakan—up until Ox chopped them down with his axe, of course." Then he turned to Tlantar. "Have the members of any of the tribes here in southern Matakan been behaving peculiarly lately?" he asked.

"Not that I've heard about," Tlantar replied. "I don't snoop around in the other tribes, though. Some of the tribes aren't too happy about this 'unification' idea of yours, so I don't go around beating them over the head with it. I just tell their chieftains what I want their tribes to do, and then I walk away. I think 'unification' is going to take several genera- tions to settle in, so I try my best to avoid irritating—or offending—tribesmen who aren't ready for it yet."

"This one's a very good chief, Dahlaine," a tall bleak- faced man wearing deerskin clothes said. "The clever ones know when to back away; it's the silly ones who cause most of the trouble."

"I think you and Tlantar will get along very well, Long- bow," Dahlaine observed. "You're very much alike."

"So *you're* the one who came up with the idea of using parts of dead enemies to kill live ones," Tlantar said to the bleak-faced man.

The one called Longbow smiled faintly. "It wasn't my idea originally, Chief Tlantar," he replied. "The shaman of our tribe is called 'One-Who-Heals,' and *he's* the one who showed me how to put the venom of dead ones on my arrow-points so that I could kill live ones faster."

"Longbow here can kill more bug-men by accident than whole armies can kill on purpose," a small Maag declared, "and he got even better after I forged him metal arrowheads."

"Ah," Tlantar said, "you're the one Dahlaine told me about, then. He seems to think that metal spear-points might be better than the stone ones we've always used in the past."

Rabbit shrugged. "That's what they're paying me for," he said. "I'll need to see one of your spear-points before I set up shop, though. I'm quite sure that you'll want the weight and size to be close to what your original stone points are."

Tlantar nodded. "If the weight's *too* much different, the spear won't go where I want it to." He handed his spear to the little Maag.

"It *is* much bigger—and heavier—than an arrow," Rabbit said, "but the general shape's the same, so it shouldn't give me too many problems. Now, then, what's this 'spear-thrower' thing that everybody keeps talking about?"

Tlantar held up his thrower. "We set the butt of the spear in this cup-shaped part of the thrower at the end, and then we whip the thrower forward. It takes quite a long time to learn how to aim the spear when you're using the thrower, but once you've mastered that, you can whip the thrower forward, and the spear flies much faster—and harder—than it would if we just threw it with our hands. A faster spear hits harder, and it drives the spear-point in deeper."

"Does it *really* work?" Rabbit asked a bit dubiously.

"We don't go hungry very often," Tlantar replied.

*   *   *

"Dahlaine told me that you've been killing the creatures of the Wasteland for most of your life," Tlantar said to Longbow as they watched the little Maag known as Rabbit pound a piece of hot metal into a rough imitation of Tlantar's stone spear-point. "He didn't tell me exactly why, though. It's really none of my concern, so if you'd rather not talk about it, just forget that I said anything."

Longbow gave him a speculative look. "We'll be working together before very long, Tlantar," he said, "so we should know each other as well as possible, I suppose." He sighed then. "When I was very young, there was a girl that I knew, and we'd decided that we should mate. On the day of our joining, she went out into the forest to bathe herself in a pool of clear water. The bug-people had been creeping through the forest near our village, and I guess they didn't want us to know that they were there, so they killed her. Now I kill them." He smiled faintly. "Word of what I'd been doing reached Zelana, and she decided that I might be useful, so she came up to our village to ask me to help her when the creatures of the Wasteland invaded her Domain. I told her no, but then the little girl who'd come with her reached out and snared me before I even knew what she was doing. If you ever come up against that little girl, be very, very careful. First she charms you, and then she grabs you."

"He's got that right, Tlantar," Rabbit said. "If you're ever in her vicinity, try to keep some distance away from her. Some people will try to make you go along with them by using threats. Eleria uses kisses instead, and she wins all the time."

"I'd pay very close attention to what Rabbit just said, Tlantar," Longbow advised. "Eleria *always* gets what she wants. Anyway, she saw immediately that I wanted to kill as many of the servants of the Vlagh as I possibly could, and she suggested that the Maags could probably kill more than I could, even if I lived for a thousand years. Then she went on to tell me that we *might* even be able to kill the Vlagh, and that's all it took to persuade me to go along."

"Who's this Vlagh that everybody keeps talking about?" Tlantar asked.

Longbow looked a bit startled. "Hasn't Dahlaine ever told you about her?" he asked.

"Not in any great detail," Tlantar replied. "He mentions the name every now and then, and I sort of get the impression that he's talking about the chief of the Wasteland, but that's about as far as he's ever gone."

"That seems to crop up every now and then, doesn't it, Longbow?" Rabbit said.

Longbow muttered something under his breath and then looked inquiringly at Tlantar. "How much do you know about bees—or ants?" he asked.

"Not really very much," Tlantar replied. "I've heard that honey tastes good, but I've never tried it."

"I think you've got a long way to go, Longbow," Rabbit observed.

"Possibly so," Longbow agreed. "All right, then, Tlantar. You're familiar with bison, so you know about herd animals. In a certain sense, you might say that bees—and ants—are herd insects. Animals think for themselves to some degree, but in a herd of insects, the queen does all the thinking."

"Queen?"

"The bee—or ant—that lays eggs. She's the mother of all the others, and they'll do anything she tells them to do— even if it is impossible. They only live for about six weeks or so, but the queen—or mother—constantly replaces them. Even if we kill a million of them, there'll be another million coming toward us in about a week or so. The only way we'll ever win this war will be to hunt down the Vlagh—the mother of *all* the creatures—and kill *her*. In most ways, the Vlagh is just another variety of insect, but she experiments, and that makes her unique—and extremely dangerous. When she sees a characteristic that might be useful, she duplicates it. That's why we keep coming up against insects that look like people—or turtles, or spiders, or, for all I know, like bears or wolves."

"What's she after?" Tlantar asked. "I mean, what does she want that's making her come out of the Wasteland to attack us?"

"She wants the land, Two-Hands—all of it in the entire Land of Dhrall. If she has more land, her servants can grow more food, and if there's more to eat, she'll be able to lay more eggs. If she succeeds, it won't be long until the entire Land of Dhrall will be crawling with her children. Then she'll move on to other parts of the world and take them as well. If she gets what she wants, it won't be long before she'll have the whole world."

"What will she do with the people?"

"Eat them, probably," Longbow replied with a shrug.

"We were closer, I think, than any other pair in the village," Tlantar told them in a sorrowful voice. "Tleri wasn't at all like the other women of our village. She did her own hunting, and that's most unusual here in Dahlaine's part of the Land of Dhrall. She hunted very well, and she cooked food even better. Then she died in childbirth, and I was alone again. The village elders told me that I should find a new mate, but I refused. Tleri had been my true mate, and I won't offend her spirit by joining with some other woman. That part of my life died with her, so I'll go on alone from now on."

"I think that you and I will be friends, Tlantar," Longbow said with a grave look on his face. "I've been gathering friends quite often lately, for some reason. Being alone is nice enough, I suppose, but you don't have anybody to talk with when you're alone."

"You know, I've noticed that myself on occasion," Tlantar replied. "Isn't it odd that we've both made this peculiar discovery?" Then he looked at the little Maag called Rabbit. "Him too?" he asked Longbow.

"We might as well," Longbow agreed. "He can be very useful every now and then, and he can be very funny when you need to laugh."

T lantar didn't entirely understand the astonishment of Dahlaine when Zelana returned and told him that the children called the Dreamers shared their Dreams with each other. If the children could *see* the future, they could almost certainly do many other impossible things as well.

Keselo the scholar seemed very disturbed by the reference to "a plague that is *not* a plague" that had come up in the children's recitation of the most recent Dream. "Are plagues really all that common in this part of the world?" he asked Tlantar when they'd all gathered in Dahlaine's map-chamber the following day.

"I've heard a few things about this new disease," Tlantar replied. "We have quite a few diseases roaming around here in Dahlaine's part of the world. Most of them are probably the same all over the world, and they're the diseases that children catch all the time. I came down with several of those when *I* was a child, and I'm still breathing. A runner came down here from north Matakan before you and your friends left Tonthakan, and from what he said, I'd say that the people up there are terrified by this ailment—*so* terrified that they won't let anybody, sick or well, get to within a hundred paces of them. I guess the thing that disturbs them the most is how fast this disease kills people. He told me that a man can be alive and well at breakfast time and stone cold dead when it's time for lunch."

"That *can't* be true, Chief Two-Hands," Keselo objected. "*No* disease moves *that* fast."

"You could go on up north and tell the dead that they aren't really dead, I suppose. I don't think they'll listen to you, though."

"Since the little girl's Dream mentioned this disease, wouldn't that suggest that the bug-people are behind it?" Rabbit said. "If one of the Dreamers warns us about something, it usually has something to do with a scheme of the bug-people."

"I think I'd better send some men up there to see if they can get some more details," Tlantar said then. "We'll need more information about this disease."

"If it really *is* a disease," Keselo added. "It *might* be something else entirely."

"Such as what?" Rabbit asked.

"Some kind of poison, I'd say," Keselo replied. "Diseases don't really kill that fast, but poisons of various kinds can kill much, much faster."

6

I don't think they'll believe you until you show them how well the spear-thrower works, Tlantar," Dahlaine said a few days later when they were alone in his map-chamber.

Tlantar shrugged. "I'll invite them to join us in a bison hunt then," he said. "Three or four dead bison should persuade them that we Matans know exactly what we're doing."

"Don't get any of our friends killed, though," Dahlaine cautioned. "All sorts of things will fall apart if something *that* disastrous happens."

"I *do* know what I'm doing, Dahlaine," Tlantar replied. "I've been taking bison for more than thirty years now, and they haven't killed me yet."

He went on outside Dahlaine's cave, and as luck had it, Longbow, Athlan, Keselo, and Rabbit were talking together just outside the mouth of the cave. "I think it's time for us to clear something up," he told the group of recent friends. "What are your feelings about a bit of hunting one of these days?"

"I'm *always* ready to go hunting," Athlan said, "but from what I've heard, my arrows might not work very well on the bison you've got wandering around out here in the grassland."

"They probably wouldn't," Tlantar agreed. "That's why I'm inviting you all to join the hunt. You'll need to see how effective the spear-thrower can be when the animal you want to kill is five or ten times as large as the deer you usually hunt. Until you see the spear-thrower kill several of our overgrown bison, you'll probably be troubled about our weapon. After you've seen what we can do, you'll probably sleep better."

"We'll probably sleep permanently if we happen to get trampled in one of those stampedes I've been hearing about," Rabbit said.

"I know of a safe place where you can stand and watch without being in any danger," Tlantar said then. "There's a rock-pile that juts up out of the meadow near a place where several bison herds go to get water. Bison run across grassland without any difficulty. Climbing up a steep pile of rocks wouldn't thrill them very much, though, and you'll be able to *see* everything, but you won't be in any danger."

"This is fairly important to you, isn't it, Two-Hands?" Longbow asked.

"I've always rather enjoyed teaching, friend Longbow," Tlantar replied with a broad grin. "This time I'll teach you and your friends not to worry so much. I'm sure you'll sleep better if you're not worrying."

"Tomorrow morning, then?" Longbow asked.

"Was there something wrong with right now? Bison graze all day, probably because there aren't any forests for them to hide in around here, so they'll be right out there in the open. Shall we go?"

The midmorning sky was cloudy when Tlantar led his recent friends down to Asmie to pick up several more hunters. Tlantar took that to be a good sign. Bison sometimes grew fidgety when the bright sun was shining down on them. He'd once seen a herd bolt and turn when the shadow of a passing hawk flickered over them on a bright, sunny day. Over the many years Tlantar had spent hunting, he'd come to realize that bison will stampede sometimes for the smallest of reasons—a flickering shadow, a tiny noise, or nothing more than a shimmer of light. On one occasion, however, he'd seen a herd calmly grazing in the middle of a thunderstorm that was shaking the very earth.

Word of the planned hunt had evidently been spreading around, and that didn't bother Tlantar at all. He was leading a group of the most experienced hunters in the village, so there wasn't much likelihood of any serious mistakes. Their friends were going to be watching what promised to be a very successful hunt, and once they reported what they'd seen, the worrying should come to an abrupt halt.

"We'll stop here," he said quietly when they reached the pile of rocks near the sizeable creek that ran on up out of the mountain range lying to the south of Dahlaine's part of the Land of Dhrall. "It might take you a while to climb up those rocks, but let's find out if there are any bison in the immediate vicinity. I sent out a couple runners a while back, and they should be coming back quite soon. The bison usually go to water about this time of day, so the hunting should be good."

"If you don't mind, I think I'd like to come with you,

Tlantar," Longbow said. He held up one hand when Tlantar started to object. "I think I'll need to see them up close," he said. Then he smiled. "Don't worry, friend Tlantar. I *do* know how to run if it's necessary, and I can run all day, if I really have to."

"Why are you suddenly so curious about these bison, Longbow?" Rabbit asked his friend.

Longbow shrugged. "You never really know when something might turn out to be very useful, Rabbit. From what I've heard, quite a few bison hunters are trampled to death by these stampedes every year up here in the North. When the creatures of the Wasteland invade this part of the Land of Dhrall, a stampede by a few thousand frightened bison could thin our enemies out quite noticeably, wouldn't you say? This *is* the native land of the bison, after all, so it's their duty to help ward off the enemies, isn't it?"

The young Trogite Keselo laughed. "Your mind is working all the time, Longbow. These bison might turn out to be almost as useful as those Church armies were during the war in Veltan's Domain. If it turns out like that, we could very well spend another war just getting out of the way, couldn't we?"

"The old ones are the best," Longbow agreed.

Then one of Tlantar's runners returned. "There's a large herd coming to the creek from the east, My Chief," he reported. "I'd say that they'll be watering in about a quarter of an hour."

"Good," Tlantar said. "Go on up to the top of this rockpile, my friends," he told Rabbit, Keselo, and Athlan. "You should be able to see everything from up there. Then, when we go back to Dahlaine's cave, you'll be able to tell everybody just how good a well-thrown spear can be. Maybe they'll all stop worrying so much then."

Tlantar stayed close to Longbow as the party of hunters crept quietly around the rocky outcrop. "Have you had much experience with crawling, Longbow?" he whispered.

"Some," Longbow quietly replied. "It's not usually necessary in the forest, though. The trees hide us when we're creeping up on a deer herd."

"We don't have that advantage here in the meadowland," Tlantar whispered. "Grass isn't as tall as trees are, so we spend a lot of time on our hands and knees when we're trying to get within range of a bison herd."

"How far will your thrower hurl a spear?"

"About a hundred paces is the limit. The spearhead has to be heavy enough to cut through the hair and hide of an adult bison, and that cuts down the range considerably. What's the outer range of your bow?"

"I've taken deer at 250 paces," Longbow replied in a soft voice. "Tell me, where do you aim when you whip your spear-thrower toward a bison? Do you try for his head?"

"No. The horns of a bison are very thick and hard. Aiming at a bison's head is a quick way to shatter a stone spearhead. This is my first hunt with a metal spearhead, so I might try for a head-shot just to see if it'll work."

"I'd wait until some other time, Two-Hands," Longbow whispered. "Right now, you're trying to impress people with the spear-thrower, so this wouldn't be a good time for experiments. Do it the old way for now."

"You're probably right," Tlantar softly agreed. He raised his head slowly and then sank back down. "About another twenty paces," he murmured. "Then I'll whistle, and we'll all stand up at the same time and run toward the bison."

"Run?"

"It adds speed to the spear if we're moving when we cast, and the extra speed can make all the difference."

"Ah. That makes sense, I guess."

They crept on through the tall grass, and then Tlantar slowly raised his head again. "Close enough," he muttered, and then he whistled.

The Matan spearmen rose up out of the grass in unison and started to run toward the bison who were drinking from the small stream. Then Tlantar gave another shrill whistle and the spearmen all launched their spears at the now-startled bison.

Several of the bison went down immediately, but a few of them staggered off quite a ways before they sank down into the grass. "I make it seven!" Tlantar cried out exultantly.

"Make that eight," Longbow said, drawing back his bow. When he released the arrow, his bowstring made an almost musical "twang." His arrow went straight and true and it struck a huge bison directly in the eye.

The bison dropped immediately.

"Did you do that on purpose?" Tlantar demanded in astonishment.

"Yes," Longbow replied almost indifferently. "He wasn't much more than seventy paces away, though, so it wasn't really all that difficult." His expression became just a bit apologetic. "Actually, friend Tlantar, it was an experiment of sorts. The bison's horns protect his head—and what's inside his head. The eye socket is an open path to the brain, though, so I thought it might be worth a try."

"That was just a lucky shot, Longbow," Tlantar said.

"Not really," Longbow disagreed. "I'm not certain that it'd work with your spear-thrower, but it works very well

when you use a bow. It's called 'unification,' friend
Tlantar. The archer must unify his eyes, his hands, and his
bow with whatever he wants to hit. If he does it right, he'll
never miss." Then he laughed. "Back when Rabbit had set
up his arrow factory in Lattash, there was a smith called
Hammer who thought that we were just wasting time and
metal. I handed him a clamshell and told him to walk down
the beach holding the clamshell up over his head. He was
250 paces on down the beach when I smashed that shell
right out of his hand. He didn't argue with us anymore
after that."

"How very peculiar," Tlantar said. And then he laughed.
"Do you think that concept might work with a spear-thrower
instead of a bow?" he asked quite seriously.

"We might want to give it a try, I suppose," Longbow
replied a bit dubiously. "You'd have to include several other
things in your unification, though, so it might be quite a bit
more complicated. We can try it and see what happens, I
guess, but I won't make any promises."

"This must be the place," a bulky fellow with a long, red
beard who was sitting on the back of a fairly large animal
said as he pulled back on the straps that appeared to be attached to the animal's mouth to make it stop walking.

"It was the last time I looked," Longbow said. "Is that animal you're sitting on one of those horses Ekial kept talking
about?"

"No, Longbow, he's just a cow who lost his horns."

"Very funny, Red-Beard," Longbow said in a flat voice.
Red-Beard looked over his shoulder at several other men
who sat on animals and were approaching. "Here comes
Ekial now," he said. "You might want to send word to

Dahlaine that we're here. Have the bug-people arrived yet?"

"Not their armies. The Vlagh has sent out its usual snoopers, though." Longbow put his hand on Tlantar's shoulder. "This is Chief Tlantar of the Matans. The Matans hunt bison rather than deer, and they use spears instead of arrows, since arrows aren't heavy enough to penetrate the skin of the bison."

"I'm honored to meet you, Chief Tlantar," Red-Beard said rather formally.

Then Dahlaine and several others came out of the mouth of the cave and Dahlaine spoke briefly with his younger brother.

"She did *what*?" Dahlaine's brother burst out.

Then their sister gave him a brief recounting of events in the Domain of their other sister. Tlantar didn't entirely understand the astonishment of Veltan when Zelana told him that the children called the Dreamers shared their Dreams with each other. If the children could *see* the future, they could almost certainly do other impossible things as well. The young fellow seemed to be profoundly disturbed by his older sister's behavior. Tlantar, on occasion, had noticed that even Dahlaine, the eldest of the gods, could be very startled when he discovered that someone was trying to deceive him. There were times when it seemed to Tlantar that the four gods of the Land of Dhrall were almost themselves as innocent as children.

After Veltan had regained his composure, he introduced Ariga and several of the other Malavi to the people who'd been living in Dahlaine's cave, and then various horsemen quite proudly demonstrated the capabilities of their animals, and they seemed to take a great deal of pleasure in the astonishment their demonstrating caused. Tlantar immediately saw how valuable the horsemen were likely to be in the upcoming war, but "showing off" seemed to Tlantar to be just a bit childish. Childishness of one kind or another kept cropping up lately, for some reason. Tlantar sighed. "Oh, well," he murmured, "if it makes them happy, I suppose I can live with it." Then he saw that the beautiful mate of the farmer Omago was looking at him with an amused sort of expression.

And then she rather slyly winked at him.

7

Early the next morning one of the men Tlantar had sent north came down to Mount Shrak with a northern tribe member called Tlorak. "This one's head seems to still be working, Chief Two-Hands," Tlantar's man said. "Most of the people up there are too afraid to even talk to me."

"It's that cursed pestilence, Chief Two-Hands," the young Tlorak declared. "Everybody's so afraid of everybody else that we can't even hold back those nitwits from Atazakan."

"You can still talk to each other, can't you?" Tlantar asked the excited young man, "even if you have to shout? Your spear-throwers can drop spears a hundred paces away. You and your friends don't have to be standing right next to each other, you know. You can stay some distance apart from each other and still be effective. You can avoid infection—if that's what it really is—and hold off the Atazakans at the same time. Just be sure that you're close enough to each other that the range of your spear overlaps those of your friends."

"We should have thought of that ourselves, Chief Two-Hands," Tlorak said rather sheepishly. "That cursed plague's got us all so frightened that our minds don't seem to work anymore."

"There's a young Trogite who works for Dahlaine's younger brother who doesn't believe that what's been killing people in the northern tribes *is* a disease. He knows a great deal about diseases, and he swears up and down that *no* disease can kill a man in just a half day. He says that diseases can't move that fast."

"What's killing our people, then?"

"The Trogite thinks that it's a poison of some kind. If the Atazaks have been sneaking around poisoning wells and ponds, everybody who takes a drink of water will die. I think that might come very close to what's *really* been happening up there. I'd say that you should tell your chief about that. If he sets men to guarding the wells, springs, and ponds up there, your people will probably stop dying."

The face of the young Matan from the north went bleak at that point. "If that Trogite's come up with what's *really* going on up there, I think that it might lead to the extinction of the Atazaks, Chief Tlantar," he declared. "When word of that gets out, it'll start raining spears over in Atazakan like a spring thunder-shower. We'll empty that part of Dahlaine's Domain in about a month."

Tlantar shrugged. "Whatever seems right and proper to your chief, my young friend," he said. "That's *his* business, not mine."

A few days later the Maags went on down into the southern mountains to begin work on what they called a "fort." Tlantar wasn't exactly sure what was involved, so he went looking for Longbow.

"The Trogites are the experts when it comes to building

forts," the tall archer explained. "The Maags are going down to Crystal Gorge to lay down a base. Then, when Narasan and his army arrive, they'll go on down there and build what's very much like a straight-up-and-down wall made of rocks. The wall will block off the gorge, and the creatures of the Wasteland won't be able to come any farther north."

"Does that really work?" Tlantar asked dubiously.

"It has in the last two wars," Longbow replied, "at least partially. During the first war, the bugs had burrows that came out in the ravine *behind* the fort. Then, in the war to the south, we had a very nice fort, but we were told to abandon it. In *that* war, we had two enemies instead of just one, and they were busy killing each other right up until a wall of water came blasting out of what *looked* like solid rock and washed *both* of our enemies away."

"From what you just told me, it doesn't sound like those forts are really all that useful, Longbow," Tlantar said. "Your enemies got behind you during the first war, and you abandoned the fort in the second one."

"Exactly," Longbow said. "When you get right down to the bottom, friend Tlantar, those forts were really nothing but deceptions. Our enemies from the Wasteland were certain that the forts were our only defense, and that kept them looking at the forts instead of paying attention to what was *really* going on. You don't need to spread this around very much, Two-Hands, but we have a friend out there who can do things that none of our gods can even *think* of doing. This friend can make mountains explode or bring whole oceans up out of the earth itself."

"Why do we need all these outlander armies, then?"

"We don't, really," Longbow replied. "I think our friend out there wants to have the outlander armies here to see just how powerful she really is. The outlanders roam the world looking for gold, and there are huge deposits of gold here in the Land of Dhrall. After the outlanders who are here see what our unknown friend can do to people who irritate her, they'll go on back home and warn all their friends to stay away from the Land of Dhrall, because if they come here, they'll surely die before they can find even one speck of gold."

"Just who *is* this unknown friend, Longbow?"

"I'm not really sure, Chief Tlantar, but I wouldn't advise getting in her way."

It was several days later when the Trogite army arrived at Mount Shrak, and it took Tlantar a while to get used to having people around who wore metal clothes.

After they'd all been introduced to each other, they went on into Dahlaine's cave under Mount Shrak and gathered in what Dahlaine called his "war-room." The outlanders carefully examined the miniaturized replica of Crystal Gorge and generally agreed that it was, indeed, defendable. "Once we have a fort in place, they won't get past us," the silver-haired Trogite commander declared.

Tlantar was still just a bit dubious about that, though. Longbow's assessment of the two previous wars strongly suggested that the forts were only for show.

Then, as Tlantar had been certain it would, the question of the pestilence came up, and Tlantar told them as much as he'd picked up so far. "It was causing the northern tribes some fairly serious problems," he continued. "The people up there were afraid to go near anybody else, so they were spread out to the point that they couldn't defend the tribal lands—even from the incompetent Atazaks. I advised them to stay far enough away from each other to avoid the disease, but to get close enough that the range of their spears overlapped. They'll still be safe from this pestilence, but they'll be able to obliterate the invaders from Atazakan."

"Did it work?" the Trogite called Padan asked.

"It should have," Tlantar replied. "I haven't received any verification from the northern tribes yet, though."

After some extended discussion, the pretty wife of the southern farmer called Omago suggested that one of the gods could pick up the body of one of the men of northern Matan and carry it on down to Zelana's Domain where an old shaman who was an expert on the peculiarities of the creatures of the Wasteland could examine the remains and determine exactly what had killed him.

Dahlaine looked just a bit sheepish when he agreed that the lady's suggestion was probably the best answer to the problem.

When Zelana, Veltan, and Longbow returned from the western region of the Land of Dhrall, they advised Dahlaine and the rest of them that the aged shaman of Longbow's tribe had found traces of snake-venom in the nose of the dead Matan, and that, of course, explained "the plague that is not a plague" that had so baffled everybody.

The farmer Omago suggested wet cloth as a protection, but Tlantar was more than a little dubious about that. He was fairly sure that *some* of the venom mist would penetrate almost anything they could use to protect themselves, and many of them would die if they were foolish enough to try the "wet cloth" form of protection. Dahlaine staunchly refused to even consider changing the direction of the wind to blow the venom back into the faces of the Atazaks and their insect allies, reminding Veltan and Zelana that they were strictly forbidden to use their almost unlimited power to cause the death of even their most dangerous enemies.

Finally, Longbow raised the distinct possibility that the "unknown friend" he'd mentioned to Tlantar probably could—and *would*—use *her* power to throw the venomous mist back onto the faces of their enemies.

"But how are we going to get word to her?" Veltan protested.

"I'm fairly sure that she knows already, Veltan," Longbow replied with a shrug. "I don't think that there's very much of *anything* that she doesn't know about when you get right down to it."

Then Tlantar saw the warrior queen Trenicia staring with obvious astonishment at the pretty wife of the farmer Omago. The pretty lady smiled, but she didn't say anything.

It was probably a slight change in the light in Dahlaine's cave that made the pretty lady's face look somewhat older and stouter, but quite suddenly, Tlantar recognized her, and hers was a face that Tlantar would never forget, despite the fact that the last time he'd seen her had been twenty-five years ago. She now appeared younger and more slender, but Tlantar was positive that she had been the one who'd tried very hard to save Tleri on that awful night a quarter of a century ago.

Tlantar began to tremble violently as confusion came crashing down on him.

THE
DEPARTURE
OF
AZAKAN

1

Longbow had set up a small camp not far from the village of Asmie late in the afternoon of the day when Narasan's army reached Mount Shrak. The people in the cave were all his friends, of course, but Longbow's years of solitude in the mountains of Zelana's Domain had made it almost impossible for him to sleep when there were other people around.

The stars were better company anyway. They were very beautiful, and they almost never snored.

He awoke at first light on the morning after Narasan's army arrived and went on back inside the cave. He followed the long, twisting passageway to the large central chamber.

Ara, the beautiful wife of Omago, was cooking breakfast there, and Longbow saw that she had added several modifications to the rudimentary stove Dahlaine had put together after the arrival of the little boy, Ashad. Longbow saw that Ara's stove was primarily a cluster of ovens—some almost right down in the fire and others farther away. Evidently, some varieties of food needed more heat than others did when they were cooking. Since Ara knew more about the preparation of food than anyone else did, Longbow was quite certain that her various ovens were exactly as hot as they needed to be. Longbow had never thought of cooking food as an art form, but Ara obviously did, and she knew just exactly what she was doing.

Eleria was seated at the table, watching with great interest. "Where have you been, Longbow?" Zelana's little girl asked.

"Visiting the Land of Dreams," he replied with a faint smile.

"Really? Did anything interesting happen while you were there?"

"It's possible, I suppose, but I was busy sleeping, so if anything unusual happened, I missed it."

"That's not very funny, Longbow," Eleria scolded.

"So beat me."

"I think you've been spending too much time with Red-Beard lately. You're starting to sound just like him, and he's not nearly as funny as he seems to think he is."

Longbow shrugged. "Nobody's perfect. Do you want to get the 'kiss-kiss' out of the way now, or would you rather wait until *after* breakfast?"

"Let's do it both before *and* after, Longbow. You owe me a lot of kisses after that 'beat me' remark."

"Does this happen very often, Longbow?" Ara asked curiously.

"All the time," Longbow replied. "Eleria *loves* kisses, and if you spend too much time in her vicinity, she'll wear out your lips."

Ara smiled. "I sort of doubt that. As soon as you two have finished your little 'kiss-kiss' ceremony, why don't you go wake the others. Breakfast is almost ready, so get our friends up and moving before it gets cold."

Despite the fact that Dahlaine's cave under Mount Shrak was extensive, the passageway that led from the cave mouth to the central chambers was narrow, and it twisted through the solid rock almost like a snake. There were also several branch passages that wandered off into the mountain, but didn't really go anywhere. Given these peculiarities, Dahlaine had decided that only the leaders—and their best advisors—should camp inside the cave. The rest of the forces should camp outside. "We could end up losing half of all the men we've brought here," Sorgan Hook-Beak agreed. "A tunnel that wanders around for ten miles or so but doesn't really go anyplace could draw off soldiers by the hundreds, and we'd never see them again."

"Well put, Captain Sorgan," Commander Narasan said.

After breakfast that morning they all returned to the place Dahlaine called "the war-chamber" to continue their study of Dahlaine's map of the North country.

It was almost noon when a northern Matan named Tladak came into the map-room looking for Chief Two-Hands. "I could be wrong about this, Tlantar," he said, "but it looks to me like the entire population of Atazakan is involved in this invasion. There are all those ones who call themselves 'The Guardians of Divinity,' of course, but there are others as well—including large numbers of women and children. That's what's giving us a lot of trouble. We don't really want to throw our spears at the innocents, but the dreadfully brave 'Guardians of Divinity' are hiding behind them."

"Did you happen to notice any very small ones that seem to be unusually pale?" Keselo asked the northern Matan.

"Oh, yes," Tladak replied. "There are hundreds of those. They don't look much like ordinary Atazaks, though."

"They aren't," Keselo said. "They're the ones responsible for this 'unknown pestilence.' They're venomous—like certain varieties of snakes—and they're spitting venom up into the air so that the wind from the east can carry it in your direction. If you're unlucky enough to breathe it in, you'll be poisoned, and you'll die."

Tladak turned to Dahlaine. "Isn't there some way you could put a stop to that?" he demanded.

"We're working on it, Tladak. For right now, though, tell your friends to avoid the Atazaks and their little friends. We haven't yet found a way to deal with this 'venom riding the wind' problem."

Then Longbow's little friend Rabbit snapped his fingers. "I *knew* that we were overlooking something!" he exclaimed.

"We've been over it a dozen times, Rabbit," Longbow said. "I'm sure that we've covered everything."

"Not quite *everything*, Longbow," Rabbit disagreed with a broad grin. "Reversing the wind and blowing the venom back into the faces of the Atazaks and their little friends might have worked out very well, except that Dahlaine and Veltan and Zelana aren't permitted to kill *anything*—not even enemies who are trying to kill *them*. If it's the *wind* that's our problem, why not just shut it down? The venom won't go *anyplace* if the wind isn't blowing, so all Dahlaine has to do is to stop the wind." He looked at Dahlaine. "You *can* do that, can't you? If you just tell the wind to stop blowing, you won't be using it to kill your enemies—even the ones trying to kill you. All you'll really be doing will be calming everything down."

Dahlaine blinked, and then an embarrassed expression came over his face.

"Were there any other problems you can't solve, big brother?" Zelana asked with a sly little grin. "If there are, just let us know, and we'll be more than happy to take care of them for you."

"I should have thought of this myself," Dahlaine ruefully said to his brother Veltan. "I'd say that Aracia's not the only one of us whose mind's shutting down."

"That's why we all went out and hired outlanders to help us, big brother," Veltan replied. "They do our thinking for us. Life's much more pleasing when you don't have to spend all of your time thinking."

They all followed Dahlaine out through the long, twisting passageway to the outside. There was a fairly stiff wind coming in from the east, but when Dahlaine raised his hand, the wind died immediately.

Veltan frowned. "I don't want to offend you, big brother," he said, "but won't shutting down the wind interfere with the seasons?"

"I doubt it," Dahlaine replied. "I didn't actually shut the wind off. All I did was reach back ten miles or so and divert it. The wind's still blowing, but it's not coming this way anymore. We only need a dead calm where the creatures of the Wasteland are standing when they start spitting venom up into the air. The wind can blow all it wants to every place else."

Sorgan Hook-Beak scratched his chin. "It's likely to take those silly snake-men a while to realize that the wind isn't there to help them anymore, wouldn't you say?"

Dahlaine shrugged. "It's possible, I suppose. Where are you going with this, Sorgan?"

"If they spit their venom straight up into the air and the wind's not blowing, it'll settle back down on top of them, won't it? Would that break any of the rules that you're not supposed to violate?"

Dahlaine smiled broadly. "None that I can think of. If they're foolish enough to poison themselves, that's not *my* responsibility." Then he looked at Rabbit. "Don't let this little man get away, Sorgan. He's one of the most valuable people we've got working for us."

Commander Narasan was frowning slightly as he looked at Chief Tlantar. "I'm not trying to be inquisitive or anything," he said, "but how did you get 'Two-Hands' attached to your name?"

Tlantar shrugged. "Back when I was a beginner learning how to use the spear-thrower, our instructor got all worked up because I could use either hand when I wanted to throw a spear. After I showed him that I couldn't miss with either hand, he started calling me 'Two-Hands,' and before very long, just about everybody in the tribe started to call me 'Tlantar Two-Hands,' as if it was a miracle of some kind. Actually, it's always seemed peculiar to me that other people favor one hand or the other."

Narasan looked at Keselo. "Have you ever heard of anything like this?" he asked.

Keselo nodded. "I had a teacher at the university who could write with either hand—or with both hands at the same time when he wanted to show off. He told us that it was quite rare. Most people favor one hand over the other—right or left—but people who don't know the difference don't come along very often." Then he looked curiously at Tlantar. "Have you ever noticed any difference, Chief Tlantar?" he asked. "I mean, will your spear go farther if you throw it with your right hand instead of the left?"

Tlantar shook his head. "They're pretty much the same," he replied. "Sometimes the spear I throw with my right hand will go a few feet farther than the one I throw with my left, but on other days, the left one goes farther. It might depend on which side I slept on the previous night."

"You're a very rare man, Chief Tlantar," Narasan said. "How much do you know about the people of Atazakan? Are they very good warriors?"

Tlantar laughed. "I wouldn't really call them 'warriors,' Commander Narasan," he said rather scornfully. "The only people allowed to carry weapons of any kind are 'The Guardians of Divinity.' Those are the lazy ones who go around threatening the ordinary people if they don't bow down quite far enough when 'Holy Azakan' walks by. They have spears, but they don't really know how to use them. They haven't moved much past poke-poke-jab. As far as I know, they've never been involved in a war of any kind, so I'd say they don't know what they're doing."

"Is there some reason that they have only spears?" Narasan asked.

"I've heard that 'Holy Azakan' has put a lot of limits on his people. He's a madman who believes that he controls the entire universe, and he spends most of his time inventing rules that don't make any sense." Tlantar laughed then. "If I understood what actually happened, he sprained his ankle once, and all the people of Atazakan had to walk with a limp for about six months, since the 'Guardians of Divinity' threatened to kill anybody who wasn't limping."

"Why do his people put up with that?" the Trogite called Padan demanded. "Why don't they just lock him away someplace, or just go ahead and kill him?"

"Probably because the first thing he did when he was crowned emperor, king, god—or whatever—was to hire hundreds of men to protect him. That was a golden opportunity for men who wanted to be important, but *didn't* want to do anything the least bit strenuous."

"That sounds a bit familiar, doesn't it, Narasan?" the warrior queen Trenicia said. "That fat priest Bersla down in Aracia's temple made a career out of talking, but not doing anything else—except eating, of course."

"There *are* a few ugly similarities here, aren't there?" Veltan suggested with a wry smile.

"We could probably send a fair number of Matans up to the north to deal with this," Keselo observed, "but wouldn't it be better to send small contingents from every army we have on up there to stamp out this idiocy? Our main battle will be in Crystal Gorge. We *don't* want to get so involved in the Atazak invasion that we lose sight of that, and we *don't* want to come up short of archers, spearmen, or horse-warriors when the *real* war starts."

"He's got a point, Narasan," Sorgan Hook-Beak said. "Then, too, if we send members of every group up there, they'll learn how to work together, in ways that might not occur to us when the snake-men come charging up that gorge. Then, after they've whomped the Atazaks, they can come back down here and tell us what works and what doesn't."

"That makes very good sense, Sorgan," Narasan told his friend. "You're getting better at fighting land wars every time we move to some other part of the Land of Dhrall. You're starting to think like a real professional."

2

Longbow spoke quietly with those who'd be joining him in the trek to the north. "We'd just be in the way here in Dahlaine's map-room," he told them, "and I think more clearly out in the open anyway."

"I'll float my stick with yours there," the scar-faced horse-soldier Ekial agreed. "There's something about having walls all around me that seems to make it impossible for me to think."

"Let's all go outside, then," Longbow said.

They trooped through the winding passageway to the mouth of Dahlaine's cave.

"That's better," Longbow said, looking out over the vast, empty meadowland. Then he turned to his longtime friend, Athlan. "Are there very many archers still in Tonthakan?" he asked.

Athlan frowned. "Most of the tribes are already here at Mount Shrak, and I don't think Dahlaine would be very happy if we filched some of *them* to go fight this second war. There *are* a fair number of tribes that live farther away, though. If I could get a messenger to those tribes, I might be able to divert them and bring them north to help us."

"I just happen to have a messenger handy who can move very fast," Longbow said, giving Red-Beard a sly sort of look.

"Somehow I knew that something like this would crop up," Red-Beard said with a gloomy sort of expression.

"You led the horse-soldiers here from the coast, Red-Beard," Longbow reminded his friend, "so you know the way. Athlan can tell you who to speak with and where you'll find them. Your horse, Seven, should get you there in a hurry. If you get word to the remaining tribes in Tonthakan and they come over the mountains, they'll probably reach northern Matakan at about the same time we will."

"All right, Longbow," Red-Beard replied. "You don't have to beat me over the head with it."

"About how many archers would you say are still in Ton-thakan?" Longbow asked Athlan.

"Six or eight thousand," Athlan replied. "That's just a guess, but it should come fairly close."

"If it's all right with you, Longbow, I think that after we get out a ways from Mount Shrak here, I'll take a hundred or so horsemen and go north," Ekial said. "We'll need the lay of the land, and we *really* need to know just how deep the Atazaks have penetrated into Matan territory. There's no real hurry, of course. We can move much faster than your people can. *If* Dahlaine can keep the wind away, I don't think there'll be much danger for us."

"Are you sure that Dahlaine will hold still for that?" Padan asked. "If I understood it correctly, he hired *you* to fight off the bug-people."

"All that's going on down there for right now is building

a fort. There'll be scouts on horseback riding out to watch for the enemy, and Ariga can take care of that. Right now, this invasion by the Atazaks is more important. We need to stop them before they come south. We *don't* want them coming at us from the rear when we're busy holding off the creatures of the Wasteland, now do we?"

"It *does* make sense, I guess," Padan admitted. Then he gave Ekial an inquiring sort of look. "I'm not at all familiar with your people," he said. "What sort of weapons are most effective when you're riding a horse?"

"We've found that lances work fairly well," Ekial replied. "That's a weapon that's very much like what you Trogites and your friends, the Maags, called a 'spear' during that war down to the south. A lance is about twenty feet long. We started using those a long time ago—except that they weren't actually weapons back then. They were just long poles with padding wrapped around the end. We used them to push cows around so that they'd go in the direction we wanted to go. It was about fifty years or so ago when somebody came up with the idea of using an iron point instead of padding. It works fairly well at a distance, but when we get in closer, we use our sabres instead."

"A sword, you mean?"

"A sabre's not exactly what you Trogites would call a 'sword,' Padan. Your swords are thick and strong and straight. The Malavi sabre is longer, and it's curved. It's made to slash, not to stab—mostly because we're moving when we use it. 'Stab' might work quite well if you're standing still, but if you're moving fast—like on horseback— 'stab's' not a very good idea. There's a fair chance that your sabre might get tangled up in your enemy's innards or caught between a couple of his ribs. If something like that happened when you're riding fast, it could jerk your sabre right out of your hand."

"That *does* make sense, I suppose," Padan conceded.

Then Ekial turned to look at Longbow. "Just how far to the north of here is this invasion from Atazakan coming across the line?"

"Dahlaine's map indicates about ninety miles," Longbow replied. He looked at Tlantar Two-Hands. "Is that at all close to being right?" he asked.

"Pretty close, yes," Tlantar replied.

"My party of horsemen should cover that in about two days," Ekial said, "so we won't have to go north for a day or so. When we get up there, we'll have a look around, and then I'll send a man down to meet you and pass on what we've seen."

"I'll let Dahlaine know that you'll be going on ahead, Ekial," Longbow said. "We want to be sure that he's shut the wind down *before* you and your men reach northern Matakan."

"Not a bad idea, Longbow." Then Ekial grinned. "If there's no wind blowing up there, my men and I might make a few charges in the direction of the Atazaks. If we can excite the venom-spitters, they *might* just eliminate about half of our enemies up there, and we won't even have to draw our sabres."

"How many men do you think Narasan will let us have?" Longbow asked Padan then.

"I'll suggest ten cohorts," Padan replied. "If Rabbit's idea of stopping the wind works like it should, we won't have any venom raining down on us, so ten cohorts should be enough. Are we going to take some Maags along as well?"

"Probably so. Sorgan's idea of mixing people together

during this little unpleasant mess to the north makes good sense. We've come up with quite a few useful ideas working that way during the past two wars, and there's no reason to believe that it won't work this time as well. Oh, tell Sorgan and Narasan that we'll be taking Rabbit and Keselo with us. Between them, those two come up with very useful ideas every now and then."

Keselo was walking along beside Ekial, and Longbow, who was just ahead of them, could hear them speaking quite clearly.

"I've been wondering about something, Prince Ekial," Keselo said. "Have the Malavi ever used horses to carry things, or are they only for riding?"

"They started out as animals that carried things for us," Ekial replied. "Riding them came a bit later. Why do you ask?"

"As you probably noticed during the war in Veltan's Domain, we had a number of war-engines that turned out to be very useful. Unfortunately, they're very heavy, so it takes a lot of men to move them. I was thinking about that here recently. This grassland is fairly level, so if we were to cobble some sleds together and mount the war-engines on them, your horses could probably pull those sleds along quite smoothly—and quite a bit faster than men could ever move them."

"You're talking about those catapult things that threw big gobs of liquid fire at the bug-people, aren't you?" Ekial asked. Then he grinned. "Dropping those gobs of fire on the Atazaks *would* make life a bit unpleasant for them, wouldn't it?" Then he squinted at Keselo. "I don't think I've seen any of your catapults up here, though."

"There wasn't enough room on our ships to bring them along when we came up here from the south, so we'll have to build new ones." Keselo looked out over the grassland. "There might be a bit of a problem, though. I don't think I've seen very many trees out here, so there's nothing we can use to build them." He sighed. "Oh, well," he said. "It was an interesting idea, but I don't see any way we'd be able to make new catapults."

Longbow turned. "Don't throw good ideas away until you've considered all of your options, Keselo," he said. "There are plenty of trees off to the west in Tonthakan, and Padan will have ten cohorts joining us in a day or so. You can take a couple of those cohorts off to the west to cut down trees and make catapults. Then you'll be able to mount them on sleds." He turned to Ekial. "Do you think you'll be able to train your horses to pull those sleds and get the catapults here where we'll need them?"

"I was going to talk with him about that. There's no real reason why the horses would have to do that all by themselves, is there? We pull things around fairly often in the Land of Malavi, but the horse has to have a rider to tell him what to do. If we tied one end of the ropes to the catapult sleds and the other end to the saddles of our horses, we'd be able to skid them along without too much trouble."

"It looks like Sorgan Hook-Beak knew what he was talking about," Keselo said then. "If you get people together from several different cultures, sooner or later they'll come up with a solution to almost any problem, won't they?" Then he straightened. "I'd better go speak with Sub-Commander Padan," he said. "We're going to need quite a few barrels of naphtha, pitch, and tar if we're going to be throwing fire missiles at the Atazak invaders."

"Do you have to wait until the last minute to mix them together?" Ekial asked.

"It's much too dangerous to mix them *before* the last minute," Keselo explained. "One spark will set fire to the mix, so we always wait until the last possible minute."

"You're the expert, Keselo," Ekial said. "To be honest with you, I don't want to get anywhere *near* that concoction."

The weather turned foul the following morning. A steady drizzle of rain mixed with snow fell out of a gloomy sky as they set out.

Rabbit came back from farther on ahead of the rest of them. "It looks to me like Dahlaine's got the wind pretty much under control," he told Longbow and the others. "This storm might hang over us for a day or so, because it's not going anywhere. The rain and snow are coming straight down, and there's not a hint of a breeze in the air."

Then Tlantar Two-Hands came back from even farther out to the front, and there was a Malavi horseman with him. "There's a sizeable bison herd about a mile ahead of us," Tlantar said. "We should probably slow down and let them go past us. We don't want to startle them."

"I'd pay close attention to what Tlantar just told you, my friends," the Malavi advised. "Those shaggy things out there are at least four times as big as our cows in Malavi are. I've never *seen* any animal that big."

"This is Skarn," Tlantar introduced his companion. "He'll be leading the Malavi who'll go off to Tonthakan to drag Keselo's catapult sleds here. I've talked with Padan, and he tells me that it won't take the Trogites very long to build the catapults and sleds once they reach the forests over there. Skarn will take his horsemen over there in a few days, and he tells me that it won't take them very long to bring the sleds back here."

"That's unless a few more bison herds get in our way," Skarn amended. "I don't mind pushing *cows* around to make them go where I want them to, but I'm *not* going to start pushing those bison around. I've done a lot of stupid things in my past, but I'm not stupid enough to irritate animals *that* big."

"They *do* provide the important part of our food supply," Chief Two-Hands reminded Skarn. Then he looked at the others in the group. "Be very careful around those bison herds," he cautioned. "There are times when almost anything can startle them, and the whole herd starts to run."

"That sounds very familiar," Skarn said. "Our cows do exactly the same thing. We call it a 'stampede.'"

"So do we," Tlantar said. "A lot of our people have been killed in those stampedes. My own father died when he couldn't run fast enough to get out of the way when a herd of bison started to run."

Ekial led his advance force of a hundred Malavi horsemen north the following day while the rest of the men continued their march. It was late in the following afternoon when they saw a peculiar-looking cloud that appeared to be ignoring Dahlaine's "no wind" interdiction.

"I thought the wind had been shut off," Rabbit said.

"It's what we call a 'whirlwind' up here," Tlantar explained, "and I don't think that even Dahlaine could order one of those to stop blowing."

"They're called 'cyclones' in some parts of the world," Padan said, "and you're probably right, Chief Two-Hands. I don't think there's *anything* that can stop them once they start to spin like that. How do your people avoid them?"

"We've had fair luck with holes in the ground," Tlantar replied. "Every village has a well-constructed shelter under the ground to protect the people. The whirlwinds don't sweep across one of the villages very often, but we don't really want to take any chances."

The dark, cone-shaped cloud moved off to the north, and Longbow and the others all thought that was very nice of it. As evening descended, they set up camp for the night and ate a rather sparse supper. It was not long after darkness had settled over the vast meadowland when a scar-faced Malavi horseman rode in. "My name is Orgal," the rider announced as he swung down from his sweaty horse, "and Prince Ekial sent me here to tell you what's been going on lately off to the north. We saw the Atazak invaders, and they don't look to me like they'll be very much trouble. There are quite a lot of them, but when we looked closer, we saw that at least *half* of them were women and children. There were a few of them who were brandishing things *they* might believe are quite threatening, but they'll need a *lot* more practice before anybody will take them seriously. I'd say that *most* of them don't even know what the word 'war' means. Of course, we were all riding horses, and I'd say that they *might* believe that the horse and the man riding him are just one creature—four legs on the bottom and two arms on the top—and with two heads of course. Whenever they see us coming, they run away."

"How far ahead of us would you say they are?" Longbow asked the Malavi.

"I'd say about sixty miles."

"It'll take us about three more days to get there," Long-bow mused. "Can Prince Ekial hold?"

The horseman grinned. "Since the enemy's too ignorant to know anything about wars, Ekial might just go on and defeat them all by himself."

"That wouldn't be at all polite," Longbow said with a faint smile. "Do you suppose you could send a messenger off to the west? We've got several tribes of bowmen coming this way and some Trogites building catapults as well. They'll all need a guide to bring them to the place where we'll need them. There's a Malavi named Skarn who's over there with Keselo, and he has quite a few horsemen who'll be able to spread the word once they know the route."

"Skarn's an old friend of mine," Orgal said. "I'll go over there and talk with him myself." And he wheeled his horse and rode off to the west.

3

It was late in the afternoon two days later, and Longbow was fairly sure that they were nearing the region of northern Matakan where Prince Ekial was holding off the invasion of the Atazaks. Unfortunately, however, Longbow and his friends wouldn't be able to go any farther today, and probably not tomorrow either.

"It looks almost like an ocean of fur out there, doesn't it?" Rabbit suggested as they all stood on a hilltop watching the huge herd of bison running in panic toward the west and totally blocking Longbow and his friends from any further progress. "What do you suppose frightened them *this* time?"

"Maybe somebody who's about ten miles away sneezed," Chief Two-Hands replied. "Almost anything will send a herd of bison running toward the far horizon. All it takes is one frightened bison to start a stampede. If one of them runs, they all run—even when they don't know what frightened the first one."

"It makes traveling in this part of the world sort of interesting, though," Rabbit added.

"I don't think I've ever seen that many animals all in one place at the same time," the archer Athlan observed.

"That's probably because you live in a forest, Athlan," Padan said. "Forest animals hide. They were probably there, but you couldn't see them because the trees were in your way."

"I don't think I'd want to try to herd animals that big around," the Malavi Tenkla said. "It looks to me like those bison run almost as fast as horses, and they're twice as big as horses. I wish Ekial had left somebody else in charge when he ran off to the north. If I happen to make a mistake, I could get a lot of the men killed." He looked at Chief Tlantar Two-Hands. "You were saying that if one bison gets frightened and runs, the rest of the herd's likely to follow him. Do they stand around looking at each other all the time?"

"I've been told that smell is involved," Two-Hands replied. "I guess that a frightened bison gives off a distinctive odor, and it's that odor that makes the rest of the herd bolt and turn."

"I've come across sailors who've been drunk for a week or so," Rabbit said. "They smelled bad enough to make *me* want to run away, too." Then he grinned. "That might just solve this problem, Longbow. If a herd of bison are blocking us off, we could get Ox drunk, and he'd smell so bad that the bison would turn around and run away."

"Very funny, Rabbit," Longbow said.

"I'm glad you liked it," Rabbit said with a broad grin.

They reached the part of northern Matakan where Ekial and his friends were holding back the invaders from Atazakan about two days later. "I was just about to send some horsemen out to find you," Ekial said. "What took you so long?"

"We ran into a herd of frightened bison," Padan explained. "They had us completely blocked off."

"Ah," Ekial said. "I should have guessed, I suppose. Were you and your friends in any danger, Longbow?"

"Not really," Longbow replied. "We were up near the top of a hill, and it would seem that bison aren't at all like goats. They don't seem to like to go uphill, do they?"

"Not that I've seen so far. If they're at all like cows, every now and then they'll stampede up a hillside, but it slows them down, and they don't seem to like that much."

"How are things going, Ekial?" Padan asked.

"*We're* having quite a bit of fun," Ekial replied with an evil grin. "These Atazaks are hopeless incompetents. They're armed with what somebody who doesn't know what he's talking about might call 'spears,' but their spears aren't very well-made, and the Atazaks haven't got the faintest idea of how to use them. We gallop at them in places where they don't expect us and skewer several of them with our lances and then gallop out again. Then, when that gets tiresome, we whip in and slash them with our sabres. I don't think they even recognize our sabres as weapons."

"I think somebody once said that a stupid enemy is a gift from the gods," Rabbit said.

"I believe I might have just seen something that'll make their lives even more unpleasant," Padan said. "There's an outcropping of hills about a mile north of here. We could build a fort out of sod blocks up near the top of those hills and then just sit there. If the Atazaks try to attack that fort, things will get *very* unpleasant for them. Then, if they try to avoid us, we can come down off the hill, kill a couple hundred of them, and then go back to the fort. Eventually they'll almost *have* to attack us, and there won't be many live ones left after that."

"And even fewer if my men and I wait out in the grass until they attack your fort," Ekial added. "We'll hit them from behind. Maybe the rest of them will give up on this silly invasion and go on back to their own territory."

Padan shook his head. "They're being controlled by our *real* enemies, Prince Ekial," he said in a bleak voice. "Let's not take chances. We don't want them coming at us from behind during our *real* war down in Crystal Gorge."

It was about then that the Malavi Orgal rode in. "Red-Beard told me to come here and advise you that he's leading the archers from Tonthakan here, and that it won't be much longer than two days before he arrives. I'm *also* supposed to tell you that Keselo's Trogites have finished building their war-engines, and they've installed them on those sleds. Skarn's men are pulling the sleds, and they'll be here soon as well."

"It just wouldn't be the same without them, Orgal," Padan said with a broad grin.

"Was that supposed to be funny?" Orgal demanded.

It was just after dawn the following morning when Longbow, Athlan, and Two-Hands joined Prince Ekial some distance off to the east to take a closer look at the invading Atazaks.

"They don't seem to have very many weapons of any kind," Longbow said quietly as they looked out across the grassland at the disorganized camp of the invaders.

"The ones with weapons are a bit farther back," Ekial explained. "The ones that are closer are just ordinary people. That's what's been bothering us quite a bit. The ordinaries aren't permitted to have weapons of any kind as far as we can tell. The ones wearing fancy clothes and carrying spears are the soldiers—or at least that's what they call themselves. They've been pushing the unarmed ordinaries out to the front to serve as a sort of walking barricade to keep my horsemen—and the local Matans—a fair distance away from the ones who think they're important. I hired on to fight warriors, not to run over innocent, unarmed common people, so I'm having the same sort of problems that Tladan and his spearmen are. I *won't* kill innocents, but they've been herded out to the front, so my men and I can't get through them to attack the ones carrying spears."

"Why don't you just herd them out of the way, then?" Longbow suggested.

"I'm not really very good at herding people, Longbow."

Longbow considered that. "I think we'll have to wait until Athlan's archers get here," he said. "Once they've arrived, you can make a false attack on the Atazak front."

"False attack?"

"Charge in as if you mean to kill every Atazak in the vicinity. The ones with spears will push the unarmed common people forward to block off your attack. Then the Tonthakan archers can shoot arrows *over* the commons and kill the ones who think they're important by the hundreds. The survivors will run back to get out of the range of the arrows. That should leave the ordinaries standing there all alone. It shouldn't be very difficult at that point to herd the innocents off to someplace safe. I don't think there'll be very many 'Guardians' left after an hour or so, and the ones who are still alive will most likely run away just as fast as they can. That should leave poor old Holy—but crazy—Azakan out there all by himself screaming orders at passing clouds, the sun, moon, and stars, and assorted other things that won't pay any attention to him. An arrow—or a lance—should quiet things down out there quite noticeably."

"What about the bug-people?" Padan asked.

"*We* know how to deal with them," Rabbit said. "The innocent ones will be safe, the crazy man and his protectors will be dead, and the bug-people won't be around anymore. Then we'll be able to go on down to Crystal Gorge and help our friends down there eliminate our *real* enemy, the one that's called 'The Vlagh.' *That's* the war we need to win. This Atazak invasion was just a hoax designed to pull us away from Crystal Gorge."

"Is this 'Vlagh' *really* just a bug?" Ekial asked Longbow.

"I've never actually seen her," Longbow replied, "but sooner or later, she and I *will* meet and settle this once and for all."

4

It was about noon of the following day when Longbow crept through the thick grass to the top of a small knoll to watch the invaders from Atazakan. They didn't seem to be very well-organized, and there was a lot of milling around out there. "The Guardians of Divinity" were easily distinguishable from the ordinary Atazaks, since they were all dressed in brightly colored clothing, and they carried crudely made spears—which the ordinary people were evidently not permitted to possess. As Ekial had said, the "Guardians" were herding the commoners out to the front to stand between them and the Malavi.

Then Rabbit came crawling up through the grass. "Are they doing anything yet?" he asked Longbow in a quiet voice.

"Nothing very significant," Longbow replied. "They've been fairly busy driving the ordinary people out to the front. They seem to *really* want a large number of unarmed Atazaks standing between them and Ekial's horse-soldiers. Ekial and his men are staying out in plain sight to make the 'Guardians' believe that they're in terrible danger. We don't want them to start finding other things in other places for the commoners to do."

"Red-Beard should lead the Tonthakan archers here sometime tomorrow," Rabbit said then. "Once the archers have pushed the 'Guardians' back a ways, Ekial can swing in and drive the ordinaries off to the north. I talked it over with him, and we sort of agreed that the safest place for them will probably be around on the backside of those hills where Padan's building his fort. He doesn't really show it, but Ekial's starting to feel very protective when it comes to those ordinary Atazaks. It's almost like they were pets of some kind."

"Cattle, Rabbit," Longbow said, "not exactly pets. The Malavi spend all of their time protecting their cattle. I suppose that Ekial sees those helpless ordinary Atazaks as something very much like a herd of cattle, and the Malavi will do anything possible to protect their cows."

"I guess I hadn't really seen them that way," Rabbit conceded. "I'm fairly sure that the ordinaries don't say 'moo' very often, but I think Ekial can almost hear them say 'moo.'" Then Rabbit laughed. "Or maybe they say 'baa' instead. They're almost like the sheep down in Veltan's Domain, aren't they? Omago's friend, that sheep-herder Nanton, did everything he could to protect his sheep from the wolves, and Ekial's behaving almost more like a shepherd than a cattle-herder."

"You don't see very many shepherds with sabre scars on their faces, though," Longbow added. "Anyway, once Ekial and his men have herded the commoners out of the way and got them to someplace safe, we can all concentrate on eliminating the 'Guardians.' It might take a while for Holy—but crazy—Azakan to realize that we've removed, or eliminated, most of his worshipers, but I'm fairly sure that he'll get the point, eventually."

Rabbit raised his head and looked out over the Atazaks who were milling around in confusion. "Is that him?" he asked, pointing at an ornately dressed Atazak sitting on a very large chair near the center of the invading force.

"I think so," Longbow replied. "He was shouting orders at the sky just a little while ago. I don't think she was paying much attention to him, though."

"Those little ones gathered around him are the poison-spitters, aren't they?"

Longbow nodded. "They look very much like the ones I've been killing for a long time now. I haven't seen any of them spitting today, though. Now that the wind's not blowing, spitting out venom wouldn't be a very good idea, since it settles right back down on them."

"I was sort of hoping they wouldn't realize that," Rabbit said. "Enemies who destroy themselves are the very best kind, wouldn't you say?"

Then the ornately dressed Atazak rose to his feet and began to bellow at the sky in a huge voice. Most of what he was shouting didn't make any sense, but as nearly as Longbow was able to determine, the crazy man was shouting orders to lightning—which wasn't around just then. "Strike down my foes!" he roared. "I command thee to strike them all down. Then clear a path for me that I might confront mine arch-enemy, Dahlaine the usurper! Do as I command, for I am the god of all of the Land of Dhrall! Ye *must* obey me, or I shall banish thee now and forever from the sky— which is *also* mine!"

"That's definitely crazy," Rabbit noted. "I don't think I've ever *seen* anybody *that* crazy before! Is there any kind of a cure for that?"

"I've had some luck with putting an arrow into the forehead of the crazy," Longbow replied, "but dear old Holy there is about three hundred paces away, and I wouldn't want to sprain my bow trying to reach out that far."

"Can a bow actually be sprained?" Rabbit asked with a fair amount of skepticism.

"I'm not really sure," Longbow admitted. "I'm not going to try it to find out just now, though."

It was late in the afternoon of the following day when Skarn rode into the temporary encampment with Red-Beard riding at his side. "The archers aren't far behind us," Skarn said, swinging down from his saddle.

"And Keselo's sleds aren't very far behind them," Red-Beard added. Then he looked at Tladak, who came from this part of Matakan. "There used to be a river that ran off to the west from here, wasn't there?"

"It went dry a long time ago," Tladak replied. "How did you know that?"

"There's a shallow sort of valley running from here on off in that direction," Red-Beard replied. "I wouldn't call it a gorge or a ravine, but it's fairly obvious that it was gouged out by running water. You get quite a bit of snow up here in the winter, don't you?"

"Oh, yes," Tladak replied.

"And that dry riverbed stops being dry when springtime rolls around, right?"

"You sound like you've been here before."

"Well, not *here*, exactly," Red-Beard replied. "The same sort of thing happened all the time in the place where I grew

up. It's sort of nice to know that some things never change."
Then he looked around. "Your camp's just a bit scruffy-
looking, Longbow," he chided.

"We aren't going to be here permanently, Red-Beard. If
things go the way we've planned, we'll be on our way back
to Mount Shrak in just a few days."

"I take it that the Atazaks don't really pose much of a
threat."

"Even less than that. They take incompetence out to the
far end."

Red-Beard looked around. "Where's Padan?" he asked.

"He's building a fort out of sod-blocks on a hill just a
ways off to the north," Longbow replied. "You know how
important forts are to the Trogites. Anyway, he's nearly finished up there. Then he's going to bring some of his men
here to build a series of breastworks off to the east to hold
back the Atazaks."

"Is their glorious leader as crazy as everybody says that
he is?"

"Even crazier," Longbow said. "Rabbit and I saw him
yesterday, and he was threatening to spank a thunderbolt."

"That's crazy, all right," Red-Beard said.

"We've been working on a way to cure him of crazy."

"Oh?"

"I think it's called 'kill,' Red-Beard. I've noticed that
'kill' cures just about everything that's bothering anybody."

"They don't look very much like soldiers, Athlan," the
young archer called Zathan said rather scornfully as he
looked down the slope at the invaders from Atazakan.

"I wouldn't call them soldiers, Zathan," Athlan replied.
"The ones down at the bottom of this slope are just common

people who shouldn't even be here. The madman who gives all the orders decided to bring them here to serve as a human barricade when the war starts. They don't even have weapons of any kind. I'm sure that they didn't *want* to come here, but the ones behind them—the ones with spears—forced them to come so that they could stand between us and the ones who think they're important. We're going to ruin their grand plan, though. That should make the crazy one even crazier—right up until one of us gets close enough to drive a dozen or so arrows into his belly. Once he's dead, everything will fall apart for the ones who think they're important, and this silly war will end right then and there."

"I like it!" Zathan said with a broad grin. "When it's all over, are we going to drag the dead ones over to the edge of Matakan territory so that they can rot and stink up the air in the land of the Atazaks?"

"We might want to see what Dahlaine has to say about that," Athlan agreed. "If that border territory smells bad enough, we probably won't have to worry about any more invasions."

"It worked pretty well for us during the war with the Reindeer Tribes," Zathan said. "If it worked once, it'll probably work again."

"We'll see," Athlan replied.

Longbow smiled. There was a simplicity about the Tonthakans that he rather liked. Simplicity was better than complicated most of the time, but Longbow was fairly sure that he'd have a bit of difficulty if he tried to persuade the outlanders that it worked that way.

5

I'm not sure just exactly why," Keselo said when he joined them the next day, "but there was a large herd of bison following our sleds all day yesterday."

"It's possible that the Malavi horses that were pulling your sleds might have had something to do with that," Padan suggested. "I've noticed here lately that those horses have a rather strong odor when they're working hard. Do you think the herd that was following you might have been one of those large ones the Malavi told us about? The ones that take a week or two to move on past you?"

"There weren't *that* many, Sub-Commander," Keselo replied.

Quite suddenly a couple of things clicked together for Longbow. "Tell me, Two-Hands, are bison at all frightened by fire?" he asked intently.

"*All* animals are afraid of fire, friend Longbow," Two-Hands replied. "Every now and then grass-fires break out here in Matakan, and the bison go into pure panic."

"Let's say that a fire broke out just behind that herd that

was following Keselo's sleds. They *would* run toward the east, wouldn't they?"

"I think I see where you're going with this, Longbow," Rabbit said, "but aren't you overlooking something? A fire won't spread out very much when it doesn't have a wind behind it, and we *definitely* don't want the wind to start blowing around here again."

"I'll get to that in just a minute," Longbow said. "Now then, Two-Hands, you and Tladak have seen these bison herds running in panic many times, haven't you?"

Tlantar nodded. "Too many times, actually," he said glumly.

"Don't be so sorrowful, friend Two-Hands. *This* might be one of the nice times. There's that large herd of bison that was following Keselo's sleds up that old riverbed. Now, *if* a fire broke out just behind them, they'd almost certainly stay down in that riverbed, wouldn't they?"

"Not necessarily, Longbow. If one of them veered off and went on up the side of the riverbed to get away from the fire, the entire herd could scramble on up to safety."

"Not if other fires were suddenly appearing right in front of them, they wouldn't."

"It's an interesting idea, Longbow," Two-Hands said, "but Rabbit just kicked several holes in this plan of yours. If a fire doesn't have a wind to drive it, it won't go very far. Were you planning to run along behind the bison with a torch and set new fires every hundred yards or so?"

"I don't think that'll be necessary, Chief Two-Hands," Longbow said with a broad grin. "I have this friend called Keselo who has a way to set fire to anything—or anybody—that he wants to. He has a special tool that was *made* to set fires, and Keselo can set fires behind the bison, or in front of any of them that want to veer off in search of safety. If Keselo is down there with his engines, the bison *will* stampede up that old riverbed, and *none* of them will get very far if they try to leave the riverbed. Once they start, Keselo can herd them up that old dried-up riverbed until they reach the top of this ridge. Then they'll run on toward the east with more fire snapping at their tails. They probably won't even notice Holy Azakan or his noble but inept Guardians. They'll just run right over the top of them without even slowing down."

"This is likely to get just a bit tricky, Longbow," Ekial said dubiously. "My men and I will have to peel off the common people and run them off to a safe place *before* Keselo starts the bison stampede, and none of us can be positive how long that's going to take. Worse yet, we'll probably be out of sight when we *do* reach that safe place. How will you and Keselo know exactly when to start setting the grass on fire?"

"It sounds to me like we'll be going back to horns, doesn't it, Longbow?" Rabbit suggested.

"I was sort of thinking along those lines myself," Longbow agreed. "You were watching us during the war down in Veltan's Domain, Ekial, and you probably heard a fair amount of toots."

"Toots?" Ekial asked, frowning slightly.

"It's a term Eleria used quite often," Longbow explained. "The Maags use brass horns to communicate with each other, and the native people of Zelana's Domain use animal horns to do much the same. If Red-Beard rides Seven and goes along with you, he can blow his horn when you've herded the Atazak commoners to a safe place. Keselo won't set fire to the grass behind the bison until he hears Red-

Beard's horn." Longbow frowned. "Just to be on the safe side, I think maybe Keselo should blow *his* horn when his catapults throw fire missiles into the grass behind the bison herd. When those of us standing behind the breastworks hear Keselo's toot, we'll kick the breastworks apart and then run away."

"You're going to destroy the breastworks my men and I built to protect you?" Padan protested.

"We don't want anything to get in the way of the bison, do we? They might not know it, but they'll be working for us. We want to make things as easy as possible for our shaggy new friends, don't we? The bison will have a nice clear path to follow, so they'll run right over the top of Divine—but crazy—Azakan and his devoted Guardians, and this 'invasion' will cease to exist along about then. 'Holy Azakan' will scream orders to lightning, wind, and, for all I know, to grass and dirt as well, but I don't think they'll listen. The nice thing about this will show up along about next spring. The grass up here will be very green, and it'll grow much taller than usual. Atazaks that have been trampled down into mush should make excellent fertilizer, wouldn't you say?"

"You are an evil man, Longbow," Ekial declared, but then he burst out laughing.

At first light the following morning Longbow and several of his friends went on up to the top of a small knoll that rose at the head of the shallow riverbed and overlooked Padan's breastworks and the gentle slope currently occupied by the Atazak invaders.

"It's still just a bit dark to see very much," Rabbit observed. "The days seem to be getting shorter and shorter, don't they?"

"That's one of the peculiarities of this time of the year," Tladan said without smiling. "Winter doesn't seem to like long days, for some reason."

"I've never actually seen it," Athlan said, "but I've heard that one of the Reindeer tribes lives so far to the north that the sun sets in the late autumn and doesn't come back up until early spring in their territory. She makes up for it in midsummer, though. She doesn't go down at all, so the people live out about a month or so without any nights. There's nothing but broad daylight up there for about forty days."

"That might make it a little hard to get any sleep," Chief Two-Hands said.

"They catch up on their sleep the following winter, most likely," Athlan said, peering down the riverbed. "As close as I can tell, Keselo's set up his engines about two miles down that dry wash. They appear to be on the outer edge of the wash. Isn't that quite a ways away from where he'll be setting the grass on fire?"

"I think his catapults might surprise you, Athlan," Rabbit said. "The Trogites were throwing fireballs a good half mile in Veltan-Land during the last war." He looked at Longbow. "Did Ekial give you any idea of just when he was going to sweep in and herd the ordinary Atazaks out from in front of the ones who carry spears?" he asked.

"I think he'll want just a little more light," Longbow replied. "He wants to be sure that he's got all of them. Then, too, Keselo will need to be able to see the bison before he starts his fires. We want those fires *behind* the herd, not right in the middle."

The Tonthakan archers were sending their arrows *over* the

unarmed Atazak commoners, and a fair number of the "Guardians of Divinity" had begun to sprout arrow feathers in places *nobody* wants penetrated.

"I thought we were going to let the bison trample those stupid Atazaks," Chief Two-Hands said.

"Not until Ekial can get the ordinaries to a safe place," Longbow explained. "Athlan and I talked it over, and it seemed to us that a brief arrow shower would persuade the 'Guardians of Divinity' to pull back. They won't be in Ekial's way now, so he won't encounter any interference when he herds the ordinaries off to safety. Then, too, if the 'Guardians' are back down the east slope a ways, the bison will have enough time and distance ahead of them to build up their speed. A running trample should work better than a walking one. Excuse me a moment." He lifted his horn and blew the agreed-upon signal. "Ekial will move now," he told the others. "We're not sure just how fast the ordinaries can move. They probably haven't been eating too well, so they might be just a little weak."

Prince Ekial and his men were surprisingly gentle as they escorted the unfortunate "ordinaries" out of harm's way. Ekial frequently assumed a pose of blunt brutality, but Longbow had been quite certain that it was nothing more than a pose. Deep down where it really mattered, Ekial was anything *but* brutal. It *did* make a certain amount of sense. After all, Ekial had spent most of his life tending his cattle, and to some degree those cows were almost pets.

Prince Ekial's pose came apart when he leaned over in his saddle and picked up a small child who'd been falling behind and carried the little boy off to safety.

"You saw that, too, didn't you?" Rabbit said with a faint

smile. "It seems that 'big bad Ekial' might just have a few soft spots in his nature."

"I wouldn't make an issue of that the next time you see him, little friend," Longbow suggested.

"I wouldn't think of it," Rabbit replied. "I might try limping just a bit, though. If I limp a lot, I might even get a free ride."

The eastern horizon had taken on a faint glow when Red-Beard's horn announced that the unarmed Atazaks had reached safety, and Rabbit raised *his* horn to pass the word on to Keselo. "Just a precaution," the little smith told Longbow and the others. "Keselo's quite a ways on down that old riverbed, and it's fairly important right now for him to start setting fires."

Longbow looked off to the east and saw that the retreat of the "Guardians" had taken them only a short distance beyond the range of the arrows of the Tonthakan archers. Evidently, Holy Azakan still held a fairly firm grip on those who were supposed to protect him.

Then the sound of Keselo's horn came up the dry riverbed, and Longbow and his friends watched as the shaggy bison were introduced to fire. Their response was very appropriate under the circumstances.

They ran.

Then, after a while, Keselo's first fire flickered and died, another one of his catapults sent fresh fire on up the riverbed, and the bison continued their flight.

"It seems to be working," Athlan observed.

"Keselo's a very dependable young man," Rabbit replied.

"We'll see," Chief Two-Hands said. "I want to find out if he can turn back any of the bison that try to get clear of that riverbed. *That's* what's going to tell us whether this will work or not. If just one bison reaches safety, the whole herd will follow him, and this will fall apart on us."

"You're a gloomy sort of fellow," Rabbit noted. "Try to look on the bright side."

"Since that pestilence came here, there hasn't *been* a bright side," Two-Hands retorted.

"We're just about to find out, Chief Two-Hands," Tladak said. "Off on the south side of the riverbed—one of the bison just started up the side-slope."

Longbow saw the fleeing bison, and he held his breath.

"Here comes Keselo's answer," Rabbit said.

They all watched the fleeing bison scrambling up the rock-strewn slope. Then, almost like a comet, a fireball came hurtling across the dry riverbed and smashed into the grassy upper side of the slope, splashing gobs of burning tar and tree pitch in all directions.

The fleeing bison wheeled around and ran back down to rejoin its herd-mates.

"Is everything all better now, Chief Two-Hands?" Rabbit asked with a knowing grin.

"Does he do that all the time?" Two-Hands asked Longbow.

"It's not uncommon," Longbow replied. "Rabbit's very clever, and he enjoys rubbing other people's noses in that. We've tried to break him of the habit, but it still pops out every so often."

Padan's soldiers and the Tonthakan archers began to tear the sod breastworks apart, moving as fast as they possibly could.

"Don't take too much time, Padan!" Longbow called. "Just shove the breastworks over. You don't have enough time to carry the sod blocks out of the way. The bison will trample them flat anyway."

"That's the way we'll do 'er, Cap'n!" Padan shouted back with a broad grin.

"Clown," Longbow muttered under his breath.

"They're slowing just a bit, Longbow," Rabbit called from the front side of the knoll. "It looks to me like they're getting a little winded."

"Is Keselo still setting his fires?"

"I think he's just about run out of grass. He's still dropping fire-missiles right behind the back end of the herd, though. Do you want me to sound the stop toot?"

"Maybe you'd better," Longbow replied. "Padan's running a bit behind."

Rabbit raised his horn and blew two sharp notes.

Keselo's catapults stopped hurling fireballs, and the flight of the bison gradually slowed.

Longbow looked off to the east of the knoll and saw that the cloud of dust the Malavi horsemen had stirred up during the rescue of the Atazak commoners had begun to settle back to earth, and the "Guardians of Divinity" that had fled the arrow-storm of the Tonthakans were more than a little distressed as they gradually came to realize that the ordinaries no longer stood between them and their enemies. The higher-ranking Guardians who surrounded Divine Azakan seemed to grasp that even more quickly than their comrades did, and they spread out and moved forward with their spears held threateningly to persuade the Atazakans who now formed the most forward ranks that the option of flight was no longer open to them.

"They spend more time waving their spears at each other

than they do when they're trying to frighten an enemy, don't they?" Rabbit observed.

"Having somebody—anybody—between them and their enemies seems to be very important to the Atazaks," Longbow agreed. "Personal safety seems to be their main concern."

Then Rabbit straightened and shaded his eyes from the light of the rising sun. "The little venom-spitters seem to have decided that they don't want to play anymore. They're crawling off through the bushes all over down there. Of course, once Dahlaine had shut off the wind, they weren't at all useful anymore, and that probably irritated old Holy no end. Irritating a crazy man isn't a very good idea, is it?"

"Longbow!" Padan called. "We've got the breastworks pretty much out of the way. Do you need us here for anything else?"

"Not that I can think of," Longbow called back. "Get your men out of there." Then he glanced down the dry riverbed. The bison were still milling around, but they hadn't gone back to grazing. "It's time to toot again," he told Rabbit. "Let Keselo know that it's all right now to start the bison moving again."

"I thought you'd never ask," Rabbit replied, lifting his horn.

There were scattered clouds hanging over the eastern horizon, and the sun, which as yet had not risen, touched them with glorious color of many shades. Longbow was still not comfortable in the treeless meadowland, but he had to admit that the sunrises and sunsets of the region were beautiful beyond belief.

He pulled his thoughts away from the scenery and peered on down the dry riverbed where Keselo's fire-missiles were dropping with great splashes of flame no more than twenty paces behind the terrified bison. The massive creatures were fleeing up the dry riverbed in wide-eyed panic.

It was quite obvious to Longbow that bison were not as clever as the deer of Zelana's Domain were—nor as timid. A herd of deer could vanish into the forest at the slightest sound. Bison, on the other hand, were not particularly timid—as long as nobody was throwing fire at them.

Then the herd of bison crested the ridge top just to the north of the small knoll where Longbow and his friends were watching.

"I hadn't realized how big they are," Rabbit said, sounding slightly awed. "They aren't likely to come up here, are they, Chief Two-Hands?"

Tlantar shook his head. "They'll take the easiest route, and that's down the slope. I'm sure that they'll want to get a long way away from that fire, and they'll run faster when they start going downhill."

"Are there any bison herds over in Atazakan?" Athlan asked.

"I've never been there," Two-Hands replied, "but I rather doubt it. Bison eat grass, not trees, so they wouldn't be very interested in forest country."

"The Atazaks have probably never even seen a herd of bison, have they?"

"It's not very likely. And even if there *were* bison over there, Holy Azakan and his Guardians live in the city of Palandor, so about the only wild creatures they've ever seen have been birds. They probably won't even realize that they're in any danger until it's too late. I think it's called 'learning the hard way,' and that's the worst way to learn anything."

"They'll be much wiser for the rest of their lives, though,"

Rabbit noted, "which might even be as long as about five minutes."

As Two-Hands had predicted, the stampede of the shaggy bison picked up speed as they fled on down the slope. The "Guardians" stationed near the upper end of the slope stood gaping at the huge creatures bearing down on them, and then they turned and tried to run away. The ones stationed farther on down the slope, however, met them with spears and commands to return to their positions.

The discussion didn't last very long, though, because the herd of terrified bison ran right over the top of both groups.

Then, in a final demonstration of his insanity, Holy Azakan rose from his ornate chair—or possibly throne—and raised one hand in a commanding sort of way. "Come no farther!" he ordered. "I am thy god! Kneel down before me lest I destroy thee, one and all. If ye do not obey me, I will punish ye all, and great will be thy suffering. I will command the earth to open and swallow ye! I shall even command the sun—which is my father—to burn ye down to ashes. I do tell ye, one and all, that ye have seen your last day, and great will be the lamentation of all of thy kind— for truly . . ." He broke off and looked around, his eyes widening in horror as he realized that he was all alone. His "Guardians" had either fled in terror or vanished, screaming, under the sharp hooves of the terror-stricken bison.

"Mother!" Azakan cried out. "Save me! Rescue me, please, mother, please! Don't let them hurt me!" Then his voice became a shrill scream of absolute terror, but the bison paid no heed, and Azakan's shriek was lost in the rumbling thunder of a thousand hooves.

"Most appropriate," Chief Two-Hands said.

"I don't follow you," Longbow admitted.

"I couldn't really swear to this, friend Longbow," Tlantar said, "but the word reached Asmie a long time back that the very first thing Azakan did when he assumed the throne of Atazakan was to order the execution of his mother and all her other children. Now that all came home to roost. He died begging his mother to save him, but she wasn't there anymore."

"There were a few of them who managed to stay alive, Chief Two-Hands," Tladak reported along about noon. "They were the ones intelligent enough—or maybe lucky enough—to hide behind large boulders on down the slope. We rounded them up and took their spears away from them. What do you think we should do with them?"

Two-Hands shrugged. "Tell them to go home," he suggested. Then he scratched his cheek and turned to look at Ekial. "You might want to tell the commoners that 'Holy Azakan' isn't around anymore and that most of his 'Guardians' are dead. Let *them* decide what to do with the survivors."

"After the way the Guardians treated then, the commoners aren't likely to treat the survivors very nicely."

"That's up to them," Two-Hands said. "We have other things to attend to right now."

Longbow walked a short distance away from the others. "Are you there?" he sent a silent thought out to Zelana.

"Of course I am," her voice replied. "How are things going up there?"

"It's all over—and I suppose you could say that we won."

"That was quick."

"We had some help."

"What happened to the crazy Atazak?"

"He isn't crazy anymore."

"You cured him? How did you manage to do that?"

"He happened to be in the wrong place at the wrong—or maybe the right—time. He doesn't have time to be crazy anymore. He's much too busy being dead."

"You stuck an arrow in his forehead, I take it?"

"No. That wasn't necessary. We *might* be able to find a few bits and pieces of him to give to your big brother, but I wouldn't make any large bets on that. He stopped being all in one piece rather quickly. Did you want any details?"

Zelana made a gagging sort of sound. "Spare me," she said. "Were you able to persuade the rest of the Atazaks to go on back home?"

"There weren't really very many of them left. It's going to take us a few days to get back down there to Mount Shrak. Ekial and the other Malavi can come on down faster if Dahlaine really needs them. Have the servants of the Vlagh started their invasion yet?"

"Not as far as we've been able to determine. Hurry on back, Longbow. Things aren't the same when you're not here."

"We'll be along in just a little while. Tell Eleria that I said hello."

"That's sweet, Longbow," Zelana said.

"Try not to get carried away with it," he told her.

THE
FORTRESS

1

It was a crisp day in late autumn as Narasan and Sorgan led the Trogite army and their assorted allies from the encampment around Mount Shrak down toward the southern mountains.

"Who's in charge of the men you sent down to that gorge to help Gunda build the foundation for our fort?" Narasan asked his friend.

"Skell and Torl," Sorgan replied. "I always put my relatives in charge when I'm not going to be there." He looked around and drew in a deep breath. "It's good to be out in the open again," he said. "You don't necessarily have to tell Dahlaine that I said this, but living in a cave for weeks on end doesn't really light my fire. I start to get jumpy when I can't see the open sky above me."

"It *does* take a bit of getting used to," Narasan agreed. "We're warriors, Sorgan. We aren't *supposed* to live inside— whether it's houses or caves." Then he smiled briefly at his friend. "I'm not sure just exactly why, but that cave seemed to shrink quite a bit when Dahlaine's little boy brought that bear into the map-room."

"He was a big one, all right," Sorgan said. "There *are* bears up in the hills above Weros over in the Land of Maag, but they'd look like midgets compared to that monster Ashad seems to believe is his brother. I didn't know that bears could grow that big."

"Different varieties, I'd imagine," Narasan said. "It might be something like the differences between you Maags and the men of *my* race. Your first mate, Ox, is about twice as big as Gunda or Padan."

"That might have something to do with it," Sorgan agreed. "Of course, Ox is one of the biggest men *I've* ever come across." He smiled. "That's always made my life much easier. When you've got somebody as big as Ox to back you up, the men in the crew don't argue with you very much. How far would you say it is down to Crystal Gorge? I don't really read maps very well. I've spent most of my life at sea, and we sort of think in days rather than miles."

"I made it to be about forty miles down to the mouth of the gorge, and Gunda's building the foundation about ten miles on down from there."

"And your men can cover only about ten miles a day?"

"That sort of depends on the terrain, Sorgan. When it's flat and there aren't many trees, we can usually walk fifteen. If it's steep and forested, we're lucky if we can cover five."

Sorgan peered on ahead. "Here comes that warrior woman called Trenicia," he said. "I never did get the straight story about her. After she threw all those jewels back at Zelana's sister and told her that she wouldn't work for her anymore, why did she decide to come north with you instead of trying to find some way to go on back home?"

"I'm not entirely sure, Sorgan," Narasan admitted. "Maybe she just wanted to see more of the Land of Dhrall—or maybe she wanted to find out if Dahlaine might want to hire her to fight in *this* war. She's a very complicated woman, and she can do things that I wouldn't even try. When we were marching from the east coast to Mount Shrak, she got bored and started ranging out in front of the army. She seemed to enjoy sneaking up on deer and frightening those huge bison. As it turned out, she's an extremely good scout. She'd come back to our camp every evening, and give us a detailed—and very accurate—description of the ground we'd cover the following day. There's *something* that she wants, but I can't for the life of me figure out just what it is."

"Women are like that, Narasan. They *always* want something, but they'll never tell you exactly what it is."

"Are we still just plodding along, Narasan?" the warrior queen demanded as she joined them.

"I'm an expert plodder, Trenicia," Narasan replied. "Is there anything interesting out to the front?"

"Not really—just more of those miles and miles of nothing but miles and miles. The mountains to the south are still a few days away."

"Did you see any of those bison herds?" Sorgan asked her.

"Not directly ahead of us," she replied. "There's a fair-sized herd eight or ten miles off to the west, but they weren't moving in this direction."

"That's a relief," Sorgan said. "After what Chief Two-Hands told us about *those* overgrown animals and what happens to people who can't get out of the way when the animals start to run, just the thought of being in the wrong place at the wrong time tightens my jaws more than a little.

If Longbow happened to be with us, I could probably relax, but he had to go north with all those other useful people to chase the Atazaks back to where they belong."

"It's not really going to take them very long, Sorgan," Narasan replied. "From what Dahlaine told us about the people of Atazakan, I don't think very many of them will survive when our people attack them."

"What I can't understand, though, is why Dahlaine even permitted the crazy man to take over that part of his country."

"Heritage, Sorgan," Narasan explained to his friend. "Dahlaine doesn't like to interfere with the people of his Domain. Azakan was the son of the former king, so he inherited the throne when his father died."

"That might be all right in normal situations, Narasan, but 'crazy' sort of disqualifies somebody for leadership, wouldn't you say?"

"That might depend on how many people the crazy one can persuade to join him—or her. Dahlaine's sister has quite a few problems, and she's been getting all kinds of bad help from her priesthood. Dahlaine should have locked her away years ago."

Then Sub-Commander Andar came back from the advance cohorts. "The Malavi called Ariga came up from the south, Commander," he reported in his deep voice. "He wanted me to tell you that he and his friends haven't encountered *any* of the creatures of the Wasteland so far."

"Have they been able to reach Gunda's wall yet?"

"Not yet, Commander. They *have* seen the northern end of the gorge. So far, they've been checking every nook and cranny down there to be certain that the bug-people aren't hiding in the bushes up here on *this* end of the gorge."

"Ah, well," Narasan said. "Apparently we're going to

have to go down the gorge by ourselves to find out how far Gunda's managed to get."

"I'm sure he's done just fine, Commander," Andar said. "Gunda's just about the best when it comes to building walls."

It was two days later when the grassy meadowland came to an abrupt stop and some very rocky mountains reared up out of the ground.

"Every time we turn around here in the Land of Dhrall, we seem to encounter more of these silly mountains," Narasan grumbled.

"They're pretty to look at," Sorgan replied.

"Looking is all right, Sorgan," Narasan said. "It's the climbing that I don't like. There are hills down in the empire, but they're a lot gentler than these piles of rocks we keep encountering here in the Land of Dhrall."

Sorgan sighed. "I know how you feel, my friend," he said. "Hills and mountains had a lot to do with my decision to become a sailor. There are big waves out at sea—sometimes almost as steep and rugged as these mountains are— but our *ships* do all the climbing for *us*."

"How nice of them," Narasan replied. Then he shaded his eyes and looked up toward the top of the steep ridge. "Here she comes again," he said to Sorgan, pointing up the slope that Trenicia was descending at a dead run. "Doesn't she *ever* run out of breath?" Sorgan demanded. "As far as I've been able to determine, she runs all the time."

"Are we still practicing our plodding, Narasan?" Trenicia called as she loped on down the slope.

"Why do you run so much?" Sorgan bluntly asked the warrior queen.

"I *like* to run," she replied with a shrug. "It's the best way I know of to stay in good shape—a much better way than sitting around drinking beer day in and day out."

"Be nice," Sorgan replied mildly.

"I'm always nice, Hook-Beak." Then she pointed off to the left. "If you and your people go that way, you'll find the going much easier. You'll start to encounter a lot of trees if you go around the other way."

"How far would you say it is to the mouth of Crystal Gorge?" Narasan asked her.

"I could run there in about three hours," she replied. "I'd imagine that it'll take you and the other plodders about two days. I'll go on ahead and keep an eye out for those enemies of yours. I'll come back and warn you if I happen to see any of them." Then she turned and ran off again.

"That woman's starting to irritate me," Sorgan muttered.

It was slow going for the next two days, and Narasan blamed Dahlaine for that to some degree. The time they'd spent in the cave under Mount Shrak rather painfully brought back the warning that old Sergeant Wilmer had repeated over and over when Narasan had been only a boy. He could almost hear the old soldier's warning, "If'n y' don't git no exercise a-tall fer three straight days, yer a-gonna stort gittin' flabby an' short-winded. If 'n y' don't stay in good shape, yer enemies'll cut y' all t' pieces the first time y' come up against 'em—an' that's the pure an' honest truth."

"I think I should have paid more attention," Narasan privately admitted.

It was about midafternoon of their second day in the rugged mountains that formed the southern boundary of Dahlaine's Domain when Ariga the horse-soldier rode up to meet them. "It's just a couple more miles to the north end of Crystal Gorge," he advised, swinging down from the back of his horse.

"Just what does this crystal look like?" Sorgan asked.

"I think it's that pale rock called quartz," Ariga replied, "only it's not quite that clear quartz that shows up now and then down in Malavi. It's got a sort of pink cast to it."

Sorgan suddenly laughed. "I think we'd better keep Eleria away from it, then—and probably Zelana as well. Just the word 'pink' perks up their ears."

"Have you been on down to where Gunda and Sorgan's men are working on the base for our wall?" Narasan asked.

"A couple of times, yes," Ariga replied. "We pretty much have to go through the gateway they've built when we need to check the lay of the land on down to the south of the wall."

"What's it like down there?"

Ariga grinned. "There are lots and lots of little side canyons that look almost like they were *made* for ambushes. I'm sure we'll be able to make life *very* unpleasant for the bug-people."

"Right up until the time that they bite your horses and you have to start walking instead of riding," Sorgan added.

"We've already taken care of that, Captain," Ariga said.

"You've been training your horses to wear those bison-hide cloaks?" Sorgan asked.

Ariga shook his head. "We decided to use boots instead."

"Boots?"

"I've never *seen* one of these bug-people but Ekial says that they're very short. All we had to do to make our horses bite-proof was wrap a couple layers of that bison hide around their legs up to the joint. Anyway, when the bug-things come up into the gorge, we'll whip out of those side canyons, kill a few hundred of them, and then duck back into our canyons."

"With the bug-people hot on your tails," Sorgan added.

"That's what's behind the whole idea, Captain," Ariga said with a wicked grin. "We've sort of joined up with the archers from Tonthakan, and they'll be hiding up in our canyons with arrows that have been dipped in that venom everybody keeps talking about. We'll rush out and sting the bugs and then rush back into those canyons like we were trying to get away. The bugs will come chasing after us, and the archers will kill every single one of them who tries to follow us."

"That's brilliant!" Narasan exclaimed.

It was late in the afternoon of the following day when Narasan and Sorgan crested a rocky little knoll in the mountains and saw the northern end of Crystal Gorge. There was a sizeable cloud-bank off to the west, and the setting sun bathed the clouds in glory.

"I wouldn't want to throw any accusations at anybody," Sorgan declared, "but that gap looks a lot like 'tampering' to me."

"I'm not really all that familiar with mountains, Sorgan," Narasan admitted, "but that gap doesn't look much like a natural formation to me either."

Sorgan shrugged. "It's Dahlaine's part of the Land of Dhrall, I guess, so if he wants to pick up an axe and chop holes in his mountains, that's up to him."

"That would have taken *some* axe, Sorgan," Narasan said, looking at the wide gap with absolutely straight walls on either side. "I can see why they call it a 'gorge,' though." He looked at the peculiar stone sides. "If I understood what Ariga was saying correctly, this 'crystal' that's part of the name is quartz. We encounter that once in a while down in the empire. It's pretty, I suppose, but it's just a bit too brittle to be of much use. I wouldn't really want to make a house out of it—not one that I intended to live in, anyway. We much prefer granite."

"It looks like Ariga was right," Sorgan said. "The side walls of that gorge are definitely pink."

"It's probably because the quartz has been contaminated by iron ore," Narasan said. "Iron ore seems to give everything around it a reddish cast."

"Maybe it's Longbow's 'unknown friend' again," Sorgan suggested with a wry sort of grin.

"I wouldn't start throwing any accusations around, Sorgan," Narasan replied. "If you happen to offend her, she might just turn you into a toad."

"I don't think that's very funny, Narasan." Sorgan squinted at the mouth of the gorge again. "It looks to me like there's a small brook wandering around at the bottom of the gorge."

"There almost has to be, Sorgan. That bear who visited us in Dahlaine's cave comes down here every year to go fishing."

The sturdy Matan called Tlodal joined them on the rocky knoll and looked down at the mouth of the gorge. "Can you believe that I've never seen this before?" he said. "Our village is no more than forty miles away, but it never even occurred to me to come down here and have a look at it. I'll admit that it's sort of pretty, but the bison herds aren't the least bit interested. They eat grass, not rocks."

"You're sort of in charge of the village of Asmie and its people while Two-Hands is away, aren't you?" Narasan asked.

"I'm not sure just exactly how much authority I have over the other men of the tribe, Narasan. They'll do what Two-Hands tells them to do, but about as far as I'll go is to make suggestions," Tlodal replied a bit dubiously. "Anyway, I've been talking with Chief Kathlak of Statha, and we've sort of agreed that his archers should concentrate on throwing their arrows at the small bug-people who'll be coming along fairly soon. The spearmen of Asmie—and the other Matan villages as well—will sit still until the larger creatures attack that wall, or fort, or whatever you want to call it, and then we Matans will take over. The Tonthakans can throw their arrows much farther than we can throw our spears, but their arrows probably won't be heavy enough to cut through anything like armor—or whatever might be there to protect the bug-people."

"You two seem to be getting along with each other quite well," Sorgan observed.

Tlodal shrugged. "We're both hunters," he said, "so we know the rules."

"Rules?" Sorgan seemed to be a bit surprised.

"There's only *one* rule, really, and it's fairly simple. It has to do with poaching. I don't try to kill *his* game animals, and he doesn't try to kill *mine*. Do you want us to set up a camp out here in the open, or should we go on down the gorge a mile or so? Kathlak and I agree that 'out here' might be better than 'down there,' but that's *your* decision. What's it to be?"

"I see that you waited until the sun was going down before you came here to ask us," Sorgan said shrewdly. "I'd say that 'down there' sort of died on the vine when the sun decided to go to bed."

"It's one of our responsibilities to make these decisions

easier for you, mighty chieftain," Tlodal replied blandly. "Do you want me to move around and tell everybody that you've wisely chosen 'out here' as the campsite for tonight, mighty chieftain?"

Narasan had a bit of trouble suppressing his laughter.

Their camp was fairly rudimentary, Narasan was forced to concede. Had the party camped there been exclusively Trogite soldiers, Narasan would quite probably have delivered a few blistering reprimands, but "neatness" and "straight lines" were alien concepts for the Matan spear-throwers and the Tonthakan archers, so Narasan chose not to make a big issue of "neat." They were going to be here for only one night anyway, so it wasn't all that important.

After a surprisingly rich supper of beans and bison meat, Tlodal, Kathlak, and Trenicia joined Narasan and Sorgan to discuss a few things. Then the Malavi, Ariga, arrived to describe in some detail what they were likely to encounter farther on down the gorge. "You'll come to some fairly rough places," he advised them, "and Gunda thought that I might be able to help you get around them."

"What exactly do you mean when you say 'rough places,' Ariga?" Sorgan asked.

"Mostly landslides—or maybe quartz slides," Ariga replied. "I guess that quartz is quite brittle, and an extremely cold winter will freeze it. Then, when spring rolls around, there'll be a quick thaw, and whole sheets of that quartz will break free and crash down on the floor of the gorge. I'm sure that you'll have to spend quite a bit of time wading back and forth across the brook. It's the only way to get around those piles of shattered quartz—unless you'd prefer to dig."

"That sort of explains why everybody was talking about

'crumbly quartz' when they were describing this end of the gorge," Sorgan noted. Then he frowned. "If it happens up here at this end of the gorge, wouldn't the same thing happen farther on down?"

"Not necessarily," Narasan replied. "Dahlaine told me that there's water involved in the process of breaking the quartz free from the wall. There are springs and brooks up on top here in the north end of the ravine, and the water seeps down through the cracks in the quartz. It's drier on down to the south, so there isn't enough water down there to break the quartz away. That means that there'll be good solid walls on both sides of Gunda's fort."

"That's all that really matters, I guess," Sorgan said. Then he looked at Ariga. "You've been up and down this gorge several times, I take it," he said.

"Often enough to get the general lay of the land," Ariga replied.

"Then you'll pretty much know where these 'wade across the river' places are located, won't you?"

"Approximately, yes."

"Where are we going with this, Sorgan?" Narasan asked his friend.

"We've got Matans and Tonthakans with us," Sorgan explained, "and they can move around in rough country quite a bit faster than your men can. Suppose that we send them on ahead of us tomorrow morning. Ariga can show them those 'wade across the river' places, and then several of them can sit down and wait for your men to come marching along and then guide them around the rough places. That should save quite a bit of time, and we *should* all make it down to Gunda's wall-base before the sun sets tomorrow.

That way, the men'll be able to get a good night's sleep, and they'll be ready to start building the *real* wall."

"You're getting better and better at this, Sorgan," Narasan told his friend. "I'd always assumed that 'planning ahead' was an alien concept for Maags, and that 'making it up as you go along' was the standard procedure."

"I've had some good teachers here lately," Sorgan said. "You're one of the best, of course, but the *really* best goes by the name of Keselo."

"You just *had* to remind me of that, didn't you, Sorgan?"

"It's good for you, Narasan," Sorgan replied with a broad grin. "I'm told that humility is a virtue, and Keselo splashes humility all over everybody who goes anywhere near him."

2

It was late afternoon, and the sky to the west was red. For some reason that Narasan couldn't quite understand, the sky here in Dahlaine's part of the Land of Dhrall was *always*—or almost always—red. Things had gone quite well that day as the horse-soldier Ariga had guided them around the numerous places that had been blocked off by the shattered heaps of quartz.

Then Narasan and Sorgan rounded a rather sharp turn in the gorge, and Gunda's solidly constructed base came into sight.

"We made good time," Sorgan noted. "I'd say that Ariga earned his pay today."

"He *was* sort of useful," Narasan agreed as he studied Gunda's base. It had been constructed out of solid blocks of the pink quartz, obviously, and Narasan was more than a little dubious about that. Quartz was pretty enough, but it was very brittle.

Then Gunda came out of the partially completed base. "What kept you?" he called.

"We stopped a few times to see if the fish were biting," Sorgan called back.

"You're starting to sound a lot like Padan," Narasan told his friend. "He comes up with that excuse every time he's late. Couldn't you have come up with something just a bit more original?"

Sorgan shrugged. "Like they say, the old ones are the best." He peered down at the wall-base. "That looks to be just about right," he noted. "Now that your men are here, they should be able to complete our fort in just a few days."

Gunda came on up the slope. "You might want to look the base over," he said to Narasan, "but I don't think you'll find much to complain about."

"Except that you built it out of quartz instead of granite," Narasan replied.

"Quartz was all we had to work with," Gunda said. "Skell and Torl went looking for granite, but the nearest outcropping of it is about ten miles on down the gorge. They said that it'd take all winter to break granite loose and drag it up here. We probably won't have that much time, so we used quartz instead. It's just a bit on the brittle side, I guess, but Torl reminded us that about the only tools the bug-people have are their teeth and knuckles. If the bug-people try to break through our wall with their bare hands and teeth, it'll probably take them ten or fifteen years to even put a noticeable dent in our wall, and by then, the only enemies we'll have out front will be toothless cripples."

"You've got some fairly massive blocks there, Gunda," Sorgan said.

"It was easier to make big ones than it would have been to make little bricks. I can flat guarantee that *nobody's* going to be moving those big blocks around—particularly not when we've got them jammed up against the walls of the gorge."

"This looks to be just about the narrowest place in the entire gorge," Sorgan said then.

Gunda nodded. "Forty feet is about all. Now we'll be able to concentrate on 'high' instead of 'wide,' and higher forts are always the best."

"How would you describe the slope on down to the south?" Narasan asked.

"Steep, narrow, and without much of anything to hide behind," Gunda replied with an evil grin. "It was just a bit cluttered when we first got here. There were quite a few large boulders on down there, but we used most of them to construct our base, and we'll probably use up all the rest when we start erecting the main wall. We won't leave any kind of shelter on that slope, so the bug-people will have to come at us right out in plain sight."

"Let's go take a look," Sorgan suggested.

"Whatever makes you happy, Captain Hook-Beak," Gunda agreed.

Narasan found Gunda's base blocks to be massive, and the numerous chip-marks strongly told him that the Maags who'd been shaping the blocks had worked very carefully.

The slope just to the south was very steep and totally devoid of anything that the bug-people could use for concealment. "Nice job, Gunda," he complimented his friend.

"I sort of like it myself," Gunda said.

"Have you installed that up-and-down gate yet?" Sorgan asked. "Keselo and Rabbit described it, but I think I should see the real thing." He paused. "Does it *really* work the way Keselo told all of us that it would? I've seen a lot of side-to-side gates, but I've never seen one that goes up and down."

"It takes a lot of grease," Gunda said, "but Ox has it pretty well moving like it's supposed to."

"How were you able to install it when the wall wasn't complete yet?" Narasan asked.

"I cheated just a bit," Gunda admitted. "We set up the frame and then braced it with quartz blocks. I was quite sure that gate would be about the first thing you'd want to see, so we went ahead and got it set up. Ox is our gate-man, and he fiddled around with it for almost a week. It does just exactly what Keselo told us it would do. Ox has a crew of men who all have shoulders about four feet wide. When *those* burlies pull the rope, the gate goes up so fast that if you blinked, you'd miss the whole thing."

"Open is all right, I guess," Sorgan said, "but wouldn't you say that the important thing is how fast it comes down?"

"That's the easy part," Gunda replied. "All they have to do when they want to close the gate is let go of the rope. The gate drops like a rock. It makes a loud bang when it hits the bottom, and that tells us that the gate's closed. When Keselo and Rabbit designed this gate, they wanted to keep the weight down to make it easier for the gate-crew to raise the thing, so they used iron bars instead of thick iron plates. I'm not sure if they saw a terrific advantage there. Our people will be able to see through the gate, so they'll know exactly what the enemies are up to. Then, if our people don't *like* what the enemies are doing, they'll be able to shoot arrows right through the gate. That should make things *terribly* exciting for anybody on the other side, wouldn't you say?"

"Let's go take a look, Narasan," Sorgan suggested. "I really want to see this fancy new gate."

      *   *   *

"Have you heard anything at all about how things are going up in the north?" Skell asked Narasan that evening.

"Much better than we'd expected," Narasan replied. "After we'd discovered that the 'pestilence' wasn't *really* a disease, things went more smoothly."

"If it wasn't a disease, just exactly what *was* it?" Gunda demanded.

"It appears that the creatures of the Wasteland are growing more clever than they were when this all began last spring," Narasan replied. "Somehow they discovered that their venom was just as deadly if the victim breathed it in as it was if they bit him and pumped some of it into his blood. They started to spit it up into the wind, and anybody who was standing on the downwind side—and breathing, of course—would inhale the venom and die within a few hours."

"That's *terrible*!" Gunda exclaimed.

"Moderately terrible, yes, but the disgustingly clever little Maag called Rabbit came up with a very simple solution."

"Oh?"

"He called it 'shut off the wind,' as I recall. Mighty Dahlaine, who can perform miracles without so much as turning a hair, looked just a bit sheepish when Rabbit explained his notion. If the wind's not blowing, spitting venom up into the air would be a *very* bad idea, since the venom would settle right back down and contaminate the air that whoever—or whatever—had spit it up would breathe in himself. They'd end up poisoning themselves—*and* the Atazaks who were on their side."

"Did it work like it was supposed to?" Gunda asked.

Narasan shrugged. "We left Mount Shrak to come on down here before any reports from the north came in, but I'd say that any time you've got Longbow, Keselo, and Rabbit working together, life will be very unpleasant for the enemy." He paused. "Can you give me any kind of an estimate of how long it's likely to take our men to complete this wall? The creatures of the Wasteland have been trying to divert us from this gorge, so I'd say that it's going to take quite some time for their main force to reach us here, but we'd better get the fort in place as soon as we possibly can."

"It won't really take us all that long, Narasan," Gunda replied. "We've got most of the Maags down here to lend us a hand. They'll carry the raw, unshaped rocks to the fort here, and our men will be able to concentrate on wall-building. I'd say give it a week or so, and then the bug invasion will stop right here."

"We didn't see anything at all down there that even comes close to mortar, Commander," a lean old sergeant reported, late the following day. "This ravine—or gorge, I guess they call it—is nothing but quartz. We could try farther on down tomorrow, sir, but I don't think we'll have any luck there, either."

"I was sort of afraid of that, Narasan," Gunda said.

"How can we build a fort without mortar?" Narasan demanded.

"We'll have to go to lock-stone, I guess," Gunda replied.

"That's sort of shaky, isn't it?"

"It's not all *that* bad. It takes longer to build, but it does the job. It's not as if the bug-people were armed—or even knew anything at all about catapults and rams. Their weapons are limited to teeth and fingernails. If they try to chew their way through our wall, it'll take them several years to get through, and it'll be sometime next spring before they can even get past the outer layer of blocks." He stamped his foot down on one of the huge base-rocks. "If we had more time, *this* would be the simplest answer. If we built the whole fort out of these foundation blocks, the silly thing would probably still be here a thousand years from now."

"I'll settle for ten years, Gunda," Narasan told his friend. "If we do things right, there won't *be* any creatures of the Wasteland ten years from now. Build your wall, Gunda. I need to go see how the men building the catapults are coming along."

He carefully lowered himself to the ground on the back side of Gunda's fort and went on back to what the men of his army called "the catapult factory," a fairly obvious variation of Rabbit's "arrow factory" on the beach near the village of Lattash.

The warrior queen Trenicia was watching as the highly skilled engineers constructed the standard Trogite catapults. "Ah, there you are, Narasan," she said. "I thought that these things were used to break down the walls of cities or forts. What good are they going to be here?"

Narasan smiled. "The catapult has many uses, Trenicia," he explained. "When we want to break down a wall, we use very large rocks, but when we want to thin out the number of enemies charging on our position, we use hundreds of smaller rocks. A well-constructed catapult will throw those pebbles about a hundred feet up into the air, and then it'll quite suddenly start raining rocks down on our enemies. Our little rock-shower might not kill *all* of our enemies, but it *will* reduce their numbers significantly. I'm quite sure that a shower of quartz fragments will be even more effective than ordinary pebbles could ever be. Quartz seems to shatter into very sharp fragments, and when *they* come raining down on our enemies, they'll cut the bug-people all to pieces."

"You people make war much more complicated than we

do on the Isle of Akalla," Trenicia observed. "We kill our enemies one at a time, and we're usually face-to-face with the one we're going to kill. You people who come from that place called civilization kill people you don't even know from a long distance away."

"The main thing in any war is winning, Trenicia," Narasan reminded her. "If more enemies are killed than your friends are, you've just won. If it's the other way around, you've lost. I'll grant you that over the years we've made things more complicated by adding machines of one kind or another, but it still comes back to killing more enemies than the enemies kill of your people."

"But are those machines you build strictly honorable?"

Narasan winced. Sometimes it seemed that every time he turned around, the word "honorable" kept popping out of nowhere.

Trenicia sat down on a large slab of quartz with a somber expression. "There's so much I have to learn," she said. "Things were happening down in the Domain of Dahlaine's younger brother that I still don't understand. I could see the value of these machines, of course, but I thought they were built mostly for knocking down the enemy's forts. Then I saw them used to throw fire at enemy soldiers. I thought that forts were the main things in civilized wars, but it seemed that as soon as your people finished building a fort, they just walked off and left it standing there."

"That was a very unusual war, Trenicia," Narasan told her. "Forts are *usually* our primary way to hold back an invasion, but Longbow's 'unknown friend' changed almost everything down in Veltan's Domain. She's capable of things that go beyond anything that Dahlaine or Zelana or Veltan can even imagine."

"I know. She spoke to me not long after we reached Mount Shrak."

"She *did*?" Narasan was startled. "Why didn't you tell us?"

"She told me not to. I do silly things quite often, but crossing *that* one would go a long way past silly, don't you think? Let's just say that she's here to help us, and let it go at that. Let's get back to these 'civilized wars.' What are they really all about?"

"Land, usually," Narasan replied, "and gold, of course. We take land away from others so that we can grow food on it. Then we sell the food to others—*if* they're willing to pay for it." He smiled faintly. "You're not really interested in gold, though, are you?"

"Not really," Trenicia said. "I prefer jewels. They're prettier and much more valuable than the yellow lead that makes civilized people get so excited. What would you say is the most important thing you want to do when you're fighting a civilized war?"

"We call it 'take the high ground,' Trenicia. You always want to be uphill from your enemy. If you do it that way, he has to climb to reach you." He frowned slightly. "When you get right down to it, that's what our forts are all about. In a sense, we *make* high ground when we build a fort."

"It sort of keeps you stuck in one place, though, doesn't it? You build a fort, and then you have to sit there. Doesn't that make your wars sort of boring? When we fight a war on the Isle of Akalla, we spend most of our time running. We run in, cut down a lot of our enemies, and then run off. Then our enemy runs after us. After we get a few miles ahead of her, we circle around and attack her from behind. After you've done that to an enemy several times, she doesn't have very many warriors left." Then she pursed her lips. "I think maybe I should have a long talk with Longbow or those archers from over in Tonthakan. If I had bows and my warriors knew how to use them, I could *own* the Isle of Akalla."

Narasan smiled. "I thought you already *did* own the isle," he said.

"Oh, I do, of course," Trenicia replied, "but there are a fair number of women there who don't quite realize that— yet."

Gunda's fort was beginning to take shape now, and Narasan began to feel just a bit more relaxed. Dahlaine had assured them that it would take their enemies quite a long time to reach Crystal Gorge, but still . . .

Ariga and his horse-soldiers had been scouting off to the south of the gorge, and as yet they hadn't encountered any of the invaders. If things kept going the way they were now, the fort would be complete long before the creatures of the Wasteland came anywhere near the gorge.

Then on a chilly, cloudy afternoon, Ariga came galloping up the gorge. "There's company coming!" he shouted as he swung down from his horse.

"Well, finally," Gunda said with a tight grin. "I was beginning to think they might have gotten lost out there in the desert." He looked rather proudly at his nearly completed fort. "Let them come," he added. "We're ready for them."

Sorgan Hook-Beak grinned. "I was starting to think that they didn't like us anymore, and we've spent a lot of time building our welcome for them, and I'd hate to see it go to waste."

"I wouldn't get too happy yet, Hook-Beak," Ariga said. "From what Ekial told me, the bug-people down in Veltan-Land didn't have weapons of any kind—except for their teeth and fingernails. That's changed, though. We saw a goodly number of them coming up the slope from that desert out there, and they're quite a bit better-armed now."

"What kind of weapons do they have?"

"You name it, and they've got it—swords, spears, axes, and clubs with iron spikes sticking out of them."

"They've started to make *real* weapons?" Sorgan exclaimed.

"I don't think 'make' had much to do with it," Ariga replied. "I'd say that 'picked up' would come closer. The swords they're carrying are the same as the ones *your* men are carrying, and the spears appear to be of Trogite origin. People *do* get killed in wars, you know, and I'd say that our enemies roamed around various battlefields picking up all those lovely free weapons."

"They wouldn't *really* know how to use them, would they, Narasan?" Sorgan asked.

"They've been watching us during the course of two wars, Sorgan," Narasan reminded his friend, "so I'm sure they've got a general idea of how to use those pillaged weapons. They won't be very good right at first, but I'm sure they'll get better as time goes by."

"It's just not fair," Sorgan growled. "Everything was going along just fine, but now we'll have to face all those thieves who've been stealing our weapons every time we turned our backs on them."

"I don't think I've ever heard a Maag use the word 'thief' before," Narasan said mildly.

It was three days later, and as yet there had been no sign of the now-armed creatures of the Wasteland, and that was making everyone just a bit edgy.

Then, not long after noon, Prince Ekial of the Malavi rode in, and as the days passed, more and more of the Malavi horse-soldiers that had been diverted to the meaningless war in the northern part of Matakan arrived in Crystal Gorge, and they ranged out farther and farther to the south to disrupt and delay the gathering of the enemy forces.

There was a kind of independence about the Malavi that Narasan found to be a bit disturbing. Soldiers were supposed to be a part of a larger entity—an army, in most cases. They *weren't* supposed to dash off and do things on their own the way the Malavi all too frequently did.

"Don't let it bother you so much," Gunda said when Narasan privately told his friend of his discontent. "They do things a bit differently, that's all. We build forts, and then we sit in them waiting—and waiting, and waiting—for our enemies to mount futile, and stupid, attacks on our impregnable defenses. The Malavi prefer to harass our enemies while they're marching toward our fort. I'm not saying that the Malavi will drive our enemies away before they ever reach our fort, but they'll probably thin out the herd quite noticeably."

"You're even starting to talk like a Malavi, Gunda. 'Thin out the herd'? That's horse-soldier talk."

"So beat me. Relax, Narasan. Our Malavi friends are having fun—*and* they're reducing the number of enemies who'll still be alive when they come here to attack our fort. Do you have any idea at all about how much longer it's likely to take Longbow and the others to get down here?"

"Ekial says just a few more days," Narasan replied. "They move independently rather than marching in groups the way we do, so they can go quite a bit farther—and faster—than we can."

Gunda rose up just a bit and looked back along the front wall of their fort. "Do you need someplace to hide?" he asked.

"Hide?"

"Here comes Trenicia. If you give her half a chance, she'll talk your ears off before the sun goes down."

"Very funny, Gunda," Narasan said.

"I'm glad you liked it."

3

It was several days later when Padan, Longbow, Keselo, and Rabbit came down through Crystal Gorge to join their friends at Gunda's wall. Narasan chose not to make an issue of it, but it seemed that just about everybody heaved a sigh of relief when Longbow arrived. There was something about Zelana's archer that seemed to give just about everybody a sense of invincibility. Longbow was one of the best. There was no question about that, but Narasan was fairly sure that it didn't rub off.

"Now we get to find out exactly what happened to the crazy man from Atazakan," Sorgan declared. "What in the world was it that made you decide to let the bison kill him instead of driving one of your arrows right through his head?"

Longbow shrugged. "They were right there, and they could do a much more thorough job than we could have. I suppose we *could* have made war on Holy Azakan and his 'Defenders of Divinity,' but a few of them would quite probably have evaded us and returned to Atazakan to stir up more trouble. The bison killed almost every one of them, and I didn't have to waste any arrows—or friends—in the process." He smiled faintly. "The nice thing is that so far as we could tell, not one single bison was killed during their stampede."

"How were you so certain that those wild animals would do what you wanted them to do?" the warrior queen Trenicia demanded.

"Everyone who lives here in Matan knows that bison are afraid of fire," Longbow explained. "Of course, almost *all* animals are afraid when fire breaks out. Keselo and his men had built catapults, and they knew the proper mixture of various liquids to make what the Trogites call 'fire-missiles.' In a peculiar sort of way, we were able to steer that bison herd in much the same way as Maags and Trogites steer their ships. All we really had to do was set fire to the grass in every direction that we *didn't* want the bison to run. We left them one option and only one, so they ran in the direction that we wanted them to run, and they ran much, much faster than anybody from Atazakan could."

"And that killed every single one of those invaders?" Trenicia asked.

"Not quite *every* one," Two-Hands said. "The bison—who probably didn't even see them—ran right over the top of them. After a thousand or so bison run over somebody, there isn't much of him left out in plain sight. *Most* of him is probably a foot or two down in the dirt in very small bits and pieces."

Trenicia shuddered. "I really wish you wouldn't say things like that, Chief Two-Hands," she said.

Tlantar shrugged. "He was one of our enemies. We *want* bad things to happen to our enemies, don't we?"

"Maybe so, but we don't have to talk about it, do we?"

*   *   *

It was early the following morning when Padan roused Narasan from a sound sleep. "We've got company," he said.

Narasan stretched and yawned. "The bug-people are coming to call?" he asked.

"I wouldn't put it that way," Padan replied. "I'm a bit surprised that you're still sleeping. The thunderclap almost shook Gunda's fort down. Actually, Lord Dahlaine stopped by—with family—to see how things are going."

"Why didn't you say so?" Narasan demanded, pulling on his uniform.

"I just did. You don't really have to rush, Glorious Commander. Gunda's taking our visitors on a tour of his fort. You know how Gunda loves to show off. I'm sure that he's boring the children almost to tears."

"Dahlaine and the others brought the children with them?" Narasan found that a bit disturbing. "That's not really a very good idea. The bug-people haven't attacked yet, but they *are* out there."

"Actually, they're not," Padan said. "The Malavi went out just before daybreak to see what our enemies have been up to, and so far as they were able to determine, there's not a single bug anywhere in the gorge. That *might* explain why Dahlaine and his family decided to pay us a call. On the bright side of this, Dahlaine brought the farmer Omago and his wife along as well, and Ara of the pretty feet is making breakfast."

"Are you having fun yet, Padan?" Narasan sourly asked his friend.

"Just doing my job, Mighty Leader," Padan replied with a broad grin.

Narasan grunted and went up the narrow stairway that led to the top of the front wall of Gunda's fort.

"Ah, there you are, Commander," the grey-bearded Dahlaine said. "I'm sorry that we had to wake you, but this sudden disappearance of our enemies is a bit disturbing. Were you able to pick up any hints about why they all went away?"

"I didn't even know that they'd left," Narasan replied. "Prince Ekial told us that they were still there yesterday evening."

"Maybe they took one look at your fort and decided that they didn't want to play anymore," Sorgan suggested with a grin.

"Their minds don't work that way, Sorgan," Zelana said.

"Are we sure that they haven't gone back to burrowing down under the ground again?" Red-Beard asked.

Longbow shook his head. "They haven't had that much time," he said. "That's not bare dirt out there, you know."

"Where are they, then?" Red-Beard demanded.

"I'll go take a look," Zelana said.

"You don't have to do that, dear sister," Dahlaine objected. "That's *my* responsibility."

"You're too noisy, big brother," Zelana replied. "*I'll* do it, and I won't shake down the walls of this gorge in the process. Just stay right here. I won't be long."

Narasan shuddered and looked away as Zelana rose up into the air without so much as making a sound. "I *wish* she wouldn't do that," he muttered.

"She's just showing off," Dahlaine declared. "She loves to startle people that way."

"We still love her, though," Veltan declared with a gentle smile. "As long as playing games makes her happy, we can live with it, can't we?"

Dahlaine gave Longbow a curious sort of look. "I'm not

trying to criticize you here, my friend," he said, "but what made you decide to goad that bison herd into fighting the battle in north Matakan for you?"

Longbow shrugged. "They were there, and I've been hearing stories about stampedes for quite some time now. The Atazaks were hopeless incompetents, but I still didn't want to take any chances with the lives of my friends. Several things came together all at the same time, and it seemed to me that stampeding the bison over the top of the Atazaks might solve several problems. It worked out even better than I'd anticipated. I'd say that no more than four or five of 'the Guardians of Divinity' are still alive—or *were*—after the bison ran over just about everything on that slope."

"You plan to rouse another bison stampede to eliminate the survivors, then?"

"The bison have done enough already, wouldn't you say? Ekial left a fair number of horse-soldiers up there to guide the ordinary Atazaks back to their own territory. I'm fairly sure that the Malavi have chased down those few Guardians of Divinity by now, so the Atazakan Nation has been purified. You might want to give some thought to finding a leader who has his head on straight to rule that part of your Domain."

"I probably should have been paying closer attention," Dahlaine ruefully admitted. "I've been just a bit preoccupied with these attacks by the creatures of the Wasteland here lately, though."

"The invasion of the lands of the Matans was a *part* of their attack," Longbow reminded him. "The servants of the Vlagh have been trying to divert us for quite some time now. They were behind Kajak's attack on Sorgan's fleet in the harbor of Kweta in the Land of Maag, as I recall, and they'd pushed the Reindeer Tribes right to the brink of a war with the Deer Hunters in Tonthakan. I'd say that the Vlagh has begun to realize that her servants are no match for us in an ordinary war, so she's doing her best to make things *not* ordinary."

Then Zelana suddenly appeared as if from nowhere. "I found them," she reported. "They're definitely up to something."

"There's nothing new about that," Veltan said. "What are they doing *this* time?"

"They all pulled back out of the gorge, little brother," she replied. "They're gathered near the southern mouth of the gorge, and they seem to be waiting for something."

"A new hatch of an entirely different breed of enemies, maybe?" Veltan suggested.

"I don't think so," Zelana replied. "I took a quick swing out over the Wasteland to see if there were more of them coming this way, but it looks completely deserted down there."

Narasan glanced on down the gorge and suddenly drew in a sharp breath. "I think we've got a problem," he told the others.

"Oh?" Gunda said. "The fort here can keep the enemy from getting anywhere close to us."

"The enemy has a friend, I'm afraid," Narasan said. "It's called 'smoke.' Look on down the gorge."

They all turned and stared at the dense black cloud of smoke that seemed almost to be boiling up the gorge.

"Cover the lower parts of your faces!" Omago shouted. "Tell your men to use wet cloth! If they breathe in too much of that smoke, they'll choke to death!"

"What *is* that?" Gunda demanded. "I've never seen smoke that black before."

"They're burning grease-trees," Omago replied. "We do that down in Veltan's part of the Land of Dhrall to drive bugs away from our orchards and crops. It kills them if they don't get clear of it."

"We aren't bugs, Omago," Gunda scoffed.

"You still have to breathe, don't you? If you breathe in that smoke, it'll kill you almost as fast as it kills a bug."

"Can you block it, Dahlaine?" Veltan demanded.

"I can hold it back for a while," Dahlaine said, "but this gorge is almost like a chimney. It's pulling that awful smoke up from down below."

"Rain," Longbow suggested. "If the fire goes out, there won't be any smoke."

Veltan turned. "I need you, baby!" he shouted.

There was a sudden flash of intensely bright light and a deafening crash of thunder, and then Veltan was gone.

"I wish he wouldn't do that," Padan grumbled.

"If it puts those fires out, I think we'll be able to live with it," Gunda disagreed.

For a short time there was an almost continuous roar of thunder to the south and jagged bolts of lightning flickering from horizon to horizon down there.

Then, as abruptly as the storm had appeared, it died out, and Veltan came flashing back, spouting curses in several languages. "It's no good," he declared. "Can you believe that they built those fires inside caves? Gather up your people, Narasan. You're going to have to get up out of this gorge, and you don't have very much time. Dahlaine and I can hold the smoke cloud back—or slow it a bit—but it *will* keep coming. If you don't get your people out of this cursed gorge, they'll die."

THE
RETREAT

1

The thick cloud of dense black smoke continued to come boiling up the gorge even as the Trogite soldiers and their Maag friends hastily gathered up their equipment and prepared for the march to the north.

Keselo had dabbled in botany a bit when he'd been a student at the University of Kaldacin, but so far as he could remember, he'd never heard of any tree or bush such as Omago had described.

"Just exactly what causes this particular tree to emit this dense smoke you mentioned?" he asked the farmer.

"I'm not really sure," Omago replied. "It's always been called 'the grease-tree,' and we've learned *not* to use it for cooking or heating. Quite a long time ago, though, the farmers in Veltan's Domain learned that a cloud of dense, greasy smoke will drive the bugs away from our orchards or crops. The smoke from a greasewood fire clogs up their breathing pits, and they die from the lack of air. It sort of comes down to 'run away or die.' Bugs aren't very intelligent, but over the years they've come to recognize the odor of greasewood smoke. I've seen several varieties of bugs that are usually natural enemies fleeing from that smoke side by side."

"Does it kill *every* variety of bugs?" Keselo asked.

"It's not limited to bugs, Keselo. Greasewood smoke kills animals as well—and also people. Every now and then, the wind changes direction and throws the smoke right back in our faces. Then *we're* the ones who start choking and running away. Wet cloth provides a *little* bit of protection, but only temporarily. I've heard that many farmers who've used greasewood smoke to drive bugs away have been trapped by a change in wind direction, and, just like the bugs, they're choked to death."

Keselo shuddered. "Sometimes it seems that being a farmer is even more dangerous than being a soldier."

"Let's move, people!" Gunda shouted. "That smoke's coming up the gorge faster and faster."

"Veltan and I'll do our best to hold the smoke back," Dahlaine told them. "We'll pull in rain clouds and unleash as much rain as we can, but this isn't a good time of the year for rain, so you'd better tell your men to hustle right along."

"I'll take the children to safety, big brother," Zelana said. "Don't let that smoke get ahead of you." Then she turned and hurried along the top of the wall to the tower where the children were staying.

"You were talking about wet cloth, Omago," Gunda said. "If we went back inside the fort and covered all the doors and windows with yards and yards of wet cloth, would that keep the smoke from reaching us?"

Omago shook his head. "You'd have to keep throwing buckets of water on the cloth," he said, "and the brook coming down through the gorge is hardly more than a trickle."

"I *hate* running off like this!" Gunda fumed. "We've got

a perfectly good fort here, but that cursed smoke's going to force us to abandon it."

"We don't have any choice, Gunda," Narasan said. "We're going to have to retreat."

"Or run away," Sorgan added, "whichever works best."

They started north from the fort at what was called "quick time" in the standard army usage. They weren't exactly running, but they were moving right along.

"This smoke sort of means that the bug-people have learned how to make fire, doesn't it?" Rabbit suggested as they splashed across the small brook to avoid another of those heaps of shattered quartz.

"I wouldn't go quite so far as to say 'make' fire," Keselo replied. "It's much more likely that they found burning branches or bushes. One of my teachers said that early man *carried* fire rather than starting it with flint sparks."

"That sort of says that the bugs are following the same road that people did, doesn't it?"

"Approximately, yes," Keselo replied, "but they're moving much, much faster than people did. These wars here in the Land of Dhrall started last spring—about six or seven months ago—and the creatures of the Wasteland have already gathered a lot of our weapons, and they seem to know what smoke can do."

"It's almost like a race, then?"

"Well, sort of, I suppose, but I'm afraid that they're moving a lot faster than *we* did way back when. It took us thousands of years to cover as much ground as *they've* covered in two seasons."

"We'd better find some way to slow them down, then," Rabbit declared.

"When you come up with something, Rabbit, let me know about it. I've been beating myself over the head about this for quite some time now, and I haven't found anything that'll work yet."

"I'll see what I can do, Keselo, but I'm just a little busy running away right now."

"How much farther would you say we've got to go before we get out of this silly gorge?" Gunda asked Longbow as they hurried along.

Longbow looked around. "I make it be about six miles, but I don't think we'll be able to stop just because we've reached the head of the gorge. We need to find someplace to get us out of the smoke."

"Like a cave, you mean?"

"It seems to be working for our enemies," Longbow replied with a shrug. "If it works for them, it should work for us."

"I don't think that's going to solve the problem, gentlemen," Commander Narasan said. "We're here to stop the enemy, and I don't think hiding in a cave is the best answer. What we *really* need to find is some way to block off the mouth of this gorge. If the bug-people manage to get out into open country, they'll spread out and kill all the people and take the land."

"We could try breastworks, I suppose," Gunda said, "but the cursed smoke coming up behind us would make that a bit dangerous, wouldn't you say?"

"I suppose we *could* collapse the mouth of the gorge," Keselo suggested.

"How could we possibly do that?" Gunda demanded with skepticism written all over his face.

"Well," Keselo said, "if I remember correctly, one of the people who described this gorge for us back at Mount Shrak said that the quartz at the upper end of the gorge is all crumbly because of the water that seeps down through it and then freezes. If there's some way that we can get people up to the top with hammers and long iron bars, they could break a lot of that quartz free, and it *would* fall down into the gorge up near the mouth."

"And that would spread that smoke out even farther," Gunda added.

"I don't really think so, sir," Keselo disagreed. "The smoke is coming up the gorge because the gorge walls are protecting it from the prevailing wind, which comes in out of the west. The smoke will have to rise up to get over our barrier, and that would get it up quite a bit higher. Then, when it came *out* of the gorge, the prevailing wind would carry it off to the east—toward a region that's almost totally uninhabited."

"Would that really work?" Gunda asked Commander Narasan.

"It sounds feasible to me," Narasan replied. "Why don't we try it and find out?"

2

It was about midafternoon when they reached the mouth of Crystal Gorge. The almost continuous crashing of thunder back on down the gorge indicated that Veltan and Dahlaine were still hard at work, and the smoke cloud had noticeably slowed.

"If those two are dropping that much rain down in the gorge, there's probably a wall of water rushing out of the southern end," Rabbit suggested. "That *might* be making things unpleasant for the buggies, I'd say."

"Buggies?" Gunda asked.

"Never miss a chance to insult your enemy," Rabbit said with a wicked little smirk.

"If I remember the map Lord Dahlaine had set up under Mount Shrak correctly, there's a fairly steep slope off to the west that leads up to that side of the gorge," Keselo said.

"It's there, all right," Chief Two-Hands confirmed.

"Then it won't be too hard for me and a crew of men to get up there and start plugging off the mouth of the gorge," Keselo said. "We don't know for sure just how far behind the smoke-cloud the bug-men will be coming, so I think we should close the door on them as soon as possible."

"This young man spends a lot of his time thinking, doesn't he?" Chief Two-Hands said to Longbow.

"Almost *all* of his time," Longbow said. "His thinking has saved us a lot of hard, honest work, though, so we try to encourage him to think as much as he can."

"All right, then," Rabbit said, hefting his hammer, "let's go up topside and start crumbling quartz."

As it turned out, the quartz wall on the west side of the mouth of the gorge was even more fragile than Keselo had anticipated, and his "crumble-crew" was mostly Maags, who were bigger and stronger than Trogite soldiers. Oddly, the Maags seemed to find shattering quartz very entertaining, and they soon had an almost continuous avalanche pouring down into the gorge. Several of them even went so far as to loop a rope around one of the many trees lining the top of the gorge and then slide down several yards and bash even more quartz off the gorge wall, shouting "Look out below!" every time they swung their hammers.

"I'll *never* understand those people," Keselo murmured to himself as he walked on down the gorge-rim to see how far up the smoke had come.

It was noticeably thinner than it had been when they'd first seen it boiling up the gorge toward Gunda's fort. The continuous rainstorm Dahlaine and Veltan had been pouring down into the lower end of the gorge appeared to be working out quite well. If things continued to go the way they were going now, the bug-people's "greasy smoke" scheme wasn't going at all the way they'd believed it would.

*   *   *

It was almost evening when Keselo and his "crumble-crew" came down the steep slope to rejoin their friends.

"This seems to be working even better than we'd hoped," Commander Narasan said to Keselo. "The smoke has to rise to get over all the rubble you and your men dropped down on the bottom of the gorge, and the wind from the west is carrying it out of our general vicinity. I think we'll want to wait until morning to make sure that the smoke *will* go away. Then we'll start building breastworks. The bug-men won't be able to come up the gorge until their fires go out, so we've got some time to play with."

"I just had an idea that you might want to consider," Longbow's friend Athlan said then. "The ground on this end of the gorge is mostly just ordinary dirt."

"There *are* quite a few rocks," Gunda pointed out, "but we'll probably be using them to build our breastworks, so what's to the front *will* be mostly dirt. What did you have in mind?"

"There *are* several streams nearby," Athlan said, "and when you mix dirt and water, you get mud, right?"

"Almost always, yes. Where are we going with this, Athlan?"

"There are quite a few swamps over in Tonthakan, and I've learned over the years that wading through soft mud makes for very slow going. If there just happens to be a lot of soft mud in front of each one of your little forts, it's going to slow the bug-people down to the point that they'll be easy targets for the archers. I don't think very many of them will reach your forts if we do it that way, do you?"

"It's called a 'fosse,' Athlan," Keselo told Longbow's friend. "They're fairly standard in the empire."

Athlan looked just a bit crestfallen. "I thought I'd come up with a notion that nobody had ever tried before," he said.

"Don't give up on it just yet," Keselo advised. "We've always used just plain water to fill the fosse to the front of any fort or breastworks. I don't think anyone's ever considered mud before. Water *would* slow the enemies down, but I think mud would slow them even more."

"It might take your people a while to divert the nearby streams," Padan said, "but we have a lot of friends here. Some of them will be helping us build the breastworks, but then there are others who'll be able to help you and your people build mud-pits."

"I think we might run out of water if we try to put these mud-pits in front of every breastworks we build," Rabbit said. "Wouldn't it work better if we just left plain, open ground in front of the second breastworks? That would give the horse-soldiers good solid ground to ride on, then they kill off all the bug-men who try to attack that second wall."

"And maybe we might want to use catapults and fire-missiles to stop the ones who try to attack the *third* breastworks," Keselo added. "The creatures of the Wasteland have a lot of trouble with changes of any kind, so if we use a different form of defense for each breastwork, we'll have some very unhappy enemies out there."

"And maybe put those poisoned stakes in front of the fourth one?" Ox added. "Then we could go back to mud-pits in front of the fifth one. After a while, they won't know *what* we're going to do next."

"We've got some very evil people working with us, Narasan," Sorgan said with a wicked grin.

"I wouldn't have it any other way, friend Sorgan," Narasan replied.

The sun had gone down, and a distinct chill settled over the mountains that lined the southern part of the Domain of Dahlaine of the North. Keselo had never spent any significant amount of time in the mountains, so he wasn't really prepared for the sudden drop in the temperature after the sun went to bed—and this was still only autumn. The thick-furred cloaks of the Matans had seemed perhaps a bit ostentatious when Keselo had seen them for the first time, but if the winters here were as brutally cold as the autumn chill suggested, the Matan cloaks might even be a little bit on the light side.

"Nippy, wouldn't you say?" Rabbit said as he joined Keselo near the mouth of Crystal Gorge.

"I might even go just a bit farther than 'nippy,' my little friend," Keselo replied with a shudder.

"Try this," Rabbit said, holding out a Matan fur cloak.

"Gladly," Keselo said, taking the cloak and draping it over his shoulders. "You didn't steal it, did you?"

"I don't steal clothes very often," Rabbit replied. "Most of the clothes on any Maag ship have never been introduced to the thing called soap, so they tend to be just a bit gamey. Actually, your cloak—and mine—are gifts from Chief Two-Hands. Since we're here to fight his war for him, he seems to want us to stay on the healthy side. How long would you say it's going to take to build those breastworks?"

"A week at the most. There are plenty of rocks lying around up here in the mountains, so things should go fairly fast."

Then there was a sudden flash of intensely bright light and a double crash of thunder.

"Guess who," Rabbit said sardonically. "Zelana's brothers are nice people, I suppose, but they sure are noisy."

"You noticed. How very perceptive of you."

Dahlaine and his younger brother joined them. "Where's Narasan?" Veltan asked.

"Most probably somewhere up that slope that slants up from the mouth of the gorge," Rabbit replied. "He and Gunda and Padan have been picking out the locations of the breastworks their men will start building tomorrow morning. Have the bug-people started coming up the gorge yet?"

"We haven't seen any of them so far," Dahlaine replied. Then he pointed at the rubble that was blocking off the mouth of the gorge. "Who came up with that notion?" he asked.

"Commander Narasan thought that it might divert that smoke," Keselo replied, "and, of course, it should make things difficult for the creatures of the Wasteland."

"How were you people able to gather that much quartz so fast?"

Keselo shrugged. "We just chipped it off the sides of the gorge," he said. "It wasn't really very hard, Lord Dahlaine. The quartz up at this end of the gorge has been fractured many times over the past several centuries."

"It might be even more useful if it were just a bit higher."

"It was starting to get dark, Lord Dahlaine. We can go back up there in the morning and pile it higher, if you want."

"Why don't *we* take care of that, brother mine," Veltan said with a broad smile. "I don't know how *your* pet feels about things like that, but *my* pet enjoys smashing things enormously. She had hours of fun when we opened the channel through Aracia's ice zone to give Narasan's army access to the Land of Dhrall."

"And it didn't really bother *you* all that much either, did it, little brother?" Dahlaine suggested with a grin.

"It was my responsibility, Dahlaine," Veltan replied in a pious tone of voice. "I always take pleasure in doing the things I'm supposed to do, don't you?"

Dahlaine laughed. "Do you ever plan to grow up, Veltan?" he asked.

"Not if I can avoid it, no."

"All right, then, let's go smash quartz for a while."

The sound was deafening, and the flashes of light were so intense that they made Keselo's eyes hurt, but the barrier across the mouth of Crystal Gorge grew higher with each clap of thunder.

"Isn't it nice to have gods around to do the hard work?" Gunda said in a pious tone of voice.

"Let's get started on the first breastwork, shall we?" Narasan suggested.

"You just had to go and say that, didn't you?"

3

It was still spitting a chill sprinkle of rain the following morning, but the scanty remains of the dense smoke-cloud were streaming off to the east as the prevailing wind skimmed them off the top of the quartz dike that now blocked the mouth of the gorge.

The standard procedure for erecting forts—permanent or temporary—had been in place since the war in the ravine above the village of Lattash in the spring of the current year. The Maag sailors gathered large rocks and carried them to the site, and the Trogite soldiers carefully put the rocks together to form the wall that was *supposed* to bring the enemy advance to a stop. It hadn't always *worked* that way, but Keselo believed that it was a good way to start.

The first breastwork was nearly finished when Athlan came by to have a word with Keselo. "It isn't working," he reported glumly. "The water doesn't sink down into the dirt far enough. We get wet dirt, but it doesn't come close to being the kind of mud we want."

"It sounds to me like another good idea just fell apart on us," Rabbit said.

A peculiar sort of notion came to Keselo out of nowhere. "Is the wife of the farmer Omago anywhere nearby?" he asked Rabbit.

"I think I saw her back behind this fort you and your men are erecting here," Rabbit replied. "Why do you ask? Do you think that she might be able to tell us how to make mud?"

"Maybe," Keselo said. "Come along, Athlan. I *think* I know somebody who might be of some help here."

They climbed over the partially completed breastworks and found Omago and his beautiful wife standing a few yards back.

"I'm not sure just exactly why," Keselo said to Ara, "but for some reason I'm almost positive that *you* can tell us what we're doing wrong."

"Oh?" she said. "Just exactly what's the problem?"

"We know that when water gets mixed with dirt, you get mud, but our friends from Tonthakan diverted several small streams into the bare dirt to the front of the breastworks, and the dirt *isn't* turning to mud."

Ara looked at the archer. "Did you stir it?" she asked him.

"Stir?" Athlan asked in a bewildered tone of voice.

"Oh, dear," Ara sighed. "You haven't done much cooking, have you?"

"I've roasted meat over open fires since I was only a boy," Athlan said.

"Cooking meat and cooking flour aren't at all the same," Ara said. "I hate to tell you this, but turning dirt into mud is going to involve quite a bit of hard work."

"When water mixes with dirt in the swamps back in Tonthakan, it turns into mud without any help from us at all," Athlan protested.

"But it takes several years," Ara explained. "It's not one of those things that happens instantly. If you want mud this year, you're going to have to stir." She frowned slightly. "Actually, the easiest way to do this would be to dig out all the dirt and pile it up around the edge of the pit. Then let water run in until the pit's about half full. Then shovel the dirt back in."

"That sounds like a lot of work," Athlan objected.

"Doesn't it, though? Nobody ever promised you 'easy,' did they?"

Athlan sighed. "It seemed like such a *good* idea."

"It was—and still is," Keselo said. "You're going to have to put in some hard work to get what we all want, though."

"I guess you're right," Athlan agreed glumly.

It was just before noon on the following day when Longbow came back on down from the rim of the gorge. "The bug-people have let their fires go out, and what little smoke is still in the gorge should drift out of the upper end before the sun goes down."

"When do you think the enemies will start to move?" Commander Narasan asked.

"They already have. They're staying a fair distance behind the last wisps of smoke, but they *are* on the move."

"Are they *really* carrying those weapons of ours that they stole?" Captain Sorgan asked.

"A few of them are," Longbow replied. "Some of them

have swords, and others have axes, but the only things *most* of them are carrying are long, pointed sticks."

"That doesn't pose much of a threat," Gunda said.

"I wouldn't be too sure about that," Sorgan disagreed. "They have that venom right in their front teeth, so they won't have to carry it around in jugs the way *we* do. All they'll have to do is spit on their spear points, and their pointed sticks will be just as deadly as ours. How long would you say it's going to take them to get up here, Longbow?"

"Not much more than a day and a half," Longbow replied. "They *will* have trouble climbing up over the rock-pile that's blocking the mouth of the gorge—particularly if Athlan's archers are up on the rim—on both sides. They *may* even try to scramble over that barricade after the sun goes down. They don't *usually* come out after dark, but I don't think we should take any chances."

The clouds Veltan and Dahlaine had used to subdue the smoke that the creatures of the Wasteland had unleashed continued to roll up the gorge for the next few days, and they were still spitting rain mixed with snow.

Commander Narasan had prudently sent several flagmen up to the rim of the gorge to keep them advised of the inevitable approach of the bug-people. Keselo was still having some trouble with the fact that "bug-*men*" wasn't very appropriate, since their enemies were female.

"One of your people up there on the rim is flapping his flag, Keselo," Rabbit said early on the morning of the third day after the smoke had been carried away by the prevailing wind.

Keselo squinted up at the rim. "He says that the enemies are coming," he reported.

"What a surprise," Rabbit said. "We already knew that they were coming, didn't we?"

"A little confirmation doesn't hurt anything," Keselo said, still intently watching the flagman's report. "He says that the archers have seriously reduced the number of enemies coming this way."

Then the warrior queen Trenicia came down from the breastworks to join them. "What's that man up there saying?" she asked Keselo.

"The enemies are on their way," Keselo replied. "What few of them are left, anyway. The flagman up there says that the Tonthakan archers have killed hundreds so far."

"They're not going to kill them *all*, are they?" Trenicia demanded, sounding more than a little concerned.

"It wouldn't hurt *my* feelings much if they did," Rabbit declared.

Trenicia scowled, but she didn't say anything.

The signalman upon the rim of the gorge continued to give them reports, but so far as Keselo could determine, nothing new or unusual was happening.

"One of them just stuck his head up over that pile of quartz," Rabbit hissed.

"You don't have to whisper," Keselo said. "They're at least a half mile away."

Then the flagman began to signal again.

"I was fairly sure *that* was going to happen before too much longer," Keselo said.

"What now?" Rabbit demanded.

"The Tonthakans are running out of arrows."

"They're *what*?" Rabbit demanded. "I made *thousands* of those arrowheads."

"Unfortunately, the Vlagh sent *more* thousands up the gorge," Keselo replied.

"Then there *will* be some enemies for us to kill," Trenicia said, sounding much relieved.

At first light the following morning the now-armed bugs came swarming over the shattered quartz barricade and crossed the open area between the northern mouth of Crystal Gorge and the edge of Athlan's mud-pit—but they did not even pause there. To the astonishment of almost everybody standing behind the breastworks, the bug-people continued to charge, despite the fact that those ahead of them sank out of sight almost instantly.

"Are they blind?" Sorgan's cousin Torl demanded. "Can't they see what's happening to their friends?"

"Bugs don't really *have* friends, Torl," Veltan explained. "They probably don't understand what just happened to the ones who tried to run across the top of the mud-pit. There's very little water out in the Wasteland, so most of them have never even *seen* mud before. They don't realize that what's there isn't solid."

"That should probably save a lot of arrows," Rabbit added. "If they're all going to drown themselves, the Tonthakans won't need to kill them. The bugs will take care of it for themselves."

Keselo frowned. "I don't think that's what's going to happen, little friend. What they're actually doing is constructing a causeway that will eventually run from the far side of the mud-pit to our breastworks here."

"Using *people* as building blocks?" Rabbit exclaimed.

"You should probably stop thinking of them as 'people,' Rabbit," Longbow said. "People do their own thinking, bugs don't. If they need a solid road across the mud-pit, the overmind will *build* that road—out of whatever is handy. Since there aren't any rocks available, the overmind will use its own bugs as building blocks—and the other bugs won't even have to carry them."

"That's *terrible*!" Rabbit exclaimed.

"Terrible is what this war is all about, little friend," Longbow replied.

"It *will* confuse them, Sub-Commander," Keselo suggested to Gunda later that morning, "*and* we won't lose any men in the process."

"I'm getting just a little irritated by this business of building forts—or breastworks in this case—and then just turning around and walking away from them."

"None of *our* people get killed, Gunda," Padan said. "Isn't that what wars are all about? Let the enemy do all the dying. *Our* main responsibility is staying alive, wouldn't you say?"

"Are you going to go along with this, Narasan?" Gunda asked rather plaintively.

"It *does* make sense, Gunda," Narasan said. "The fort—and the mud-pit, of course—*have* killed several thousand of our enemies, and it hasn't cost us any of our own men. *If* the breastwork is deserted when the enemy reaches it, they'll be very confused for at least a day. Then they'll try another one of those senseless charges, and the Malavi will run right over the top of them."

"And then we abandon the second breastwork as well?" Gunda asked.

"I don't see any reason why we shouldn't," Narasan replied. "When the bug-people try to attack the third breastwork, they'll come face-to-face with catapults and fire-missiles. There's a fair chance that we'll be able to eliminate about a million enemies in these first three breastworks, and it won't cost *us* a single life. It doesn't get much better than that, Gunda. That thing called Vlagh *will* run out of soldiers—eventually."

The Tonthakan mud-pit was quite a bit deeper at the center than it had been at the southern end, and more and more of the bug-people sank out of sight as the day wore on. Longbow spoke with his friend Athlan and Athlan's chief, Kathlak, and the archers began to concentrate their arrows on the poorly armed bug-men who were crossing the improvised causeway.

"If we're going to abandon this first breastwork after the sun goes down, we probably won't want the servants of the Vlagh snapping at our heels," he explained. "If they still have a few hundred feet to cross tomorrow morning, it'll most likely be about noon before they find out that we aren't here anymore. Then they'll mill around here in the first fort while the overmind considers the options. I'm fairly sure that they won't come any farther until the morning of the day after tomorrow."

"When did you want us to jump them?" Ekial asked.

"I'd say along about noon, wouldn't you, Keselo?"

"That should probably work out for the best," Keselo agreed. "We'll need some time to abandon the second breastwork, and I don't think we'll want the enemy close enough to interfere. They always seem to stop when the sun goes down—probably because they can't see very well at night. Do you think they'll pull back when it gets dark, Longbow?"

"They always did during the last war. It's probably instinctive. We can start pulling out of the second fort as soon as the Malavi hit the enemy."

"And then the poor little buggies will wander around in that second empty fort for a day or so looking for somebody to kill," Rabbit added.

"Buggies?" Narasan asked, looking slightly confused.

"Rabbit came up with that a few days ago," Gunda explained. "He seems to think it'll insult the enemies and hurt their feelings or something."

"How many more of these walls have your people erected so far?" Chief Kathlak asked.

"Eight, isn't it?" Gunda asked Commander Narasan.

Narasan nodded. "Andar has people working on two more. He's getting fairly close to the top of this slope. We might have to come up with something a bit stronger when we reach the top. We *don't* want the enemies to get past us until the weather turns bad. Once winter arrives, I'm sure that *this* particular war will grind to a stop."

"What a shame," Sorgan Hook-Beak said with mock regret.

4

It's different," Sorgan's younger cousin Torl declared, gesturing at the glorious sunset late that afternoon. "It's pretty enough, I suppose, but it's not too much like the sunsets out at sea. Mountains seem to do peculiar things to the sky."

"It's the clouds, Captain Torl," Keselo explained. "Most of the time, I'd imagine, the clouds out over the sea sort of plod along from here to there. When they come to mountains, though, they have to climb up one side and then slide down the other. That sort of scrambles them, so they're thicker in some places and thinner in others. That's why we see so many different shades of red in a mountain sunset."

"Did you study *everything* when you were going to school?" Torl asked.

"Well, not quite *everything*, Captain," Keselo replied. "My father had plans for me that didn't thrill me very much, so I spent my years at the university stalling. I wasn't interested in politics or commerce, so I dawdled a lot. Then I joined Commander Narasan's army—probably more to irritate my father than out of any great enthusiasm."

"Over in the Land of Maag, there's really only one career for us to follow," Torl said. Then he laughed. "When Skell and I were only boys, we used to slip into ships in the harbor of Kormo, hoping that we'd be a long way from shore before the sailors found us. You wouldn't *believe* how many times Skell and I got thrown into the bay when we were young. We both got to be very good swimmers, though." Torl squinted across the steep meadow that lay between the first breastwork and the second. "Nothing even resembling cover of any kind," he noted. "I think life will get very unpleasant for the bug-people when the Malavi gallop over the top of them."

The second breastwork was very much like the first—or like all the others Narasan's army had been erecting for the past several generations, for that matter. Soldiers *were* creatures of habit, after all, and as long as something worked the way it was *supposed* to work, nobody ever tampered with the original design.

The first breastwork was about five hundred yards to the south. The distance between the two was a bit farther than was customary, largely at Prince Ekial's request. "We'll need quite a bit of room, Narasan," the horseman had explained. "We're going to hit the enemy several times, so don't crowd us." Then he'd grinned. "Just remember that every one of them we kill out there in the open will be one less that'll attack your fort."

It was about midmorning before Keselo saw any movement in the now-abandoned first breastwork. He shuddered back from trying to make any estimate of just how many of their enemies had been mindlessly sacrificed to provide a causeway for the main force to follow to safely cross Athlan's mud-pit.

Since the first breastwork was some five hundred yards to the south, Keselo couldn't see many details in the activity of the bug-people down there, but it seemed to him that the invaders were more than a little confused.

"I see that they finally made it across the mud-pit," the youthful Veltan observed as he joined Keselo near the center of the breastwork. "Are they doing anything interesting at all?"

"It's a bit difficult to see any details," Keselo replied. "It's quite a long way down the slope from here."

Veltan peered down at the first breastwork. "From what I can see, they're all very confused."

"I didn't think an insect was capable of confusion," Keselo said.

"As an individual, it isn't," Veltan said. "It's the overmind that's confused. We just did something that no insect in all the world would *ever* do."

"Oh? What's that?"

"We abandoned our nest."

"Nest?"

"Insects wouldn't understand the meaning of the word 'fort,' Keselo. From *their* point of view, all these assorted fortifications are nests, places designed to protect *our* queen and all of her offspring. The ones that finally managed to get across the mud-pit are searching that breastwork, probably in the hope of finding *our* queen—and all of her puppies, of course—so that they can kill *her,* and eat all of her children, *and* the eggs that haven't hatched yet. There are a few lifeforms that are more primitive, but insects aren't really that much ahead of them. Life's extremely simple for an insect. Their first obligation is to protect mother at all cost. They'll even starve themselves to make sure that mother has enough to eat. If she doesn't eat, she won't lay eggs. That translates into 'extinction' in the minds of insects."

"They seem to be approaching 'honorable,' don't they?"

Veltan smiled. " 'Honor' is an alien concept for insects, Keselo. That's a human term and a human concept. Insects wouldn't recognize honor if it walked up and slapped them across the face—of course, they don't even *have* what we'd call faces. The insect queen—the 'Vlagh,' in their terminology—instills the need to protect *her* at any cost, and that need is paramount in the bug world. Bugs don't think for themselves, Keselo. 'Mother' does *all* the thinking, and what my big brother calls 'the overmind' is the instrument of her thoughts. What *she* thinks, they *all* think. It's a very simple kind of thing, but it works. The Vlagh has been around for millions of years, and she's still there. That means that they're doing *something* right, wouldn't you say?"

"I think she just changed her mind, though," Keselo said. "Quite a few of the bug-people just left the first breastwork behind, and they're coming up the slope toward us."

"Well, now," Veltan said, "that's *very* interesting. I'd have sworn that she wouldn't do that until sometime tomorrow. She seems to be growing up. I wouldn't have been the least bit surprised if she'd ordered her children to take that first breastwork apart, stone by stone."

Keselo caught a flicker of movement out of the corner of his eye, and when he looked more closely, he saw the Malavi horse-soldiers gathering among the trees off on the east side of the slope. Then he turned and looked toward a similar patch of trees on the west side. He wasn't really surprised to see Malavi gathering there as well. "I think we might be in for a surprise, Lord Veltan," he said.

"Oh?"

"If you look carefully, you'll see horse-soldiers gathering off to the west. Then, if you turn, you'll see more of them on the east side. I'd say that the bug-people are in for a very nasty surprise. It's quite obvious that the Malavi will strike from both sides at the same time, and there won't be many live bugs left after that."

"That's *awful* !" Veltan exclaimed.

"We *are* talking about our enemy, Lord Veltan," Keselo reminded his friend.

There came a sudden shout from the west, and Keselo recognized the voice of Prince Ekial. The Malavi swept out of the forests to the east and to the west at a dead run. The west side seemed to be slightly uphill from the east, but not really all that much. The enemies that had been coming up the slope seemed to be caught up in confusion, not knowing which way to flee. A few of them brandished their stolen weapons, and others awkwardly raised what passed for spears, but they were obviously no match for the charging Malavi.

In the space of just a few minutes, there were only a few enemies left standing. Then Ekial shouted again, and the two bodies of horse-soldiers whirled around and rode their horses right over the top of those survivors.

Keselo shuddered. "Remind me *never* to insult the Malavi, Lord Veltan. I don't think there's anybody in the whole world that could survive an attack like that."

The Malavi completed their second charge, brandishing their sabres in what seemed to Keselo to be a grossly over-dramatic fashion.

The slope leading up from the first breastwork was now littered with dead enemies, and so far as Keselo could see, not a single one of them was even twitching.

"It gets more'n a little tricky, Subaltern Keselo," the red-faced Sergeant Shwark said a few days later as the two of them stood beside a catapult just behind the front wall of the third breastwork. "Fire-missiles don't behave exactly like rocks do, and catapultin' *anything* downhill is a lot more difficult than uphill or straight across flat ground. A man what don't know exactly what he's doin' will almost always overshoot."

"You're the expert, Sergeant," Keselo replied. "I'd look sort of silly if I tried to tell a man who's been catapulting rocks and fire at enemies for the last twenty years how he should do his job, wouldn't you say?"

"Not out loud, I wouldn't," Sergeant Shwark said. "It ain't none too polite to say nasty things about our officers."

"You have very good manners, Sergeant," Keselo said. "What I'd really like to see is a way to make a fire-missile break up into a lot of smaller fragments. I think we'd like to see them scatter—or spread out—*before* they hit our enemies. If the fire-missile stays all in one piece, it might engulf four or five enemies in fire, but these particular enemies wouldn't really pay much attention to that."

"Now *that's* downright dumb, Subaltern."

"I'd say that 'dumb' is a fairly accurate description, Sergeant."

Sergeant Shwark squinted down the slope. "A skip-shot *might* work," he said. "I don't know that anybody has ever tried skip-shots with fire-missiles afore, but it'd prob'ly give you what you're after."

"Good," Keselo said. "Now why don't you tell me what you mean when you say 'skip-shot'?"

"It's a notion we sorta stole from another ormy a while back, sir," the sergeant replied. "Most always, catapults is used t' fling boulders at folks y' don't like much. That there other ormy thunk it over a bit, an' it sorta come t' 'em that flangin' a whole lot of smaller rocks at the ormy they didn't like would most likely kill a lot more than jist the four or five as would git skwarshed by a great big boulder. We tried it out a few times back in our home fort in Kaldacin, an' it done real good—or seemed to. We couldn't tell fer certain sure that it'd work on people as well as it seemed t' work on tree stumps. Then a young soljer as warn't none too bright in the first place come up with the notion of flangin' them small rocks at the ground right in front of the soljers we didn't like. He tole us it *might* work the same as a flat rock skippin' over water does. Well, we give it a try a couple times, an' believe me, sir, you wouldn't want t' be anywhere *near* where them little rocks come a-skippin' after they hit solid ground. Now, iff'n we was a-usin' *fire* instead of pebbles, thangs would get purty awful in a hurry."

"I think you just earned your pay for this whole month, Sergeant," Keselo said with a broad grin.

"I'm almost positive that it'll work, Commander," Keselo declared in the customary meeting the following morning. "If we use that 'skip-shot' Sergeant Shwark described, we'll scatter lumps of fire all over the downhill slope to the front of this breastwork."

"It *sounds* like it might work, Narasan," Padan said. "I'd say let's give it a try. The bug-people might not pay very much attention to their friends if all they do is just fall over dead, but if somebody *I* knew suddenly caught on fire, it'd get my immediate attention."

"And if it *doesn't* work, we could go back to throwing big gobs of fire at them," Gunda added. "I'll go along with Padan this time. Let's try some skip-shots and find out if they work like they're supposed to."

It was shortly after noon when the first bug-men tentatively came out of the second breastwork and started up the slope. It seemed to Keselo that their enemies had broken out in a rash of wariness. They'd encountered some very nasty surprises in the last few days so they had no idea of what *might* happen *this* time.

"It's up t' you, Subaltern," Sergeant Shwark said, "but if'n it was me, I'd wait a bit. Let more enemies get out in the open afore we stort settin' 'em on fire."

"I shall be guided by you, Sergeant," Keselo replied.

"I'm a-thankin' that y' *might* just have spent more time at that there school in Kaldacin than y' really should have, Subaltern. *Real* people don't hardly never talk so formal."

"I know," Keselo replied. "I'm *hoping* that it'll wear off—eventually. Have you any idea at all of what we should expect, Sergeant?"

"Nope. As fur as I know, nobody's ever tried it afore."

"We're breaking new ground, then," Keselo said. "I think that maybe we'll call this 'the Shwark maneuver.' You'll be famous, Sergeant."

"Only if it works, Subaltern," Shwark said. "Iff'n it happens t' fall apart, I don't think I'll want my name attached to it."

Keselo grew more and more tense as more and more of their enemies came out of the lower breastwork and started up the slope. It was growing increasingly obvious that the Vlagh had available servants beyond counting.

"I just came up with another idee, Subaltern," Sergeant Shwark said enthusiastically. "What say you to the notion of *not* settin' no fire t' the first one we fling out at them folks a-comin' up the slope. If we was t' splash the stuff that burns all over most of them, an' *then* threw fire down the hill, they'd almost *all* catch on fire, wouldn't they?"

Keselo blinked. "That's *brilliant,* Sergeant!" he exclaimed. "How in the world did you come up with that—just at the last minute?"

"I ain't all that shore, Subaltern," Sergeant Shwark replied. "It just seemed t' come a-poppin' outta nowhere."

"Do it that way. Let's see what happens."

"Keep yer fingers crossed," Shwark said, grinning. Then he ran over to the first catapult and took the torch away from the soldier who usually ignited the fire-missile. "All-right, shoot!"

"But—" the igniter protested.

"Keep your mouth shut!" Shwark barked. Then he glared at the catapult-crew. "I said shoot!" he barked. "Do it! Now!" The crew-leader jerked the release lever and the thick liquid that was normally on fire was hurled high into the air and then showered down on the advancing enemies.

Shwark turned sharply to the second catapult. "Touch off the fire!" he shouted.

The igniter laid his burning torch on the thick liquid in the catapult cup, and flame and smoke came pouring out.

"Shoot!" the sergeant roared.

The crew-leader jerked the release lever and the ball of fire flew out above the slope. It slanted down above the steep slope and then crashed down, almost exploding into hundreds of flaming gobs.

That in and of itself would have been disastrous for the advancing enemy, but the as yet unburning liquid launched by the first catapult suddenly took fire as well, and the entire slope was in flames.

Keselo stared down the slope in horror. No matter where he looked, he saw burning enemies—and they were mindlessly running in all directions at the same time. The fumes rising from the first catapult launch were suddenly ignited, and hundreds more enemy soldiers caught fire, and they too ran in all directions, igniting still more.

"A little extreme, perhaps," the Maag ship captain Torl noted, "but it *might* even get the attention of the Vlagh herself."

Then the warrior queen Trenicia, closely followed by Commander Narasan, came running up to the top of the wall. "What are you *doing*!" Trenicia screamed.

"It's called 'war,' Your Majesty," Keselo replied respectfully. "A bit unusual, perhaps, but it *does* seem to be working."

"Wars are supposed to be fought with *swords*!" she fumed.

"The older ones were, I suppose," Keselo admitted, "but fire is much more efficient. Look on the bright side, though. Your sword didn't get so much as a single dent in the blade this time, and we still won." He paused. "Isn't that just dandy?" he asked her in wide-eyed innocence.

"Be nice, Keselo," Commander Narasan murmured, trying his best to conceal the broad grin on his face.

INFERNO

1

It seemed to Ara that Dahlaine's decision to concentrate on Crystal Gorge was very sound. There were other passes that led up through the mountains standing between the Wasteland and the North country, but after Ara had sent out her awareness to examine those other passes, she was positive that the servants of the Vlagh would concentrate on Crystal Gorge, since the other passes all led into that single ravine which was the only route through the ridge-line that effectively blocked all other possible invasion routes.

The fort the Trogites had erected near the lower end of the gorge should have most effectively stopped the incursion of the creatures of the Wasteland, but the servants of the Vlagh found a way to assault the Trogites and their friends rather than the fort itself.

Ara found that to be most irritating. What made it even worse, she felt, lay in the filching of the use of smoke as a way to drive the outlanders out of the gorge. The Vlagh was a thief—a very *good* thief, but a thief all the same.

The Trogites and their friends had devised many ways

to block the creatures of the Wasteland. The barrier that now stretched across the north end of the gorge seemed most effective, and the mud-pit *would* have been a stroke of genius *if* their enemy had been human. The servants of the Vlagh were not intelligent enough to be afraid, so they crossed the mud-pit with an enormous loss, and they took the first breastwork.

The savage attacks of the Malavi slowed the advance of their enemies, but not by very much.

It was the use of what the Trogites called "fire-missiles" that was most effective. Ara found the innovation of the "skip-shot" by the humorous old veteran called Shwark to be a stroke of pure genius. She had come up with a way to make it even more effective, and it hadn't been difficult to pass that on to Shwark at the last minute. Fire, it appeared, was the one thing that actually frightened the creatures of the Wasteland, so it seemed to Ara that fire *might* just be the best possible weapon to use in this particular war. This was confirmed by the mention of "a fire unlike any fire we have ever seen" in Lillabeth's dream. It didn't seem to make much sense to Ara, however. Fire *was* just fire, after all, and they all looked more or less the same.

The smoke that had driven their friends out of Crystal Gorge had pretty much died out by now, and the clouds Dahlaine and Veltan had called in to douse the gorge with rain had moved on, and the sky above was once again a glorious blue.

Then the word "blue" seemed to jump out and seize Ara. Of course! *That* was what Lillabeth's dream had described. Blue fire *would* be most unusual, but not here in the Domain of the North. The archer Athlan had spoken of "swamp-fire," and the overly clever Trogite Keselo had mentioned something he called "methane," or "coal-gas." He'd told his friends about a coal mine down in the Trogite Empire that had been on fire for seventy years and would probably continue to burn for several centuries. The notion of a blue fire that would burn forever cleared away Ara's doubts and confusion. All she had to do now was to locate a deposit of what Keselo had called "coal."

She released her awareness and sent it probing through the ridge-line that stood on both sides of the gorge. She encountered several extensive layers of coal, but they weren't exactly where she wanted them.

She probed deeper and came to the one she wanted. It ran along the ridge and lay just below the floor of the upper end of the gorge. Better still, there were large pockets of that coal-gas Keselo had described. "Now we're getting somewhere," Ara murmured. She'd have to crack a few rocks to release the coal-gas, but that wouldn't be much of a problem.

Then she stopped, and her awareness seemed to freeze inside the coal-bed. The prevailing wind in Crystal Gorge went up toward Dahlaine's part of the Land of Dhrall, and sending perpetual fire in *that* direction could be disastrous. Fire was nice enough, Ara conceded, but only if it went in the right direction.

"I think I'll have to work on this a bit," she murmured to herself, rising back up through the hard stone and gleaming quartz.

She sent her memory back into the distant past, long before the Land of Dhrall had been separated from the rest of the world. At that time, this region had been covered by a dense forest of primeval trees that, in a certain sense, had been the grandparents of what Keselo had called "coal." The region had been marshy, so the tree roots had not been firmly attached to the ground beneath them, and even a minor windstorm had uprooted them. She realized that those short-lived trees had been the ultimate source of what Keselo had called coal, *and* of the gas that was the source of the blue fire. That explained what had seemed to Ara to be a contradiction. Down at their core, swamps and mountains were not really unrelated.

The more Ara considered her scheme, the more she came to realize that success or failure would depend almost entirely on the direction of the wind—and its strength. There *was* a certain kind of windstorm that might just work out fine. The natives here in northern Dhrall called them "whirlwinds," and Keselo had referred to them as "cyclones." They were enormously powerful, and that made Ara quite dubious. A bit of experimentation seemed to be in order here.

She sent her awareness on up to the northernmost region of the Matakan Nation and started to play with the wind. It wasn't easy, of course. Whirlwinds seemed to have minds of their own. After several tries, however, Ara came up with a way to steer the silly things. She *would* have to warn the outlanders, of course, but she knew exactly whom she should turn to when the time came.

Ara considered her options then. It seemed to her that the fire driven by the whirlwind should be enormous. First it would purge Crystal Gorge, that went without saying. There *were* all those secondary passes to the south of the gorge as well, though, and Ara wanted to clean those also. If she did this right, she could obliterate an entire hatch of the servants of the Vlagh in no more than half an hour. "That might persuade her to go play somewhere else," Ara murmured.

There still seemed to be something missing, though. "I

think that maybe I'll need a second fire—somewhere near the southern mouth of the gorge. The Vlagh can be very stubborn sometimes, so I'd better make it clear that she's *not* going to be able to come this way ever again."

She sighed and began to probe the southern end of the gorge. It *was* getting just a bit easier, she was forced to admit. Coal had a distinct odor, and Ara had noticed that she could actually *taste* what Keselo had called "coal-gas."

There was definitely a deposit of coal near the southern end of the gorge, and as Ara homed in on it, she suddenly burst out laughing. She was positive that it hadn't been intentional, but Gunda's fort lay right above the deposit. The fort itself was *relatively* impenetrable, but the fort bathed perpetually in blue fire would take "impenetrable" out to the far end.

"First things first, though," she reminded herself, and she went in search of Longbow.

Night was descending on the Trogite breastworks to the north of the gorge, and when Ara touched Longbow's mind, she found that he was already asleep.

"Don't get excited, dear one," she told him. "It's only me."

"Again?" Longbow's thought replied. "Do you want us to run away some more?"

"Not really," Ara replied. "Warn our friends that a windstorm's coming, so they'd better take cover. Caves might be the best. The wind won't be just a gentle breeze. You'd *also* better pull all of our friends off the rim of the gorge. The wind might be a bit hard to control, so the gorge rims—both east and west—could be dangerous. There's *also* going to be fire down in the gorge, and it might spill over now and then."

"You don't sound too sure of yourself this time."

"I've never done this before," Ara admitted. "It *should* work the way we want it to, but let's not take any chances. Go back to sleep, Longbow. I'll take care of everything. I hope so, anyway."

Then she drifted away. She still had one more important decision to make. Right at first it had seemed that Yaltar, who was really Vash the younger god, might be the most suitable Dreamer to unleash this upcoming disaster, but if it was going to be the whirlwind that would drive the blue fire down through Crystal Gorge to the Wasteland, weather would be far more important. Enalla, known now as Lillabeth, had already contributed much to this third war, but Enalla lacked a certain amount of subtlety, and she was a long way away. Since the whirlwind would be their main weapon this time, the Dreamer would almost have to be a girl, and that left Balacenia, of course. The more Ara thought about it, the more convinced she became that Balacenia—known to the humans as Eleria—would be the perfect Dreamer to permanently block all passes from the Wasteland to the Domain of Dahlaine of the North.

Ara reached out to Mount Shrak, where Zelana was minding the children, and gently touched Balacenia's sleeping mind. "Sleep on, dear child," Ara said, "but join your mind with mine that we may once again confront the servants of that called 'the Vlagh.'"

"Well, it's about time," Balacenia replied. "Did you forget that I was here?"

"I never forget you, dear one," Ara replied. "Yours is the finest mind of all the children—and of the old ones as well. Do you think that you could unleash a whirlwind?"

"I see no problem with that," Balacenia said.

"Perhaps not in bringing it to life, dear one, but we need to send it down along a specific path."

"I was fairly sure that's what we would need. I might have to sit on it a bit to keep it from roaming up out of Crystal Gorge, but it *will* do what I want it to. What have you come up with to produce this 'fire unlike any fire we have ever seen' Enalla's Dream mentioned?"

"It's going to be blue, child."

" 'Swamp-fire,' you mean?"

"It goes just a bit further than swamps, dear," Ara said. "The gas that comes out of rotting trees in swamps also lies under the ground in beds of coal. There's a vast pocket of that inflammable gas in a coal-bed that lies under Crystal Gorge. We'll want to shatter the rock plate that's holding the gas in the coal-bed. That's where the whirlwind comes in. Not only will it push the gas south toward the Wasteland, but whirlwinds create a great deal of lightning, so it'll ignite that gas, and there'll be a huge wave of blue fire rushing down toward the Wasteland."

"You're going to create another inland sea, I take it," Balacenia said shrewdly. "The one in Veltan's Domain was water. The one up here will be fire. Their colors will match, though. Veltan will love that. He *adores* the color blue."

"You're not supposed to make these jumps ahead without letting me know, Balacenia," Ara scolded her.

"A habit of mine, I suppose," Balacenia confessed. "I'm very sorry, Mother. Can you ever forgive me?"

2

The weather had turned cold, and Sorgan Hook-Beak was very grateful for the bison-hide robe Chief Two-Hands had given him to ward off the chill. He squinted up at the bright blue sky just after sunrise. "At least it isn't snowing yet," he muttered. He'd been here in the Land of Dhrall for almost a year now, and he still remembered the deep snow that had been piled up on the village of Lattash when he'd arrived there with his fleet.

At least he'd been more or less in charge of things during that first war, but as more and more outlanders arrived here in the Land of Dhrall, he felt that he wasn't really all that significant anymore.

That didn't sit too well with him, for some reason.

He decided that he should probably go have a few words with his friend Narasan. There was yet another peculiarity about this part of the world. If someone had told him a few years ago that he would *ever* be friends with a Trogite, he was sure that he'd have laughed in the fool's face. Narasan had been a little stuffy right at first, but as the two of them had come to know each other better, that stuffiness had faded away, and they now got along very well together.

"You're up early, Sorgan," the dark-haired Trogite noted as Sorgan joined him on the west side of the breastworks.

"Not really," Sorgan disagreed. "The sun comes up later, that's all. I'm having a bit of trouble with some of the things the bug-people did when they attacked your first breastwork. I was almost positive that the mud-pit would stop them dead in their tracks, but it didn't seem to slow them down very much. Of course, the idea of their using their friends as building material to get across that pit never would have occurred to me."

"That's probably because we don't think the way bugs do, Sorgan," Narasan replied. "It startled me probably even more than it startled you. I'd say that there's no such word as 'friend' in the language of the bugs. What they did sickened me right down to the core, but it *was* extremely practical. They needed to pile up *something* to build a road across that mud-pit, and since there wasn't anything else nearby, they used their fellow bugs instead."

"You're probably right," Sorgan conceded. "Do you think there's any way at all for us to get back down to that fort we built near the bottom of the gorge?"

"I wouldn't get my hopes up, Sorgan. Now that the bug-people have run us off once, they know exactly how to do it again."

"Maybe the horse-soldiers could rush into those caves and put out the fires. That fort would have stopped the bugs right there if it hadn't been for that cursed smoke."

"I wouldn't make any large wagers on that, my friend."

"Your people *have* found a way to get the bug-people's immediate attention, though. Those fire-missiles your men threw at them yesterday worked very well. When you set fire to anybody—or any*thing*—he seems to forget all about whatever he's supposed to be doing."

"It worked out even better than we'd expected. The only problem is the fact that the bugs have fires of their own now. If we throw fire at them too often, they'll probably steal our idea and start throwing fire at us."

Sorgan squinted off toward the south. "I'm not really very useful here right now, Narasan," he said. "Your people—and the horse-soldiers, of course—seem to have things under control. I think I might just drift on down along the rim of the gorge and see just how many of the bug-people are coming this way. That's one of the things we really need to know."

"You're going to take up scouting as a hobby, Sorgan?" Narasan asked with a faint smile.

"I need something to *do,* Narasan," Sorgan declared. "I feel so *useless* just sitting here watching my friends fight this war."

"It's not really such a bad idea, Sorgan," Narasan replied thoughtfully. "You've got a steady mind, and younger scouts tend to get excited, and they exaggerate things. Older soldiers are much more dependable. Why don't you take Padan along? He's got a good mind, and you two seem to get along quite well."

"Iff'n that's the way you want 'er, we'll do 'er that way," Sorgan said, grinning at his friend.

"Clown," Narasan accused.

And then they both laughed.

It seemed to Sorgan that it might not be a bad idea to take another friend or two along on the expedition down the rim of the gorge. The bug-people were very unpredictable sometimes, and there was no real reason to limit their party to just two men. Longbow would have been his first choice, of course, but Longbow seemed to be *everybody's* first choice, so Sorgan went in search of relatives instead.

Skell seemed to be in a bad humor, however. The abandonment of the fort at the bottom of the gorge had *really* irritated Sorgan's cousin.

"We spend weeks and weeks building that fort, and then the bug-people drive us out in less than a day. We aren't getting paid enough for *this* silly war, cousin. If things don't start getting better, I think I'll just pack up and go on back home."

"We took the gold, Skell," Sorgan reminded his cousin. "We're pretty much obliged to stay here now."

"Just exactly what do you expect to see down in that gorge, cousin?" Torl asked.

"I'm not sure," Sorgan admitted. "That's why I think it might be a good idea to go have a look. The bug-people are full of surprises, and getting surprised during a war is the best way I know of to end up dead."

"He makes a lot of sense, big brother," Torl said to Skell. "Why don't you stay here and try to get over your grouchies. I'll go along with cousin Sorgan and see if I can keep him out of trouble."

"Thanks a lot, Torl," Sorgan said in a flat, unfriendly tone.

"Family responsibility, cousin," Torl said, shrugging. "Who else will be coming along? If that warrior woman will be one of the party, I might just change my mind, though. She gives me a lot of creepies, for some reason—probably because she never learned how to laugh."

"Do you get along with Padan at all?" Sorgan asked.

"Very well," Torl said. "Padan can be almost as funny as I am."

"We're not going down there to laugh, Torl."

"I'll try to keep it under control. Let's go find Padan and get started."

Padan was waiting for them near the third breastwork up the hill—the one where Narasan's men had doused the charging bug-men with fire. "Narasan told me to join up with you on your scouting expedition down the rim of the gorge, Captain Hook-Beak," he said. "What are we supposed to be looking for?"

"If I knew that, we wouldn't have to go," Sorgan replied. "Those fires your men splashed all over the bug-men worked out very well."

"I sort of liked it myself," Padan replied. "I just wish that somebody could come up with a way to throw fire at our enemies without using those cumbersome catty-pults."

"Catty-pults?"

"There was a sergeant back when we were only boys in the fort in Kaldacin," Padan explained. "For some reason, he just couldn't pronounce 'catapult.' Every time he said it, it came out 'catty-pult.' I've got a sort of a hunch that the first time he ever heard the word, 'catty' was right there at the beginning."

Torl laughed. "I did that to a fisherman one time. I deliberately mispronounced the names of certain kinds of fish, and after that he'd talk for hours about 'habilets' and 'clod-fish.' It drove the other fishermen crazy, but he just couldn't help himself. Just exactly what do you think we should be looking for down in the gorge, cousin?"

"Numbers, for the most part," Sorgan replied, "but I think that what we *really* need to know is whether or not the bug-people have picked up bows and arrows, and whether they know how to use them or not. We *definitely* don't want to come up against bug-men who can shoot arrows at us."

"Let's get started, then," Padan suggested. "If there *are* any bug-archers charging up the gorge, we'd better come up with some way to kill them off *before* they get up here. Things are likely to fall apart on us if the bug-people start showering us with arrows."

They climbed up the steep slope to the west side of the Trogite breastworks and then went on down to the little brook that crossed the mouth of Crystal Gorge. Sorgan tried his very best *not* to think about how long it must have taken for a stream *that* small to eat its way down through solid rock to form its current bed. Sorgan knew exactly what the word "hundred" meant, but when numbers wandered off toward "thousand"—or even "million"—and the people who used those terms were talking about *years,* Sorgan's mind shied back in horror.

The sun was all the way up now and the shadows back under the stunted mountain trees had that bluish cast to them that always seemed to come out in the early morning up in the mountains. Sorgan rather grudgingly admitted that mountain country could be very beautiful—not as beautiful as the sea, of course, but not really all that bad.

They followed the little brook on upstream until they reached the steep slope that led up to the rim of Crystal Gorge. "You missed a lot of fun up here, cousin," Torl said. "You should have come along when we helped Keselo fill the mouth of the gorge with chunks of that pink quartz. If I understood what he told us right, there are a lot of cracks and fissures in that quartz. A good healthy sneeze is all it takes to break the quartz loose, and it tumbles on down to the bottom of the gorge. I had a good solid iron pry-bar, and I broke loose about a half acre of quartz in one afternoon."

"That Keselo for you," Padan declared. "He can come up with the most exotic things I've ever seen or heard of every time he blinks his eyes."

"He's good, all right," Torl agreed. He squinted up the steep slope. "Here comes the chief of Athlan's tribe. I think his name is Kathlak," he said. "He might be able to give us enough information to save us the long hike down to the bottom of the gorge."

"You'd better let me do the talking, Torl," Sorgan said. "These natives are very formal, and I'm sort of what they'd call 'the chief' of the Maags around here."

"Was there something you needed?" the silvery-haired chief of the Deer Hunter Tribe asked.

"Mostly just information, Chief Kathlak," Sorgan replied. "The bug-people have been attacking for the past several days. Are there very many more of them coming up the gorge?"

"Oh, yes," Kathlak replied in a somber tone.

"Is there trouble of some kind?" Torl asked.

"The young men of my tribe made a foolish mistake, that's about all. The bottom of the gorge was completely covered with our enemies, so our young archers had many, many targets to shoot arrows at, and they got carried away. Can you believe that they wasted all of those metal arrowheads that the little fellow from the Land of Maag made for us? Now we'll have to go back to using the old stone ones."

"I'll have a talk with Rabbit when we get back," Sorgan promised. "We'll have him set up his arrow factory again."

"I'd appreciate that," Kathlak said.

"The bug-people we've seen so far seem to be carrying various kinds of weapons, Chief Kathlak," Sorgan continued. "I'd say that it's likely that they wandered around the battlefields during the first two wars stealing the weapons of our dead friends. We've seen them carrying swords and axes and spears."

"We've seen those as well," Chief Kathlak replied.

"Now we come to the important question. Have your people up here seen any of them at all that were carrying bows?"

"I believe there *was* one," Kathlak said, squinting down the slope. "I wouldn't worry about him too much, though. I'm sure that he didn't understand at all what it really was. He'd cut off the bowstring and used it to tie a spear-point to one of the bow-tips."

"You're not serious!" Padan exclaimed.

"Nobody's ever accused our enemies of being very bright," Kathlak replied. "I think 'very dull' would come closer."

"Have you happened to see any peculiar-looking ones?" Sorgan asked. "We encountered some of them during the last war that looked like a cross between a bug and a turtle. When Longbow's archers shot arrows at them, the arrows just bounced off those turtle-shells."

"Athlan warned us about those. His friend Longbow described them. I thought he was just joking, though."

"Longbow doesn't know *how* to joke," Torl said. "Have any of the bug-people tried to climb up the quartz walls to these rims?"

"A few tried that," Kathlak replied, "but about all they did was cause us to waste more arrows. Those of us on *this* side picked off the ones on the other wall, and our friends of the

Reindeer Tribes cleaned off *our* wall. Those bug-things climb very well, don't they? There's nothing at all like handholds on these quartz walls."

"Bugs don't *have* hands, Chief Kathlak," Padan said. "Flies can walk on the ceiling if they want to."

"How have things been going up beyond the gorge?" Kathlak asked.

"Not bad at all. You should be very proud of your man Athlan, Chief Kathlak. He came up with an idea that's never even *occurred* to those of us who fight wars for a living. The Trogites had built a sort of low fort-wall to hold our enemies back, and Athlan suggested that a mud-pit to the front of the wall would slow the enemies down quite a bit."

Kathlak smiled. "That's Athlan for you," he said. "How did it work?"

"Not quite as good as it should have. The bug-people decided that a raised-up road would give them a way to cross the mud-pit to attack that wall, and they used their friends to *build* that road."

"I wouldn't *want* friends who could do something like that."

"We got even with them later, though," Padan said. "We splashed burning tar—or pitch—all over the ones who were trying to attack us on up the hill a ways. There were burning bugs running in all directions up there. Over the years we've found that one of the best ways there is to distract an enemy who's charging you is to set him on fire."

"You people are *very* good," Kathlak said.

"We try," Padan said modestly.

3

It was about midmorning when a stiff, chill wind came in from the west, carrying dark clouds that strongly hinted that stormy weather was on the way. Sorgan periodically looked down into the teeming gorge. It seemed to him that the bug-people stretched from wall to wall across the narrow valley. They were almost all carrying weapons of one kind or another. There were a *few* that had obviously been picked up during the two previous wars, but the vast majority of the bug-things carried nothing except for sharp-pointed sticks. A pointed stick wouldn't be much in the way of a weapon, but just the fact that the bug-people had moved up from using nothing but their own teeth and claws worried Sorgan more than just a little. It seemed to him that the creatures of the Wasteland were becoming more and more intelligent every day. If that happened to continue at its current speed, it wouldn't be very long before the bug-people outclassed the people-people in the world of intelligence. There was an old saying in the Land of Maag that declared that a stupid enemy was a gift from the gods. A suddenly *intelligent* enemy would be much more like a curse. "I think it might just be time to kill every last one of those cursed things down there in the gorge and then sweep on out into the Wasteland itself and kill every one of them out *there* as well."

"I didn't quite catch that, cousin," Torl said.

"Just thinking out loud, Torl," Sorgan said. "Let's step right along here. We've got a few miles between us and the south end of the gorge. Let's go take a look at that, and then hustle back on up to the north end. Narasan's waiting for information, so let's get back up there as quick as we can."

By midafternoon, the wind coming in from the west was howling through the mountains, and the clouds it carried had gone even darker. Sorgan glared at the sky. "Can't you go someplace else to play?" he growled.

"Cap'n!" he heard a shout coming from behind them.

It was Rabbit, and the little smith seemed to be running just as hard as he could. "You'd all better get as far back from this rim as you possibly can, Cap'n," he shouted, "and then we'll probably need a cave to hide in for a few hours."

"What are you talking about, Rabbit?" Sorgan demanded.

"Longbow's 'unknown friend' is playing games again, Cap'n," Rabbit said. "This time I think she's going to use one of those land-bound waterspout things."

"A cyclone, you mean?" Padan asked.

"I guess that's what the land people call them," Rabbit replied. "What they're called doesn't really matter all that much, though. Longbow told me that there's one of those spin-around winds that's going to zip right on down through this gorge. It'll pick up the bug-people and throw them up about a thousand or so feet up into the air. That's *one* of the reasons we're going to need shelter. After that spin-around wind goes on down the gorge, it's probably going to rain bug-people around here for an hour or two at least."

"Aw," Torl said with a broad grin, "what a shame. I'd say that we're just about to hear 'splats' coming from all over the place, and I surely wouldn't want some bug going 'splat' right on top of my head."

"We'd better get some warning to the Tonthakan archers up at the head of the gorge," Padan said. "If it's really going to be a cyclone, they'd better get back at least a mile from the rim."

"I already took care of that, Padan," Rabbit said. "They were running when I left. Now *we* need shelter ourselves."

"There, I think," Padan said, pointing at a nearby cluster of grey-colored boulders. "We should be able to find a cave—or at least a well-sheltered place—in that rock-pile."

"We'd better hurry," Rabbit suggested, looking off to the north. "I don't see anything coming our way *yet*, but it probably won't be very long before it shows up. Longbow's friend can move very, very fast when she thinks it's necessary, and I'd say we're getting real close to the edge of 'necessary,' wouldn't you?"

"Let's go!" Sorgan said sharply.

They reached the pile of mossy boulders, and as Padan had suggested, there were a goodly number of passages running between the huge rocks. When a large rock leans against one of its neighbors, it forms what almost looks like a tunnel.

"Let's try that one over there," Padan suggested. "The boulder that's facing the probable direction the cyclone will follow is as big as a house, and when a cyclone is coming your way, you want something big and heavy standing on the windy side."

"Here it comes," Torl shouted. Then he stopped dead in his tracks. "Good god," he exclaimed. "The silly thing's on *fire*!"

Sorgan whirled and stared at the approaching whirlwind. As Torl had observed, the spinning wind was definitely burning—but it was no ordinary fire. Normal fires are yellow or red.

This one, however, was blue.

4

Sorgan and his friends crouched in the sheltered passageway between the two enormous boulders, listening to the shrieking roar of the wind. Rabbit, however, frequently crawled on his hands and knees to the narrow opening between the two boulders. "I think we're safe," he shouted over the roar of the whirlwind. "The storm's on fire, that's for sure, but the fire's staying down there in the gorge. A few flickers come up above the rim, but they aren't spreading out much."

"That curiosity of yours is likely to get you killed one of these days, Rabbit," Sorgan shouted.

"I don't think so, Cap'n," the little smith replied, "—at least not when Longbow's friend's involved. She did this to kill the bugs—not us. The color of the fire that windstorm is pulling along behind it says that it's that gas that burns across the top of a swamp or comes boiling up out of coal-mines—except that it's not very likely that anybody's digging coal out of *this* one. I *think* I know how she did it, if you're curious, Cap'n."

"I'll listen," Sorgan replied.

"I'd say that she found a huge pocket of that gas that burns blue somewhere down below the floor of the gorge at the upper end. Then she cracked open the solid rock that was holding the gas back. Then, after quite a bit of the gas had built up, she reached out and grabbed this whirlwind and threw it in this direction."

"Nobody could do things like that, Rabbit," Torl scoffed.

"We're not talking about just *anybody,* Torl. This is the lady who turned miles and miles of sand into imitation gold and then broke open a mountain to unleash an underground ocean on the bug-people and the Church people. I'd say that there's almost nothing that she *can't* do, if she really wants to."

"All right, then," Torl said, "how did she set fire to the gas?"

"We've all seen those waterspouts out at sea. I don't know if you've ever looked hard at one of them, but it's always seemed to me that every one of them had lightning jumping around as it went by. If you want to set something on fire, lightning will do it faster than just about anything else. I'm just guessing here, but I think her plan went something like this: First she turned the gas loose, then she set fire to it with lightning, and *then* she sent that whirlwind roaring down the gorge. The wind's pulling the fire along behind it, and I'd say that's what this is all about. A solid wall of fire is rushing down the gorge, burning every one of the bug-men who was rushing on up to attack the Trogite breastworks right down to little clumps of ashes. *And*—knowing Longbow's friend and how she thinks—I'd say that the fire won't stop at the bottom of the gorge. It's probably going to sort of imitate that wall of water she used down south. The fire will most likely rush out into the Wasteland and set fire to every single bug-man within a hundred miles of where we are right now."

"A sea of fire instead of a sea of water?" Torl asked.

"I'd say so, yes," Rabbit agreed.

After the shrieking of the whirlwind had begun to fade off to the south, Sorgan and his friends cautiously came out into the open again to see what had happened down in the gorge.

There were no longer thousands of bug-people eagerly rushing north, that was obvious. Many of the bugs had been covered with those peculiar shells Sorgan and the others had seen during the war in Veltan's Domain. Keselo had referred to those shells as "outer skeletons." Evidently, *some* varieties of bugs wore their bones on the *outside* of their bodies rather than the inside. Sorgan saw that armor of any kind would be a bad idea if the enemy was using fire. Getting burned a bit around the edges was one thing. Getting cooked alive was quite another.

There was a thick layer of ash covering the bottom of the gorge, stirred occasionally by the vagrant breeze. Since there were no plants down in the gorge, the ashes were almost certainly all that was left of hundreds—or even thousands—of bug-people. Sorgan shuddered. The bugs were enemies, certainly, but still . . .

Though it was probably not really necessary now, Sorgan and the others went on down the west rim of the gorge to have a look at the fort they'd been forced to abandon some time back. Sorgan told himself that Narasan *would* like to know if the fort was still standing, so it *was* proper to have a look at it. Then too, there was now no *real* need for them to hurry back. Their enemies didn't exist anymore, after all.

Sorgan privately admitted to himself that it was pure curiosity that pulled him the last few miles down the rim of the gorge.

The fort itself appeared to be intact, but there was a very noticeable difference now. The fort was bathed in blue fire that came boiling up out of the earth.

"Now *that's* what I'd call a miracle!" Padan exclaimed. "There's a fort that doesn't need any soldiers at all. The blue fire is doing all the work."

"Our 'unknown friend' must really *hate* the bug-people," Rabbit said. "That first blue fire is still rushing on down to the Wasteland, burning bugs every inch of the way. Just on the off-chance that her first blue fire burns itself out some-time next year, she reached down and unleashed a *second* fire that'll keep burning for the next hundred years or so."

"I suppose we might as well turn around and go on back up to Mount Shrak," Sorgan said. "That fire—or the two of them, actually—put an end to this third war. Our 'unknown friend' ended the second war with a sea of water, but she ended *this* one with a sea of fire."

"Three down, and one to go," Padan noted. "If we step right along, we *should* be able to finish that last war before next spring rolls around. Then we'll all be able to go on home and spend the next thirty or forty years counting all the gold we made *this* year."

THE RETURN TO THE LAND OF DREAMS

1

Balacenia was alone in a seldom-used chamber in Dahlaine's cave under Mount Shrak. There were several things she needed to consider, so she'd separated her awareness from the sleeping Eleria so that she could be alone with her thoughts.

She had been more than a little startled by just how far Mother had been willing to go to halt the invasion of the North by the creatures of the Wasteland. Unleashing perpetual fire seemed to be more than a little extreme.

"It *was* necessary, Dear Heart," Mother's voice came out of the darkness near the back of the cave. Her presence didn't particularly surprise Balacenia. Mother had almost always appeared when Balacenia was troubled.

"I don't see just exactly why, Mother," Balacenia replied. "The outlanders had things pretty much under control, and I'm sure they'd have defeated the servants of the Vlagh."

"But not in time, Balacenia."

"Is time really all *that* significant, Mother?"

"More significant than you could ever imagine, Dear

Heart. If something doesn't happen when it's *supposed* to happen, the servants of the Vlagh will overcome our friends, and then the world will be hers. *Her* children are advancing much more rapidly than you could ever imagine, Balacenia. If we don't destroy them all very soon, they'll become more intelligent than people, and people will go down the path to extinction. We must move against the Vlagh now."

"*We?*"

"You and the other children, Dear Heart. I love the elders dearly, but they're too close to the end of their cycles to be of much use. That's why the Vlagh waited so long. Her observers had described the slowing of thought that infects older ones, and she deliberately waited until now to unleash her servants. The local natives and the outlanders are still more clever than the creatures that serve the Vlagh, but that superiority won't last very much longer, I'm afraid. The servants of the Vlagh are filching thought from people. It's been less than a year since the incursions began, and the creatures that serve the Vlagh have already learned the value of weapons, and also the importance of fire. I shudder to think of how far their minds will have gone by next spring. Gather up your brothers and sister, Balacenia, and take them to that Land of Dreams you and Vash created. We need to make some decisions, and we don't have very much time."

"We need to talk, Eleria," Balacenia said, sending her thought out to her sleeping alternate.

"Who are you?" Eleria mumbled in her sleep.

"I am you, Eleria. I'm who you'll become when you grow up."

"I don't understand."

"Yes, you do—if you'll think about it a little."

"You've come back to visit me from the future?"

"Or the past. We're in the Land of Dreams now, Eleria, so time doesn't mean anything. Mother needs our help."

"Why didn't you say that before? I'll do whatever Mother wants me to do."

"I know," Balacenia replied. "I feel much the same." She hesitated. She and Eleria were one and the same, but there were several differences, and she didn't want to disturb her other self. "There are going to be a few times in the not-too-distant future when I'll have to step in and take over for you, Eleria. Some things are about to happen that we *must* prevent. I'm more experienced than you are, so I'll be able to deal with those things more smoothly than you will. Please don't fight me when I do that, Eleria."

"Well—all right, I suppose," the child replied, "but it's going to cost you quite a few kisses."

Balacenia laughed. Eleria, it seemed, was much more advanced than she seemed at first glance. Something came to Balacenia that would probably never have occurred to her if Eleria hadn't mentioned kisses. "I was going to visit a certain place alone," she said to her alternate, "but maybe you might want to come along."

"Where is it?"

"In my imagination, dear—mine and the imagination of our brother Vash—or Yaltar, if you'd prefer."

"What's this place called?"

"It's the Land of Dreams, Eleria. I think you'll like it. I know that Mother does."

"Will she be there?"

"If you want her to be, yes."

"Let's go, then," Eleria said enthusiastically.

*   *   *

There was an almost homelike familiarity about the Land of Dreams Balacenia and Vash had created in years long past. The dark forest was still uncluttered by bushes, the streams of clear water showed no trace of mud, and, most beautiful of all, the multicolored aurora seethed above the horizon like a rainbow that had finally found its native home.

"Your imagination does nice work, Balacenia," Eleria observed.

"*Our* imagination, child," Balacenia corrected.

"Not entirely, alternate me," Eleria slyly disagreed. "You left out the sea, and there's hardly a trace of my pink pearl."

"Can you ever forgive me?"

"I'll think about it."

Then Vash, Dakas, and Enalla came out of the forest, but they stopped, staring in open astonishment and disbelief at Eleria.

"Was it really a good idea to bring her here, Balacenia?" Vash asked in a slightly worried tone.

"A *very* good idea, Yaltar," Eleria said, stepping past her older identity. "I'd have nagged poor Balacenia for weeks if she hadn't brought me along. She told me—or probably would have eventually—that Mother comes here quite often. I really want to see Mother, and to talk with her."

"About what?" Balacenia asked, greatly puzzled.

"You'll find out all in good time, Big-Me," Eleria replied with a grin.

"Whatever seems best to you, Little-Me," Balacenia said. Then she looked at her brothers and sister. "I'm not trying to tell you what to do," she told them, "but I'm almost positive that you'll all have to do exactly what I just did. When Dahlaine snatched us up while we were sleeping and pushed us back to infancy, he separated us from our previous identities. Eleria is *me*, of course, but she's *not* the me you all know and love. The same will be true of Yaltar, Ashad, and Lillabeth. They've encountered things that we've never seen, and we need to know about those things."

"They all know that, Big-Me," Eleria said. "I think you'd all better start smiling. Mother's coming."

Balacenia turned quickly, and sure enough, Mother, surrounded by the seething colors of the aurora, was walking down through the imaginary sky. "Are we having a little family get-together again?" she asked with a slightly amused expression.

"I thought it might be best to share what you told me about the possible extinction of people, Mother," Balacenia replied, "and Eleria wanted to talk with you."

Mother gave child Eleria a startled look. "You brought her *here*? What were you thinking of, Balacenia?"

"It's not her fault, Mother," Eleria said. "I *wanted* her to bring me here. She's already explained to the other members of our generation that when Dahlaine seized us while we were still sleeping and then hurled us back to infancy, he was splitting us right down the middle. Doesn't that sort of mean that when the elders go to sleep, there'll be eight of us instead of just four? We may be taking on our tasks in just one body each, but we're different enough now that each of us will have separate personalities. That might be all right, though. We little ones will probably be able to suggest alternatives to the big ones—and *we* know much more about what's happening out there in reality than they do. You told Big-Me—Balacenia—that the Vlagh thing wants to make people stumble off toward extinction. *We* know people better than our elders do, so we can help keep people around when we need them."

"She *could* be right, you know," Mother told Balacenia and her relatives.

"Of course I'm right, Mother," Eleria said. "I'm *always* right—or hadn't you noticed that? Now I think you owe me a whole *lot* of kisses, don't you?" And she held out her arms to Mother.

2

Narasan and Sorgan had only recently returned to Mount Shrak from the upper end of the now eternally burning Crystal Gorge. After they'd reported what had happened in the gorge, they went outside to privately discuss what was almost certain to come up before long.

Balacenia was there, of course, but *not* there at the same time. The Eleria part of her had been aware of Mother's clever trick, and it hadn't been difficult to duplicate.

"You *do* know what's going to pop up very soon, don't you, Sorgan?" Narasan asked his friend.

"Let me think about it for a moment or two," Sorgan replied with an imitation frown. Then he snapped his fingers. "I think *somebody* might just come along and offer us tons of gold if we'll agree to fight still another war in some part of the Land of Dhrall that hasn't been invaded yet."

"There's *only* one left, Sorgan," Narasan replied.

"Why, now that you mention it, I *do* believe that you're right, friend Narasan. Isn't it odd that it never occurred to me?"

"Have you just about finished having fun?" Narasan asked.

"You seem just a bit grumpy for a man who's been on the winning side in three wars, my friend," Sorgan said.

"I'm not really grumpy, Sorgan," Narasan replied. "I'm sure there'll be a lot of screaming and weeping, but I will *not* work for the queen of the East, no matter *how* much gold she offers."

"Bite your tongue," Sorgan said. "We work for gold, Narasan, and we always win because we *love* gold."

"*I* don't," Narasan replied, "at least not enough to spend any more time with Divine Aracia. Just the sight of her makes me want to vomit."

"Don't look at her, then. *I'll* take care of the negotiations and all that. And no, I won't cheat you out of your share. Were your people able to pinpoint the most likely route the enemies will take?"

"It wasn't all that hard, Sorgan. It's called 'Long-Pass,' and it's the only possible route our enemy will be able to follow. The mountain range blocks everything else off."

"That makes things even simpler," Sorgan said. "My men and I'll go down to 'temple town' and swindle our employer out of just about everything of value. I'll tell her that you're busy building forts, so you don't have time to pay her a call."

"I *still* think I'd rather just go on home, Sorgan," Narasan said. "I'm not really sure that I'll even be necessary down there. Our 'unknown friend' might fry another ten thousand or so enemies before you and I can even reach for our swords."

Then Ekial and Trenicia came out of Dahlaine's cave to join their friends. "Have we made any decision yet?" Ekial asked.

"We've sort of worked our way around a little problem,"

Sorgan said. "Our friend, honorable Narasan here, doesn't want to have anything to do with Zelana's older sister. I think she rubbed him the wrong way a few times while he was down there. Anyway, I think we might have come up with a way to keep him away from her—far enough away from her, at least, to keep him from trying to chop her all to pieces."

"Are you *really* considering going back there, Narasan?" Trenicia demanded.

"Sorgan sort of rubbed my nose in 'obligation,' Trenicia," Narasan replied. "In a way, I suppose he was right. Our war with that thing out in the Wasteland isn't over yet. We might not *like* Aracia very much, but if we abandon her, we'll put her relatives in great danger."

"If you're going to defend her, you'll almost *have* to be in her general vicinity, won't you, Narasan?" Ekial asked.

"Not really, Prince Ekial," Narasan replied. "The invasion of her Domain will almost certainly come down Long-Pass, and we'll need forts there to hold back the bug-people. I'll take my men up there, and we'll build forts. Sorgan has volunteered to handle the negotiations with unspeakably holy Aracia. Our dear friend Sorgan here is a master swindler, so he'll probably empty Aracia's treasury down to the last penny, but *I* won't even have to look at her."

"Swindler?" Sorgan protested.

"It's a step or two up from 'thief,' friend Sorgan," Narasan said with a faint smile.

"I'll go with you to the temple, if you don't mind, Captain Hook-Beak," Ekial said. "I know of several ways to bump up prices, so I might be useful."

"And I'll stay with Narasan," Queen Trenicia said. "Just

keep that liar away from me. Just the thought of her makes my sword start to itch."

"There's one problem we'll have to solve before we go much farther, though," Narasan said, "and that has to do with smoke. We can build forts from one end of Long-Pass to the other, but they won't be worth a thing if the bug-people send clouds of greasy smoke rolling down the pass."

"I'm sure that we'll be able to find a way to deal with that, Narasan," Trenicia declared.

"I wouldn't worry too much about it," Sorgan told her. "Longbow has that 'unknown friend' who can do almost *anything* that needs doing."

Balacenia smiled. Mother's reputation seemed to be growing every day.

"It's always seemed to hit her earlier—and harder—than it hits the rest of us," Zelana was saying to her brothers a bit later when the three of them were alone, they thought, in Dahlaine's map-room. Balacenia was there, of course, but the elders seemed to be unaware of her presence.

"I think that might be the fault of that idiotic priesthood," Veltan declared.

"No, little brother," Zelana disagreed. "This was turning up long before the emergence of people. Aracia just can't bear the idea that Enalla will be taking over in the East after we all drift off to sleep. If I remember correctly, the same sort of thing happened when the only living thing in the entire Land of Dhrall was grass. Aracia just can't accept the idea that she won't be in charge of everything after she goes to sleep. I think she actually *hates* Enalla."

"That doesn't make any sense at all," Veltan objected.

"I know. When you get right down to it, Aracia has *never*

made much sense. She cherishes her position so much that it's unseated her mind. I shudder to think of what she might have become when we complete this particular sleep cycle."

"We can deal with that later, dear sister," Dahlaine said. "Right now, though, we've got this other problem. How are we going to deal with the Vlagh?"

"The Trogites seem to have found a way to persuade the servants of the Vlagh to go play somewhere else," Veltan said. "Even the most devoted servants of the Vlagh seem to get distracted after they've been set on fire."

"That *does* seem to work," Zelana agreed. "Unfortunately, the Vlagh's an imitator, so I'm sure it won't be long before the creatures of the Wasteland start throwing fire at *our* friends. I'm not sure if it would work the way we might want it to, but eight or ten feet of wet snow *would* make it very difficult to start fires, wouldn't you say?"

"We might want to plant that notion in Lillabeth's mind," Dahlaine said.

"Or possibly Eleria's," Zelana added. "I hate to say this, but Aracia *might* interfere if we depended on Lillabeth."

"We can deal with that later," Dahlaine said. "Right now I'd say that we should concentrate on moving the outlanders down to Aracia's Domain."

Veltan followed his older brother out of the map-room, but Zelana lingered for some reason. "All right, Balacenia," she said when she was sure that her brothers were out of earshot, "what are you up to now?"

"Just gathering information, Beloved," Balacenia said, mimicking Eleria's voice and her traditional form of reference.

"Don't do that," Zelana scolded. "You're *not* Eleria, and I know that as well as you do."

Balacenia shrugged and stepped out into the open. "It was worth a try, I suppose. Stay calm, Zelana. Eleria and I know each other now, and we know that we're not exactly the same person." She smiled. "She's the most delightful person I've ever known."

"You've actually spoken with her?" Zelana sounded astonished.

"Of course. We're making our own plans for the war in Aracia's Domain. Please don't interfere, Zelana. We *do* know what we're doing. I'm sure that you've noticed that Eleria can bring just about everybody around to her way of thinking. I'm sure that it won't be long before she's kissed Mother herself into submission."

"Are you saying that she's *met* Mother?"

"Oh, yes. Mother loves her already, but there's nothing new or different about that."

"I'm not trying to insult you, Balacenia, but you don't sound at all like Eleria."

"I don't go around begging for kisses, you mean? Dahlaine's idea was very interesting, but he separated us. Eleria's *not* me." Balacenia smiled. "I was just a little startled when she called me 'Big Me.' It sort of rubbed off, and now I call her 'Little-Me.' She put her finger immediately on something that had never occurred to me. *Our* cycle this next time will have *eight* divinities instead of only four." She gave Zelana that wide-eyed look of total innocence. "Won't that be fun?" she said.

When Balacenia went looking for Longbow in Dahlaine's cave, he was nowhere to be found, and when Balacenia realized that several of the other significant natives were also missing, she was sure that Longbow had taken them aside to discuss some things they didn't want the outlanders to know about.

It took her a little while to find them. Longbow was very good when it came to concealing himself. "We don't need to make a big issue of this with our outlander friends," he was saying to the others, "but I'm catching a strong odor of reluctance from several of them to go down to Aracia's Domain to fight the last war here in the Land of Dhrall. After Aracia tried to conceal Lillabeth's Dream, our friends came to realize that she wasn't to be trusted. I know several of them who don't want to have anything to do with Zelana's older sister."

"I wonder why," Red-Beard said sarcastically.

"There's one thing that our friends from other parts of the world don't seem to realize," Longbow continued. "The Vlagh steals ideas, rather than gold, and ideas are making her servants grow more and more intelligent. When they reach the point that they're more intelligent than people are, people are going to start to die out—and it won't just be here in the Land of Dhrall. The Vlagh wants the whole world, and once people are gone, she'll *get* what she wants."

Balacenia saw Mother's fine hand at work there. Mother had obviously told Longbow exactly what she'd mentioned to Balacenia herself in Dahlaine's cave a little while ago.

Then Kathlak, the chief of the Deer Hunter Tribes in Tonthakan, said, "Why don't we come right out and tell the outlanders that if the servants of the Vlagh win *any* of the wars here, there won't be *any* live people anywhere in the world before very long?"

"They wouldn't believe us, Kathlak," Tlantar Two-Hands said. "The outlanders are positive that they're much, much more intelligent than we are—largely because they discovered metal before we did."

"When you get right down to it, we don't really *need* the outlanders anymore," the archer Athlan declared. "We might want to hold on to Rabbit—and maybe Keselo—but if something comes up that we can't deal with ourselves, Longbow's 'unknown friend' will probably take care of it for us. She built a sea of water down in Veltan's Domain, and then she built a sea of fire up here. If we have a friend who can do things like *that*, why do we need any outlander armies?"

Balacenia decided that it was time to take steps at that point. She assumed Eleria's form and joined the assorted chieftains. "That was a nice idea, Athlan," she said, "but aren't you overlooking something? *If* the Vlagh sees that the outlanders aren't with us anymore, she'll become more and more certain that she's going to win this war after all, and that means that she'll throw everything she's got against us, and the Vlagh can spawn out new servants—millions and millions of them—when she wants to. Bugs become adults in about a week or so, and that means that every warrior here in the Land of Dhrall will have a thousand or so facing him during the war in the East. Then, after she's killed off *all* the people here in the Land of Dhrall, she'll spawn out even *more* servants, and she'll take the whole world. We might not *like* the outlanders all that much, but we *do* need them."

"What if they decide that they don't want to play anymore?" Kathlak demanded.

Balacenia shrugged. "We can always offer them more gold, can't we? If you give an outlander more gold than he can carry, I'm sure that he'll do almost anything that you want him to do."

It was somewhat later that afternoon when Dahlaine announced that it was time for the traditional victory celebration. Balacenia found it to be somewhat amusing when she realized that Mother, who'd *won* the war in Crystal Gorge, was now preparing the feast that would be a major part of the celebration.

Balacenia moved quietly and inconspicuously around Dahlaine's cave listening as the outlanders spoke with each other in awed tones about the conflagration of blue fire that had incinerated the servants of the Vlagh in the space of only a few minutes.

The somewhat overly educated young Trogite called Keselo spoke at some length about the enormous power of what the outlanders called a "cyclone."

"Normally, a fire would have gone *up* the gorge rather than down," Keselo declared, "but when you're dealing with a cyclone, normal goes right out the window. A cyclone can *almost* tear down a mountain. The cyclone that went down Crystal Gorge pulled the blue fire along behind it, and the fire burned anything the cyclone hadn't smashed down into tiny fragments. The enemies that hadn't been ripped to pieces by the cyclone were incinerated by that blue fire." Keselo paused, squinting at the ceiling. "I'd say that we had a case of 'tampering' again. A normal cyclone would almost certainly *not* have followed the gorge all the way down to the Wasteland. A cyclone is wind, and wind goes where it wants to go. Somebody grabbed hold of that cyclone and literally hurled it down the gorge."

"Then we probably owe Longbow's 'unknown friend' a whole *lot* of kisses, wouldn't you say?" Balacenia added.

"*I'm* not going to kiss somebody who can do things like *that*," Sorgan's cousin Skell declared. "If I just happened to get it wrong, she could jerk out all of my insides—through my *nose*—if she really wanted to."

"Or, she might decide to turn you inside out, brother," Torl said with a grin. "You'd look very peculiar with your insides right out in the open like that."

"Please don't say things like that, Torl," Gunda said. "*That* one almost took a big bite out of my stomach."

"So beat me," Torl replied with a broad grin.

"Supper's ready," Mother announced. "Come and get it before it turns cold."

Balacenia had a peculiar sort of thought then. Since Mother enjoyed cooking as much as she obviously did, why was it that the gods of the Land of Dhrall didn't eat?

"We'll talk about that some other time, Dear Heart," Mother's voice said softly. "Now go eat your supper."

After the guests had all finished eating, Dahlaine of the grey beard rose to his feet to make a speech. For some reason,

Dahlaine made speeches almost every time he turned around. "I most definitely want to thank our friends from the other side of the world for the victory we've achieved here in the North. I must advise them, however, that there still remains one part of the Land of Dhrall that has not yet known war, since it's quite obvious that the Vlagh will *not* just walk away and leave sister Aracia's Domain behind. An attack on the East will certainly come before long; we should make plans to protect the East."

"If I may," Narasan said, rising to his feet with a certain reluctance. "My men and I spent some time in Lady Aracia's Domain, and I sent Sub-Commander Andar out to speak with the natives and make an assessment of the defensibility of Lady Aracia's temple-town *and* of the capabilities—or lack of them—in the local population. Why don't you tell our friends what you encountered, Andar?"

The deep-voiced officer rose to his feet. "As nearly as Brigadier Danal and I were able to determine, the place called 'temple-town' is totally indefensible. It has no walls, and no fortifications of any kind whatsoever. As for expecting any help at all from the local population, forget it. They don't even know what weapons are." Andar scratched his chin. "Commander Narasan was finally able to persuade Lady Aracia to create what we've come to call a 'lumpy map.' Brigadier Danal and I examined that map quite closely, and, so far as we could determine, there's only one possible invasion route. It's called 'Long-Pass,' and it's definitely long, but 'pass' may not be quite so accurate. It's an ancient streambed that wanders quite a bit. There are several excellent places for forts, and I strongly suggest that if we *are* going down there, we should concentrate on building those forts."

"Aren't you forgetting the smoke the enemies unleashed on us down in Crystal Gorge, Andar?" Gunda said.

"I was just getting to that, Gunda," Andar replied. "In that region, the prevailing wind comes in from the sea that lies along the east coast. That means that the smoke—if the enemy decides to use smoke again—will go from east to west. Our forts will be on the east side of the pass, and the wind will push at our backs and not at our faces. *If* the enemy is stupid enough to try burning greasewood trees, that prevailing wind will push the smoke into the enemy's face, not ours."

"Thank you, Andar," Narasan said, rising to his feet again. "I think that just about covers everything, Lord Dahlaine. My men and I will build forts in Long-Pass and defend them from our enemies—for appropriate payment, of course. There *is* one stipulation I'm going to add this time, however."

"Oh," Dahlaine asked, "and what's that?"

"You *will* keep your sister away from me. If she comes up there with that fat priest, Takal Bersla, my men and I will pack up and go home. I will *not*—under *any* circumstances—take orders from your sister. Keep her away from me, and I mean it."

"Do you really dislike her all that much, Narasan?"

"I wouldn't say 'dislike,' Lady Zelana," Narasan replied. " 'Contempt' comes much, much closer."

Balacenia carefully covered her mouth so that nobody would be able to see the wicked grin that had just come across her face.

About the Author

DAVID EDDINGS published his first novel, *High Hunt*, in 1973, before turning to the field of fantasy with The Belgariad. He went on to write The Malloreon, The Elenium, and The Tamuli series, as well as *The Redemption of Althalus*. Born in Spokane, Washington, he served in the United States Army and taught college English.

LEIGH EDDINGS has collaborated with her husband for more than a dozen years on numerous bestsellers.

More
David and Leigh Eddings!

Please turn this page
for a preview of
THE YOUNGER GODS,
the stunning conclusion to
The Dreamers series.

Available in bookstores
everywhere.

1

It took the better part of two days to get Sorgan's army ashore, and then Sorgan and Padan rowed over to *The Victory* to speak with Brigadier Danal.

"That takes care of things here, Danal," Sorgan told the lean, stubborn officer. "Convey my thanks to Narasan, and tell him that I'll stay in touch."

"I'll do that, Captain," Danal replied.

"How long would you say it's going to take you to get the rest of his army down to the mouth of Long-Pass?"

Danal squinted. "The ships will be empty when we go north," he said, "and that should save us a day. Loading the troops on these ships will take a couple of days, and then four days to the mouth of the pass. Then two more days to unload. I make it to be twelve days to two weeks. Even if the bug men have reached this side of the Wasteland, the Malavi and those archers from the north will be able to hold them off until Gunda's got some forts in place." Then he smiled slightly. "You don't necessarily have to tell Narasan that I said this, but your little side-trip gave me a wonderful opportunity to avoid all that tedious business of building forts."

"That's what friends are for, Danal," Sorgan said with a grin. "If you happen to meet Lady Zelana up there, tell her that I said hello."

"I'll do that, Captain Hook Beak."

"Oh, and tell Narasan that I'll keep *The Ascension* here. I'm going to need a private place to confer with my men. I don't want one of Lady Aracia's fat priests eavesdropping when I'm telling my men what to do."

"I'm sure he'll understand, Captain," Danal replied. "You have a nice war now."

"I'd hardly call what we're going to do here a war, Danal. It's just going to be an imitation."

"Those are the very best kind," Danal said with a grin.

Sorgan and Padan climbed down the rope ladder to their skiff. "I like that man, Padan," Sorgan said. "We get along just fine."

"He's a very good soldier," Padan agreed.

They rowed across to *The Ascension* and joined several Maags in the rear cabin.

"All right, then," Sorgan said. "The Trogite fleet will sail at first light tomorrow, and they'll pick up the rest of Narasan's men and take them on down to the mouth of Long-Pass to fight the *real* war. In the meantime, we'll get started on the imitation war here. I don't *think* Aracia has any people up in that vicinity, but we'll want to make sure that no word of what's happening up there reaches her. I don't think she'd pay much attention to anything that's not going on here in the vicinity of her temple, but we should probably block off any roads or trails coming down here from up in the Long-Pass region."

"I'll send some men up there to take care of that, cousin," Torl said.

"Good," Hook-Beak said approvingly.

"Have you worked out a plan yet?" Padan asked the Maag.

Sorgan grinned. "Oh, yes," he replied. "I'm going to take some men to Aracia's throne-room. I'll tell her that they're scouts, and they'll find out what they can about the upcoming invasion of the bug-people. Then I'll tell her how dangerous things are going to be for those scouts and make a big issue of how many varieties of invaders we'll come up against. Then I'll send the men on their way, and they'll march out about a mile or so and then set up camp in some fairly well-concealed place."

"Wouldn't you say that a mile is just a little too close?" Padan asked.

Sorgan shook his head. "I want them to be close enough to be able to hear the sound of a horn. I'm going to work on Aracia to build up her fright. Then, when she's filled to the brim with terror, I'll send word out to the west side of her temple, and one of men there will toot a horn. When the imitation scouts hear it, they'll come running back and start piling 'awful' all over Aracia and the fat ones who worship her." He squinted. "Torl," he said to his cousin, "I'll send Rabbit out there with you. He's very clever, and between the two of you, you should be able to come up with stories that'll send Aracia and her fat priests screaming and searching for safe places to hide. I'd say that you two should put things together so that this non-existent invasion by the bug-people starts out with moderately awful and then builds up to pure horror. You'll have several days to work on these stories, so use lots of imagination. Then too, I think you all might want to practice looking frightened. Bulge out your eyes, shiver like crazy, and scream once in a while. The whole idea here is to frighten everybody to the point that they'd sooner die than go outside the temple and have a look for themselves. *If* we can scare them enough, the notion of going north to pester Narasan will never occur to any of them. They won't know that Narasan's there anyway, but I want those priests to be so frightened that they won't even *consider* following an order to go anywhere away from this central temple. We'll use terror instead of bars, but this silly temple *will* be a prison if we do this right."

Padan was just a bit surprised by the level of sophistication Sorgan's scheme indicated. "Maags aren't supposed to be that clever," he murmured to himself.

"I think you'd better come along, Padan," Sorgan said when they went out onto the deck of *The Ascension.* "I'm going to be playing a game of sorts, so I might miss a few reactions of Aracia or her assorted priests. If you happen to notice any degree of skepticism, let me know immediately. We *don't* want any doubts floating around at this point." Then he turned to his cousin. "Gather up the men who'll be going with you and come along. I'll give you your marching orders right there in the temple. I want Aracia and her priests to see you leave so that they'll recognize you when you come back. Try to look brave and strong when I send you out, and frightened and timid when you come back. I'll make an issue of how skilled you are as warriors when you march out. Then, when you come back whimpering, Aracia will believe just about everything you tell her about all the awful-awful you've witnessed."

"This is a side of you I don't think I've ever seen before, cousin," Torl said. "You're an excellent deceiver, aren't you?"

"I'm probably the best," Sorgan replied. "Let's go frighten Zelana's sister for an hour or so, and then *I* can come back to *The Ascension* and rest for a while. I've been running steadily for about three days now."

They rowed on to the beach just below Aracia's temple and then walked on up to the golden door. Evidently word had gotten out, and no priest—or priestess—tried to interfere as they marched on along the corridor that led to the throne-room.

The fat priest Bersla was delivering another oration of praise when they entered Aracia's throne-room. His majestic voice faltered when Sorgan marched in, however.

"Are you just about through?" Sorgan asked in a flat, unfriendly tone of voice.

"I was just about to leave, mighty Sorgan."

"No," Sorgan said abruptly, "stay. There's something I want you to see."

"As you wish, Mighty Sorgan," Bersla replied in a squeaky sort of voice.

Sorgan approached the throne. "I've looked around your temple here, Lady Aracia," he said, "and we've got a lot of work ahead of us, I think, but right for now we need information—what kind of bugs are coming this way, anything new and unusual approaching, how close they are to where we are right now." Then he gestured at Rabbit and Torl. "These men are the best, so they'll be leading the scouting parties. I'm *hoping* that some of them will live long enough to bring back the information we need. There are many different varieties of bug-people. We know about quite a few of those, but there might be others as well. If there are, I want to know about them. We *don't* want any surprises. We already know that bugs can come at us from under the ground, from up in trees, and even out of the empty air. There's one variety that's part bug and part bat, and it flies around biting people, and the people die immediately."

Aracia shuddered. "How in the world did these things come into existence?"

Sorgan shrugged. "Their queen—the one called 'The Vlagh'—comes up with the idea for these various creatures, and then she lays eggs. When the eggs hatch, there's a whole new variety of bug. Worse yet, she lays those eggs by the thousands."

"They'd only be infants," the priestess Alcevan said. "They wouldn't be much of a danger for quite some time."

"I see that you've never spent much time around bugs," Sorgan said. "Bugs only live for about six weeks, and then they die. The infancy of a bug only lasts for three or four days, and then it's a full-grown adult, and it'll kill anything the Vlagh wants it to kill. They're not intelligent enough to be afraid of anything. I've seen two or three of them still attacking a fort after we've killed thousands of their friends. They just keep coming until they die."

"That's absurd!" Bersla declared.

"You'd better be ready for *lots* of absurd when the bug-people attack," Torl said. "About the only thing we've found that gets their attention is fire. When you set fire to something, it tends to get a little confused."

Then Sorgan gestured toward the door. "Take your men and go out there and see what you can find out. Don't get *too* many of your men killed by taking chances. I need information, not dead friends. Find out what you can and then hurry back, and be very careful. You can die some other time. *This* time I want live men who can tell me what I need to know."

Sorgan had moved his main force to the far western side of Aracia's temple. "If there really *was* going to be an invasion by the bug people, they'd reach this part of Aracia's temple first," he told Padan. "That means that we'll need some kind of fort here to persuade Aracia and her priests that we *are* going to protest them. It won't have to be *too* close to a real fort. The temple itself isn't really that well-built, so the priests wouldn't recognize *real* construction even if it walked up and bit them on the nose. We'll move a few of the building blocks and maybe knock down a tower or two. Then we'll have the men pretend to be building some kind of fort and let it go at that. What we'll *really* be doing will be terrifying Aracia and her priests to the point that they'll be afraid to come out of the central temple."

"If this works out the way we want it to, we'll have pulled off one of the greatest hoaxes of all time, Captain," Padan said.

"Naturally," Sorgan boasted. "No matter what I do, I'm always the best." Then he laughed. "Sorry, Padan," he said then. "It was just too good an opportunity to let slip by."

"Where's Veltan?" Padan asked. "I haven't seen him for the last few days."

"He's nosing around over in the main temple," Sorgan replied. "I need to know how much of our silly story the priests—and Aracia, of course—have swallowed whole. If there are any doubts over there, we might have to play some more exotic games." Then he shivered. "Let's get in out of the weather, Padan," he said. "I *hate* winter."

They went on back inside to a room that had a stove, and it wasn't too much later when Veltan joined them.

"Well, Sorgan," he said, "you've managed to terrify my sister's priesthood."

"That was sort of what we had in mind, wasn't it?" Sorgan asked. "That's why we've been waving bugs around every time we're near any priest."

"It's *you,* not the bugs, that has them worried, Sorgan. They're desperately trying to come up with some way to reduce your grip on Aracia. They're afraid of you, and they hate you. It seems that you've got a tighter grip on Aracia than even *we* could imagine. I think it all goes back to Bersla. He had Aracia wrapped around his little finger with those stupid orations of his. Then you came along and pushed him back into a corner and threatened to kill him if he said one more word. He's had Aracia under his control for years now, and then you walked in and took her away from him in just a day or so. Aracia had the title, but Bersla had the power. Now he doesn't any more."

"Poor, poor fat Bersla," Sorgan murmured smugly.

"Now we come to the interesting part, Sorgan," Veltan said. "Bersla wants to kill you—or persuade some lesser priest to do the job for him."

"They don't even have weapons, Veltan," Sorgan scoffed.

"They *do* have knives, you know. They're made of stone, but a good hard stab in the back with a stone knife will penetrate your skin and go in far enough to do very serious damage to your vital organs. Bersla's doing everything he can think of to persuade some minor priest to stab you in the back. Quite a few of them are very interested by the offers

Bersla has been waving in their faces. Instant promotion to the higher priesthood sounds very nice to young, ambitious priests who don't stand too high in the church of Aracia."

"It sort of sounds like I should have borrowed one of those iron breastplates from Narasan before I even came down here," Sorgan muttered.

2

After a bit of thought, Hook-Beak spoke briefly with his first and second mates, Ox and Ham-Hand, and after that, the two big Maags followed their captain wherever he went to Aracia's temple. Ox was carrying his huge battle-axe, and any time Hook-Beak spoke with one of Aracia's overfed priests, the hulking Maag touched up the already razor-sharp axe-blade with a hefty whetstone that made a shrill sound as Ox drew it across the axe-blade.

The priests of Aracia got the point almost immediately.

Veltan, who had frequently demonstrated his ability to listen without being seen, advised Sorgan that the priests of Aracia had stumbled over a truth in their desperate search for some way to loosen Sorgan's grasp on Aracia. They had taken to denouncing Hook-Beak and his men as opportunistic swindlers. "They keep telling each other that there's no such thing as a bug-man, Sorgan," Veltan reported. "They're claiming that you and your men are waving 'bug-men' around as a way to leech more and more gold out of Aracia."

"That's ridiculous, Veltan," Sorgan protested. "I know for a fact that Lady Aracia has actually *seen* the bug-people. I was standing right beside her down in your Domain when the bug-people and the Trogite priests were busy killing each other."

"I know," Veltan replied. "I think big sister has been keeping that to herself. The last thing she wants here is to have all of her priests come down with panic. If they run away, she'll be all alone here."

"We're going to have to do something about this, Veltan," Sorgan said. "The priests are obviously scraping this off the wall, but it looks to me like they've accidentally stumbled over the truth. Bug people are real, but they aren't coming through *this* part of Aracia's country." Then he looked speculatively at Veltan. "You can make people believe that they're seeing something that's not really there, can't you?" he asked.

"If it's absolutely necessary," Veltan replied. "I'd have to stay a long distance from Aracia, though. She *can* sense things like that if I'm too close—or if I leave the illusions in place for too long."

"I think a few brief glimpses might serve our purpose, Veltan. We want to confirm Aracia's belief that the bug-men are invading *this* part of her Domain, *and* to persuade the priests that I'm not lying and that Aracia *knows* that I'm not. I think I'll go have a little talk with Torl and Rabbit. If they come running out of that farmland off to the west and there are images of several huge bugs right behind them, Aracia will probably go into hiding and this scheme the priests came up with will fall apart right then and there, wouldn't you say?"

"I think it's worth a try, Sorgan," Veltan agreed. "I've

briefly touched Aracia's mind a few times since we arrived, and she's absolutely convinced that the Vlagh is out to get *her* personally. She's sure that the Vlagh wants to kill her, and she's terrified."

"She can't actually die, can she? I mean she's immortal, isn't she?"

"Yes, she is, but she's drifting toward senility, so she's not sure of *anything* any more. This has happened several times before. All of us get a little vague when we're approaching the end of one of our cycles, but Aracia tends to take it to extremes."

"I had a talk with Torl and Rabbit last night," Sorgan said the next morning in the cabin of *The Ascension*. "Now they know about Veltan's illusions, and they'll make some show of fighting them off. The only problem we might have is that Aracia has to *see* this imitation skirmish, and she almost never comes out of that silly throne-room of hers."

"We've got some time to play with, Sorgan," Padan said. "You might want to have your men get started on the fort. Then, when its base is in place, you could invite holy Aracia to come out and have a look." Padan scratched his bearded cheek. "I suppose that technically you'll need her permission to continue, so a visit would be very appropriate. If Veltan and your scouts know when she'll be there, they'll be able to put on a show for her that'll send her running for cover—*and,* after that, she'll dismiss any priest who tries to tell her that you're a swindler." Then he laughed as he remembered something that had happened in Kaldacin several years ago.

"What's so funny?" Sorgan asked.

"The Church of Amar down in the empire has a fair number of dungeons scattered about. When a priest blunders and insults one of his superiors, they lock him in a hole in the ground and throw away the key. I'd imagine that Bersla would lose quite a bit of weight if Aracia had him locked up in a dungeon where all he had to eat would be bread and water."

Sorgan frowned slightly. "I wonder if we could get away with that," he murmured.

The Maags were busy knocking down walls that afternoon. Padan saw that they were very good at destroying things. Building, however, might cause them a few problems.

A young priest came scurrying out of the central temple with a look of horror on his face. "What are you *doing*?" he screamed.

"We need a fort to hold off the bug-people," Sorgan replied. "When we saw that nobody lives here in this part of the temple, we decided to modify it just a bit. There are quite a few similarities between forts and temples. Did you ever notice that? Anyway, things are going along fairly well. Give us a week or so, and the invasion of the bugs will stop right here." Then he looked rather speculatively at the young priest. "He looks pretty husky to me, Padan. If Lady Aracia wants this fort in place to defend her temple, she might just order all of her priests to come here and lend us a hand. The exercise would probably be good for them wouldn't you say?"

"I'm sure it would," Padan agreed. "If we were to sweat some of the fat off them, they'd probably live longer." He looked at the now horrified young priest. "If you were to step in and lend us a hand with our fort here, you *might* even live past your thirtieth birthday. And if you were to *really* bear down, you *might* even live to be forty. Look at all the extra life you'll get out of a few weeks of hard work."

The young priest turned and fled at that point.

Sorgan laughed. "I think that might eliminate any further objections," he said. "The notion of doing *real* work doesn't seem to sit very well with Aracia's priesthood."

"What an amazing thing," Padan agreed.

Their imitation fort was coming along quite well now that Sorgan had leaned on his men and ordered them to follow Padan's instructions. They had what *looked* like a solid base about ten feet tall running along the west side of Aracia's temple.

"It's not really all that substantial, Sorgan," Padan admitted, "but Aracia wouldn't even recognize a *real* fort. I don't know that you want to wait too much longer. I'm sure that her priests are trying everything they can think of to discredit you. Let's not give them *too* much more time before she sees the skirmish between your men and the imitation bugs Veltan's going to conjure up. That's going to verify our scam and scare Aracia's stockings off. After that, we'll be home free."

"You're probably right, Padan. I'll have a quick talk with Veltan, and he can go on out and start Torl and Rabbit this way while you and I go to the throne-room and tell Aracia that we want to show her what we've accomplished so far."

"What are you going to do if she refuses to come out here?"

Sorgan shrugged. "I'll tell her that all work stops until

she comes out here and approves of what we've done so far. No matter what her priests have been telling her, she's still terrified by the Vlagh, so she won't take any chances. She knows that her priests would be useless in a war, so she'll do just about anything to stay on the good side of me."

Bersla was orating again, but for once Aracia didn't even seem to be listening.